Esperanza

TOR BOOKS BY TRISH J. MacGREGOR

Esperanza

TRISH J. MACGREGOR

Esperanza

A Tom Doherty Associates Book

New York

ESPERANZA

Copyright © 2010 by Trish J. MacGregor

All rights reserved.

A Tor Book
Published by Tom Doherty Associates, LLC
175 Fifth Avenue
New York, NY 10010

www.tor-forge.com

Tor® is a registered trademark of Tom Doherty Associates, LLC.

ISBN 978-0-7653-2602-7

First Edition: September 2010

Printed in the United States of America

0 9 8 7 6 5 4 3 2 1

For Rob and Megan,
con mucho cariño siempre

And many thanks to Al Zuckerman
and Beth Meacham,
whose insights vastly improved the story

Book One of
The Hungry Ghosts

· · · · · · ·

Prologue
THE CITY OF ESPERANZA, ECUADOR

Dominica watched the pretty young woman standing on a dark, windy corner in the oldest section of the city, known as El Corazón, the heart. She liked what she saw. A foreign tourist, mid-twenties, beautiful figure, pale, flawless skin as smooth as a river stone. The woman's colorful skirt rustled in the chilly breeze, her fingers fumbled with the zipper on her jacket, then tucked her thick black hair behind her ears.

Dominica wondered if the woman knew that in 1530, on this very street, the last emperor of the Incas had marched against the Spanish. The colonial buildings behind the woman covered an Incan site where Inti, the sun god, had been honored with daily sacrifices. The restaurant where the woman had just eaten had been built over an Incan altar used for divination during *ayahuasca* ceremonies. Did the woman have any grasp of this?

Well, it didn't matter. Physically, she fit Dominica's needs—young, attractive, foreign, and probably healthy.

Dominica moved toward her. Most people couldn't see a *bruja*, but because human awareness varied widely this woman might be an exception. If she perceived Dominica, it would be as a shadow in her peripheral vision. So Dominica approached her slowly. Sudden moves could startle her or prompt a hasty retreat back into the restaurant.

As she came up behind the woman, Dominica's eagerness to feel the physical world again was so great that she struggled not to rush. Up the street, people emerged from a hotel, their laughter drifting in the night air. Headlights from approaching cars washed over the woman, revealing the angular flare of her hips, the tumble of her beautiful hair past her shoulders. *Steady, steady.* Then Dominica summoned her strength and swiftly seized the woman's body.

She gasped and staggered back, aware that something had happened to her, but what? Dominica worked quickly, adjusting her essence to the size and shape of the woman's body, taking control of her brain, her organs, limbs, even her voice. When a scream was about to explode up the woman's throat, Dominica stifled it so it emerged as barely a hiss.

The woman's heart and lungs pumped furiously. As oxygen flowed into the body, Dominica gulped at it. That first delicious breath shocked her. It always did. Then she tasted dampness, a promise of rain, and smelled flowers, grass, earth, exhaust fumes, and the woman's perfume. Then the rhythmic beating of the woman's heart and the rushing of blood through the body's arteries and veins empowered her. Dominica was fully in control of the woman's body, and the sensory feast of physical existence was now hers again and she drank it in.

The colors. Even at night, the colors she now saw were radiant compared to the grayness in which *brujos* existed. The vibrant greens of the pines looming in the park across the road looked as if they had spilled from an artist's palette. The glow of the street lamps was the color of melting butter. The blues and violets in the woman's skirt reminded Dominica of a dusk in Spain, where she had been born centuries ago as Dominica de la Reina, the only daughter of a wealthy landowner. In that life, she had died of a broken heart at thirty-six.

The sweet chill of the high mountain air smelled of pines. Stars burned like tiny suns in the black sky. Music pumped from an open window somewhere and Dominica tapped her foot to the rhythm, three quick beats, then two, then four. She held out her arms, turned her palms upward, flexed her fingers, then ran them through her hair. This body felt magnificent and Dominica fit into it perfectly, as if it had been created for her. An ideal host.

Claire: the woman's name was encoded in her body's cells.

Dominica now felt Claire's essence recover from the shock. She started struggling, twitching, jerking, creating spasms in her muscles as she screamed to go one way and Dominica forced the body in the opposite direction. Quick. Around the corner, where the shadows were thicker, deeper.

Claire's essence shrieked. Dominica quickly formed a metal box in her mind, shoved the woman's essence into it, slammed it shut. Only now was the body wholly hers.

Dominica walked rapidly, deeper into El Corazón, where Esperanza's history was also her own. Each block held a memory. Here at the corner of Trujillo Avenue and Francisco Street she had seized a man in Pizarro's army as the Spanish had surrounded Atahualpa's army and forced him to flee. And over there, in 1862, she had seized a local woman, a peasant, and spent wondrous days on horseback, riding through the countryside outside of the city. In 1918, on the corner in front of her, she and Ben had seized an Asian couple. And so it went, block after block of memories, every step a glorious celebration of physical life.

Outside the Internet café where she was supposed to meet Ben, she paused. People with laptops and BlackBerries occupied the sidewalk tables, sipping their fancy coffees. Tourists. The locals knew better than to be out on the streets this late, when her kind was likely to attack.

Were any of them the friends or family members of *brujo* victims? Rumors swirled that a massive retaliation against *brujos* was being planned among such people. But there were always rumors. Even if this rumor was true, it would take tens of thousands of human beings armed with flamethrowers to overcome her tribe, the largest in all of South America. She reminded herself to check the Internet for the genesis of this rumor. But not right now. Ben first. Then everything else.

Dominica sensed Ben's presence nearby, but couldn't see him. Her perceptions were now connected to this body, limited in its ability to perceive *brujos*, but enhanced in so many other ways. She didn't have to see Ben to know he was surveying possible hosts. She knew that he would choose a young man, virile, healthy, someone she would find irresistible.

She pulled out a chair at a vacant table, eyeing three men who would fit Ben's desires. Black, Asian, Caucasian. She felt attracted to all of them and smiled, wondering which he would select. *Surprise me,* she thought.

Deep down in her metal box, Claire's essence kept screaming and shrieking and banging her puny fists against its walls. The turmoil distracted Dominica. She pressed an imaginary button and, in the blissful silence that followed, checked out the woman's health.

During the centuries of her existence, Dominica had learned much about the human body and its physiology. She had once spent a year using the body of a physician, her essence dispersed throughout his cells so that she could absorb his knowledge. Claire's body felt in excellent health. A nonsmoker, no addictions, heart and lungs perfect. Claire's pancreas seemed a bit off, due only to all the alcohol she'd been drinking since she arrived in Ecuador five days ago. Kidneys worked well, liver and stomach in good shape. Allergic to codeine, didn't eat red meat, took a lot of vitamins.

Suddenly, a man barreled around the corner, shouting, "Claire, hey, Claire."

It took a moment for Dominica to find his name in Claire's memories. Lewis. Her husband.

He stopped at the table, breathless. "My God, Claire, what're you doing here? I thought you were going to wait for me just outside the restaurant."

Down in the metal box, Claire's essence went ballistic, screeching for help, hurling herself against the walls. Dominica tightened her control. "Calm down, Lewis. I just came here to get a couple of coffees. The hotel restaurant is closed now."

"You should've said something." He jerked out the chair across from her, sat down. "I didn't know what the hell had happened to you. Did you order yet?"

Just then, a muscle tick appeared under one of Lewis's blue eyes and his shoulders jerked, as though his shirt were too small for him. Ben obviously had arrived.

The twitching and spasms lasted for another minute. When Ben fully controlled the husband's body, a kind of bliss settled across his expression. "My God," she heard Ben whisper. "I always forget how incredible it is."

Dominica reached across the table and touched his hand, the first time she had felt the skin of another in more than a month. "We chose well this time."

He clasped her fingers and brought her hand to his mouth, kissing each knuckle slowly, his eyes never leaving hers. "Where're they staying? This guy is blocking that information."

"Posada Andres, three blocks from here."

They stood at the same time, their hunger for each other urging them on. Dominica tugged back on his hand. "Let's slow down a little. We don't want to attract attention."

She feared the locals knew what to look for—erratic, jerky movements, twitches and spasms, uneven gaits. There hadn't been a full-scale *brujo* attack here for several months, but people remained wary. And with good reason. For ten years, Dominica and her tribe had terrorized this city, using bodies in a frenzy of sex and excess. Her tribe occasionally attacked en masse, moving within the fog that rolled in from the countryside. But mass attacks led to great precautions, giant fans to keep the fog away, shutters slamming shut across windows and doors, the locals disappearing into tunnels and underground bunkers. So now her kind usually attacked in small groups or pairs, as she and Ben had tonight, seeking the pleasure that only physical life could provide.

For five hundred years, since Esperanza had become a physical place, the prize that *brujos* sought had not existed here. Before that, the city and every place south of it to the Río Palo had been an etheric construct for the dead or the near dead. Souls had journeyed to Esperanza to learn about the afterlife. Those in comas or who were nearly dead could decide whether to return to physical life or to pass on. In those days, *brujos* had seized souls whenever they wanted to, claimed those souls' bodies, and lived out their natural lives. Compared to that, her brief excursions into the physical were paltry. But it was all she and Ben could have for now.

Their dream was to claim Esperanza and every place southward to Río Palo by seizing every resident and tourist, man, woman, and child. A city of *brujos,* living out the mortal lives of their hosts. But if they attempted this, Dominica felt sure the *cazadores de luz,* the light chasers, would intervene and the battle that ensued would be far worse than the battle five centuries ago. So for now they satisfied themselves with these small forays, hesitant to do anything that might prompt the chasers to get involved.

"I'm going to devour your body," Ben said, drawing her closer, nibbling at her ear.

"Maybe we should take it easy, draw out the fun so these bodies last us a while."

"No, it's been too damn long for that."

He pulled her into a narrow, dark alley and they pressed back against a wall of stone, hands and mouths everywhere at once, their lust like that of some starved beast. They broke apart at approaching footfalls and voices, and stood motionless against the wall, his hands trapping hers against the stone, his mouth at her neck. When the passersby had moved on, she and Ben hurried on toward the inn.

A few hours, that was all they would get with these bodies. As they neared the inn, Ben ran his fingers through her hair. "You're beautiful, Nica," he said, and kissed her, and they staggered back against a wall.

She and Ben, like all *brujos,* could make love, but it was smoke and mirrors, as was their entire existence. Nothing they could do really equaled this, the raw physicality of lust, passion, and sensuality that humans experienced. His hands were now under her skirt, her breath came in short, staccato bursts, and she kept murmuring, "Not here, Ben, not here." But she didn't push him away.

The street suddenly lit up like high noon, sirens screamed, a high-pitched, terrible bleating followed by explosive shrieks. Like air raid sirens during wars, these sirens warned that *brujos* or the fog in which they often traveled had been sighted and shelter should be sought immediately. Tourists who had no idea what the sirens meant panicked and rushed into buildings. A fortunate minority followed locals into the underground shelters.

She and Ben leaped apart, fumbling with their clothes. Certain they would now be hunted down by bands of men armed with flamethrowers, they had to either vacate these bodies or hide. They looked around wildly.

But shutters rolled across windows and doorways, sealing up buildings, closing them out, giving people inside time to get into the tunnels and bunkers where *brujos* loathed to venture.

Ben grabbed her hand. They raced across the road, plunged into the park, and ran beneath the tall pines, the monkey-puzzle trees, into and out of the brilliant glare of the lights. Around them, panicked pedestrians tore toward the public shelters, cars screeched to a halt. Drivers and passengers leaped out and loped toward the nearest building before shutters clattered closed and buildings went into lockdown.

Dominica realized that the chaos worked to their advantage. People were so terrified, so concerned for their own safety, that no one paid attention to them. They would not be robbed of their communion. Ben read her thoughts and they ran toward an abandoned car, scrambled into the back seat, locked the doors, slid down against the cool fabric, and surrendered to their hunger.

Within minutes, their violent lovemaking taxed the bodies they'd borrowed and Ben's beautiful blue eyes leaked blood, the beads of sweat on his face turned red, and blood oozed from his nostrils, the corners of his mouth. Her body's heart stuttered and strained. She felt blood rolling down the sides of her face and the back of her throat, and started choking on it. These bodies were used up, bleeding out. Lewis was losing consciousness with shocking swiftness. Unless Ben escaped Lewis's body before that happened, he would be obliterated.

"*Now,*" she gasped, and leaped from Claire's body, then pulled Ben free.

For moments, they drifted inside the car, nothing more than puffs of smoke next to Claire and Lewis, who twitched and jerked, dying in the back seat. She and Ben were too depleted to move away from the car. Sirens kept shrieking, security lights still flashed and strobed, and tomorrow morning the authorities would find the bodies of Claire and Lewis, and would dispose of them. The true cause of death would never be revealed.

More rumors would circulate on the Internet, on conspiracy and travel sites, and for a while, tourism in Esperanza would drop. But in the twenty-first century, where news consisted of sound bites, memory was short, Dominica thought. Eventually, tourism would pick up again and Claire and Lewis would be forgotten.

Dominica melted into Ben and together they moved through the windshield and out into the bright, empty road. They lifted above the tall pines and drifted off into the darkness, hungry ghosts once again.

The Town

. . . .

Life is a great surprise. I do not see why death should not be
an even greater one.

—Vladimir Nabokov, *Pale Fire*

One

The back of her neck felt as if insects were burrowing under the skin. She thought she could hear them, too, nibbling through her tissue, a dry, whispery sound, like callused fingertips sliding over paper.

Tess kept running her hand up under her hair, certain she would discover tiny furrows in her scalp, proof that her body was under attack. But the skin felt fine. She realized someone was staring at her, the sensation so strong that she turned slightly in her seat and searched the rows of faces.

The rickety bus that sputtered and backfired its way up a steep and winding road in the Ecuadorian Andes was crowded, three and four people to a row meant for two. She couldn't tell who was staring. As a tall blonde in a country where ninety-nine percent of the population was short and dark haired with dark eyes and olive complexions, she stuck out. People stared all the time. It didn't mean anything.

But if true, why had all the passengers avoided her, so that she had an entire seat to herself?

The left side of the bus consisted mostly of Quechua Indians—women holding children in their laps, men clutching canvas bags, all with colorful wool blankets wrapped around their shoulders. Large families traveled with crates of noisy chickens, bleating goats, skinny dogs, even a friendly pig sprawled on the floor in the back.

On the right side, her side, sat the tourists with their electronic toys—iPods, laptops, BlackBerrys, PDAs, DVD players. European, Asian, South American. She saw only four who looked like Americans, a mother and father with two young children.

Tess turned around again and rubbed the heel of her hand against the foggy window, creating an aperture through which she could peer out. Not much to see. Bits of fog threaded through the branches of trees that grew at lopsided angles along the road. No people or animals in the fog—no donkeys, no dogs, just the white stuff, eddying and moving like a living thing.

Heat burst intermittently from the vents, erratic hiccups that didn't do much to mitigate the chill. The cold, thin air seeped in through the edges of the windows. When she exhaled, she could see her breath. Tess zipped up her leather jacket, blew into her hands to warm them. The altitude had turned her sinuses so dry that the air she inhaled felt almost abrasive.

The bus's engine growled, straining as it climbed yet another ridge. How many more ridges lay beyond this one? A dozen? Fifty? Each one would be higher and already she found it difficult to catch her breath. On a family vacation when she was a kid, she remembered throwing up from altitude sickness while crossing the continental divide. She didn't feel nauseated now, but bands of pressure kept tightening across her chest. Her pulse raced. She tried to relax by sitting back, breathing deeply, shutting her eyes. But as she did so, that eerie sensation crept up her neck; the watcher was staring again.

Tess glanced back and this time she saw him, caught him just before he averted his gaze. A short Quechua man. Intense eyes. Thick red and blue blanket around his shoulders. His black braid crossed his left shoulder and fell halfway down his chest. His face vanished beneath the brim of the white Panama hat that he'd tugged over his forehead.

The Quechua. The face of Ecuador. They graced postcards, Web sites, travel posters, men and women in boldly colored, layered clothing, children with huge, liquid eyes, faces that hinted of an ancient lineage, a people descended from the Incas. They numbered in the millions and were one of the largest indigenous populations in South America. Known as a spiritual people, loyal to their families and communities, they were said to be neither political nor materialistic. Herders of llama and sheep, weavers, farmers, they were abysmally poor. Their language had been spoken long before the Incas and was still one of the official languages of both Bolivia and Peru. She loved its musical intonations, but didn't understand a word of it.

Maybe the guy just didn't like blondes, she thought, and faced the front again.

Her cell jingled, a bar from Bruce Springsteen's "The Ghost of Tom Joad." Tess dug it out of her jacket pocket and smiled when she saw the text message was from Maddie, her eighteen-year-old niece.

Hey, Tesso, u out of Quito yet? Lauren's in fretting mode, says she's been sending u txt messages u don't answer Luv u, M

Tess's mother had gotten an iPhone for her birthday last year and hadn't yet mastered the text-messaging feature. Lauren balked at asking her eighteen-year-old granddaughter for help, but Maddie, like many kids her age, was a whiz with this stuff. Since she had moved in with Lauren last fall, the household had become a techie hub. Maddie and her computer-savvy friends had set up their own server to host their Web sites, where they posted freeware they wrote for fun and sold the software they wrote for profit. With the money, Maddie was paying her way through junior college and had enough saved to start at the University of Florida in the fall.

Before Tess had left on this trip, she, her mother, and Maddie had agreed they would text frequently. *If you disappeared down there, we wouldn't know where to begin our search,* her mother had said the day she'd left. So Tess pressed reply and typed.

Doing fine. Headed to Tulcán, northern Ecuador. Will send L an e. Can u give her 10 lessons on iphone? Got a cute pig on this bus! Miss u guys.

Maddie's response came back quickly.

Doc's hounding L 2 give him another chance. Ha. He has to get past me 1st. luv, M

A couple of years ago, her mother had gotten involved with an ER doc in Key Largo where she was director of nursing. He was Lauren's age, sixty-three, and like her, an ex-hippie. But Doc, as Tess and Maddie referred to him, had lost his rebellious soul somewhere along his trek from the sixties, and was pro everything her mother was against. He also had baggage, two dysfunctional adult children and an ex-wife with a bad attitude. Doc and Lauren had split a few months ago, for the umpteenth time. If the past was any indication, he probably was calling her at odd hours, e-mailing long missives about why they should get back together.

What's w/ doc bugging her again? Remind him stalking is a crime.

Tess sent the text message, then navigated to her e-mail.

Hey mom, was in Quito 4 several days and it reminded me of the time I spent there after dad died. A couple of times I felt him around. My floor lamp blinked off and on one night, the TV came on by itself, stuff like that. M tells me doc has been making noises for reconciliation. Tell him 2 go pound sand, mom. Ask M 4 help on txt messaging. More later.

Luv bigger than google

She pressed send and hoped the e-mail would go through. Up here in the Andes, she wasn't ever sure what languished in cyberspace and what actually made it to its destination. Tess turned off the cell to preserve the battery and glanced out the window again.

The fog looked thicker, like cotton candy. Her reflection in the window was ghostlike, blue eyes as pale as distant smoke, blond hair tangled and falling to her shoulders in unruly waves, mouth quiet and still, as if waiting for something. She hoped her pallor was just the dirty glass and not a sign that she was getting sick.

Tess blew into her hands again and wished she had something hot to drink. Tea, coffee, chocolate, it wouldn't matter. She rubbed at the fogged glass once more. Here and there, the snow-capped peaks—volcanoes—loomed above the thick fog and burned with the afternoon light.

At the back of the bus, the pig snorted, some of the chickens started clucking, one of the dogs barked sharply. The vehicle smelled like a barn and her hunger made the odors almost painful. Her snacks were gone, her water bottle empty. She wished she had taken a plane to Tulcán.

Deal with it.

Oddly, she couldn't recall where she'd caught this bus. Was it in Guayaquil or Quito? Guayaquil was on the coast. Could she have gone there from Quito? But she hadn't been anywhere near the ocean in days, maybe weeks. She had a memory of a crowded bus station, though that might be from an earlier trip, when she had taken a bus from Quito to Otavalo and then on to Baños.

The nagging confusion troubled her. Yet it also seemed par for traveling in Ecuador. Here, her American life seemed less real and she felt closer to this country, as if Ecuador were a truthful reflection of where she was in her life right this second. If you needed an ancient mysticism to soothe your soul, then your Ecuador experience would attract Quechua, tribal healers, vestiges of the Incas. If you needed something from Ecuador's visible, conscious world, as she did, then you apparently froze your ass off on a bus that churned up the spine of the Andes.

Ten years ago, after her first year in law school, Quito had given her solace from her father's death. As she had walked, she had moved back in time through the labyrinth of Quito's old city, where Indians lived on the streets, cooked on the streets, made love and raised their children on the streets, all in the gloomy shadows of ancient stone buildings. But now, as she traveled ever higher into the Andes, her cold misery reflected the purpose of this trip—track the Colombian bastard who had turned a stellar FBI counter-feiting bust into a fiasco that enabled him to abscond with more than five million. Or, as she had learned from a lead in Quito, track the woman to whom he had entrusted the five mil.

True, the FBI had no jurisdiction here, but it was believed the guy had fled to Ecuador. If she found him or the woman to whom he allegedly had given the money, she was supposed to contact her Miami office and they would alert the Ecuadorian authorities. Her partner, Dan Hernandez, had congratulated her on an all-expenses-paid trip to Ecuador. But Dan was just trying to make her feel better because she was being blamed for the sting going south. Her boss had implied as much. *Around here, memory is short, Tess. A couple of months out of sight, and when you return, everything will be just as it was.*

Right now, Tess was no longer sure that she wanted to return to the Bu-reau. Eight years, since graduating from law school, and she was feeling the symptoms of a massive burnout. Since landing in Quito, she had been flirt-ing with different options—private practice with a law firm in Miami that had offered her a job several years ago, working for the Florida state attor-ney's office, even opening her own firm, maybe in the Keys. Nice idea, but it would require more capital than she had.

Another possibility was moving to Key Largo, where her mom and niece lived. She could work at one of the dolphin centers or perhaps sign up with one of the marine rescue groups and save sea turtles. Her B.S. in marine bio-logy might get her in. At thirty-three, she just didn't see herself grinding away for the Feds for the next twenty years.

And she sure as hell didn't see herself tracking a mark—or his lady friend—around Ecuador. If the informant's lead about the creep's where-abouts didn't pan out, she might as well spend the rest of her time here en-joying herself. A flight to the Galápagos. Follow Darwin's path through those islands. Tortoises the size of condominiums. Penguins that weighed just five pounds. Marine iguanas. Rare birds. An animal lover's carnival. And then she would head out to Easter Island to wander until she had a plan—or ran out of money.

A dilapidated building took shape in the fog, one story made of wood and tin that looked like something the big bad wolf might blow down with a single puff. BODEGA DEL CIELO read the sign on top. Store of the Sky. Over it stood a large neon Coca-Cola sign, burning blue in the fog. Scrawny dogs and cats skulked around, no doubt hoping for handouts. Half a dozen men and women, some sipping from tin cups, waited out front with their packs and bags.

The driver pulled on the emergency brake, stood up, pointed at Tess and the four Americans. In Spanish, he told them another bus would be along shortly that would take them on to Esperanza. She liked that word. It meant "hope," but she felt sure she hadn't bought a ticket to a place she'd never heard of.

"Excuse me," she said in Spanish. "I didn't buy a ticket to Esperanza."

The driver snapped his fingers impatiently and in fairly good English said, "Let me see your ticket, please."

"We didn't buy tickets to Esperanza, either." The American guy with the two kids had an irritating twang in his voice.

The driver patted the air with one hand, and held up Tess's ticket with his other hand. "Here." He indicated the red number stamped at its bottom. "Eight means Esperanza. If this is not right, talk to the agent inside."

"Eight?" the man called out. "What kinda weird system is *that*? Why do other passengers have tickets with the *name* of their destination?"

The driver looked flustered, then agitated, and Tess wondered if the altitude was getting to him. She wished that rude American would shut up.

"Señor, in Ecuador, there are many systems," the driver replied. "One man cannot know them all. Please, you and your family must get off."

"Christ Almighty." He rolled his eyes and urged his family forward. Tess fell into step behind them, heavy pack over her shoulder.

The two kids whined, rubbed their eyes, complained about the cold. The girl, the youngest, clutched her teddy bear in the crook of her arm and held on tightly to her mother's hand. She kept glancing back at Tess, her dark eyes pools of misery. The collar of her heavy parka, zipped to the throat, swallowed most of her chin. Just as she and her mother reached the door, the girl started coughing and suddenly doubled over and vomited.

"For Chrissake, Gretchen," her father snapped, and hauled her off the bus.

Tess stepped around the puke and into the cold, foggy air. The child was sobbing, wiping her hand across her mouth. Tess dug around in her pack until she found a packet and went over to them. "These papaya enzymes should calm her stomach," she said to the mother, and offered the packet. "Have her chew a couple. If you can find an actual papaya, she should eat some of the seeds."

The woman took the packet and raised her rheumy eyes to Tess's face. "Thank you. It's probably just the altitude. But thank you."

"You bet."

The people waiting now boarded. The driver counted heads, passengers handed over tickets. No crated chickens or pigs on leashes in this haul. Moments later, the bus pulled away into the fog.

She felt uneasy stranded here in the middle of nowhere. She brought out her cell to update her mom and Maddie, but didn't have a signal now. She would have to wait. But she also needed to update Dan.

As she turned to go into the building, she found herself face-to-face with the watcher from the bus. He looked half a foot shorter than she, five feet four if that, slender, with bladelike cheekbones, a badly pocked face, and scary eyes. *"Permiso,"* she said, and moved to the right.

He also stepped to the right, blocking her, and his mouth swung into a mocking smile. He flicked his thick braid off his shoulder. She moved quickly to the left and pushed past him, but he grabbed the back of her jacket and jerked her around.

Tess nearly fell into him and he grasped her forearm, as if to steady her. His fingers sank into the underside of her wrist, gripping tightly. Their faces were so close she could smell his breath: garlic, onions, and something else, something gross, decay, as though his teeth had rotted in his gums.

"Go home, *gringa.*" The words ground out of his mouth, and the pressure of his fingers against her skin burned. "You are an intruder here."

Tess wrenched back, but his grip was too strong. He laughed softly. "You cannot escape me. You cannot escape *us.*"

She jerked her arm upward, twisted, broke free, and darted toward the bodega. She glanced back once and saw him standing there, staring after her with his mocking smile, his eyes seeming to burn through the fog.

The building was larger than it looked and was jammed—locals and tourists at the ticket counter, the food counter, milling around in the waiting area. She clearly wasn't the only confused traveler.

She got in line for the restroom, dismayed at the crowd in front of her. She kept looking around, worried. Would he follow her inside? Three dark blue bruises were forming on the underside of her wrist, the imprints of his fingers. Though armed, Tess didn't want to display a weapon, not here. But if he came at her again, she would.

The line barely moved. She began feeling nauseated by the odors— roasting chicken and pork, the stink of smoke and unwashed bodies. So when someone announced there were outhouses, Tess made her way through the crowd and stepped outside into the chilly, pine-scented air.

Two wooden outhouses with tin roofs perched at the lip of a precipice, beneath a row of crooked trees. The lines were shorter and as soon as she entered an outhouse, she saw why. The toilet looked as if it had stood here fifty years and never been cleaned. The sink was practically falling out of the wall. Sit on it? No telling what germs were crawling around.

As she squatted over the seat, she noticed a scar on her right thigh, but couldn't remember what had caused it. And why did it now throb and ache?

Tess stood, turned on the sink faucet. The water was icy cold, but it felt good against her face. She longed for a steaming hot shower, fluffy towels, a soft bed. *Soon.*

When she emerged, she was alone. The fog had rolled up over the edge of the cliff and swirled so thickly across the ground she couldn't even see her feet. She stumbled over something, looked down, gasped and wrenched back. The watcher lay there, sprawled on his back, staring vapidly upward, his eyes pink with blood that oozed from their corners. Blood glistened on his lips, under his nostrils, even on his earlobes. His fingernails were red, blood speckled his arms, stained his blanket, his white shirt and pants.

He'd bled out.

A scream clawed up her throat, she spun away and burst through the door of the building, shouting in Spanish. "*Someone get the police, there's a dead man outside.*" Total silence. Everyone stared at her, no one moved. "*A dead man, outside.*"

Tess stabbed her hand toward the open door, but no one reacted until streamers of fog swirled across the threshold and a woman in line at the ticket counter pointed frantically at the fog, screaming "*Neblina!*"

A short man with salt-and-pepper hair leaped out of another line and threw himself against the door. It crashed shut so hard the windows trembled. He slammed a bolt into place, turned, made a hasty sign of the cross on his forehead. "*El jefe, dónde está el jefe?*" he called.

Weird. No one had reacted to her shouts about the dead man outside, but two people had freaked about fog streaming in. What was *that* about? Then she heard voices, a scuffle, and saw an Ecuadorian man in a tattered uniform stumble out of the food area. The local cop. He tugged at his jacket, straightened his sleeves, hoisted his cop belt. "*Aquí, estoy aquí.*" He weaved through the crowd, obviously drunk, and stopped in front of the man who had slammed the door.

Tess hurried over to them. "Excuse me, there's a dead man outside by the outhouses."

Her Spanish was good, not great. But she might have been speaking Swahili. The cop could barely stand upright without tilting in one direction or another. She started to bring out her FBI badge, but the cop belched, "*Gringa,*" then sank to the floor.

"Are there any other police?" she asked the man who had shut the door.

Although she had spoken in Spanish, he replied in English. "We call by radio. You not worry, señorita. We take care of body. Your ticket, which bus you on?"

As he spoke, he urged her along through the crowd until they had reached the calmer side of the building. The people in the food line eyed them, but didn't stare. In fact, most of them deliberately looked away.

He called out something in Quechua and a group of men and women hastened to the windows along the back wall and peered through the windows. But no one stepped outside. The man folded her ticket and pressed it into her hand. "You get in line for food, drinks. You must be on that bus, Señorita Tess."

He moved away, vanishing into the crowd. *What the hell.* Tess was certain she had not told the man her name.

Two

Ian heard a woman screaming something in Spanish. He didn't speak the language, but recognized the alarm in her voice and glanced around, through the sea of faces. So many people were jammed into the building that it was difficult to see anything. Customers were lined up at the counters, in front of the restrooms, and more people poured through the doors and occupied the old plastic chairs along the walls. Someone bumped into him from behind. A baby's cries echoed in the stuffy air.

Christ, he just wanted to get his ticket straightened out and grab a bite to eat. He'd been booted off his bus and told to arrange his transportation to Guayaquil and the Galápagos at the ticket counter. But that line moved slowly and his stomach rumbled with hunger, so he slipped into the food line. He couldn't read the menu. What were *plátanos? Legumbres?* Luke would know. His son spoke Spanish.

But Luke was in Minneapolis, Ian didn't have a Spanish-English dictionary with him, and didn't know how he'd ended up in this crammed building in the middle of nowhere. His memory seemed to be riddled with holes. He couldn't remember much of anything about this trip prior to arriving here at the bodega. He desperately wanted to believe the altitude and fatigue accounted for it.

Someone tapped him on the shoulder, a slight woman with Shirley Temple curls and a dimpled smile. "Excuse me, but do you know what's happening over there?" She gestured toward the other side of the building where the scream had come from. "My Spanish isn't that good, but I thought I heard a woman shout about a dead man outside." She nervously smoothed her hands over her wrinkled slacks and jacket. "I mean, my daughter has altitude sickness, my husband is ready to strangle someone, we got kicked off our bus, we—"

"I don't have any idea what's going on," he said.

"I'm Stephanie Logan, from upstate New York." She thrust out her skinny hand.

"Ian Ritter, Minneapolis."

"Do you think it's safe here?" She looked around uneasily. "My husband just took the kids out back to the outhouses because the line at the restroom is so long."

"I'm sure it's—"

"Jesus God," huffed the plump guy who hurried over to them, herding two kids into the line behind Ian. "There's a dead man outside. On the ground. By the outhouses. Covered in blood." His young daughter rubbed her little fists against her eyes and started to cry. Her brother took one look at her, threw his head back, and began to wail. Stephanie's husband snapped his hand against the side of the boy's head. "Stop it. Now." He jerked on the girl's arm. "Look what you made your brother do. Shut up, just shut up."

Stephanie looked embarrassed, then angry as she drew the children up against her. "You're scaring them, Jim."

Ian slipped away from them and made his way through the crowd, toward the windows where people huddled together, peering out. He squeezed into a spot at the window and pressed his face to the glass, but all he saw out there was fog, rolling in through the trees, thickening like soup.

He moved toward the door, turned the dead bolt, pushed it open. Streamers of fog swirled in, wrapping around his feet and ankles, chilling him. He stepped outside, trying to see through the fog. He detected the shapes of outhouses and of trees that leaned in toward the bodega. Then, as the fog parted slightly, he saw someone on the ground, a man, motionless and bloodied. *Dead.* As he was about to move forward, someone yanked him back, slammed the door.

Ian spun around, facing a benign-looking man who spoke in tortured English. "No outside. No safe. Bad." He shook his finger in Ian's face as though he were a naughty child and spat, "You get ticket, Señor Ritter."

What the fuck? How did this guy know his name? Before Ian could ask, the crowd closed in around him, cutting him off from the man, the cop, the door, the windows. Ian hastened back to the food line, unnerved by what had just happened, but grateful to find that Stephanie and her family had moved on.

Never mind that he couldn't read the menu. He would point at anything, eat anything, drink anything. And then he would dare the ticket line and get his itinerary squared away. Galápagos. Darwin. *Please.*

Tess was shocked that people continued to peer through the windows of the building, yet no one had ventured outside. Maybe just as well. Her federal badge wouldn't mean much here and she didn't want to get stuck answering questions. She had been inside the outhouse. She didn't know what had happened. But she probably was the last person who had seen the man alive, so it all could end up like something out of a Graham Greene novel. American Fed held for questioning. American Fed jailed. American Fed never heard from again.

Finally, at the front of the line, she bought a thick, hot coffee, three steaming vegetable empanadas, a couple of mangos, a papaya, a knife and spoon, and two more bottles of water. These rich odors exacerbated her hunger and she quickly unwrapped one of the empanadas, bit into it. The crust and vegetables tasted so fresh they melted in her mouth. She stood there feeling like a fool, devouring the whole empanada, licking her fingers, unable to recall when she had eaten last. She was tempted to wolf down the other two empanadas as well, but remembered how hungry she had been on the first bus trip and decided to save these.

"Excuse me."

Tess looked up at the man who towered over her and felt as if she nearly swallowed her tongue. George Clooney. Here. In Ecuador. Speaking to her. He seemed taller in person than on the screen, at least six three. Gray threaded through his beard, his eyes were dark pools into which she might fall. He appeared to have the body of a runner, hard, compact, lean. She didn't remember seeing him on her bus.

"Uh, yes?"

"An American. Fantastic. Can you read Spanish?"

She couldn't take her eyes off him—and not just because of his resemblance to Clooney. There was something undeniably sensual about this man—the shape of his mouth? Those eyes? His lean body? All of it. Then she realized he had asked her a question and she still hadn't answered.

"On a good day I speak Spanish passably," she said, and he laughed and showed her his ticket.

"My bus just dropped me here, supposedly because that's what's on my ticket. What's this say?"

Tess took a look. "You're headed to Esperanza—that's apparently what the eight means—on bus thirteen, which leaves here at four-ten."

"What the hell? I'm supposed to be on a bus to Guayaquil so I can fly from there to the Galápagos."

Her dream trip. "You may not get it straightened out quickly." She nodded toward the growing line at the ticket counter. "I thought my bus was headed to Tulcán until I got kicked off and was told to speak to the ticket agent." She was about to tell him about the dead man, to blab about what had happened, but changed her mind. "I figure I'll be lucky to get out of here before midnight."

"Maybe the line moves faster than we think. Listen, could you translate what's good on that menu up there? By the way, I'm Ian Ritter, from Minneapolis."

What? George Clooney traveling incognito? "Tess Livingston, Miami."

When they shook hands, his touch electrified her, unnerved her, and it definitely wasn't his resemblance to Clooney. It was as if they had been lovers in the distant past and she couldn't remember. Clearly absurd. He was not the sort of man she would forget.

She had been involved with her Bureau partner, Dan, for the last two years and they had discussed moving in together. Tess had resisted it. She loved her privacy, her space. At the moment, she could barely remember Dan Hernandez's face. She knew she had to figure out these glitches in her memory, but wasn't sure how.

"That's some nasty bruise on your arm," Ian remarked.

The marks were now a deep purple. "Some guy outside grabbed my wrist and told me I was an intruder."

"A local?"

"I don't know. But he was Quechua." *And then he turned up dead outside.*

"I saw a dead man outside by the outhouses," he confided, glancing around uneasily.

Ripples of shock tore through her. *It happened, here's your confirmation.* She kept her eyes fixed on the floor and whispered, "I don't think we should talk about this right now." Then she raised her head and pointed at the menu. In a normal tone of voice, she discussed the menu posted on the wall. *Plátanos* were plantains, a kind of banana, served baked or fried. *Pollo* was chicken, *legumbres* were vegetables. "It's smart to stay away from pork and beef. Chicken's probably okay, but vegetables are safer, the hotter the better. And bottled water is safer than soft drinks with ice. Or any drink with ice."

"Got it. Thanks."

She desperately wanted to linger, to continue talking to Ian. But her attraction to him was so strong that it troubled her. It might be too easy to allow camaraderie on the road to turn into a sexual adventure that she'd regret. She hadn't come to Ecuador to get her heart broken. "I need to get my ticket stuff straightened out. Excuse me."

But even when she got into the line at the ticket counter, she glanced back at him, drinking in the sight of him, unable to satisfy a need to look at him, to make sure he was real.

She noticed that people still peered out the window, the drunken cop still argued with someone, the door remained shut. *Not my business.* Tess checked her cell. No signal. But it looked as if her message to Maddie earlier had gone through. She typed a message to Dan in the hopes that once she was out of this valley, she might have a signal again. She updated him on the lead she'd gotten in Quito and her detour to Esperanza. She wanted to add something personal, that she missed him. But she didn't. In fact, she felt conflicted about writing him at all, and what was the point if she didn't have a signal?

She turned off the phone, slipped it back into her pocket. The American family waited just in front of her. The little girl was no longer crying, the boy had fallen asleep in his father's arms, and the wife seemed distraught. But Tess saw a plump, ripe papaya sticking up from her shoulder bag.

The girl looked back at Tess and said, "I feel better now. Thanks." She held out her teddy. "This is Roo. He feels better, too."

"Roo looks cold. Maybe you should tuck him inside your jacket."

The mother smiled nervously at Tess, tugged on her daughter's hand, leaned down and whispered something to her. Probably, *Don't talk to strangers, she found a dead man outside . . .*

Except she wasn't a stranger. She had given the woman all of her papaya enzymes.

When she reached the ticket agent, he listened with patient boredom. He said she had two choices—to return to Quito, a trip that would take about fifteen hours, or take the bus to Esperanza and make her travel arrangements from there to Tulcán.

"When does the bus leave for Quito?" she asked.

"Tomorrow morning."

"Where's the nearest hotel?"

"No hotels. You sleep here." His sweeping gesture encompassed the waiting area—plastic chairs lined up along the windows and walls, most of them occupied, the dirty concrete floor, dozens of stranded passengers.

No, thanks. Esperanza it would be. "Is my ticket set to go?"

He stamped it, gave her a thumbs-up. "Set to go."

Tess navigated through the crowd again and made it outside. The fog seemed thicker, and the cold, damp air penetrated her jeans, socks, jacket, chilling her to the bone. She wished she had one of those colorful wool blankets the Quechuans wore.

Two buses pulled up, Otavalo 12 and Baños 18, expelled passengers, and the drivers called out destinations. She felt uncomfortable in the crowd and moved to a bench against the wall, under the eaves. There. Better. A wall at her back, her own little space on the bench, food in her pack. She was good to go.

Ian Ritter came through the door, spotted her, and joined her, ticket in hand. "Esperanza on bus thirteen," he said. "It's better than staying in that lobby, with the dead guy outside. The body's still out there."

"I'd feel better about it if it weren't bus thirteen."

"Yeah, I know what you mean." He gave a soft, nervous laugh. "Listen to us. Superstitious grown-ups."

"Hey, I've yet to find an elevator with a floor thirteen listed."

"So you think the superstition is universal?"

"You look like George Clooney," she blurted.

"You remind me of Lauren Bacall in *Dark Passage.*"

Wow. Bacall? The only other person who had ever told her that was her dad. "One of my all-time favorite movies."

"You like old movies?"

"Some of them. You make it sound like that's rare."

"Rare for me. So why is *Dark Passage* one of your favorites?"

"Bogie and Bacall. How can you not like everything they were in together? Okay, so the premise is simple. Man is convicted of murdering his wife and goes to prison. He escapes to prove that he's innocent, Bacall helps him remain free, and he has plastic surgery to change his appearance. But it's the way it was done—how we don't see Bogie's face until the bandages come off. Up until that point, the entire perspective is through his eyes. It tells you a lot about what lies beneath appearances." *Why the hell did I say that? It sounds like I'm coming on to him.*

Well, wasn't she?

"I think *The Big Sleep* is a better movie," Ian said. "But in *Dark Passage,* you could really feel their chemistry." He flashed a quick smile. "You know what Bacall's nickname was?"

"Slim." Her dad used to call her that. *Hey, Slim, let's get a move on.*

Ian looked delighted. "You win the 1957 T-Bird."

She laughed and decided it didn't matter if her heart got broken here.

"Now, who the hell is George Clooney?" he asked.

Yeah, okay. Ian from Minneapolis had been living under a rock for the last twenty years. "An actor."

"Never heard of him. What movies has he been in?"

She'd seen all of Clooney's movies, but only recalled one. "*Ocean's Eleven.*"

"I thought Frank Sinatra and Dean Martin were in that."

"Well, yeah, in the original. But they did a remake."

He seemed confused now and she wondered if the altitude was affecting his memory, too. She returned to the number thirteen. "Okay, number thirteen. Among the Greeks, the bad luck day is Tuesday the thirteenth. On most planes, you don't find a thirteenth seat or a thirteenth row, at least not in planes where the first twelve rows are first class. In some cultures, there's a superstition that if thirteen people sit at a table for a meal, one of them will die in the next year. And it goes on like that, in country after country, culture after culture."

"If I remember my trivia correctly, I think the fear of the number thirteen is called 'triskaidekaphobia.'"

"That's a mouthful," she said, laughing.

One of the scrawny dogs, a black Lab, crept over to them, tail between his legs, as though he expected to be hit. But his tea-colored eyes, so wolflike, so primal, denied that impression. He looked up at her and Tess brought out an empanada, broke off a piece, set it on the ground in front of him. The dog hesitated, eyes flicking from the food to her face, as though he thought it might be a trick to grab him, haul him off. He finally drew closer and gobbled up the food. She put a second piece in the center of her palm, held out her hand. The dog wagged his tail, sniffed her hand, and delicately took the piece of empanada. Then he sat right up against her legs, shivering from the cold. She stroked his head, ran her nails down his sleek coat, finally put her arm around him.

The dog licked her hand. "So what should we call you?" she asked.

The Lab whined and pawed at the ground. Ian scratched the dog behind his ears and gave him the last bite of his empanada. She liked that, a man who fed strays. "When my son was really young," Ian said, "we had a yellow Lab we named Old Yeller, after the dog in the movie. We were convinced she had a human soul."

"How old is your son?"

"Twenty-one. He's a senior at the University of Minnesota."

She noticed he didn't wear a wedding ring. Divorced? Widowed? "You don't look old enough to have a twenty-one-year-old son."

He seemed flattered. "Forty-four last month. You have kids? Pets?"

"No kids yet, no pets now." But before law school and the FBI, she'd always had pets. Dogs, cats, birds, guinea pigs, gerbils, a regular circus. "What're you doing in Ecuador?"

"Vacation. You?"

"Same."

A bus emerged from the fog, smaller, more compact, painted in festive colors, bright red, bold yellow, celery green. Large black letters across the side read: ESPERANZA 13. It didn't shudder and backfire like the first bus. Piled high on its roof rack were bags, crates, packages. It stopped, the door sighed open, no one got off. But a young man with high cheekbones and a smile filled with teeth as white as a picket fence appeared in the doorway.

"Esperanza." His voice echoed through the fog like a cry to arms. "*Número trece a Esperanza.*"

As Tess and Ian got up, the dog started barking, tail whipping back and forth, and tore toward the bus. The driver stepped out and threw open his arms, laughing. "*Nomada. Caramba, perro.*" The Lab leaped up, knocking the driver back onto the steps, and covered the man's face with wet, sloppy kisses.

"He's got friends and a name. Let's get outta here," she said.

"Can't be too soon for me, Slim."

Slim. Yes, this guy intrigued her.

They walked over to the bus, where Nomad now sat at the top of the steps, panting, and the driver was brushing off his jacket. "Esperanza, right?" Ian asked.

"*Sí, señor. Bienvenidos.*" The driver took their tickets and they got on.

"Is Nomad your dog?" Tess asked.

"No, no." He shook his head vigorously, still smiling, and replied in heavily accented English. "Nomad belongs to everyone. He often rides the bus to Esperanza."

The bus was completely empty and nicer than she had expected, tourist transportation, clean and spacious, with a restroom, and a TV screen mounted up front. She chose an aisle seat halfway down and slipped her pack under the seat in front of her. Ian claimed a seat across the aisle and Nomad then settled in the aisle between them.

Through the window, Tess saw the American family huddled together, the mother stabbing her hand toward this bus, the husband pointing at the bus that had pulled up behind them. Beyond the Americans, slouched in the doorway of the bodega, was the drunken cop. Tess wondered if he was looking for her, for an official statement, to detain her. She turned away.

"Are we it?" Ian asked. "The only people headed for Esperanza?"

"There's a second bus behind us. I talked to that family earlier."

Ian slid open his window, took a look, pulled his head back in. "Yeah, I did, too. They're from upstate New York and headed to Esperanza."

The driver shouted out their destination again and when no one else came forward, he shut the door and turned to Tess, Ian, and the dog. "Amigos, welcome aboard."

"That bus behind us," Tess said. "Is it going to Esperanza, too?"

"Yes. But we are the express. My name is Manuel Ortega and I am honored to be your driver between here and Esperanza." He spoke carefully, as if testing each word in his head first. "And you are . . . ?"

Tess and Ian introduced themselves.

"We have much room, and on the screen behind me, we will be showing one of my favorite movies. *The Graduate.* In the back of the bus you will find a cooler with cold drinks and snacks. No popcorn, I am sorry to say, but I believe I have included some delicious treats for our dog, Nomad."

Nomad's ears twitched at the sound of his name. Manuel laughed and sat down. "And so, amigos—"

Banging on the door truncated his announcement. Manuel pressed the lever, the door whispered open, and a man lurched up the steps, clutching an old duffel bag. An icy horror swept through Tess: he looked like the dead man's twin, except he was taller and his braid was mostly gray.

Nomad lifted his head, a low, feral growl issuing from him, and Manuel shot to his feet and shouted, *"Vete, hombre. No hay bienvenido aquí para tí."*

A heated exchange ensued in Quechua. Nomad was now on his feet, snarling, lips drawn back, exposing his teeth, body hunched and ready to spring. The man gestured wildly at Tess and Ian. "You heard Manuel," Ian said, moving up the aisle. "Get the hell off the bus."

The man's expression didn't bode well. Tess had seen it on the faces of other foreigners when dealing with Americans, a kind of, *Who the fuck do you think you are?*

The man threw his head back, laughing. "What? A gringo tells *me* what to do?" He grabbed the front of Ian's jacket, and even though the Quechuan was much shorter and Ian outweighed him by probably sixty pounds, he jerked Ian forward and spat at him. The glob of spittle rolled down his cheek.

Ian wrenched free and pushed the guy away. The Quechuan stumbled back, Nomad charged, Tess leaped out of her seat, but already the man was falling out through the doorway, arms pinwheeling for balance, eyes wide with shock. He slammed into the ground and Manuel hurled his bag through the opening and shut the door. A heartbeat later the bus shrieked away into the fog and the gathering darkness.

Ian gripped the backs of the seats, body swaying with the motion of the bus. The dog seemed frozen, body hunched, fur standing up along his spine. Manuel drove like a man possessed. Tess, feeling shaken, made her way toward Ian and Manuel.

"What was *that* about?" she asked Manuel.

He waved her away. "Not to worry. These crazies are everywhere."

"C'mon, that guy wasn't a crazy. Everything he said and did seemed deliberate. And there was another man earlier, who grabbed my arm and told me I was an intruder and then ended up dead behind the store."

Manuel looked horrified. "He *touched* you, this man?"

She turned her arm so he could see the bruise.

"Dios mio," he whispered, and crossed himself. *"Mala sangre."*

"Bad blood." She could translate it, but didn't know what it meant in this context.

Ian said, "There were other Americans getting on that bus behind us. A family with two kids. Why did he target us?"

"He is *brujo*," Manuel spat. "He said you were not supposed to be on this bus."

Go home, gringa. You are an intruder here.

"Brujo," Ian murmured. "That means 'witch,' doesn't it?"

"Sí, señor, but no broomsticks, eh? They are crazy, like I say before." Manuel now laughed like it was no big deal. Every day here in Ecuador, his laughter said, weirdness happened, it was a way of life. "You must not worry. Nomad and Manuel, we take care of things."

Tess pressed him. "Why would he want to take us off the bus?"

"Quién sabe?" Who knows? Manuel made a dismissive gesture. "Please, watch the movie. Have something to eat and drink. In a little time, we will be in Esperanza." Then he fiddled with dials on the dashboard and the screen in the back of the closest seat flickered and there was Dustin Hoffman, a young kid in *The Graduate*, dubbed in Spanish.

Ian hesitated, then made his way back down the aisle, the black Lab following him. He sank into his seat. Tess continued to the rear, craving foods that were familiar, known, and discovered all of them. Gala apples, containers of yogurt, bags of Fritos, a brick of sharp cheddar. The situation wasn't just strange. It had gone well beyond that when she was booted from the first bus. She now felt as if she had walked into *The Twilight Zone*.

Three

Hours later. Ian didn't know how many hours, but Manuel had pulled off the road for a long time because the fog was just too thick to proceed safely.

The Graduate had ended and his body felt sluggish, thick, welded to the seat, as if he had been onboard for weeks. Blackness pressed up against the windows. The bus's headlights burned through a lighter fog now, glanced off trees. Here inside, the noise of the tires against the road seemed abnormally loud, deepening his concern that they were, including the dog, only four. His ears kept popping, a sure sign they were climbing higher into the mountains. The bus churned on through the darkness.

Shortly after the movie had started, he had moved across the aisle to sit next to Tess and now she dozed with her head resting against the window, hair falling like a veil across the side of her face. Bacall in repose. Jesus, she was easy on the eyes. He found himself staring at her for long periods of time, his mind a merciful blank.

When she pressed her stocking feet up against the chair in front of her and yawned, stretching her arms over her head, he looked quickly away from her to the dog, snoozing and snoring on the floor just up the aisle. Tess raised the armrest. He hoped it was an invitation to intimacy. But it might be nothing more than what happened on airplanes sometimes, when you and the stranger next to you acknowledge that the sardine space you share might be improved, however slightly, by raising that armrest. So he probably read too much into it.

But as their arms brushed, he felt the electrical connection like a series of shocks throughout his body. It was then he knew his first impression was correct. Intimacy, not just more stretching-out space.

"Where are we?" she asked.

"Beats me."

Tess leaned toward him. "Just curious. But do you get the feeling that something is wrong with this picture?"

His eyes pinned her, an insect under glass. "Which picture?"

"The whole damn thing."

"I get the impression that nothing here is what it appears to be."

"Most of South America feels that way to me. It's like the myths are alive, reaching out to us, and if we find a story that resonates for us, we get to stick around and explore it."

"What do you do?" he asked.

"You mean, like, for a living?"

He nodded.

"I'm . . ." She laughed. "I want to say that I'm a woman who hides out in South America when stuff goes wrong in her life."

It sounded like something Bacall would say, he thought, and waited for her to continue.

"I work for the FBI. I'm tracking a counterfeiter who is supposedly in Tulcán. What about you?"

"I teach journalism at the University of Minnesota. I also write a weekly column in the *Minneapolis Tribune*. This week's column is on empanadas in Ecuador."

They cracked up, snickering and snorting like kids who had just heard a fart joke. Ian reached for her hand and turned it over, looking at the ugly bruise. He liked the softness of her skin. "It looks like a neon sign of fingerprints." He withdrew his hand. "You said the dead guy was covered with blood, Slim. But what's that mean? Had he been shot? Stabbed? What?"

She had explained in more detail during the movie. "He looked like he had bled out. Not exactly empanada material, is it?"

"Why do you use that term? Bled out? How do you know that's what happened to him? Do you have medical experience?"

"My mother's a nurse. When my dad was dying, he bled out—not exactly like the dead man, but similar. I know what it looks like when someone bleeds out, Ian."

He heard the defensiveness in her voice. "Sorry, it's the journalist in me. I seem to have this obsessive need for objective proof. When I suspected my ex was having an affair, when everything pointed to that, I hired this private detective to follow her, take pictures, document it. He did. Pictures don't lie. I filed for divorce."

Divorce. Why did he tell her that? Why divulge it? Well, that was easy. He'd said it to let her know he was single and available.

"Actually, pictures *do* lie," she said. "Any image can be altered. But if we know there's something really wrong with *this* picture, how come we're still on this bus?"

He tapped his knuckles against the dark, frosted window. "Hey, I don't have any idea where the hell we are. It's dark and cold out there. In here, it's warm, we have food, a restroom. We even have a *dog*. And the company is great. That's why we're still on the bus." He didn't know what her quick smile meant.

"When we get to this town," she said, "I think we need to consider how to proceed. How I can get to Tulcán. How you can get to the Galápagos."

You go your way, I go mine. "Sounds like a good plan." The thought that they would head in different directions depressed him. He broke eye contact and stared at the snow-filled TV screen.

Then he astonished himself by looking at her again, touching her chin, turning her head toward him. Their eyes locked, the air crackled with sexuality, and he brought his mouth to hers. The kiss was light, exploratory, a scene from one of the old black-and-white movies that they both loved. But in those movies, he thought, it didn't go beyond this kiss, not on screen. Ian pulled back.

"Hey, if your counterfeiter can wait a few days, how about if you take a detour to the Galápagos with me?" he suggested. "Are you allowed to do that?"

"*Allowed?*" She seemed to nearly choke on the word. "The last time someone asked me that, I was maybe six years old, allowed to walk *here* but not *there*, allowed to do *this* but not *that*. Fuck the Bureau. I can do whatever I want to do, whenever I want."

"What about the counterfeiter?"

"Hey, if I don't find him, so what? The world won't end. The Bureau won't collapse. Sure, I'm allowed, I'm a grown-up."

When he kissed her again, an image bloomed in his head of the odd angle of the dead man's feet, out there by the outhouses.

Inside the greenhouse, Dominica followed the peasant woman beneath the soft lights as she pruned strawberry plants, plucked ripe papayas from the trees, picked weeds from a garden of herbs. She loved the certainty with which the woman's fingers moved, how she hummed quietly as she worked, patting the rich, black dirt with her hands and talking to the plants, urging them to grow more quickly. But what was she doing alone in the greenhouse at this time of night? Even in the countryside, the locals knew the dangers.

She contemplated seizing her just to sample the details of who she was, the flavor of small-town rural life. But she felt a disturbing rift in the web that connected the *brujos* of her tribe, and was compelled to follow it. She thought herself toward the disturbance and it led her to a narrow, twisted road high in the mountains. A lone bus chugged upward through the starlit darkness, the bright glow of its headlights glancing off the sheer faces of the peaks. Puzzled by why a bus would cause any disturbance in the *brujo* web, she drifted in closer and read the words on the side: ESPERANZA *13*. A tourist bus?

She drifted alongside it, peered in through the dark windows. Except for the driver, it looked empty, yet she sensed three other bodies inside, probably asleep. Dominica hovered over the roof for a moment, moving right along with the bus, then drifted down through the packages and bags strapped to the top, down through the metal and into the twilit interior.

A man lay on his side, body stretched out across three seats, jacket pulled over him, head resting on his pack. On the other side of the aisle, a woman sprawled across three other seats, long blond hair hanging over the edge, jacket bunched up under her head, arms clutched tightly against her body. Tourists who had caught the last bus out from wherever? But why would these two draw her here?

Dominica moved in closer to the man, intrigued by the shape his body assumed as he slept—a lightning bolt. It meant that he attracted the unforeseen, that he himself was a lightning rod. She liked that. She also liked that he was as handsome as a movie star. Could she take him? Could Ben? Wouldn't these two make ideal hosts for her and Ben?

She considered assuming a tenuous human form, something any *brujo* could do north of the Río Palo, so that she could follow his breath, the smell of it, back through time. She wouldn't be able to hold the form very long, but it would provide her with temporary sensory ability—more than what she had as a *bruja,* yet pitifully short of what physical life offered.

The problem was the driver. If she assumed a temporary form, she would be visible to him. And he had a flamethrower tucked nearby. Fire was the preferred weapon against *brujos* when they were in their phony human forms. Or in their natural forms. It didn't matter. It could obliterate her. So she satisfied her curiosity by leaning in closer to the man—and suddenly wrenched back, shocked to realize he wasn't physical. His body was elsewhere, dying, in a coma, at the brink between life and death. *You're a transitional. The first in five centuries.*

Impossible.

Dominica stared at him, unable to wrap her mind around it, around him. She finally moved closer to the woman and realized that she, too, was a transitional, nearly dead in the physical world. It meant that both were in deep comas in their respective physical bodies, perhaps on life support machines, and what she saw here were their souls, the essence of who they were. *Two in one day.*

Would Esperanza accommodate their illusions? Of course. It already had. They looked as solid and physical as any human being and would be seen as such by any people with whom they came into contact. They would believe they were alive, that their encounters with people and everything they experienced and felt were real. Their cell phones would respond to conditions of altitude and weather, just as they did in the physical world. Reception would be spotty, but when their cells had signals, they would be able to send and receive text messages and would be able to leave and receive voice mails, all of it based on their own memories and expectations. They wouldn't be able to have actual conversations with loved ones, but everything else would be like physical life. They would be able to touch each other, make love, converse, eat and sleep, even dream.

But how had they found their way here? Five hundred years ago, when Esperanza had been brought into the physical world, it had been closed to transitionals. So who had thrown open the gates? The chasers? If so, why? What did it mean? And if two transitionals had gotten through, then perhaps more would, too, and the feasting days of the distant past would return. Her hope soared at the thought. But caution instantly intruded. *It may be a trick, a ploy by the chasers.*

Dominica moved swiftly up the aisle and suddenly a black dog leaped off a seat, blocking her way to the driver, and snarled, back hunched, fur rising along his spine, teeth bared.

The driver's head snapped around as he reached for the flamethrower. *"Epa, perro, qué pasa?"*

She recognized the driver. Manuel Ortega lived outside Esperanza, in one of the rural communities, and worked part-time for various inns and hotels in Esperanza. But she knew little else about him. He slowed the bus, glanced back at the road, then eyed the dog in his rearview mirror. "Are we good? Are we safe?"

Low, feral sounds issued from the dog. Dominica couldn't tell if the animal really saw her or only sensed her presence. Didn't matter. She drifted back, not willing to provoke the dog into attacking. It couldn't hurt her, she was already dead. But its attack would signal Manuel that a *brujo* was nearby and the call would go out to Esperanza and all the defensive measures would be taken. Sirens, shutters, bunkers, cops with flamethrowers.

"Is something here, Nomad?" Manuel asked.

The name shocked her. *Nomad? Here?* Why hadn't she recognized him? Because there were thousands of black dogs in Ecuador. Because it wasn't like their paths crossed frequently. Because she hadn't laid eyes on Nomad for decades. But there was only one black dog with the eyes of a wolf, and seeing him here, now, tore at her.

For nearly a century, they had run together, Nomad her most trusted companion, not a *brujo* but a shape-shifter capable of transforming into a man with the face and body of a god. And one night in battle, he was critically injured and given a choice. *Join us or die.* And when he had joined the chasers, he had lost his ability to shift and was forever imprisoned in the body of this skinny black Labrador with the eyes of a wolf and the mind and heart of a man.

I mean you no harm, she thought at him.

He bared his teeth. *The only things you understand are harm, despair, death. Leave.*

But this is unprecedented, two transitionals who—

Leave, Nica.

I don't understand how—

Go fuck yourself, Nica.

Then he sprang, his body arching through the air, jaws snapping. Manuel veered the bus to the right and it tore across the shoulder of the road, stones pinging against the sides. He slammed on the brakes and she was catapulted through the roof like some Olympic gymnast. She hovered there for a time, above the motionless bus, clouds of dust mixing with the fog. But she couldn't bring herself to enter the bus again.

Just as well. Manuel scrambled out, his flamethrower whipping from side to side as he shouted in Spanish, *"I know you're here. Show yourself and let's finish it."*

Right. Like this fool with his fancy flamethrower would finish anything. Her tribe of *brujos* numbered more than sixty thousand. The population of Esperanza was twenty thousand, with another ten thousand scattered through the countryside north of the Río Palo. *Brujos* outnumbered humans by at least three to one. This arrogant young bastard pissed her off. But could he be one of those rumored to be planning a retaliation against the *brujos?* She still hadn't checked the rumor mill on the Internet, but would do it as soon as she returned to the city.

She quickly thought herself into her favorite human form, her *virtual* form, a tall, muscular woman armed with an AK–47. Manuel took one look at her and started laughing. "Are you kidding me?" he finally managed to say in between guffaws. "An AK–47? Why not arm yourself with a surface-to-air missile?"

He mocked her so openly that she just stood there, stunned. Why wasn't he tearing for the nearest shelter? Why wasn't he racing away from her, shrieking with terror? Why wasn't he terrified? A part of her began to believe this rumor about retaliation. She'd never encountered a local so bold.

"Who . . . who the *fuck* are you?" she stammered.

"Not anyone you want to cross," he said, and suddenly flames shot from his thrower and Dominica was forced to shed her virtual form and move away, quickly.

She remained above him for a few minutes, watching as the fog twisted around his ankles, his knees. Nomad now stood beside him and Manuel's body swiveled back and forth, his flamethrower steady. Then his head suddenly dropped back, as if he sensed where she was, and flames shot upward, brilliant, orange, dangerously hot. Dominica thought herself away, fast.

Ian woke sporadically during the night and hoped the movement of the bus and the drone of its engine would lull him back to sleep. He had moved next to Tess again and she had nodded off with her head against his shoulder. He remained wide awake, staring out into the darkness, unease seeping through him. He couldn't shake it.

He tried to focus on the scent of Tess's hair, an aroma like roses and mint. Strands of it rested against his shoulder and upper arm and he drew his fingers over it, marveling at the softness, the pale gold color. He longed to kiss her once more, to see if he felt again what he had experienced when his mouth first touched hers, as if the earth's tectonic plates were shifting. A Hemingway moment. But he was reluctant to wake her.

Part of his unease concerned the holes that riddled his memory. He couldn't remember anything about this trip prior to arriving at the Bodega del Cielo. The altitude and fatigue might account for it. But it didn't explain why he was on a bus bound for a town he'd never heard of, accompanied by a black dog and a woman who looked so much like Lauren Bacall that it made his heart ache. And how could she be an FBI agent?

When he first had seen her back in the bodega, standing in the food line, he had pegged her for a teacher, a lawyer, a nurse, but also as something of a rebel in her personal life. He figured her for the type who sought out Middle Earth on weekends, got high with her boyfriend, demonstrated against the war, and ate organic foods.

But FBI? And that dead body back at the bodega?

He knew that he lived in Minneapolis and vaguely recalled a flight from there to Miami to Quito. Other than that, he wasn't sure of anything. Mulling this over only made him more anxious and Ian finally shut his eyes. Almost immediately, his left brain shut down, his anxiety ebbed. He didn't give a shit. He didn't need all the answers this minute. Right now, the bus was the most comfortable choice.

When he opened his eyes again, the foggy windows fractured the light.

He rubbed his fist against the glass and peered upward into Jimi Hendrix's *Purple Sky*. Plum-colored and streaked with blinding white light, it was the kind of sky that urged him to believe in miracles. But the fog still hugged the windows and he couldn't see much of the landscape.

Tess now leaned away from him, head resting against the window, jacket pulled over her shoulders. Nomad snoozed on a seat, the bus barreled on through the dawn. Ian straightened, knuckled the sleep from his eyes, and got up to use the restroom. He took his toothbrush with him. He could deal with nearly anything if his teeth were clean, probably a vestige of a childhood spent on military bases, where home was what you carried with you.

Home is where your toothbrush is, son, his old man used to say.

Sure. That explained why his father hung himself in a bathroom, a toothbrush sticking out of his shirt pocket. *My home is death.*

Ian slipped into the bathroom, shut the door, locked it. Laughable. Locking it against who or what? Tess? Manuel? The dog?

The bathroom was as spacious and clean as the rest of the bus. Plenty of hot water poured from the faucet, and the soap smelled like some herb he used when he cooked. Basil? Mint? Cilantro? Maybe a combo of all three. He liked that the scents were familiar to him. But when he raised his eyes to his reflection, he didn't like what he saw. A haggard face. Tight, anxious mouth, terrified eyes that ached from lack of sleep. A man at the edge. But at the edge of what? Just what scared him so badly that his hands now shook? Well, it was obvious, wasn't it? Bathroom, toothbrush: *you don't want to end up like him.*

Ian squeezed his eyes shut, but it already was too late, he was *there,* a seventeen-year-old kid running down the hall to the shower one morning only to find his father hanging from a rope. He still could hear the way the rope creaked, see how his father's eyes bulged in their sockets, tongue lolling from his mouth, face a ghastly blue. Nearly thirty years hadn't diminished the clarity of this memory.

He gripped the sides of the sink, struggling to shake off the rest of the memory, but couldn't. The wound had been torn open, the past spewed forth. He saw his younger self staggering back from his father's body, horrified, relieved, then eaten up with guilt. He saw himself and his mother moving out of the base housing in Stuttgart, Germany, where his father had been stationed at the time. He remembered that in the ensuing months, the suicide always stood between them, an uninvited guest. The only time they had spoken of it, at Ian's high school graduation, his mother had referred to his father's "death" and Ian had snapped, "He fucking killed himself. There's a difference." They never again mentioned his old man.

Ian didn't have any idea why his father committed suicide. His knowledge of the man didn't extend beyond his career military mind-set—*tuck in the corners of your bed; it's "yes, sir" and "no, ma'am"*—and what he was like when he was drunk, demons released by booze, belt whistling through the air as he shouted, *You'd best remember who's boss here, you little shit.*

But Ian was not his father. Since his son's birth twenty-one years ago, he had taken great care to be the father his old man hadn't been. When his wife sank into a terrible postpartum depression after Luke's birth, Ian took a six-month sabbatical from the University of Minnesota and cared for his infant son. When Louise returned to her job as an accountant for a real estate firm, Ian arranged his teaching schedule so that one of them was always home to take care of Luke. Then it was Little League games, Boy Scouts, fishing and camping trips, late-night talks around campfires. They were tight long before Ian's marriage fell apart and remained close afterward. They shared a love of the outdoors, sports, politics, music, books and old movies. Anything that interested Luke, interested Ian.

Even with Luke's busy schedule now, in his final year of college, they still managed to get together for fishing trips to northern Minnesota, for Twins games, for concerts. Ian felt genuinely sorry for Louise, that it drove her nuts when Luke took time to be with Ian, yet couldn't make it to Sunday dinner with her and her new husband. But Luke detested her husband, didn't get along with Louise, and stubbornly refused to pretend otherwise.

Ian pressed paper towels against his face. *Breathe through it.* When he finally tossed the wad in the trash, he glimpsed movement in his peripheral vision, and spun around, breathing hard, the small of his back pressed against the sink. The hairs on his arms stood up, a cold tongue licked its way up his spine. But the restroom was empty, he was alone. Of course he was.

He remembered that in the weeks immediately after his old man's suicide, he had felt as edgy as he did now, constantly looking over his shoulder, as if he had expected his father to suddenly appear and announce that he wasn't really dead, after all. The feeling that he was being watched had persisted until he had left Germany for Minnesota. But what spooked him now? Hadn't the ghosts of his childhood been put to rest?

He peered in the mirror again, searching his face for signs that he might be getting sick. He pressed his hand to his forehead. No fever. If anything, his skin felt abnormally cool. He murmured, "I am . . ."

I am Winnie the Pooh, Luke used to say when he was a kid. The I Am game evolved over the years from I am Pooh to I am Bond, James Bond. If he and Luke had been playing that game right now, it would be, *I'm feeling troubled and fucked up and I'm not sure why.* Had he spoken to Luke since leaving the U.S.? It seemed he had, but he wasn't sure. He needed to call him as soon as they arrived in Esperanza. Luke would be worried if he didn't hear from him at least once a week, and since Ian hadn't known where he would be staying, Luke couldn't call him.

Ian opened the door and made his way up the aisle, past the snoozing dog, past Tess still curled up with her head against the window, and came up behind Manuel. "What time is it?"

"Six-twenty. We are nearly there. Besides the delay from the fog, I had to pull over in the night because of the rain. So I went to sleep. It is why we did not get here sooner."

"Tell me how that TV screen up there works."

Manuel laughed. "I am no technician. I cannot even tell you why a lamp comes on when I stick the plug into a socket."

Fair enough. Ian couldn't explain it, either. "Then tell me about the *brujos.*"

Manuel pressed the heels of his hands against the steering wheel. "That is a difficult question."

"Give me a simple answer."

"Lost souls. That's what the *brujos* are."

Lost souls. Fine. But was he speaking in a religious sense? Metaphorically? And what did he mean by "soul," anyway? Before Ian could ask, the bus drew up in front of a huge metal gate with a high concrete wall shooting off on either side of it and disappearing into the fog. Manuel flipped a switch on the dashboard and the gate swung open, creaking noisily.

Manuel drove through and continued along a narrow, twisted dirt road lined by the oddest-looking trees. They looked like a cheerleader's pom-poms, tufts of green sprouting from the branches in uneven clusters. "Those are monkey-puzzle trees." Manuel pointed off to the right. "And over there, through the opening in the fog, see the alpacas?"

A group of them grazed in the dawn light, beautiful creatures with long legs and necks, short tails and small heads, most of them perhaps three feet tall. Interspersed among them were their llama cousins, who looked nearly identical except that they were taller and weighed more.

"Do you have alpacas or llamas where you live, señor?"

Ian laughed. Alpacas and llamas in Minneapolis? "Nope. Are they friendly?"

"They can be shy, but they love people. Here in Esperanza, they supply wool and are used to carry heavy loads. The alpaca wool is the best, soft, like cashmere."

"Can we take a closer look at them?" Tess asked, joining them.

Ian noticed that her request surprised Manuel. "You do not want to go first to your hotel? To rest until later?"

"The hotel sounds great, Manuel, but I'd like to stretch my legs first," Tess said.

"Me, too," Ian agreed. Nomad barked and trotted up behind them, slipped past Ian and stopped in front of the door, tail thumping against the floor of the bus.

"The majority wins, eh?" Manuel stopped the bus, opened the door. The dog bounded off first, with Tess and Ian close behind him.

The fog swirled across the damp ground, twisting vinelike around their legs. But it burned off quickly as the sun pushed higher into the sky. Ian now had a clear view of the alpacas and llamas in the distance. Their heads seemed to swivel around, mouths chewing patiently, and although they gazed curiously toward the humans, they didn't move any closer. Ian and Tess made their way toward the creatures, Nomad trotting alongside, Manuel hanging back, calling, "Please, my friends, do not go too far."

Ian raised his arm, indicating they heard him, but he and Tess kept inching closer until maybe eight yards separated them from the animals. "They're beautiful," Tess breathed. "Their eyes are huge."

The sun broke through the fog, showering the alpacas and llamas in a soft, celestial light that tinged their fur a reddish gold. Spellbound, Ian wished he had a camera. Then the fog closed in again, rolling toward the animals on every side, thickening, rising. Something spooked them and they turned in unison, like dancers in some choreographed ballet, and tore off across the grass, headed for the far trees.

At the same moment, Nomad started barking fiercely, the fog rolled toward them faster and faster, every hair on Ian's body stood on end. Nomad suddenly sprang at him, knocking him back.

"Hey, what the hell is wrong with you, Nomad?" Ian snapped.

The dog barked again and dashed off into the fog. "I think he wants us to follow him," Tess said.

"Suits me. It's eerie here. Let's get back to the bus."

The fog now surrounded them. Although Ian could hear Nomad's barking, it echoed in the thick whiteness. Wind rustled through trees, but Ian realized it was a soft whispering, insidious, mocking. And then the whispers became voices, a strange, haunted chanting that sounded like, *Find the body, fuel the body, fill the body, be the body,* over and over again, louder and louder.

"Jesus," he whispered. "Do you hear that?"

Alarm filled her eyes. "It sounds like—"

Suddenly, a group of men emerged from the fog, six, eight, then ten. They wore dark shirts and trousers, with white wool blankets wrapped around their shoulders. Their eyes seemed to be all pupil, shiny black surfaces that reflected nothing. Some had long braids, others had short hair, some wore shoes, others were barefoot.

"*Campesinos,*" Tess whispered. "Peasants." But where had they come from? Ian wondered. "*Buenos días.*"

"*Buenos días,*" one of them replied.

Ian nodded and looked away from them. He and Tess walked faster. Two more men appeared on either side of them and fell into step alongside them.

"*Buenos días,*" Ian said again.

"*De dónde vienen?*" the man on the right asked.

"What's that mean?" Ian whispered to Tess.

"They're asking where we're from. This is seriously creepy, Ian."

As the man repeated his question, Ian took Tess's hand, gripping it tightly. He no longer heard the chanting and wondered if they had imagined it. He and Tess walked faster, the two men fell back. When Ian stole a look behind, he saw at least two dozen of them now, fanning out behind them in a half-moon, the men at either end closing in, tightening the semicircle. Then nothing registered except his certainty that he didn't want these men to touch him. "Run," he rasped.

They raced forward, he tripped over something on the ground, lost his balance and flew forward. Tess's hand slipped away. He slammed into the ground, air rushed from his lungs, and Ian lay there, unable to breathe. Nothing in his body worked, except for his brain, and it shrieked, *Get up now, fast, run.* And, somehow, he did, lurching to his feet with the gracelessness of Frankenstein.

Only then could he suck air in through his clenched teeth. He raced toward Tess's vanishing shape in the fog, toward Nomad's frantic barking, toward the roar of the bus's engine, all these sounds concentrated in one area of the fog.

But the men surrounded him—and closed in on him. Ian feinted to the right, the left. They moved as he moved, as if they were connected to him, as if they were all part of the same wave, the same netting, the same huge piece of seaweed. He saw a tiny opening, dived, struck the ground, rolled, leaped up, and raced away from them. The bus roared into view and Tess swayed in the doorway, shouting at him, gesturing wildly. He loped toward her, toward the bus, the men pursuing him, nearly reaching him. Tess leaned out and grasped his hand and pulled him aboard, her strength as shocking as the fact that he had escaped at all.

The doors shut, he and Tess stumbled back against the seats. Manuel shouted, *"Hold on, amigos,"* and executed an erratic ninety-degree turn away from the group.

Tess fell into the nearest seat, her head cut off Ian's line of sight. Then she shot to her feet and grabbed onto one of the bars above her head as Manuel swerved into another ninety-degree turn. The bus skidded back onto the dirt road, tires kicking up dust and stones, and raced ahead, engine roaring, and broke free of the fog.

Ian grabbed onto the armrests, Nomad sprawled against the floor, Manuel drove madly. When he finally spoke, he sounded angry. "You cannot leave the bus again. Not until we arrive at the hotel."

"You haven't told us shit," Ian spat. "Neither of us remembers buying tickets to Esperanza. Neither of us has a clue what the hell we're doing on this bus. There's a dead man back at that bodega that no one seems too concerned about. Who the fuck *were* those men?"

"I cannot explain all the—"

"We need answers, Manuel," said Tess.

"And if we don't get them, we're finding the fastest way out of this place," Ian added. "So either you give us the answers, Manuel, or stop the goddamn bus so we can get off."

The bus stopped and Manuel shot to his feet, marched over to Ian, and leaned in close, planting his hands on the armrests, effectively trapping Ian in his seat. "I do not have the answers." He spoke quietly, a threatening edge in his voice. "I wish that I could make a list for you. One, two, three. But I cannot. I do know this. Those men were *brujos,* señor. In the recent history of my city, the *brujos* never have been so bold. *Never.* An assault on Señorita

Tess. You, surrounded by these men. It means you both are important to them. It means . . ." Manuel suddenly paused, blinked. All the anger seemed to hiss out of him. He stood up straight again, so that Ian was no longer trapped in his seat, and his arms dropped to his sides. Nomad growled softly and Manuel glanced at him, then back to Ian, at Tess. "The dog should stay with you. When he growls, when he barks, when he becomes agitated, it means the *brujos* are nearby."

With that, Manuel started back to his seat, but Ian grabbed the hem of his jacket. "Hold on just a goddamn minute, Manuel."

Manuel jerked free of Ian's grasp, eyes burning with anger. "I have told you all that I know."

"I don't believe in witches, so what are these *brujos*?"

"They are *real,* my gringo friend, and it doesn't matter what you believe. That dead man behind the bodega? The *brujos* were responsible for that. The mark on Tess's arm, you being surrounded by them out there . . . *Real.* So if you cannot believe in *real,* then you have a very big problem."

He spun and hurried toward the front of the bus. Moments later, they drove on.

Four

Tension clung to the air like Velcro to cloth. No one spoke. Tess and Ian glanced at each other and he rolled his eyes and shook his head, as if to say he didn't have any idea what had happened. Manuel drove with his shoulders hunched and tight, eyes fixed on the road ahead. Tess felt sorry for him and even more anxious to get to the city.

When they were free of the fog, she drank in the stunning landscape. Sheep and goats, cows and horses grazed in the rolling pastures and emerald fields on either side of the bus. Beyond the fields rose spectacular mountains and volcanic peaks that seemed to reach for the sky as if to embrace it. A few buildings appeared, wooden structures with tin roofs, like the Bodega del Cielo, that looked like they were held together with Super Glue and duct tape. An occasional old, rusted car bounced by, tires kicking up dust. But the road was used predominantly by peasants, hauling their goods in burro-drawn wooden wagons or carrying their wares on their heads and shoulders.

The road turned from dirt to cobblestone. More buildings cropped up, more cars appeared, most of them small and old—VWs, Renaults, Peugeots, and lots of motorbikes and scooters. But pedestrians and people on bicycles outnumbered cars.

As the city took shape around them, Tess's first impression was of antiquity, evident in the bleached stone of the colonial buildings, the looming churches, the maze of narrow streets. Every few blocks, parks appeared, filled with monkey puzzle trees, pines, flocks of hummingbirds, and bustling outdoor markets. Wooden wagons brimmed with fresh fruits and vegetables, men and women hawked jewelry, art, woven hammocks.

As the street widened into four lanes and filled with traffic, restaurants, cafés, and businesses became more numerous. Sleek buildings of steel and concrete appeared. This city, like Quito, seemed to have two distinct sections to it—the old and the new. In between lay the residential area through which they now drove, homes and apartments rising from hilltops, tall, snow-covered peaks looming behind them, embracing the city, protecting and isolating it. And there, distant but approaching, a magnificent condor drifted on a current of air. Tess nudged Ian, pointed out the window. Despite the earlier weirdness, this certainly wasn't a bad place to end up in accidentally.

The bus finally pulled up in front of Posada de Esperanza, a colonial-style building that appeared to lie at the border between the old and new parts of the city. Made of bleached stones and wood, with large bay windows, the inn's single story was shaped like a half-moon. To either side of the double doors stood huge ceramic pots filled with blue and lavender flowers and emerald-green ferns that would cause her mother to swoon with admiration and envy.

As the doors opened, Nomad bounded off first and trotted over to the doorman, a handsome young man with high cheekbones and a winning smile. He greeted the Lab with a pat, a grin, and a treat that Nomad leaped into the air to catch. The dog's lungs, Tess thought as she stepped down, were definitely made for this altitude.

"Welcome to the posada." Manuel swept his arm grandly toward the building, then pointed at the plaque above the front door. "*Mi casa es su casa.* My house is your house."

His eyes looked strangely smooth and bright. A sense of familiarity swept through Tess, as it had several times since she'd first seen Manuel. It puzzled her. It was as if he were an old friend whom she recognized intuitively, but not consciously. Yet, she was sure she'd never met him before.

"It is the most comfortable lodging in Esperanza," Manuel added. "Excuse me, I will be right back."

He headed toward the doorman and Tess stood in the inn's shadow, the early morning chill nipping at her face and hands, her stomach cramping with hunger. She watched the activity on the street—a bus, two men speeding past on bikes, cars, kids in uniforms on their way to school. Ordinary life here didn't seem all that different. Except for these *brujos*.

Manuel and the doorman conversed like old friends and kept glancing toward her and Ian, then both of them came over. Introductions ensued. Juanito Cardenas looked to be in his late twenties and his facial features said he was part Quechua. He tugged nervously at the lower edge of his jacket, and didn't seem to know whether to smile or frown.

"Juanito will speak to the clerk and make sure that you have comfortable rooms and everything else that you need," Manuel said.

"You have no more luggage?" Juanito asked.

"Nope, this is it," Tess replied.

"Never have I seen Americans travel with so little. It is a good thing, eh? It means that you are decisive, certain."

Tess almost laughed. Decisive? Certain? No way.

"Right now, we're just tired and hungry," Ian said.

Juanito flashed his dimpled smile. "I understand."

They entered the posada. The most unusual thing about it was that no one objected when Nomad tagged along. She couldn't remember dogs being allowed in motels and inns in Quito. If anything, Quito was overrun with strays and, like most domestic animals in South America, they were treated like shit.

Ian apparently noticed this oddity, too, and asked, "Is Nomad allowed inside?"

"Everyone knows him," Manuel replied, as if this explained it all.

In the lobby, leather couches and chairs were draped with Ecuadorian blankets, native art festooned the walls. The roaring fireplace reminded her of a ski lodge in Colorado, people sitting around and reading newspapers, sipping coffee. A black and white cat wound his way through their legs, purring loudly. He trotted up to Nomad, they touched noses, then the cat moved on and finally settled by the fireplace. In the bay window, an Amazonian parrot with flaming blue and scarlet wings moved back and forth along a massive perch, greeting everyone who passed.

"*Buenos días, cómo está, bienvenidos.*" Now and then it emitted a wolf whistle as some beautiful babe passed by. When Nomad sat in front of the perch, the parrot gazed down at the dog and greeted him in perfect English. "Hello, Nomad, welcome." Then the bird squawked, picked up a piece of dried fruit from her bowl, tossed it, and Nomad caught it.

"*Cómo te llamas?*" Tess asked the parrot.

The parrot looked her over, whistled softly. "*Me llamo Kali.*"

"Wow, Kali, as in consort of Shiva?" Ian asked.

"Supreme deity of Hinduism," Manuel added, and pointed at Juanito, now talking to a bald man at the front desk. "The manager is Ed Granger. He and Juanito will take care of you from here. If I can be of help, amigos, here is my card." One for each of them. "I can drive you around, take you to wonderful restaurants, show you marvelous sights, drive you to the volcanoes, *me entiendes?*"

Ian, evidently feeling guilty for his outburst on the bus, quickly dug cash from his pocket and pressed it into Manuel's hand. "Thank you for everything, and I apologize for getting angry."

"It is nothing, señor. I understand. Dealing with *brujos* . . ." He shrugged. "No two people react the same."

Manuel extended his hand to Tess, but she hugged him instead. That sense of familiarity rushed through her again. She stepped back, frowning. "I feel like we've met before, Manuel."

His quick smile lit up his face. "I know what you mean. But I think not. You are not one I would forget, Señorita Tess."

"I appreciate everything you've done."

As they crossed the lobby, Tess noticed more of its details—the beautiful light that spilled through the glass domes of several skylights, the intricate designs set into the floor tiles, the magnificent craftsmanship of the woven rugs. Music played in the background, something familiar with a Latin rhythm. The faint scent of smoke from the fireplace mixed with the richness of freshly brewed coffee.

"Hey, it could be a lot worse," Ian remarked. "We could've gotten stuck in that bodega for the next three days."

No argument there.

At the desk, Juanito introduced them to Whiskers, the black and white tuxedo cat Tess had seen moments ago, now curled up on the counter near Ed Granger. Granger looked like an ex-wrestler—a slick, shiny bald head, massive shoulders, a colorful and elaborate tattoo that decorated his right arm and the back of his right hand. "Mates," his voice boomed. "Juanito tells me you are North American allies."

The phrase struck Tess as strange, as though a war had been declared and Americans and Aussies were on the same side. She could tell from the expression on Ian's face that he found it odd, too.

"Uh, yes, that's right," Ian said. "We'd like two rooms."

Ed's smile shrank. He said something in Quechua to Juanito, who looked flustered, replied in Quechua, then shrugged and hurried off. "We have just one room at the moment, actually a cottage, with two double beds. I hope that won't be a problem, mates."

Not for me, Tess thought.

"We should have something else by tomorrow," Granger continued. "Juanito went over there now to make sure the refrigerator is stocked with food. He'll make you tea that helps counteract the effects of the altitude."

Ian looked over at Tess, who said, "It's fine with me. Right now, a bed in a stable would be fine."

"A stable." Granger exploded with laughter. "Oh, I assure you, mates, the cottage far surpasses any stable." As he slapped a key on the counter, the tattooed figures on the back of his hand seemed to move, dance, undulate. "Go down the first hall to the right, out the first door. Cottage thirteen is on the east side of the courtyard."

Thirteen. That number again, Tess thought. "Do you take credit cards?" She reached into her pack.

"Credit cards, cash, a check, traveler's checks. But don't worry about it now. We'll settle the bill when you leave. I just need to see your passports."

Passport. She couldn't remember the last time she'd shown hers. But she slipped it out of her pack and turned it over to Granger, just as Ian did. Maybe it was her imagination, but it seemed he studied their passports just a tad too long.

As Granger started filling out forms, Ian said, "You know, we both seem to be having memory problems. We can't even remember getting on buses that dropped us at Bodega del Cielo. Tess was headed to Tulcán, I was going to the Galápagos."

Granger made a dismissive gesture. "Not unusual. The bus system in this part of Ecuador is confusing. People end up on the wrong buses all the time. As for your memory, it's the altitude, mate. Once you cross the Río Palo, the road climbs to over thirteen thousand feet. Esperanza is at thirteen-two.

Don't drink alcohol for at least twenty-four hours. Stay hydrated. Sleep all you want. You'll feel a hundred percent better in another day."

"I don't remember seeing any river," Tess said.

"You crossed it shortly before you reached the bodega." Granger finished his forms and handed the passports back to them. "As the crow flies, Esperanza isn't very far from the bodega. But the road twists upward for more than seven thousand feet. It's like going from, oh, maybe Denver to the continental divide."

"Where can we make travel arrangements?" Tess asked.

"And I'd like to make a call to the States," Ian added.

"Calls can be made from the cottage. As for travel, we can arrange things for you here at the desk. Or there're bus stations in town. But I recommend resting up for a day or two. And while you're here, you might as well see our marvelous city. If you're hungry, we have a great restaurant here in the inn, open twenty-four/seven. Or there are other restaurants throughout Esperanza. And your cottage will have food in the fridge. We also have shops in the immediate vicinity where you can buy whatever you may have left at home." He slipped their passports and two maps across the counter. "City maps, so you can find your way around. The town can be confusing to newcomers."

"What's the population of Esperanza?" Tess asked.

"About twenty thousand. We lose young people every year, you know how it is—the bigger cities beckon, they go off to the university, find better-paying jobs." He leaned forward, lowered his voice. "I heard about what happened on your way in. The fog. The, uh, *brujos.* They often travel in the fog, for cover, so it's a good idea if you don't wander outside of town."

"What exactly are these *brujos,* Mr. Granger?" Ian asked. "Back at the bodega, one of them grabbed Tess's arm and then later on he turned up dead outside."

"Dead?" Granger looked as if Ian had just told him a UFO had landed on the White House lawn. His gaze flicked to Tess. "You're sure it was the same man?"

"Yes. He looked like he had bled out." *Tick-tock,* whispered the clock on the wall. Tess watched the hands click forward and realized a full thirty seconds passed before Granger spoke.

"What did the police do?"

"The only cop there was drunk," she replied. "He didn't do anything."

Granger clicked his tongue against his teeth, shook his head. "I'm really sorry you had to go through that." His soft, conspiratorial voice struck Tess as phony. "These *brujos* fight among themselves all the time. They're crazies. Outcasts."

"Outcasts from where?" Ian asked.

"Mate, if I knew the answer to that, I'd be happy to share it. But no one really knows. My theory is they're thieves, drug runners, undesirables from all over South America who are looking to make Esperanza their home base. They seem to have some sort of, I don't know what you call it. Unusual abilities?" He shrugged, palms aimed at the ceiling. "Sara Wells will want to talk to you as soon as she returns. She's the expert on these *brujos*. She'll be eager to hear all about your encounter with them in the fog, Mr. Ritter."

"And she'll be back when?" Tess asked.

"In a few days." The phone behind him rang just then and he excused himself.

"I guess we should go find cottage thirteen," Ian said.

Nomad barked and trotted off ahead of them. The tuxedo cat leaped off the counter and followed, and the parrot swept through the air, joining the procession.

Dominica watched Juanito Cardenas hurry along the path, carrying several fabric bags probably filled with groceries. He looked around uneasily, but she doubted that he sensed her presence. Ever since she and Ben had taken his parents some years ago, paranoia had been his normal state.

It surprised her when he unlocked the door of cottage 13 and slipped inside. Thirteen was reserved primarily for guests who had been targeted by *brujos* in some way, a signal to the inn's staff to remain vigilant. Did Ed Granger know the man and woman were transitionals? Undoubtedly. Manuel, the wild card who had mocked her there outside the bus, probably told him. And if Granger knew, then Juanito and everyone else who came in contact with the couple would find out, too.

The man and woman emerged from the main building, flanked by Nomad and a black and white cat, with an Amazonian parrot flying low overhead. Now that Dominica saw the woman awake, moving, she got a good look at her—a knockout, nearly six feet tall, slender, curves in the right places. She moved with the grace of a dancer, her long blond hair shining in the early light. The man, bearded and so stunningly handsome, intrigued her. Such a perfect profile, a seductive mouth, long, certain strides.

She still couldn't quite bring herself to believe what had happened. The first transitionals in Esperanza in five hundred years. Even though she hoped it meant that more transitionals were on the way, she couldn't move beyond her suspicion that it was a light-chaser strategy, perhaps concocted to divert the *brujos* from further attacks on the city. *Dangle the carrot, distract them, make them believe the city is open to transitionals again.* But surely the chasers didn't believe the *brujos* were that stupid.

Right now, she was the only one of her kind who knew about the transitionals. It was up to her to find out as much as she could about who they were, how they'd gotten here, if they were really protected. Back there on the bus she had been at a disadvantage, unable to assume a virtual form because of the risk it would pose to her from the driver and Nomad. But the dog had sensed her anyway and when she had assumed a form outside the bus, Manuel mocked her and turned the flamethrower on her.

But once Juanito fixed them herbal tea to induce a deep, heavy sleep, she would be able to study the man and woman more closely. The herb grew in the greenhouses outside of Esperanza and while it probably did help to counteract the effects of altitude, it was primarily a sleep aid. And with these two, it was a protective measure. *Keep the targets sedated until a strategy can be implemented to keep them safe.* And ignorant of the fact that they were in comas, nearly dead.

She imagined Juanito in the cottage, putting away groceries and supplies, chatting amiably with the couple as he fixed the sleeping tea. Nomad and the cat would curl up by the fire and the parrot would find a perch, completing the silly picture of domestic bliss. Goddamn dog, cat, bird. Goddamn Juanito. Goddamn all of them.

She waited within a light fog at the edge of the posada courtyard, wishing she could think herself into an insect form, a mosquito, a fly, something small with wings so she could get into the cottage to watch and listen. But even the magic of Esperanza couldn't make such a thing possible.

The sun rose higher, spilling light across the inn's courtyard. The fog burned off. She finally saw Juanito slip out of cottage 13 like a guilty thief, Nomad trotting alongside him, the parrot riding on his back, the cat trailing behind them. Why hadn't Juanito left Nomad behind to guard them?

Halfway up the path, the dog paused again and glanced out toward the back property and the trees. *He senses me.* Just as he had sensed her on the bus. But he apparently couldn't *see* her because when Juanito called to him, Nomad trotted on and he and Juanito vanished into the main building.

There, Juanito would report to Ed Granger that the transitionals were sedated. Granger would get in touch with Sara Wells, a cultural anthropologist, another interloper, and with Illika Huicho, the leader of the Quechua,
they would come up with a plan. Let them plan.

She finally left her hiding place and paused at the door of cottage 13, listening for sounds within. Electricity hummed through the wires, but she
heard nothing else and slipped inside. Logs crackled in the fireplace, the
air smelled of smoke, sugar, something mildly bitter. She moved on into the
bedroom, paused between the beds, listened to their breathing. Definitely
drugged.

Dominica moved toward the man first. He slept in the bed under the
window, one hand tucked under his jaw, legs drawn up toward his chest so
that his body formed a sort of lightning bolt, as it had on the bus. Now that
she was alone with them and they were sedated, she felt safe enough to create a tenuous form, a simple farm woman. She leaned in close to the man
and inhaled the air that he breathed, trying to trace it back through time.

She found his name, embedded in his smells. Ian. She caught a whiff of
soap, the most superficial odor. He'd showered before he'd fallen into bed.
She inhaled more deeply and uncovered the scents that told of his journey
to Esperanza—a hospital, medicines, the smells of a particular type of sickness. Heart? This felt right. He'd had a massive heart attack. Then she smelled
dust, earth, rocks, odors that had come after he slipped into a coma and his
soul left his body and crossed the Río Palo. At this point, his soul apparently
assumed its human form, which would explain the sharp tang of food, probably from the bodega, and a strong smell of hormones. She examined that
last scent more closely and knew it was associated with his deep attraction
to the woman.

She ran her hand over his hair. Like silk. What an opportunity he pre-
sented, this transitional. She could seize his soul and it would take her to his
comatose body. If she could heal his body, she could live out his mortal life.
Even though she preferred women, she believed in making do with what
was available. But perhaps Ben could take Ian and she could take the woman
and . . . *You're getting ahead of yourself.*

Dominica sat at the edge of the woman's mattress. A bed hog. She
sprawled on her back, arms flung out at her sides, mouth slightly open. She
noticed the bruise on the underside of her wrist. The longer Dominica
looked at it, the stranger it seemed. She thought it emitted a sound, a high-
pitched hum, but maybe she was imagining it. Dominica leaned toward

her, inhaling deeply. Name first. *Tess.* Ian and Tess. Nice ring to it, like Adam and Eve. She inhaled Tess's breath, moving past the scent of tooth-paste to the deeper odors.

Violence, gunfire, blood. Dominica jerked back, alarmed. Tess looked like a model, not a warrior. But the odors didn't lie. She leaned in closer again, struggling to trace the smells of violence back to their source. There. *Go deeper. Hold it.* A warehouse. Police? No, federal agents. Dozens of them. Something went terribly wrong, Tess was in the crossfire, took a bullet to her thigh, nearly bled to death, flatlined during surgery, was revived but slipped into a coma and her soul took flight.

Dominica sensed a lot of people around Tess, caring for her, talking to her constantly to draw her out of the coma. But what connected her and the man?

She brought her mouth close to Tess's, pulling her breath deeply into herself. She moved back to Ian and did the same thing. Molecules braided together, each strand a story. She couldn't follow every plot line, but the bottom line was obvious: Esperanza was their destiny. Before they were born as Tess and Ian, their souls had agreed to this experience. They shared a lack of belief in an afterlife and yet both carried a kind of blueprint of the other, an ineffable, powerful need to find their other half. A love that spanned many lifetimes had brought them here.

It scared her. She understood this kind of need, the power of an insa-tiable hunger for another. They weren't like her, they would not settle for loving the one you were with.

Dominica thrust her farm woman's hand into Tess's chest and smiled when her body twisted away from the pain. *She feels it, the intrusion.* Do-minica quickly shed her form and allowed her essence to settle over Tess's body, to sink into it through her hair, scalp, chest. She was immediately hurled out. Enraged, she threw herself onto Tess, so that they would merge, and was instantly catapulted upward.

Impossible. In six hundred years, she had never been *unable* to seize a human. There were bodies she found distasteful or repulsive, too ill or filled with toxins to be used for more than a few minutes. Frequently, seized humans fought back and occasionally the struggle was so brutal that Dominica simply vacated the body. But that she was *unable* to seize a hu-man, especially a transitional soul, was almost beyond her comprehension. Who or what protected Tess? Was it that mark on her wrist? Did it protect her somehow?

She looked at Ian. *What about you? Are you protected, too?* Dominica dived at him—and was flung so violently upward that she passed through the ceiling and sailed out into the blue morning sky.

Her emotions lurched from confusion to indignation to rage. She thought herself into the main building, past the front desk where Granger busied himself with paperwork. She briefly toyed with the idea of seizing him, this Aussie bastard who worked so hard to defeat the *brujos*. But he disgusted her. She went into his office, assumed the form of a cleaning woman, an inn employee. The shape was too weak to last more than a few minutes, but it was all she needed.

His computer was on. She moved the mouse, the screensaver vanished, and an Internet site filled the screen, something called *liberationblogspot.com*. As she clicked through it, horror seeped into her, a toxic gas. *A rumor no more.*

The blog appeared to have been started five years ago by Vivian Ortiz from Guayaquil whose parents had bled out simultaneously on a beach. Their deaths initiated Vivian's search for answers and that search had intensified when the autopsy results determined that no virus or bacteria was to blame. Cerebral hemorrhages had taken them both. She had reached out to others who might have lost friends and family in the same way and, over time, stories had poured in from all over South America.

Vivian studied the stories like a forensics expert and eventually put together a kind of MO—identifiable symptoms that victims exhibited before their deaths, the types of people most likely to suffer bleed-outs, why they might be occurring. When her search led her to the mythology of Esperanza—and to the *brujos,* a word she didn't use, but a phenomenon she described as parasitic—the tone of the blog had taken a radical change. *We will take back our freedom when they least expect it and extract our revenge. We will vindicate the deaths of our loved ones and take back Esperanza before this parasite infiltrates the entire continent.*

Dominica heard noises just outside the door. *Hurry.* She clicked on the map of South America and it suddenly filled with thousands of red dots. At the bottom of the screen, a number and description appeared: *22,162 cerebral hemorrhages reported since 2003.* The figure shocked her, filled her with fear. If those victims had at least one person who had joined the liberation movement as a result of the deaths, it meant more than twenty thousand avengers who hoped to obliterate *brujos.*

Dominica made note of the URL, then went into Granger's e-mail, brought up his sent mail file. The most recent e-mail intrigued her.

Effective immediately, all wireless devices, including laptops, cell phones, iPods etc must be kept in the storage area during work hours. & no Internet. The new arrivals, the American couple, must be treated cordially, but nothing can be revealed to them. Alert me if either of them is sighted. Their passport photos are attached.

Why the caution about wireless devices, the Internet, cell phones? Granger had sent the e-mail to every Internet café, restaurant, shop, and church in the city, to all employees at the inn, to everyone who was anyone in the Esperanza hierarchy. He was scared. And because he was scared he had contacted Sara Wells and told her the impossible had happened. *Two transitionals have arrived.*

The next e-mail, sent around the time Dominica was inside the bus, mystified her, too. It had been addressed to "undisclosed recipients," and read: *Alert Charlie. They've been identified.*

Was "Charlie" some sort of code or a person, perhaps connected to the liberation blog?

Voices on the other side of the door. Dominica pressed another key, shed her form, fled the posada grounds.

She headed for the Lago del Sueño, a hot spring at the foot of a hundred-foot cliff behind the posada. She created a new form, one of her favorites, an Amazonian warrior queen, a ballbuster. She didn't care that it flickered uncontrollably, that she was too weak to provide the solidity she needed to feel the cool earth against her bare feet, make out the color of the sunlight, taste the moisture in the air. Even in her depleted state, this form was such a powerful symbol for her that she almost felt physical.

Almost. Such was the curse of the *brujos.*

She crossed the beach and climbed gradually uphill to the place she loved, the caves. She entered one she had visited numerous times, and half a mile in, she paused in front of the petroglyphs. No one knew for sure who had drawn these extraordinary images. The elders in her tribe believed the petroglyphs were thousands of years old, created by a culture that existed long before the Quechuans, the Incas, perhaps as far back as the Paleo-Indian era. Even she was not that old.

The story the images told haunted her. All of them—*brujos* and humans alike—were only as real as the stories they lived. It didn't matter whether their stories were good or bad, tedious or carefree, defined by love or hatred, good or evil. It didn't matter if the stories were political or religious, about families or loners or aliens from Pluto. They were all aliens—to each other and to themselves. They created stories to explore who they were and what they might become.

And at least part of her story was told in these frames. She could never move beyond the implications of what it might mean. There she was, a *bruja* depicted as a smudge of dark ash, running with a wolf or a dog who became, in the next frame, the man she had loved before Ben, the man No-mad had been. Over there, drawings depicted the last battle between the *brujos* and the chasers. And here were images that depicted the future, several possible versions, nothing set in stone. Whoever had painted these images—shamans, seers, the light chasers themselves, or some ultimate prophet or being—could see only possibilities this far into the future.

"Waves of probability" the quantum physicists called it. Her tribe had one such scientist, a man obsessed with the puzzles and mysteries of the universe. His rage at the scientific community had triggered a massive heart attack at the age of sixty and had brought him to her tribe and kept him here. He had no desire to return to physical life, where his peers had considered him a lunatic, his theories too far *out there* to be taken seriously. So now he worked as assiduously for the *brujos* as he once had worked for science in the physical world. But such luminaries among the *brujos* were rare.

They had no Einsteins, Picassos, Beethovens, Kerouacs, Hesses. A few poets joined them from time to time, but always moved on. The politicians and CEOs who arrived were an obnoxious bunch, control freaks with axes to grind, and they rarely lasted long among her kind. Prime ministers, presidents, cabinet members, dictators, popes and priests, rabbis and ministers, evangelicals and crazies: the *brujos* had seen them all. Decades ago, a Dalai Lama had appeared among the *brujos*—not as one of them, but to understand them. He had been in the between and no *brujo* had seized him. A few hours among her people had convinced him he had seen the face of evil and he had dived back into his body.

Those who stayed with the *brujos* for any length of time tended to be rebellious souls who had chafed against the conventions of the time into which they were born. Some had been famous in the physical world, most had not. Some had held positions of power or influence, most had not. Many were ordinary people like herself whose hopes and dreams had been dashed by circumstances or their own blunders. They had died young or suddenly. Or both. About half believed in some sort of afterlife. A quarter did not. The last quarter hadn't even thought about it. But the numbers of *brujos* had grown so great in the last fifty years that she was no longer certain about her statistics. Maybe the majority of the more recent *brujos* believed in nothing except their own rage, intolerance, racism, envy, cruelty, and sadism.

Dominica ran her warrior hand over the rock, over the panel of the wolf/dog, then over the man he became. Cool, even to her flickering touch. It seemed that the ancient rock came alive, vibrating through her warrior fingertips and igniting such sorrow in her warrior heart that she began to weep, then sob.

Then she was on her knees before these images, her form flickering, weakened by her surrender to such shattering emotions.

Fuck them. Fuck all of them.

She lifted her head, swiped at her eyes, reared up and screamed, *"You will never defeat us, drive us out."*

Her voice echoed throughout the cave, raging but impotent. Then she threw off the warrior form and fled.

Five

It rained for three days, a cold, steady drizzle that kept them in the cottage. Tess was fine with it, but felt disappointed that nothing more happened between her and Ian.

She suspected the intimacy they had shared on the bus, those promising exploratory kisses, had happened too quickly for him. Or maybe Ian just wasn't interested in anything more. Whatever the reason, she was too worn out to think about sex, to look for her lost cell phone, too tired to do much of anything but sleep and read. She felt as if she had been injected with sludge and couldn't remember altitude ever affecting her like this.

The cottage lacked television, but had a large library. During the day, she and Ian read propped up on the two couches in the living room, near the fireplace, their reading broken up by conversation. At first, it was impersonal—books and movies, their travels, jobs, the inclement weather. It gradually grew more personal—his father's suicide, her father's death from cancer, his divorce, her atrophied relationship with Dan, his erratic relationship with Casey O'Toole, an English professor. They were equally comfortable discussing the inconsequential, as if they had been together for years and were accustomed to sharing such small details.

It was obvious that the altitude had zapped them and eventually they would have to leave the cottage to replenish their supplies. But neither of them seemed in any hurry to venture outside or to request separate cottages.

Whiskers, the tuxedo cat, hung around the cottage for the first day, either curled up in Tess's lap or snoozing next to Nomad in front of the fireplace. Periodically, Nomad would lick and preen the cat, but eventually Whiskers slipped outside and probably moved on to another cottage. The dog left every so often and usually returned with a juicy bone or some other treat.

Besides the cat and the dog, Kali the parrot dropped by, squawking happily, always grateful for a treat—a grape, a strawberry, or her favorite, a cherry. Wildlife was often visible from the cottage windows—condors, hummingbirds, rabbits the color of the fog, silver chinchillas, deer the size of large dogs. Little wild guinea pigs sometimes scurried to the front door, then reared up on their miniature legs and made squeaking sounds, as if asking to be let in.

On the third evening, Tess and Ian rummaged through the pantry and fridge, taking stock of their diminished supplies to find something suitable for dinner. "Okay, it's official," Ian said. "Dinner's going to be simple. Ravioli with a red sauce. I think we've got enough fruit for a salad. But we need to go shopping tomorrow, Slim."

"I'll be ready to venture out tomorrow."

"I realized that other than opening the front door to step outside for a closer look at those condors, I haven't moved more than five yards from these rooms in the last three days."

"The farthest I've gone is the back porch to refill the hummingbird feeder. This is the first time since we got here that I've felt almost normal." On an upper pantry shelf, Tess found a bottle of Chilean red wine. "Hey, look at this." She held it up. "Grab us some glasses, Ian."

Moments later, she clicked her glass against his. *"Salud,"*

"Salud!" he echoed, and began to prepare dinner.

Tess settled on a stool and watched. Throughout much of her childhood, her dad had cooked evening meals and he had been the kind of cook Ian was—a dash of this, a pinch of that, toss in herbs, sauces, mix it all together, and voilà, a gourmet meal. Ian, like her dad, used flavors in unusual ways, as if his intention were to awaken the palate by shocking it. Even the desserts Ian concocted were like this and usually involved chocolate, for which he confessed a weakness.

"Where'd you learn to cook?" she asked.

"After my dad's suicide, my mother was so depressed she didn't get out of bed for weeks. So my choices were to get takeout, starve, or start cooking. Then in college I worked part-time as a cook. Since Louise hated to cook, it just continued after we got married." He shrugged and flashed one of those complicated George Clooney smiles. "Nothing glamorous like a French cooking school. Where do you want to eat?"

"By the fire."

"It'll be ready in a jiffy." Ian handed her the bowls of fruit salad to take into the living room.

Tess set the bowls on the coffee table, pulled the table closer to the fire, and dropped two cushions on the floor. While Ian finished his culinary magic, she used the cottage phone to call her mother and Maddie. But like every other time either she or Ian had tried to place a call from the cottage, the operator said the circuits were busy and to try again later. Since she had lost her cell and Ian didn't seem to own one, the cottage phone was the only option.

"Circuits still busy?" he asked as she walked into the kitchen.

"It's ridiculous. No phone system can be that incompetent."

"We'll get through." He passed her a bowl of steaming ravioli and a basket of hot bread, then picked up the bottle of wine, his glass and bowl, and they went into the living room. As they settled on the pillows by the fire, logs crackling at their backs, Nomad trotted over and sat down, waiting for handouts. "I fed you, big guy," Ian said.

The dog barked twice. Tess laughed and tossed him a square of ravioli, which he caught in midair. The meal was delicious, surpassing anything her dad had ever cooked. She left a couple of bites for Nomad, set her plate on the floor next to Ian's, and the dog lapped it up.

Ian refilled their wine glasses. "You know, the more I think about it, the stranger this all seems. I've been in other high-altitude cities, but I've never felt so out of it. Maybe something in that tea Juanito made didn't agree with us."

"Or there was something in those empanadas. Write about that in your column. The Empanada Altitude Strangeness."

They laughed hysterically, just as they had that night on the bus. She knew the silliness was exacerbated by their mutual anxiety that something eerie was happening to them, even if they didn't know what it was, but she couldn't stop laughing. She finally rolled onto her back, her hands creating a billboard in the air. " 'If you eat the empanadas at the Bodega del Cielo . . .' That's your lead, Ian. I can see it."

She looked over at him, but his eyes were fixed on her already, staring in a way that made her heart somersault. He flashed a quick, complicated smile, then rolled once and hovered above her, his fingers sliding through her hair, his face dangerously close to hers. The fire snapped and hissed, his eyes undressed her. He lowered his mouth to hers and for long moments, the only thing that existed was the texture of his tongue, the heat of his breath, the reality of his hands slipping under her sweater, cool against her skin.

She felt, suddenly, like a teenage girl seized and betrayed by her own hormones. They were crossing the threshold, she didn't care. It felt good to be touched and caressed by this man. Their clothes melted away, they rolled onto their sides, and everywhere he touched her, her skin exploded with heat and desire.

His tongue slipped from her throat to her breasts, circling them, teasing. They rolled again, so that Tess was on her back, and his mouth moved lower, tongue inscribing her hips and belly with a secret language, and then sliding lower. Tess gasped and her hips lifted from the rug, her pleasure so intense she thought she might implode. He slipped inside of her and repeatedly brought her to the edge, then took her over it, a free fall.

Ian drew an alpaca throw over them and the fabric felt sensuous against her skin. He stretched out on his side and raised up, head resting in the palm of his hand. The fire's ambient light cast the room in a surreal glow and threw half of his face into shadow.

"Ever since I saw you in the bodega, Slim, I've wanted this to happen."

"I thought you'd lost interest."

"No way." He smiled, the corners of his eyes wrinkling like crepe paper. "Until this evening, I barely had the energy to keep my eyes open long enough to eat and shower."

Her fingertips traced those lines at his eyes, each one the groove of a story. There, his father's suicide. Here, Luke's birth and childhood. There, Ian's divorce, his columns for the *Minneapolis Tribune*, stories he hadn't shared yet, the good and bad, the ugly and the glorious. "Maybe it's not the altitude, but something else."

"Like what?"

"I don't know." But day three was gone and they still hadn't left the cottage. Bizarre. She wanted to blame it on the cold rain and the sludge that moved at a snail's pace through her veins. Yet, she sensed something deeper was at work, knew it fell into the same realm as the hiccups in her memories. She should examine it more closely, but it was easier to ignore it. That bothered her, too. "I feel like people are listening to us." She pulled the throw over their heads, creating a little cocoon. "Do you know what I mean?"

"Yes." He brought his mouth so close to hers she could feel the warmth of his breath against her lips, the tip of her nose. He whispered now. "That first day, after Juanito had left and we'd finished drinking that tea he'd made, I didn't think I was even going to be able to make it to the bedroom to crash. And I woke only once in—what? fourteen hours? I've never slept that long in my life."

"Same here. And I don't think I woke at all."

Still whispering, he went on. "What woke me was a . . . I'm not even sure how to describe it. It felt . . . like something was slamming against me. Trying to get inside of me." He laughed nervously. "Did you experience anything like that?"

Tess started to say no, but a vivid memory surfaced. A sharp pain in her chest, heart racing, fear so intense that it paralyzed her. She blurted all this, then added: "I was so paralyzed I couldn't even wiggle my fingers or toes. I must've fallen back to sleep. A *brujo?*"

"Not with Nomad inside," he said.

"He left with Juanito after we drank that tea."

"I forgot about that. So it could've been a *brujo.*"

"Maybe. But here's something else that's weird. I've never gone to a foreign country and just hung around my hotel room for days, without venturing out at all. Even when the weather was shitty. Have you?"

"No. Never." He put his arms around her, holding her close, their legs intertwined, his hands cool against her spine. "We'll figure this out." Then he began to touch her again. "But not right now."

Ian bolted upright, heart drumming furiously against the tight, uneasy silence. His eyes darted nervously around the room, through the fading firelight. Nothing moved. Shadows pooled in the corners, blackness pressed up against the windows. Tess sighed in her sleep and pulled the blanket up higher around her shoulders. Hours ago, they had moved from the rug to the pull-out couch and Nomad had curled up in front of the fire. Now Nomad was gone. But that wasn't what had awakened him.

Ian swung his legs over the side of the bed, listening. Suddenly, he heard it, a high-pitched whining, a distant noise, like that of a high-speed drill. Then silence. Then the whining again, but closer. He swept his jeans and sweatshirt off a nearby chair, pulled them on, and hurried across the cold stone floor to the window. It was so chilly in the cottage he could see his breath when he exhaled.

He pressed his face to the glass, hands cupped at the sides. No starlight, no moonlight, too dark to see anything. The whining stopped, a sixty-second pause. When it started once more, he realized the noise he heard wasn't the whine of a drill, but the shrill cries of voices out in the courtyard, hundreds of them, a strange, almost melodic sound, like the keening of dolphins.

"What the hell." He hurried to the front door.

Before he removed the chain, ribbons of fog slipped through the crack under the door, eddying, shifting, then whipping back and forth, snakelike, across the floor. Ian leaped back, the keening got louder, a kind of atavistic fear seized him. He spun and ran over to the couch, shaking Tess awake. "They found us," he hissed.

She sprang out of bed, swept up her clothes, jerked them on. Ian snapped a blanket off the bed and ran back to the door.

The fog wrapped around his ankles, a cold that bit to the marrow. He fully expected *campesinos* to materialize, for that insidious whispering and chanting to begin, like what had happened in the field the day they arrived. He quickly stuffed the blanket into the crack and the bands of fog around his ankles abruptly loosened, dropped away from him, then writhed and twisted against the floor as if in agony. Ian grabbed the fire poker, slammed it down through the snakelike streamers, and he and Tess backed away, staring in horror as the streamers split in half and struggled to merge with other streamers. It was like watching beheaded chickens flailing around, wings flapping until their bodies keeled over. In moments, the stuff dissipated.

"Jesus, Ian, look." Tess pointed at the windows to their right.

Fog twisted up and across the glass like rapidly growing vines, each shoot thickening, spreading, until it covered the windows. He glanced quickly up at the skylight. Fog blanketed it. He grabbed Tess's hand, and they raced toward the back of the cottage.

The whispering grew louder, the *brujo* voices rasping like wind through trees. They flew into the bedroom, slammed the door, tore sheets and quilts off the bed. But the fog had found these windows already, wisps slithering through crevices, into the room.

"The bathroom, Slim. Fast. No windows in there."

"Tape, we need electrical tape. Or duct tape." She jerked open a nightstand drawer. "I saw a roll of something in here."

Ian ran into the bathroom, hit the wall switch, dropped the quilts and sheets on the floor. As he snapped towels off the rack, Tess barreled in, waving a roll of tape and a pair of scissors. She dropped her linens, kicked the door shut, and they stuffed a sheet into the crack, sealed it with strips of tape, then pressed towels and quilts over the sheet, and scooted back, eyeing the door.

Stupid, totally stupid, he thought, that towels and quilts and tape could keep sentient fog from reaching them. But it was equally insane to think the fog was sentient. Yet, he knew it was.

The keening grew louder, abrasive, almost unbearable. He clenched his teeth, slapped his hands over his ears. In moments, wisps of fog slipped through the vertical crack just above and below the hinges and along the top edge of the door. Ian shot to his feet, Tess struggled to cut long strips of tape from the roll, and he pressed them into place, sealing the door completely. The keening escalated until it felt as if long, hot needles were being thrust through his ears, tearing away cartilage, tissue, penetrating bone. It drove him, wailing, to his knees. Even with his hands squeezed over his ears, he could hear it, feel it in his teeth, and knew he was minutes from passing out.

Suddenly, Tess started shrieking, a sound so primal and savage that it hardly sounded human. She kept it up, her shrieks battering against the keening, driving it back, and lurched to the towel rack. She grabbed several, tossed one to Ian, and he wrapped it around his head, turban style, so that it covered his ears. It helped to muffle the intensity of the noise so that he didn't think he would pass out now.

While Tess wrapped a towel around her own head and kept on shrieking, Ian flipped over the metal clothes hamper and beat his fists against it, playing it like a drum. She kept shrieking and turned the shower on full blast, adding the pounding of water to the cacophony. He didn't know how long it went on, but when the keening abruptly ceased, the silence felt tight, eerie. She turned off the shower, whispered, "Is it over?"

"Maybe it's a trick," he whispered back.

A great clanking and clattering erupted in the bedroom and spread quickly to the rest of the cottage, echoing, vibrating against the walls. Then this, too, stopped, and a silence so profound and strange gripped the building that he and Tess strained to hear anything at all.

They finally tore away the tape, Ian picked up the poker, opened the door slightly. He didn't hear or sense anything and opened the door all the way. As he and Tess stepped into the bedroom, she flicked the wall switch to her left, turning on a floor lamp.

The room was empty, but something now covered the window—and it wasn't fog. It seemed to be some kind of metal shutter. "It's like an aluminum hurricane shutter," Tess said, coming up behind him. "Electrically controlled. And since it probably didn't shut on its own, it must be *remotely* controlled."

"So Granger or someone else knew the cottage was under attack."

"It looks that way. This is what they do in prisons. At night. Or when someone has escaped. Lockdown. Fuck this. They can't lock us in here."

She made a beeline for the bedroom door. Ian turned the lock, raised the window, ran his hand along the bottom edge. Airtight. No sign of fog. He couldn't even feel the chill of the night air. Impressive. And undoubtedly expensive. Was every building on the grounds equipped with shutters like this?

When he emerged from the bedroom, the kitchen and living room blazed with lights, and Tess was pounding her fists against the shutter across the front door. "Hey, we're trapped in here, I didn't sign up for this shit!"

Ian realized these shutters had also closed off the skylights, every window, the rear door to the back porch, even the pet door Whiskers and Nomad used. They apparently were prisoners. He marched over to the fridge, threw open the door and determined, in a quick glance, what might make a good breakfast. Mushroom omelets with cheese. A side dish of sliced mangos. Mugs of rich Ecuadorian coffee. He found celery and tomatoes and chopped with a kind of vengeance. He whipped four eggs with a frantic rhythm, a drumbeat for war. Slammed the knife through a brick of cheese, *chop chop, chop chop.* The preparation of food became his weapon, his defense.

Tess ran into the kitchen. "What're you doing? We need to get the hell out of here."

"Out of *here*? Where the hell is *here*? We don't have any idea where we are with respect to any other point in this country."

Then an assault began and it sounded as if the hounds of hell had been turned loose. The rooms echoed with the clamor, a battering storm like hail or rocks pounding the shutters as *something* fought to get in. Paralyzed, he and Tess stared at each other, then Ian forced himself to turn back to the counter, to finish the omelets.

"Are you nuts?" Tess burst out. "You're *cooking* while we're under attack? Jesus, Ian, we need weapons." She jerked open one of the drawers, grabbed a long, sharp knife. "We've got to be able to defend ourselves."

He looked at her, spatula in hand. "Against what? *Brujos?* What the fuck are they? We don't know. How'd we get here? We don't know. What's happening? We don't know. What's really going on, Tess? *We. Don't. Know.*"

Her eyes widened. "You're deaf? You can't hear this attack?" She threw her arms out at her sides. "Something is attacking this cottage and if . . . if it breaks through, if . . ."

"We don't know shit." He poured the whipped eggs into the frying pan, grabbed the spatula, folded celery, tomatoes, and mushrooms into the eggs. "And I'm hungry. I'm going to eat."

Just like that, the assault stopped. Silence suffused the cottage. Tess's arms fell to her sides, she stared at the shuttered windows, the door, and dropped her head back and looked up into the dark belly of the skylight. Then she spun around with the knife clutched in her hand and vanished into the living room. Ian turned back to the stove, the frying pan, the omelets, to what he understood and could control.

With the abrupt cessation of the assault, Tess's desperation for light and visibility propelled her straight to the front door. If these shutters were anything like the ones at home, then they would have an inside lock, something simple that could be turned quickly.

She threw the door open, ran her hands over the flat, smooth surface. This shutter wasn't an accordion; it was a metal panel, flush against the door. But down near the bottom, she found a turn lock, flipped it, then leaned into the panel, pressed her hands against it, and pushed. It slid slowly to the left, admitting early morning light, a chill, the sweet scent of pine.

As she started to slip through the opening, Ian grabbed her arm, bellowing, "*No! We don't know if it's over.*" He jerked her back so hard she nearly tripped over her own feet.

Tess wrenched her arm free, furious that he had attempted to restrain her. "Don't *ever* do that." The vitriol in her voice shocked her. Ian looked as if she had slapped him. "You said we don't know shit. It's true. And it's time to find out what's going on."

She brushed past him, pushed the door open wider, and stepped out onto the porch. An overturned cleaning cart blocked the path from the main building, a bank of fog rolled away from her on the left. Then Nomad shot past her, a blur of black, his snarls and frantic barking shredding the air. Behind him thundered an army, thirteen men stampeding down the path, waving rifles, pitchforks, machetes, flamethrowers. Ed Granger was in the lead, a bald John Wayne without a horse, shouting, *"The bitch fled into the fog! Mow her down!"* He gestured wildly at Tess. "Get back into the house, it's not safe out here!"

Tess hurried down the porch steps, stopped right in front of him. "The cottage was attacked and suddenly we found ourselves prisoners in there." She stabbed her hand toward the building. "We deserve some answers, Ed."

"*Brujos.* Juanito, get her into the house."

Granger and his men raced on and Juanito Cardenas waved his rifle in a vaguely threatening way. "Go inside, please. It is safer."

"Hey, hold on." Ian loped over, clutching the iron poker. "We're guests here. You can't order us around. You can't put us into lockdown. You—"

Juanito whipped his rifle up, aiming it at Ian. *"Get inside now."*

"Fine, fine, we're going."

But as Juanito moved toward them, Ian slammed the poker down over his rifle, and as it clattered to the ground, Tess hurled herself at Juanito. He was at least half a foot shorter and forty pounds lighter than she and went down like a shoot of trampled bamboo. Tess swept up his rifle and she and Ian raced away from him, following the other men into the fog.

She immediately regretted it. The fog was thicker and higher than it looked, a soup that darkened and curdled, swallowing brush and trees. She couldn't see more than a few inches in front of her, but shouts and Nomad's frantic barking rang out clearly. She and Ian kept angling toward the barking, stumbling over flower beds, through trees.

"Quick thinking back there, Ian."

"Ditto, Slim. But will a rifle kill a *brujo*?"

"I don't have a clue. Why would they be carrying them otherwise?"

"They're also carrying flamethrowers. I assume you've shot a rifle before?"

"Yeah." And this one was a Winchester Super X3, a model she and Dan had practiced on last year, during a special training session. It was capable of shooting twelve shells in under two seconds and was touted as the fastest shotgun in the world. "How many of them do you think there are?"

"It sounded like hundreds."

"We can't handle hundreds. We've got a dozen shots. And that's only if the rifle is fully loaded."

"We do what we—"

The rest of his sentence was truncated by a man flying out of the fog on their left, one of Granger's men swinging a shovel, bellowing and snorting like a wounded animal. He crashed into Ian and they slammed to the ground, grunting and punching, bodies so tightly pressed together she didn't dare fire. Ian hollered, "*Run, Slim, go, go.*"

She tore deeper into the fog, toward Nomad's barking, but no longer knew why she was running, what the goal was. Her bare feet felt like blocks of concrete, she couldn't see much of anything, and had no clear idea what was happening or what *had* happened. Her frames of references had been torn away from her.

She clutched the rifle more tightly and moved toward Nomad's frenetic barking. When the dog went silent, Tess stopped, dropped to a crouch, listened hard. Then shapes appeared in the fog, voices took on volume, substance.

The rest of the *brujos* had fled, so it was just her and Nomad, staring at each other in the dark fog. Despite Dominica's form as a cleaning woman, he recognized her. His amber eyes fixed on her with such precision and hatred that she knew she would be annihilated if he attacked. But she didn't think he wanted to fight her. He was warning her. So she tossed him a sock with a note attached to it. Written in Quechua, it read:

> *Oh, Ed. Really. Give it up. The transitionals are ours. Sooner or later, we'll get them and then we will take Esperanza back. The land is ours. It has always belonged to us.*
>
> *Yours always,*
> *Dominica*

Nomad nudged the sock with his nose, as if its scent might tell him her true intentions, and looked up at her again.

"Take it," she whispered. "Just take the damn thing."

But suddenly, Nomad's bones cracked and popped, his spine elongated, his ears melted into his head, his tail shortened and vanished altogether. His front legs pulled back into his belly, as if through an extraordinary gravity, and the bones rearranged themselves and extended into arms. His rear legs went through the same process and became human legs. His jaw widened, bones moving and wiggling beneath the skin like something living. His snout shrank, reshaping itself into a human nose, mouth, cheekbones. Then his fur disappeared and human hair raced up his arms and down his legs and across his skull. It happened at such luminal speed that when she blinked, Nomad was gone and Wayra stood before her in all his blinding, breathtaking beauty. Wayra, whose name in Quechua meant "wind."

"They're protected, Nica. So give it up. You can't seize them."

Shock tore through her—at the sight of him, the sound of his voice, that he was here at all. "How . . . I . . . thought you . . . lost the ability to shift centuries ago . . . when you were wounded. I—"

"That is only a lie you have told yourself. And over the centuries, you came to believe it was true."

"You . . . you betrayed me, Wayra."

"You betrayed yourself."

"You chose . . . the chasers over me."

"You chose the *brujos* over *me*. It works both ways."

He moved toward her and slipped his long arms around her, pulling her gently against him. Even though she was only a virtual form, she felt the strength of his arms, inhaled the familiar, wild scent of his skin. When he slid his hands up through her hair, drawing her head back so that she was forced to look into his eyes, she saw him as he had been centuries ago, in the 1400s, when they had both been physical, a proud Spaniard whom she had loved unconditionally.

Her father in that life, a wealthy landowner with a great deal of power, had hated Wayra and forbade her to see him. He then had married her off to a nobleman, who eventually cast her aside when she had proven to be barren. She had spent the rest of her life searching throughout Spain for Wayra, only to discover that her father had killed him. She died at the age of thirty-six from tuberculosis and a broken heart—and Wayra was waiting for her when she had crossed over.

He read her thoughts now. "We are no longer those people, Nica." Then he brought his mouth to hers, hard, insistently, and her pathetic virtual body melted into his, sobs clawing up her throat, her hunger and lust for him unabated after all these centuries. She ran her hands slowly over the back of his neck, across his shoulders, her memories coughing up the contours of his flesh, the shape of his bones, all the joy this man had given her. "Join me," he whispered, his mouth moving against her neck, her throat. "It's not too late." His hands slipped under her skirt and between her legs, exciting her. "Together, we can end this ancient battle."

She pulled back slightly. "We can rule Esperanza, Wayra. I command the largest and most powerful of all *brujo* tribes. We will lack for nothing. And now that two transitionals have arrived, the—"

"No." His hands dropped away from her. "There is only one way."

Her heart shattered into a million pieces. "But—"

Suddenly, shouting erupted nearby, men crashed through the brush. For a long moment, Wayra's eyes held hers, his expression inscrutable, then he whispered, "Run now and you will run forever, Nica."

She had no choice. The men were too close, their voices too angry. She shed her human form and thought herself upward, watching as Wayra's body quickly transformed again. As Nomad, he picked up the sock she had tossed him moments ago, and trotted on through the fog, the trees.

Coward, she thought at him.

She knew he heard her, but he didn't reply. Crushed and stricken with grief, she thought herself home.

The fog thinned rapidly and now Tess could see Granger and his men huddled in the courtyard. There, off to her left, from the same direction where the voice had been, Nomad emerged from the fog, carrying something in his mouth. The men couldn't see him yet, but the dog saw Tess and immediately turned toward her, his strange eyes regarding her with what seemed like astonishment and an underlying fear.

Baffled, Tess got to her feet and looked around quickly for some sign of the woman she'd heard talking about betrayal and tribes. But she seemed to be the only woman in the immediate vicinity. Nomad reached her, dropped a sock at her feet, then sat back, tail wagging.

"I bet you saw them," Tess said. "The man and woman who were talking." Tess picked up the sock, a note attached to it. She couldn't read the language in which it was written. "Let's go find Ian, Nomad."

As they came out of the trees, men were huddled around Ian, who sat at the edge of the courtyard fountain, a towel pressed to his bleeding temple. It wasn't immediately clear to her what was going on. "Ian, you okay?" she called.

Heads turned her way. "For the moment," he said.

"He'll need a couple of stitches," Granger said. "We've called the doctor."

"How gracious of you, since one of your men tackled him out there in the fog."

"It was a misunderstanding," Granger replied quickly. Too quickly. "And I'll take that shotgun, mate. It belongs to Juanito."

"I'll be glad to return the shotgun after you translate this." She thrust the sock at him. "Nomad came out of the fog with it."

He glanced at the note, shook his head. "Can't read it. Sorry. English and tortured Spanish are the limits of my linguistic skills."

"Then maybe you can tell me what a *transitional* is, Ed."

"A transitional?" He blinked rapidly, as if he had dust in his eyes. "Well, I know what 'transition' means, but I can't say I've ever heard the word 'transitional.' Why?"

"You're a lousy liar." She threw down the sock, tossed the rifle on the ground. "We'll be checking out as soon as we find other accommodations, Mr. Granger. Please have our bill ready and open up those goddamn shutters."

She strode past them, to Ian, who was already on his feet, looking pale, shaken. As they headed back toward the cottage, Nomad following them, Ian said, "What the fuck happened out there?"

"I'm not sure. I heard a man and a woman talking, but I couldn't see them. I don't have any idea who the woman was since I'm the only female out here. How bad is your head?"

"When the bastard tackled me, my head hit a rock." He moved the blood-soaked towel away. "How's it look?"

She winced. "Awful. There's a first-aid kit in the cottage. I'll work on it till the doctor arrives."

"And once he does, you go on into town and find us a way out of here. Bus, train, a driver, I don't care what it is. We shouldn't stick around here any longer than we have to."

She agreed completely. "If I can't find public transportation, I'll offer Manuel a sum he can't refuse to drive us to the nearest airport."

Six

Dominica waited on a dirt road without shelter from the bitter wind, in a place so devoid of beauty that it tore at her. In the distance, across the miles of flatness, an object sped toward her, a storm of dust following it. Ben, driving his favorite car, a 1992 Mercedes Benz 500 SL.

Moments later, the car roared up alongside her, stopped, and Dominica climbed into the passenger seat, suddenly and completely exhausted. "Worn out?" Ben asked.

"Very." She would not tell him about Wayra, and quickly locked that information deeply within herself, where even Ben wouldn't be able to find it.

"And?" he asked eagerly. "What happened with the raid?"

"It failed. They stayed hidden in the cottage and someone in the main building activated the shutters."

"Are they transitionals?"

"Yes."

He let out a whoop of delight. Dominica couldn't bring herself to tell him the rest of it yet, that these transitionals were untouchables. Let him enjoy the moment.

His usual virtual form, the Ben she knew, looked like a California surfer, blond and tan, with vivid blue eyes. Her usual form was a slender brunette, the beauty she had been in her Spanish life. In *brujo* time, he was relatively young and she was not.

Brujos had the ability to travel through time, and during such a sojourn, she had found him in one of Henry Ford's factories in 1914 and seized him as he was leaving work one evening. She used him for five months, living through him vicariously, getting a taste of life in that period. Then one day he became aware of her, thought he was losing his mind, and took a gun to his head. The gun clicked but didn't fire, saving her from annihilation because she wouldn't have been able to escape his body before he died. So she'd seized his brain violently as she abandoned his body, and when he'd died of a cerebral hemorrhage, she had been there, waiting for him. They had been together ever since. She felt responsible for him.

Ben remained with her tribe because he believed it was his best chance to seize a body and live out that person's life, the ultimate goal of every *brujo*. Over time, her tribe had enjoyed some impressive successes. But it was never easy, there were no guarantees. *If* you conquered the temptations of immediate gratification, *if* you could keep the body's personality subdued or subsume it altogether, you still inherited all the personality's emotional baggage. And *if* you even recalled who *you* were, it was exceedingly difficult to achieve anything. The suicide rate among returns was high. The mental breakdown rate was even higher. Maybe one in five survived it.

But she and Ben were fortunate. They had experienced several such lives together. The worst was as teens, disastrously short lives that nonetheless expanded their venue. The best was a Kansas life in the 1950s, where they had spent thirty years together in physical life. They'd tasted other lives between then and now, stints as long as several years in order to study a particular time and place. Full lives, however, were rare.

"Can we take them?" he asked.

She held her hands to the heat pouring from the vents. Heat and cold for *brujos* weren't like they were in a physical body. She felt only a phantom sensation, similar to what an amputee experienced. In the old days, when her people controlled Esperanza, their senses had been sharper. But that time was long gone and here she was, racing through cold sunlight in a vehicle that cost a ton of money in the physical world but that, here, was created from intent and desire. Chimeras, her stock-in-trade.

"Nica?"

"No, we can't seize them. I tried, just to see if it could be done, and was hurled out."

"*What?* But . . . that's impossible."

Impossible, perhaps, but it had happened. "What do we know about Manuel Ortega? He drove the bus that took these transitionals to Esperanza." She explained what had happened on the bus—and outside of it when Manuel had mocked her and turned the flamethrower on her. "I know that he works for the Posada de Esperanza, does odd jobs around Gigante. Other than that, he's a blank."

"I'm not familiar with him. But I'll check into it."

"Do we know of anyone named Charlie?"

"Last name?"

"I don't know." She told him about the e-mail she had found on Ed Granger's computer.

"He sounds important in the chaser scheme of things."

Dominica thought immediately of Nomad. *They're protected, Nica. So give it up. You can't seize them.* Now that she knew Wayra could still shift, she doubted everything she thought she had known about him. Was he one of the chasers or simply a surrogate? Did the distinction even matter? Either way, he worked with them. More to the point, had she actually revised her own history? *That is only a lie you have told yourself. And over the centuries, you came to believe it was true.* Had her memories over the six hundred years of her existence betrayed her?

"So how do we get to them?" Ben asked.

"Wrong question. How did the transitionals get in? Who opened the gate? And *why?*"

"We could seize Ed Granger and Sara Wells and find the answers quickly."

"They may not have the answers. Ed Granger recognized them as transitionals, but I think he's as mystified as we are. Besides, we'd have trouble getting into the city now. The fans will be on everywhere." For the last ten years, since she had ordered the attacks on the city, the fans had run after every sighting, every attack, to blow away the fog in which *brujos* often traveled. "How large are we, Ben? Sixty thousand?"

"Sixty thousand, eight hundred and twenty-six as of yesterday."

Ben, the numbers man, the tribal accountant. "And our totals?"

"Over two million, spread across the globe, but most of them concentrated in small tribes. Many of our members are still feeding off the ongoing disasters in Haiti, the Sudan, Darfur, Indonesia, you name it. As the hurricane season ramps up, they're salivating over possibilities in the Gulf that Katrina didn't finish off."

Vivid picture, that. "Have you heard of *liberationblogspot.com?*"

Ben's expression tightened, she could almost smell the fear that rolled off him. "Yes. We're keeping tabs on them. We have *brujos* in Guayaquil who are looking for the woman who started the blog. But so far we haven't located her. It's difficult to know how well organized they are, but they seem to be planning something."

"If twenty thousand humans armed with flamethrowers descended on Esperanza, Ben, we would face extinction."

Ben flexed his fingers against the steering wheel. "All the more reason to do things my way, Nica."

His way was to turn the tribe loose on Esperanza and every village and town north of the Río Palo, seize every resident, and once and for all turn Esperanza into a city of *brujos.* "The chasers would intervene."

"They haven't intervened since we began seizing people here ten years ago. I don't think there're enough of them to fight us. The whole playing field is different than it was during the last battle for Esperanza, Nica. We outnumber them. We've evolved beyond anything they ever imagined five centuries ago. If they were going to intervene, they would have done it by now."

"Maybe the appearance of two transitionals is the first step in some new grand plan they have for defeating us."

"How?"

"I don't know." She didn't have any answers. But the chasers were up to something, this liberation group disturbed her, and the appearance of the transitionals frightened her. She suddenly felt threatened from all sides and wasn't sure what to do, which way to turn.

Ben opened the Mercedes up wide. It tore across the barren land, tires kicking up dirt and dried brush, mile after mile of flatness until the twin peaks appeared beneath a sagging gray sky, their bases ringed by a thick, dark fog. Home, she thought, and felt depressed by the thought.

After the chasers had crushed the *brujos* in the battle five centuries ago, many of them had sought release from their existence. The chasers swept in and supposedly guided these *brujos* to other realms within the afterlife. Dominica still wasn't sure what that meant. What other realms? The only realm she knew of was this one. The only certainty was that the battle had left most *brujos*, Dominica among them, with a deepening hatred toward the chasers and a greater hunger for physical life.

Many *brujos* had left Ecuador after that battle and journeyed out across the globe. They began to form tribes and learned how to seize bodies for physical pleasure or to familiarize themselves with the world as it marched through time.

Twenty years ago, she and Ben had returned to this barren valley, which was nearly as ugly as it was now, a flat wasteland. They had summoned *brujos* from every corner of the world, and those who had answered the call had become part of her tribe. Through their collective intentions and desires, they had erected twin peaks that rose a mile high. Then they had created their world inside of it. None of it was real in the physical sense. It was akin to a mirage, invisible to humans. But it was from here, their home base, that they had ventured for the next decade, spreading throughout South America, seizing bodies here and there. She'd always believed they hadn't seized enough bodies in one place to attract the attention of the chasers. But apparently they'd seized a sufficient number so that through the miracle of the Internet, victims' families and friends had coalesced around a single purpose: to annihilate the *brujos* and take back Esperanza.

The Mercedes plunged into the fog. Ben reached up to the remote control device clipped to the visor, pressed it, and the door in the mountain slid open. He drove in, honked twice, and the door shut, sealing them within. Lights winked on in the cavern, simulating daylight in a parking lot anywhere in America or Europe. Since physical life was so coveted, great care had been taken to create an atmosphere that mimicked it. Even the other cars parked here reflected it faithfully—hybrids, trucks, sedans, SUVs, Jeeps, a couple of Smart Cars, even some electric cars. Above this parking garage were the accouterments that reflected physical life: downtowns, shops, restaurants, cafés, small businesses.

She and Ben took the elevator to the third floor and caught a train downtown to their town house. En route, she put out a call to Rafael and Pearl, two loyal members of her tribe. They were waiting on the platform when the train pulled into the station.

Because of their physical histories, their afterlife forms were predictable— Rafael as a black Clark Gable to Pearl's pristine white Vivien Leigh. They had died in the United States in the early 1960s, a black man and a white woman in the heavily segregated South, when blacks and whites had their own restrooms, restaurants, and seats on the bus. Their relationship had threatened the status quo in their backwater Alabama town—he had been hung by the KKK, she had killed herself. Their rage had brought them to Dominica's tribe. They rarely indulged in sexual excursions like she and Ben and other members did. They were just happy to be together and looked ahead to the big picture. A city of *brujos*.

Hugs all around, *brujos* were always affectionate. "There're rumors," Rafael said as the four of them headed toward the sidewalk below. "Are they true?"

"Yes," Dominica said.

Pearl emitted a delighted squeal, hooked her arm through Rafael's, and did a funny little jig there on the sidewalk, in the shadow of their phony buildings, on the phony concrete sidewalks of their phony goddamn world. And Rafael, usually so reserved and serious, burst out laughing and indulged her, dancing along with her.

"But they can't be seized," Ben said. "They're protected."

Elation hissed out of Rafael and Pearl like gas from a balloon. "How . . . can that be?" Pearl stammered.

"Ridiculous," Rafael added. "Unprecedented."

"But true." Dominica proceeded to explain what she knew, suspected, hoped, and needed to know.

By then, they were inside the town house she and Ben shared, an ultra-modern environment—movable walls, hardwood floors, electronically controlled blinds, breathtaking views of lakes and volcanic peaks, parks and mysterious neighborhoods, all of it as phony as everything else that surrounded her. Phony but comforting. She and Ben even had several dogs and cats and birds, abused in physical life and pissed by the hand that had been dealt to them. Here, they were protected and loved. The animals changed as their understanding of *brujo* dynamics changed, and moved on, so right now they were down to one of each. A golden retriever puppy, a dusky conure, a white Persian. They slept together, ate together, and by tomorrow, one of them might be gone—to where? She had no idea. Now wasn't the time to think about who went where.

They gathered in the front room, talking quietly while Dominica did her phony hostess routine, cheese and crackers, sliced celery and a dip, a red Chilean wine, slices of fresh mango, papaya, kiwi. They conjured only the best, she and her tribe.

"If we can't take them, what's the point?" Pearl was saying when Dominica joined them with the goodies.

"We need information," Dominica told them, and brought them up to speed. "What do Ed Granger and Sara Wells know? Who is Charlie? How did Manuel Ortega know about the transitionals? Who instructed him to pick them up at the bodega? Is he part of this liberation movement? Why isn't he afraid of us? He had the audacity to *laugh* at me, to actually tell me he wasn't someone I wanted to cross. Can you imagine?"

Rafael sat forward, frowning. "We know about this liberation group. But their blog entries are coded, secretive, rather obscure at times. It's hard to tell how many there are, what their plans are. But we need to pay closer attention to their activities."

"I think they're potential threats," Pearl said. "If a group like this was large enough and swept into Esperanza with flamethrowers, when we were in virtual forms or using bodies, that would be the end of us. Or we would have to flee Esperanza."

"Never an option," Ben said. "We can't assume virtual forms anywhere else. We're powerless elsewhere."

Dominica patted the air with her hands. "Let's not get ahead of ourselves. Right now, you two should shadow Ed Granger and Sara Wells. Ben and I will follow the transitionals and see what we can find out about Manuel and this mystery man, Charlie."

"And that's it?" Rafael looked horrified. "*That's* the fucking plan?"

"You have a better plan?" she shot back.

"Yes. We sweep into Esperanza and take everyone." He laughed. "Imagine the chaos."

"That would bring out the chasers, Rafael. We would have flat-out war."

"Maybe it's time for war. Why're you afraid of them, Nica? The chasers haven't done anything since the first attacks started ten years ago. They're cowards, just like the locals. We have successfully intimidated them. Fear and terror work."

"And by seizing everyone," Pearl went on, "maybe we would put a stop to any plan this so-called liberation group has."

"The chasers aren't cowards, but I feel there's something else going on, some grand scheme they've concocted," Dominica said. "It's wiser to move cautiously now than to be reckless and lose Esperanza for good."

Rafael nodded thoughtfully. "Look, Pearl and I are with you and Ben. But if we can't find answers and still can't take the transitionals, then I say we seize the initiative and launch our offensive by attacking en masse and taking the city."

"Exactly," Ben agreed.

Dominica disliked the direction in which this conversation was moving. Rafael and Pearl were well liked among her tribe and could easily win backing by the majority. It angered her that Ben sided with them. She was only as powerful as the *brujos* she commanded and in the event of a coup within her own tribe, she could easily find herself sidelined. Such a drastic possibility prompted her to make a radical suggestion.

"*If* the chasers are the ones who allowed these transitionals into the city, then we can be sure it wasn't to benefit *us*. So you're right about one thing, Rafael. It's time we launched an offensive. I think we should kill the transitionals."

"How can we kill them if we can't seize them?" Pearl asked.

"We tell them they're both in comas, that they're nearly dead. That should scare them out of here. We follow them back to their bodies, seize the nearest people, force those people to kill them. This will effectively neutralize whatever plans the chasers have and send a direct message that they can't fuck around with us."

For moments, none of them said anything. Then Rafael's face lit up like a Halloween pumpkin. "It's brilliant. And once they're dead and the chasers are off balance, we move fast and attack Esperanza."

She resented Rafael for attempting to call the shots. But she didn't call him on it. Let him think what he wanted. "We work in pairs," she said, and explained the rest of her new plan.

Seven

Dr. Paco Faraday swept into the cottage with Ed Granger and pumped Ian's arm as if he intended to draw water. "Nice to meet you, Mr. Ritter. Ed mentioned you suffered a mishap, so if you could sit over here by the light, I'll take a look at it."

"What took you so long to get here?" Ian asked. "Ed said he called you an hour ago."

"The sorry roads, landslides, herds of llamas. Hey, this is Ecuador. I'm from Chile, where we don't have these kinds of problems unless there's been an earthquake."

Paco reminded Ian of a professor in his department, a man so uncomfortable with silence that he never shut up. Tall and thin, with a fussy mouth and thick, dark hair combed back dramatically from his forehead, Paco moved the same way he spoke, rapidly, with a staccato rhythm. While he examined the gash at Ian's temple, he chattered on about how backward Ecuador was in the high mountain areas, how the abject poverty kept the area from fully developing. "Looks deep, Mr. Ritter. It'll take four or five stitches, but that should have you nearly as good as new."

"Just do it," Ian said. "Make it stop bleeding."

"Of course he'll do it, mate," said Granger, pacing, sweating, visibly nervous, like a man who either had plenty at stake—or plenty to hide. "That's his job."

Why was Granger still here, hovering, offering his two cents? "Ed, I appreciate your bringing Dr. Faraday to the cottage, but you really don't have to hang around."

"I don't mind, mate. I feel responsible for what happened to you. Where's Tess?"

"She went into town." *To find us a way out of here.*

The doctor injected something cold in the skin right around the gash. A jab here, there, four in all. "Nomad went with her?" Paco asked.

"Nomad *left* with her. Beyond that, I don't know." Ian noticed a perceptible change in Granger's expression. "Why?"

"It's smart that she took Nomad," Paco said. "But I'm sure Ed warned you both about not traveling too far outside of Esperanza."

"You bet I did," Granger piped in.

"After one of Ed's men tackled me in the fog, Tess and I decided to look for other accommodations."

Paco's mouth tightened with what Ian sensed was fury. "Jesus, Ed, your posse needs to calm down or you're going to be losing business left and right. This kind of shit isn't exactly great for tourism."

"They attacked the cottage," Granger snapped. "We had to go after them."

"And trample a guest as well," Paco remarked dryly. "What an excellent business practice."

"I hope our bill is ready, Mr. Granger," said Ian.

Granger glared at Paco for another moment, then forced a smile. "I'll head up to my office and get it done now. Again, I apologize for what happened."

He slammed the door on the way out, eliciting an expression of disgust from Paco. "They're zealots when it comes to these *brujos*. Does it feel numb yet?"

"Very."

"If you feel pain at any point, just holler and I'll stick you again."

As Paco stitched, Ian felt only greater anxiety about getting out of here, finding Tess, and joining her in their exit from Esperanza. "Where's the nearest bus station, Dr. Faraday?"

"In the old town. But only local buses are running until the day after tomorrow. The long-distance buses never run on Sundays and Mondays. And they closed the airport years ago. It's too risky flying into Esperanza because of the way it's situated in these mountains. We're quite isolated here, really. So if you're looking to get to Quito, you'll have to hire a driver."

A driver it would be. "What's the story with these *brujos*, Dr. Faraday?"

"Eerie fucks, that's the story. You don't want to mess with them."

"But what the hell *are* they?"

He paused in his stitching and regarded Ian with a kind of incredulity that hinted at a massive breakdown in communication somewhere. "You mean, no one's told you?"

"Let's just say I've heard different theories and opinions."

His dark eyes narrowed. "Well, then, let me provide you with the facts, Mr. Ritter. *Brujos* are hungry ghosts, spirits who are stuck. They know they're dead, but for whatever reason they can't seem to move into any other after-world realm. Their ultimate goal is to become human again, to live in the physical world, and they do this by seizing humans and living out their mortal lives. When they do this, they take over completely—your brain, limbs, voice, memories, personality. When a full life isn't possible, they seize bodies to use for sex, to explore physical life. They often move within the fog, manipulating it, and suddenly, you're surrounded by *brujos*. That's what happened to you and Tess in the field."

Ian burst out laughing. "C'mon, Dr. Faraday. *Ghosts? Possession?* Those *brujos* outside of town looked as solid as you do."

"Anywhere north of the Río Palo, they can assume a human form for a short time, a kind of virtual form. That's what you saw. They're real in the sense that they look, speak, and act like humans and can interact with physical matter. But they're as ephemeral as smoke. Usually, they can't hold these forms very long. I'm shocked that Ed didn't tell you any of this."

"It wouldn't matter if he had. I don't believe in ghosts, hungry or otherwise."

"I know how preposterous it sounds. But if you look across various cultures, you find this belief is prevalent. In my own country, specifically on the island of Chiloé, there's a widespread belief in a different kind of *brujo*—the ghost ship *Caleuche,* allegedly crewed by men in black who come ashore at certain times of the month and abduct humans. In Brazil, there's the Bag Man, a hobo who collects disobedient children to sell. In Bulgaria, the Torbalan kidnaps children if they misbehave. In your own country, the UFO phenomenon with its abductions and men in black is similar. Ghosts are endemic to nearly every culture."

"If everything you say is true and these *brujos* are destroying life in Esperanza, why don't you leave?"

Paco dabbed something cool on his suturing job and Ian clearly recognized sadness and resignation in his eyes. "Esperanza is my home."

"As Hitler was rising to power, there were people who saw what was going on and fled their countries."

"In this area, many of those who could flee have done so."

The way he phrased it sounded odd, too careful. "What's that mean? Those who *could* flee . . . You could leave, you're not handicapped."

He resumed his stitching. "In a way, I *am* handicapped. Many here are."

"I don't understand."

"How old do you think I am, Mr. Ritter?"

"Late thirties, early forties."

He finished stitching and pressed a bandage over the sutured gash. "I arrived in Esperanza on my thirty-ninth birthday. And that was forty-two years ago."

What the fuck. "You're *eighty-one?* But . . . that's impossible."

"People who live north of Río Palo don't age. Or they age very slowly. If I left this area, it would be only a matter of hours before I would look every second of my real age. There are others who are much older and would turn to dust. That's why so many of us haven't left. We can't. When I came here, Mr. Ritter, it was as a gift to myself. I had been diagnosed with leukemia and given three months to live and I wanted to enjoy whatever time I had left. Within a week of my arrival, all my symptoms were gone. I was cured."

From ghosts to miracle cures and long life. "What about infants? Do they stay that way forever?"

"No, they grow normally until adolescence, when hormones kick in. Most of them leave Esperanza after high school—to attend universities, for jobs, to start families, whatever—and age normally. Many of them then return in their thirties or forties and live out long and healthy lives. They often bring outsiders back with them, which we encourage. That keeps the area diverse. Tourists who stay here for any time marvel at how much better they feel, how invigorated. On the far side of the Lago del Sueño there's a spa and health resort that's enormously popular with upscale tourists. People who arrive with chronic health problems often leave completely cured. I know this because I'm one of their on-call physicians."

"How is that even possible? Is it the water? The soil? What?"

"No one knows for sure. Physiologically, it seems to be connected with the master gland—the pituitary. But in a deeper sense, I believe it's related to Esperanza's extraordinary history, it's—"

The doctor suddenly started twitching, shoulders jerking one way, then the other, eyes darting right, left. His arms flew up, hands fisted, his head dropped back and his mouth fell open as if to scream, but only gurgling sounds spilled into the air. His face contorted in excruciating agony, his head snapped upright again, eyes wide, shiny, almost all pupil, and pinned Ian like a butterfly under glass.

Like the men in the field.

"Know this," he said in a quiet, slippery voice that made Ian feel as if he were inhaling wet moss. "We want you because you're in transition. There hasn't been a transitional soul in Esperanza since it became a physical place five centuries ago. And now, suddenly, there are two of you. A kind of Adam and Eve, if you're the religious sort."

Ian couldn't speak, couldn't breathe, but as Paco moved toward him, he grabbed his pack and swung. It struck Paco in the side of the head and he stumbled back, eyes wide with astonishment, breath exploding from his mouth. He crashed into the end table and a lamp toppled, books slid to the floor, a pair of coffee mugs shattered.

Paco lay there, groaning, then the *brujo* inside him forced him to rise up on his elbows and explode with laughter. In that same wet, slithering voice, he said, "You had a heart attack, Ian Ritter. You're on life support. In the between. Not here, not there. Tess Livingston was shot, she's in a coma. Not here, not there. And since we covet physical life and appreciate it more than your kind, let me sink into your skin. Let me live out your mortal time. We'll be partners you and me, we'll be—"

"*Shut up, you brujo fuck.*" Ian spun around, swept Tess's pack off the couch, and tore out of the cottage, that hideous laughter and voice pursuing him.

"*You cannot escape us, Ian Ritter. We can find you anywhere there is fog.*"

A blind, white panic propelled him up the path, past other cottages, past the main building. He raced out onto Calle Principal and plunged into the stream of pedestrians, slowing down slightly so that he didn't attract attention. *You had a heart attack, Ian Ritter. You're on life support.* Lies, just lies to deepen his terror. He obviously wasn't on life support. The dead didn't make love or bleed. His heart beat, he slept and dreamed, he was moving, scared, hungry, and he desperately wanted to find Tess and get out of here.

But he didn't know where to look for her, so he kept moving with the crowd, deeper into El Corazón, the old city. He didn't see a single bus station or car rental agency. But on every corner, huge fans whirred incessantly and more air blew up through grates in roads and sidewalks. It wasn't like the city wilted in heat. The air was chilly. The only possible purpose the fans could serve was to keep away fog and, therefore, *brujos.* Insanity. But no less nuts than the idea that a *brujo* possessed the doc.

C'mon, c'mon, you need a goddamn plan. Great urgency seized him and with it came clarity. He figured that Tess had learned the same thing he had about the buses and had headed directly to Manuel's. Ian dug out the man's business card, memorized the address. He had no idea where the town of Gigante was or how he might get there, but intended to find out.

Ian loped across the road to a huge park lined with vendor stalls and wooden bins overflowing with fruits and vegetables, freshly baked breads and pastries, kiosks selling coffee. He ordered a café con leche from a diminutive man with several missing teeth. The man returned with a tiny plastic cup half filled with a tarlike coffee and a second, larger cup that held steamed milk. He poured the viscous stuff into the cup of milk, gave it a quick, vigorous stir, and set it in front of Ian. The man picked up the dollar Ian had left on the counter, counted out change, but Ian shook his head. *"No cambio. Gracias."* He showed the man Manuel's business card. *"Autobús? Gigante?"*

The little man gestured off to his left and rattled away in Spanish. The only part Ian understood was "four blocks" and "Gigante 11." *"Es lejos?"* Ian asked.

"Veinticuatro kilómetros."

He understood *kilómetros* as "kilometers," but didn't know what the rest of it meant. He held up five fingers. "This many?"

"No, no, señor." He flashed ten fingers twice, then held up four fingers.

Twenty-four kilometers. That was about fifteen miles, he thought, and moved on to a wagon filled with fresh fruits and vegetables. He bought two ripe mangos for fifty cents. He needed to eat something before boarding a bus, so he headed into the park and found a vacant bench.

The current gringo wisdom about South America, at least in Minneapolis, was that if you bought from a street vendor, you would end up with Montezuma's revenge. But once you'd been stalked and chased by *brujos* and one of them claimed you were on life support, what was a little Montezuma's revenge?

Anxiety ate away at him and he continually looked for Granger or Juanito, certain one of them would barrel into the park, perhaps with cops, and accuse him of taking off without paying his bill. But he felt protected here, surrounded by so many people, and if he did see either man, he could easily lose himself in the crowd.

Eerie fucks, Paco had said moments before he started to twitch and jerk. Was that the instant when a *brujo* had seized him?

You had a heart attack, Ian Ritter. You're on life support. In the between. Not here, not there. Tess Livingston was shot, she's in a coma. Not here, not there. Ian took another sip of the strong, sweet coffee, savoring it, then peeled the top off one of the mangos and bit into it. The taste was exquisite, sweet and warm, the texture soft. The juice dripped between his fingers.

I taste, smell, see, touch, hear. I'm alive.

Monkey-puzzle trees rose everywhere, birds flitted through their branches, singing and occasionally hopping around on the ground, seeking food. Hummingbirds congregated around a nearby feeder and just above him, a pair of condors circled against the brilliant blue sky. They were larger than the ones he'd seen outside the inn, wingspans at least ten feet across. They drifted on the air currents, conserving energy, and gracefully spiraled lower until they were just above the treetops.

Across the Andes, these magnificent birds lived at anywhere between ten thousand and sixteen thousand feet of altitude and these two were the most magnificent he'd seen. Everyone in the park watched them until they lifted upward again, shrinking to dark dots against the blue. People on life support couldn't see condors, couldn't drink in or appreciate such breathtaking beauty: stunning snow-covered volcanic peaks, cobblestone roads twisting up and down hills that rivaled San Francisco, the explosive carnival of color in the flowers, the sky. Homes and apartment buildings basked in sunlight on the nearby hillsides. Except for the *brujos,* Esperanza secretly enchanted him.

People who live north of the Río Palo don't age. Was it true? He looked around at other people in the park, studying their faces. How old were the two teenagers tossing crumbs to a flock of pigeons over by the fountain? And what about that elderly man snoozing on another bench? He looked seventy, but might be twice that.

"Hey, hello," someone called.

A short, thin woman hurried toward him, waving. He recognized her bouncing curls and the dimples as deep as craters at the sides of her mouth. Stephanie Logan, the American woman from the bodega. He barely resisted the urge to pretend he hadn't seen her.

"I remember you," she said breathlessly, stopping in front of him. "The bodega. Yesterday. Or was that the day before yesterday? Or five days ago?" She rubbed her hand nervously against her cheek. "I'm so mixed up here. We spoke briefly at the bodega. You're Mr. Roiter, right?"

"Ritter." He continued to consume the mango.

"Right. Ian Ritter." As her head bobbed, her eyes darted about uneasily. She sat beside him on the bench, emitted a long, dramatic sigh. "I'm so relieved to see a familiar face. That awful bus we took from the bodega left us off in some godforsaken town and we had to wait around for another bus to bring us here. The driver gestured uptown. That's where the hotels supposedly are. I mean, can you believe this place? Where are we?"

In the between, he thought, if he could believe what the *brujo* had said. *Maybe you're a transitional, too, Stephanie. Or maybe you're dead.* "Where's your family, Stephanie?"

She waved across the park. "Somewhere around here. My husband was trying to find a restroom for the kids and a place to charge up our cells." She touched his arm and spoke in a soft, conspiratorial tone. "I think there's something really strange about all this."

Tell me about strange. He wondered what she meant by "cells." "Strange how?" *Enlighten me. Tell me you know you're dead.*

"Nothing feels right to me. I mean, I'm known to be a bit fey, and from time to time I sense things. And I have to tell you, Mr. Ritter, that my senses have been going haywire since we got kicked off the bus at Bodega del Cielo. I mean, honestly, I can't remember a damn thing before the bodega. Don't you think that's a tad strange?"

"Yeah. I don't recall anything before the bodega, either." It still disturbed him and he didn't want to discuss it with Stephanie "a little bit fey" Logan from upstate New York. He polished off the rest of the mango, tossed the seed in the nearest trash, stood. "And that's part of the reason I'm leaving. Did you happen to see a bus station on your way in?"

"I'm not sure. I wasn't really paying attention. There're so many distractions. But could you stick around for a few minutes and repeat what you just said to my husband? He thinks I'm making this stuff up even though he can't remember anything, either."

For all he knew, Stephanie and her husband might be *brujos* in their phony human forms. "I really need to get moving. Good luck, Stephanie."

Ian hurried away from her. *Brujo* or something else, she was the type, he felt certain, who might follow him and prove to be the ugly American stalker, whose persistence, rudeness, or tenacity doesn't just embarrass you, but becomes a thorn in your side.

Sure enough, she ran after him, shouting, waving her arms, begging him to stop, drawing attention from anyone who could hear her. Pedestrians stepped out of her way, bicyclists swerved clear, and when she pursued him across a street, cars slammed on their brakes to keep from hitting her.

Ian pounded up and down hills, around corners, into and out of alleys. By the time he lost her, he was completely disoriented. Since he had left his city map in the cottage, he picked a direction and started walking. How many of the people around him were *brujos* in human form? Or were possessed by *brujos?* What was he supposed to look for?

Black, glossy eyes.

Twitches, erratic movements.

Ian now scrutinized everyone—men and women in business attire, obvious tourists, Quechuans, locals, even kids. And suddenly, it seemed they all had black, glossy eyes and moved erratically, that he traveled through a city of *brujos.* Panicked, he barreled through the crowds, his mind empty, and when the muscles in his legs screamed for a respite and he couldn't catch his breath, he stopped, backed up to a wall and bent forward, hands clutching his thighs, gasping for breath.

People who passed eyed him curiously, stared, or looked away. He felt exposed and vulnerable out here on this narrow, shadowed, labyrinthine street, and quickly ducked through the nearest door, into the Incan Café.

Eight

Throughout the bus ride to Gigante, Tess's emotions fluctuated wildly between highs and lows, euphoria and despair. When she thought of returning to the Bureau, the prodigal daughter welcomed back to the tribe and her old routine with Dan, she felt nauseated. When she thought of staying with Ian, her heart sang. So it went, mile after mile. The deeper she moved into this country, the deeper she traveled into those parts of herself too long neglected, shoved aside, or buried altogether.

The bus stopped every few blocks until they were out of town, then continued nonstop for miles. Buildings gave way to open countryside. Deep green hills rolled away on either side of the road, thickets of monkey-puzzle trees and pines sheltered horses, llamas, birds. Acre after acre of windmills stood tall against the clear blue sky, dozens of greenhouses dotted the landscape, the air filled with hummingbirds.

Tess and Nomad got off at the sign for Gigante, population 4,567. The air felt warmer, the sun burned white against a blue continent of sky. A gorgeous day for walking. No giant fans out here. This entire area looked rural, with pastures and fields, humble homes, a smattering of stores that resembled Bodega del Cielo. She passed silos, concrete buildings, warehouses, more windmills. Quechuan peasants herded goats and sheep. Several kids on donkeys called out greetings to Nomad. The dog had his own fan club.

Gigante—giant—hardly qualified as a punctuation point and probably was named after the snow-covered volcano that overshadowed it. The main street boasted a theater showing an old Fellini movie, a drugstore, several restaurants, cafés, a market. Bicycles outnumbered cars. The beautiful weather had lured people outdoors.

Up and down side streets, she caught sight of neighborhoods of wooden homes with tin roofs, small concrete houses with jalousie windows. Laundry hung from clotheslines, dresses and shirts swaying in a slight breeze. Most homes had small gardens—tomato vines, herbs, great leafy sprouts that might be broccoli or cauliflower. How did any of this grow at an altitude of more than thirteen thousand feet? Her imperfect memory of her trip across the continental divide was of barrenness. No trees, not even aspens.

Tess didn't see any street signs, so she ducked into a café to ask directions to Calle Libertad, Manuel's street. When Nomad slipped inside with her, no one objected.

On a rack to the right of the door were prepaid cell phones and other cell and iPod supplies. Tess selected a cell with two hundred minutes on it, went over to the counter. The young man who waited on her didn't even seem to notice the dog. His nametag read Hank, and he looked to be fresh out of college. When he spoke, she pegged his accent as either Midwestern or Canadian. How had some kid from either place ended up in this rural Ecuadorian town?

"What can I get you?" he asked, all smiles.

"A café con leche." More caffeine. What the hell. "And the cell."

"Sure thing." He looked at Nomad, then leaned forward, elbows resting against the counter. "If you're with Nomad, the coffee is on the house. The cell is thirty bucks. I'll activate it for you."

When he returned with her coffee and cell phone, she said, "What is it with this dog? Everyone knows him."

"Nomad means you're from the Posada de Esperanza. If you're in cottage thirteen, then you've been marked by the *brujos.*" He smiled nervously, lowered his voice. "But you never heard any of that from me." He tossed Nomad a doggie treat. "Lemme me get you some water, guy." Hank filled a bowl with water, stepped out from behind the counter, set it on the floor.

As Nomad lapped it up, Tess said, "We're on our way to see Manuel Ortega, who—"

"Calle Libertad, one block north. Hang a left. Third house in on the right. You'll know it's the right house because there are always dozens of cars in the driveway. Your name's Tess Livingston, right?"

"How—"

"You should know that I'm supposed to contact the inn, let them know you're here." He looked about warily, like some paranoid stoner who believed that everyone over thirty might be a drug cop. "Several days ago, they sent out an e-mail about you and Ian Ritter. How you might be visiting Manuel and were probably traveling with Nomad. Now how do *they* know this kinda Big Brother shit? That's what troubles me."

"Who sent this e-mail?"

"Ed Granger. He and Sara Wells—you met her?"

Not yet. "No."

"Well, they're pretty high up in the governing hierarchy of the town and when they send out a notice like this, people pay attention. Personally, I think it has to do with the *brujos'* interest in you and your friend." Hank stepped out from behind the counter, spoke quietly. "Look, a lot goes on here that I don't understand."

"Thanks, Hank." She sipped from the mug. "I appreciate the information. Where're you from?"

"Wisconsin. Came down after college to see South America, met a woman who lives here, we moved in together. So here I am. The cost of living is next to nothing, the expat community is growing, hiking is fantastic, locals are friendly. We're saving money to start a bookstore and Internet café. What's there not to like?"

"The *brujos.*"

"Well. Yeah. There's that." He smiled quickly. "But we work around them. Look, if you're going to hire Manuel to drive you to Quito, it'll take eight hours *if* he's got a lead foot."

Eight hours. She paid, and as soon as she and Nomad were outside again, she punched out her mother's cell number, Maddie's, then the house phone. Busy signals. Tess typed a text message to her mother and Maddie: *I met someone. Journalism prof at U of Minn. Game changer. More later, luv.*

She pressed send and smiled when the envelope icon sailed off into cyberspace.

Nomad suddenly barked and dashed toward a house with six cars in the driveway and several bikes on the sidewalk. The windows were open, music drifted out into the cool air—John Lennon crooning to give peace a chance. She caught up with the dog and before she could knock, the door was flung open.

Manuel stood there in jeans, a dove-gray pullover sweater, black running shoes. His dark hair was combed away from his face, revealing an unlit cigarette tucked behind his ear. His face collapsed with astonishment. "*Dios mio.*" He stepped out onto the porch, shut the door, scratched Nomad behind the ears, and glared at Tess. "You should not be here. It is much less safe than the city."

"That's why Nomad is with me. I need answers, Manuel. And I'd like to hire you to drive Ian and me to the nearest airport."

He touched her elbow, urging her down the driveway, the dog trotting along behind them. "We'll go someplace safe to talk. Where we won't be interrupted."

Or seen, she thought.

They walked in silence for half a mile. She sensed his unease, but couldn't tell if it was due to her unexpected arrival or that he was afraid to be outside, here and now, with her. The road turned to gravel and dirt, houses thinned out, thickets of scrawny pines appeared. Except for a scudding of clouds to the west, the sky was a pure, unadulterated blue.

"Señorita Tess," Manuel began.

"Please call me Tess. The 'señorita' stuff makes me feel old."

For the first time since they'd left his house, he smiled. "You are many things, but *old* is not one of them." Manuel gestured toward a large greenhouse. On either side of it was a fenced pasture where horses grazed. "We can speak freely in there."

"Why can't we speak freely right *here*? No one's watching. No one can hear us."

Manuel shifted his weight from one foot to the other, looked around nervously. "It is too easy to be surprised by *brujos* out here."

"Let's start with these *brujos*. What are they, Manuel?"

His frown forced his dark, bushy brows closer together, so they looked like feathery wings that might lift off his face. He slipped a Zippo lighter from his sweatshirt pocket, plucked the cigarette from behind his ear, lit it with a flourish. As he snapped the lid shut, Tess remembered that her dad had owned an identical silver Zippo lighter that he kept with him even after he'd quit smoking. Whenever he was preparing for a case, he used to snap the Zippo's lid open and shut, just as Manuel had, but repeatedly, so that it clicked like castanets. She and her mother used to joke that without the lighter, Charlie would be a mess of nervous tics.

Manuel inhaled deeply, with obvious satisfaction. "I told you already." He dropped his head back, blew smoke rings into the air, snapped the lighter open and shut. "They are lost souls."

"That's an expression. To me it means someone is screwed up." She stabbed at her temple. "*Loco.* Crazy. Nuts. Is that what you mean?"

"They are . . . spirits. *Fantasmas.*"

"*Ghosts?*" She balked. "You people are terrified of *ghosts?*"

Manuel blew more smoke rings, kept snapping the lighter's lid. Nomad sat between them, vigilant, tense. "Let me try again." He switched to Spanish and proceeded to describe a worldview that was so far removed from her beliefs and experience that it sounded like fantasy. Hungry ghosts stuck in the dimension closest to physical life. Ghosts that could possess humans. Ghosts that assumed human form anywhere north of the Río Palo by drawing on the residual power of the area from when it was a nonphysical location. Whatever *that* meant.

It all sounded nuts. *He* sounded nuts. When you were dead you were dead, that was it, end of story. Except that she didn't really believe that. In Quito, she had felt her dead father around, lights had come on by themselves, she'd even caught a whiff of the aftershave he often had used. But before she could say anything, Manuel's eyes fixed on something over her right shoulder and Nomad emitted a low, throaty growl, the fur along his spine rising. Manuel dropped his cigarette, crushed it with his shoe, then touched her elbow, urging her forward, toward the greenhouse.

"We must go inside, Tess. Quickly."

The urgency in his voice alarmed her. Nomad darted out in front of them, leading the way. Off to her left, through the trees, fog rolled toward them. They broke into a run.

Manuel pushed the door open and they darted into the warm, humid building. Tall mango and papaya trees brushed the skylights, branches sagged with ripe fruit—oranges, grapefruits, avocados. Colorful patches of lettuce, broccoli, tomatoes, and cauliflower covered the ground. It smelled like high summer in Florida, when the rains came and heat and humidity hung so thickly in the air that you could almost taste the soil, salt, ripening fruit, fertile earth. Manuel quickly shut the heavy metal door, bolted it, pressed a green button on the keypad to the right of the door. Somewhere in town, a siren started shrieking. Another button activated the accordion shutters outside and they rumbled and clattered, closing off the greenhouse walls, the skylights.

As light inside the greenhouse diminished, emergency beacons winked on. Nomad barked and tore up a row lined with banana trees. He finally stopped and started digging frantically. Manuel dropped to his knees beside the dog, dug his fingers down into mulch and soil, pulled open a trapdoor. A hinged, wooden ramp unfolded, Nomad raced down it. Tess and Manuel hurried after him, footfalls echoing as they descended fifteen feet through twilight.

Above them, the assault began, a relentless pounding and battering muted by the mounds of earth that covered them. At the bottom of the ramp, Manuel punched a button on yet another keypad, the trapdoor shut, emergency lights flared. A flight of wooden stairs took them down even deeper and the assault now sounded distant, unreal.

She followed Manuel into a long corridor so narrow that she couldn't extend her arms without knocking something off the dozens of wall shelves that held bags of rice, canned goods, thirty-gallon containers of water, tools, even propane tanks. The corridor emptied into a dimly lit but comfortable room where Nomad already lapped water from a bowl on the floor. Manuel hit a switch for the lights and the room lit up with floor lamps, coffee table lamps, recessed lighting. He locked the door, Tess looked around slowly.

What the fuck. "A panic room." But far more comfortable. Couches, beds, a table, sink, faucets, TV. "My God, Manuel, who built this?"

"A rich colonel from Gigante provided the money for our few shelters like this one. We're about forty feet underground. The fog cannot penetrate here. We have learned to defend ourselves."

"*Defend* yourselves? Jesus, you're like kids terrified of the bogeyman. You're not defending yourselves. You have *defenses.* There's a difference."

Something dark and terrible entered his eyes. He spoke in a hoarse, choked voice. "Ten years ago, when the attacks started, my sister and I were riding horses in a field behind our house. A fog rose. It moved over us so swiftly that my sister didn't escape. I felt it the moment she was seized. I heard her calling to me as she emerged from the fog. I saw her outstretched arms. And I ran. When the *brujo* used up her body, she started bleeding from her eyes and nose, her skin, from beneath her toenails, her fingernails. I *saw* it all, Tess. And so yes, I hide well and deeply."

He had just described a bleed-out, like that of the man outside the bodega. Even though his description was vivid, she felt it had happened to someone else, not to Manuel personally. Why would he pretend these events had happened to him? But she couldn't bring herself to disbelieve him, either. He felt too familiar and trustworthy.

"Where is Ian?" Manuel suddenly asked, as if just remembering him.

"At the inn, waiting for the doctor." She told him what had happened at the inn earlier, about Granger and his men holding her and Ian at gunpoint, chasing *brujos* into the fog, about Nomad and the sock with the message pinned to it.

"I am so sorry, Tess." Misery carved deep lines into his face. "Granger and his men were supposed to protect you and Ian, not harass and antagonize you. Nomad once ran with the *brujos*, with Dominica, who commands the largest tribe of them. He knows the *brujos* better than any of us. What did the message say?"

"I don't know. I think it was written in Quechua. Manuel, I'd like to hire you to drive us to Quito."

"Wait, is Ian in the cottage *alone?*"

The way he said it made her feel guilty that she hadn't waited with Ian until the doctor had arrived. But Ian had been insistent that she go on without him and find a way out of the city as quickly as possible. "By now the doctor has gotten there."

"But you don't know for sure."

"Ed said he called the doctor. Why would he lie about it?"

"It's not that he would lie, but that *brujos* might use the situation to their advantage, to harm Ian."

"Why would they harm him? Why did they attack the cottage we're staying in? What the hell's going on, Manuel?"

He ignored her question, brought out his cell. "I need to call the inn, but the cell doesn't work down here. I have to get closer to the surface. I'll be right back. Nomad will stay with you."

Manuel hurried out and as soon as the door shut behind him, Nomad ran over to it, whining and pawing at the wood. Then he leaped up, his powerful legs slammed against the door, paws pressing down against the latch, and it swung open.

Nomad tore out of the room, Tess's stomach churned with anxiety. Why had everyone they'd met here ignored their questions? How could a dog run with ghosts?

Tess burst through the door, into the narrow corridor. The emergency light was still on, but in her haste to reach the greenhouse, she knocked canned goods and tools off the shelves, stumbled over them, nearly lost her balance. At the end of the corridor, she felt inexplicably winded, her heart hammered, and she had to pause to catch her breath. She peered up the flight of stairs to the ramp and, beyond it, the open trapdoor to the greenhouse. It suddenly seemed an impossible distance, even though she knew it wasn't.

Move. As she started up the stairs, she suddenly felt on the verge of passing out. She sank to her knees on one of the steps, then doubled over, allowing the blood to rush into her head. For a moment, she thought she heard her mother calling to her—*Tess, hon, we're here*—and the scar on her right thigh itched and throbbed terribly. Then the dizziness passed and she was able to move forward again, to the top of the stairs and then onto the ramp. She rubbed at her leg, alarmed by what had just happened. Was that a telepathic SOS? Was her mother in some sort of trouble?

Her leg muscles ached as she went up the steep ramp. The cacophony outside now sounded so loud, it was as if meteorites were crashing against the greenhouse shutters. And where was Manuel? He'd said he had to get closer to the surface, not that he needed to go into the greenhouse.

She hurried out into the echoing greenhouse, the soft glow of the emergency lights. At the end of a row of fruit trees, Manuel was arguing with a tall, thin man whose black hair brushed his shoulders. *Brujo?* Had to be. Nothing human could penetrate this fortress. But Manuel had said no *brujo* could get through it, either.

From where she was, she couldn't tell if Manuel was scared, but he definitely looked pissed. She darted up another row, body shielded from their view by the trees and thick bushes. She couldn't hear them over the echoing clamor, but now and then she caught sight of Manuel, then of the mystery man. He didn't look any more ghostlike than the men in the field had. If anything, he looked Spanish, exotically handsome with a strong, square jaw, eyes set deeply into their sockets, mouth proud.

She slipped into the trees, moving quickly, and glimpsed them through the low-hanging branches. As the interloper grabbed hold of Manuel's arm, Tess slammed her bag into the back of the man's head. He lurched forward, hands to his head, and was just turning when Tess tackled him. They slammed to the ground, rolled once, Manuel dancing around them, waving his arms, shouting shit she couldn't hear. Then, between one blink and another, Tess felt the man's bones popping and rearranging themselves, his body shrinking, arms pulling back into his chest and reemerging as something bonier, covered with thick hair. She knew that something hideous and extraordinarily strange was happening and leaped away from him.

The clamor suddenly stopped, she heard the sharp, startled explosions of her own breath as she stared in horror. Her brain refused to translate what she saw. The *thing* on the floor in front of her was neither man nor animal, but some grotesque amalgam—the ears and rear legs of a dog or a wolf, the nose, mouth, and arms of a man; human skin on the arms, fur covering the rear legs; the shape of a human spine vanishing, a tail appearing. And then the abomination became a black dog with tea-colored eyes. Nomad.

"Sweet Christ."

"*Carajo*," Manuel spat, raking his fingers back through his hair.

Nomad's ears twitched, his eyes bored holes through her.

"What . . . what do I call it, Manuel? What . . ."

"Wayra is a shape shifter. The last of his kind."

Awe and revulsion rushed through her. This creature had been in the living room when she and Ian had made love, had been a part of their lives since they'd arrived four days ago, had heard everything they had whispered. They had befriended him outside of the bodega, he had ridden on the bus with them to Esperanza. She had sensed his unusual intelligence, but *this*? The stuff of legends and myths here in front of her? Friend, companion, sentry, shape-shifter. *Uh-huh, right, lock me up.*

"Look, I really need to know what's going on, what Esperanza is, how—"

"Tess, I'll answer all your questions, but not right now. We don't have much time. I just spoke to Ed, who said that Ian fled the inn a while ago. We must find him. He's in danger. He—"

"*I'm not moving until you answer my questions.*" She didn't realize she shouted until she heard her voice echoing in the cavernous greenhouse. "Please," she finished, her voice softer, controlled.

Manuel raised his hands, patting the air, trying to calm her. They both looked at Nomad, who sank to the floor, doing dog things—scratching at himself, sniffing, then moving off into the trees. *Even shape-shifters have to take a piss.* Manuel now spoke English clearly, without hesitation or accent, as though it were his native language. That was nearly as strange as what he said.

"Myth and folklore tell us that thousands of years ago, Esperanza was a nonphysical place, a kind of virtual world for the dead, the near dead, the comatose. It was where the soul could explore the afterlife and realize that death isn't the end, that it's just another state of consciousness. Here, the soul could choose to pass on or to return to physical life."

"Excuse me, but this sounds a lot like fiction, Manuel."

"Isn't myth a kind of archetypal fiction?"

One point for Manuel. "Go on."

"During this time, *brujos* permeated Esperanza. Their ultimate goal was to become physical, so they *seized* souls and lived out the physical lives of the transitionals who stood at the threshold between life and death. Five centuries ago, a group of more evolved souls fought the *brujos*—"

"Evolved souls. What's that mean?"

"They were called *cazadores de luz*—light chasers. Their job was to help these *brujos* forward in their afterlife journey. A difficult task because most *brujos* were—and still are—stuck close to physical existence, held there because of emotions and beliefs they carried with them into death. Rage, hatred, racism, envy, intolerance, sadism, cruelty, revenge, terror."

"So, we're talking about angels and demons?"

"The terms vary from culture to culture, religion to religion. But forget labels. I'm speaking in the language of myth, archetypes, legends. And in this story, the chasers crushed the *brujos* in that battle five centuries ago. Some were so shocked and demoralized by the loss of the battle that they sought release from their lives as predators and the chasers were able to guide these *brujos* to other realms within the afterlife. But for most of them, their defeat only increased their hatred of chasers and their hunger for physical life."

"What happened after the defeat?"

"Esperanza was brought into the physical world and closed to transitional souls, which essentially cut off the source of the *brujos'* endless feasting. After the defeat, most of the *brujos* left Ecuador and spread out across the world. They grouped into tribes, learned how to seize bodies for physical pleasure or to familiarize themselves with the world as it marched toward the twenty-first century. They *evolved*. Now the chasers are fewer in number. They can mitigate but not stop the incursion of *brujos* into Esperanza and the larger world."

"That's quite a mythology, Manuel. How does it fit with *brujos* now? Has the myth leaped to life?"

"The attacks have been happening here in Esperanza for the last ten years, sporadically, often on tourists, but also on locals. We can defend ourselves, but don't know how to defeat them."

"Why're they after Ian and me?"

"I don't know."

She stabbed her thumb toward Nomad, who paced restlessly. "So where's he fit in that mythology?"

"Other than what I told you, I have no idea. You'll have to ask him. We need to get moving, to get out of here before the next wave of attacks."

"And go where? I thought you said we're safe here."

"There's a lull. They're regrouping. We need to leave while we can. This place isn't completely secure. There was a call from a café in Esperanza, where Ian is. He apparently took refuge there after the doctor was seized and threatened him. Juanito will pick him up, we'll meet at another location."

She felt used up, her head ached, she had more questions. But she trusted Manuel and his sense of urgency and nodded. Manuel snapped something in Quechua to Nomad and the dog bolted forward and raced up the corridor, through the immense silence. Tess and Manuel followed him, fast.

The Incan Café, deeper than it was wide, provided a welcoming fireplace to the left, a serving counter on the right, tables and chairs in the middle. Farther back stood bookcases and more tables, and beyond that lay a third area where people appeared to be sitting in front of small TV screens. Behind the counter, a young woman with beautiful skin and long black hair, who looked to be about his son's age, had an object pressed to her ear. "*Sí, sí, claro,*" she was saying. "*Tengo que ir, mi amor.*" Then she slipped easily into English. "I'll call you later." She snapped the object shut and hurried over. "*Buenos días, señor.*" Her name tag read CONSUELO DE COLOMBIA.

"A café con leche, please." Ian gestured at the object in her hand. "What is that, anyway?"

"This?" She seemed surprised by his question. "A cell phone." She flipped it open, revealing a small screen and keypad with numbers.

"A *telephone*?" Without a cord? Unconnected to anything? Smaller than her palm?

"You don't have these where you're from?"

"No. Where can I get one?"

"We sell prepaid cells here. I'll bring you one with your coffee."

As Consuelo turned away, Ian glanced at a sign on the counter: FREE WI-FI AND DSL FOR JUST A BUCK AN HOUR! Cell phones, Wi-Fi, DSL: he felt like he'd dropped down the rabbit hole.

Consuelo returned with his coffee and a bright blue cell phone. "This one's got a hundred prepaid minutes. It's thirty dollars and I can activate it for you."

"Fantastic. Thanks." Now he could call Luke. "What do you have to do to activate it?"

"*Caramba,* you're really new at this. I'll show you. We have DSL now and it's *magnífico.*" She brought her fingers to her lips, kissed them. "You blink and are on."

He had no idea what she was talking about, but followed her into the back room with his coffee and new cell phone. A dozen people sat in front of small TV screens.

"Here you go. Number thirteen."

Thirteen. Again.

He realized that what he'd mistaken for TV screens were something altogether new to him. Resting on a square pad to his right was an odd-looking plastic gizmo. Ian set his coffee down, pulled out a wooden chair, sat.

"What browser do you use?" Consuelo asked.

Browser? What the hell was *that?* "You pick for me."

She placed her hand on the gizmo, jiggled it slightly, and the screen lit up with a photograph of the café—and dozens of symbols. "Left click on the logo for Firefox," Consuelo said. "Like this."

A white page appeared with letters across the top of it: a blue *G*, red *O*, yellow *O*, blue *G*, green *L*, red *E*. Google. What the hell was a Google? To the left of it were: *more, gmail, shopping, news, maps, images, web.*

What the fuck? He sat with his hand over the gizmo, but didn't know what to do with it.

"You don't have DSL where you live?" Consuelo asked.

"Uh, no."

"You're still on dial-up? *Qué barbaridad.*"

What was dial-up? "I live in rural Minnesota. We don't have anything like this yet. What do I do?"

Consuelo's expression made it abundantly clear that he was the white elephant in the café. "*No* Internet? *No* cells? *Ay, señor.* Even in the small towns in my country, everyone has a cell and Internet." She sat beside him. "Many expats come through here. You're the first I have met who has never used the Internet. So let me activate your cell, then give you a lesson."

She whizzed through the activation and proceeded with a short lesson in the use of the Internet. Most of it seemed to revolve around Google, which she referred to as a search engine. "You can enter anything in Google and if there's information anywhere in the known universe, it'll come up. Just give me a word, a term, a name, anything."

"Esperanza, Ecuador."

"Perfect." Consuelo typed the words into a space she called the search bar. The screen filled with phrases—links. "You click on a link, then press this button here if you want to print. Try the Wikipedia link. It's an open-source encyclopedia. Anyone can enter information into Wikipedia."

"Thanks very much, Consuelo."

As soon as she turned away, he clicked on the Wikipedia link and scanned the article. Some of the information echoed what Paco Faraday had told him and much of it pertained to the myths and folklore about Esperanza—that the city had once been a nonphysical location for souls in transition, about some big battle between *brujos* and light chasers five centuries ago. He skipped to the factual aspects.

This town of 20,000 is located at 13,200 feet in the Andes. Esperanza is nearly impossible to get to without a local guide. This difficulty is due, in part, to the roughness of the terrain. The roads are bad, the volcanos are unpredictable, the mountains rise nearly 8,000 feet from the nearest outpost.

Local myths and legends claim the area retains some of the mystical qualities it possessed as a nonphysical location—that it is home to shape-shifters, that residents enjoy extraordinary health and longevity, that desires manifest more quickly. But in the last decade, the homicide rate has spiked significantly, tourism has fallen, and the city struggles to hold on to its younger population, who increasingly seek lives elsewhere.

In the late 1960s, a cultural anthropologist from Berkeley, 35-year-old Sara Wells, won a Fulbright to study the beliefs in *brujos* in Esperanza. She disappeared in the Andes and is presumed dead. Her sister launched an extensive search for Wells, but nothing came of it. Her disappearance certainly remains one of the more mysterious stories in the history of this mysterious place.

(See: International Herald Tribune, Journal of Cultural Anthropology, San Francisco Chronicle, L.A. Times)

His mind raced. Was this Sara Wells the same one that Ed Granger had mentioned? *Sara Wells will want to talk to you when she returns. She's the expert on these mala sangres.*

He returned to Google, typed in Tess's name: 52,196 hits. He added Miami, Florida, to her name and learned he could obtain a credit report, the White Pages with an address and phone number, and find out whether she'd been sued, declared bankruptcy, married, or divorced. He could buy the information for $29.95, credit card or PayPal, whatever that was. But even more puzzling than any of this was the date at the top of the page: late January 2008. That had to be a mistake.

Back on the Google page, Ian clicked news and scanned the headlines and excerpts. He didn't recognize any of the presidential candidates. He read that global warming was spawning entire new industries, stem cell research held great promise for diseases like Parkinson's, Alzheimer's, cancer. A dead satellite was to be shot down. The space station had been expanded. Something called "blogs" buzzed with political rumors. AIDS continued to ravage Africa. In entertainment news, the writers' strike in Hollywood was sinking the L.A. economy. *The Simpsons* movie was now available on DVD.

He printed out some of the articles, feeling as if he had stumbled through the looking glass without a compass, dictionary, or rudimentary knowledge of the language or culture. Ian took the printed pages from the tray, folded them, slipped them in the pocket of his jacket. Shaken, he got up, returned to the front room, paid Consuelo, and asked for a city map. She handed him one, then leaned toward him.

"I just received this strange e-mail from Ed Granger, at the Posada de Esperanza. That's where you're staying, right?"

"Yes." But what was an e-mail? "So?"

"It's the second I've gotten in the last several days and it was sent to all the businesses in town. The first one said no computers, cells, Google, or e-mail for you or your friend, Tess. The second one, sent an hour and a half ago, says you're in danger from the *brujos* and if you're sighted, we have to call in. Whenever the *brujos* are involved, the procedure is mandatory. So I had to call, Mr. Ritter. But I really dislike the way they do this, like a Gestapo, *me entiendes?* So it's up to you. Stay here and they'll pick you up or, if you move fast, you have a lead of maybe five minutes."

"Thanks, Consuelo. Where do I catch a bus to Gigante?"

"Two blocks east, in front of a place called Books of Hope."

He burst through the café door and raced up the street, his new cell phone clutched in his hand, backpack banging against his hip, sutured temple throbbing, throat raw and dry with fear.

Nine

When Dominica gave the signal, the assault on the greenhouse ceased and the fog, shrouding a thousand of her tribe, withdrew into the nearby woods. There, her *brujos* chattered, their collective voices like the susurrus whisper of wind through trees. But to the living who could hear it, those voices probably sounded insidious, obscene, and hungry.

"Why'd you do that?" Ben demanded, materializing beside her in his California surfer form.

"To lure them out." And because she'd heard a distress call from Rafael apparently meant only for her. "If they leave, follow them in the fog, Ben." She sensed that Nomad and this Manuel character had some location that was more secure, someplace she didn't know about. "Then signal me."

"I say we summon the rest of the tribe and move into the city, Nica."

"Not yet. First we scare the transitionals back into their bodies and kill them. It's our best insurance."

With that, she thought herself to Rafael. He and Pearl, wearing their virtual forms, argued on an abandoned spit of sunlit beach by Lago del Sueño. Dominica ran toward them in her Amazon warrior queen form, shouting, "Enough, enough!"

Pearl whipped around, a barefoot beauty in hip-hugging, bell-bottom jeans, a white cotton top with a scoop neck, hippie beads draped at her throat. "He's freaking out, Nica," she hollered. "Do something. I can't talk to him."

Sobbing into his hands, Rafael was so distraught that he couldn't hold his *campesino* form together. It flickered, faded, vanished, and appeared again. Alarmed, Dominica grabbed him by the shoulders. "Calm down, Rafael, take deep breaths, that's good. Now tell me what happened."

His hands fell away from his tear-streaked face, dark eyes filled with such excessive emotion that she almost believed he really *was* human.

"You . . . told Pearl and me to stay close to Ian, to frighten him when we got the . . . the chance." He balled his hands into fists, ground them against his thighs. "He got hurt . . . when one of Ed's men tackled him. So Ed called the doctor, and when . . . Ed left the cottage, I . . . I waited for the right moment and . . . seized him. Seized Paco Faraday. I . . . he . . . fought me, Nica, he . . . wouldn't cooperate, he wouldn't do what I told him to do . . . And I . . . shit, he pissed me off and I . . . squeezed too hard and he . . . bled out and Pearl had to . . . to pull me out before he died."

Rafael, whose life as a black man in the segregated American South had ended when he was hanged by racists, had never seized a human and caused the host body to bleed out. He couldn't kill. It wasn't in him. In her calmest voice, Dominica said, "It's okay, Rafael. It's not your fault, it—"

"I'm not here to kill anyone," he screamed. "I'm here to be with Pearl, to . . . to create a city of *brujos,* where we just *use* bodies to enjoy physical existence. I don't want to *kill,* I can't become like the . . . monsters who hung me. I can't. It's not who I am."

Then he sank to his knees in the sand, weeping uncontrollably. It hurt her to look at him. In Rafael, she saw her own failings, that she hadn't foreseen this possibility, she'd neglected to connect the dots. No wonder Rafael and Pearl never joined her, Ben, and other *brujos* on their sexual excursions, where the risk always existed that you might have to cause the host body to bleed out.

She drew Pearl aside. "What happened to Ian?"

Pearl was so upset that her form also flickered. "He fled the cottage. Rafael told him that he was on life support, that Tess was in a coma, but he . . . he didn't freak out, Nica. He didn't cower in some corner and curl up in a fetal position. He just . . . took off. I got Rafael out of there before Ed Granger and his goddamn vigilantes showed up and found Paco's body. I brought him down here to the beach, then returned to the inn. They were all there by then—Ed, Juanito, Sara Wells, Illika Huicho . . . and the sirens went off and . . . and . . ."

"Bottom line, Pearl."

"Ian was sighted at the Incan Café. Juanito Cardenas is on his way over there now, to pick him up."

Juanito. Good. She could handle him. "Take Rafael back to the twin peaks. Stay with him. Have him talk to a counselor, Pearl."

She looked horrified. Counseling was one step removed from tribal

banishment. "It just . . . caught him by surprise, that's all. I'm sure he's going to be fine."

"Your job is to take care of him and make sure he gets the help he needs.
I'll be in touch." Dominica turned and raced back up the beach, shedding
her warrior form in pieces—an arm, a leg, her head. When she was free of
it, she thought herself toward Juanito Cardenas.

But Juanito was a sly one, wise to the *brujo* ways. A native of Esperanza,
born eighty-plus years ago, he'd gone to Quito in his late teens, then to
Buenos Aires for college. He'd made a lot of money in real estate and returned here in his early thirties with his wife. They had bought a home near
his parents and sister and started a family.

Ten years ago, Dominica and Ben had seized his sister, and ever since,
he'd worked with the Esperanza hierarchy of chaser helpers to defeat the
brujos. He knew what they knew—how to camouflage himself when he
needed to, where their sanctuaries were, what the larger plan was, who
the chasers were, what they were up to. Juanito had discovered that *brujos* in their phony human forms could be annihilated by fire and, ever
since, Granger and his ilk—like Manuel Ortega—had been armed with
flamethrowers.

Who the fuck are you? she had stammered to Manuel when they were
outside that bus.

Not anyone you want to cross.

As if he, too, had knowledge, power, answers. She wanted to know who
he was, why Ben hadn't been able to find any information on him, and
what Manuel and Nomad had been doing inside that greenhouse with Tess.
She was sure Juanito could enlighten her.

She focused her attention on a mental image of Juanito and allowed that
image to direct her to an old truck speeding through the back roads of
the city. She moved closer to it, saw Juanito inside. Instead of dropping
through the roof and seizing him instantly, she followed him to the Incan
Café.

Brujos rarely entered this place because the young woman who managed it, Consuelo from Colombia, could sense them, see them. In certain
circles, she was known as the *brujo* bullshit detector. Rumors said that Consuelo had suffered a near-death experience when she was a kid and had
been able to see and communicate with the dead ever since. Did that mean
that Ian and Tess, if they survived the returns to their physical bodies,

would be able to do the same? Was that the real reason the chasers had allowed these two transitionals into Esperanza?

Is it that simple?

The mere possibility staggered her imagination. Yet, the more she thought about it, the more likely it seemed. Perhaps this answered the most pressing puzzle of the last ten years—why the chasers had not intervened in the *brujo* attacks on Esperanza. Could it be that there weren't enough of them? That these so-called evolved souls were simply outnumbered by those like her?

Juanito didn't stop in front of the café, but drove past slowly, talking on his cell, and vanished into an alley. She didn't like narrow alleys any more than she did underground bunkers, the tightness of boundaries, the tomb-like claustrophobia. But when the truck popped out on the other side of the alley and screeched into a right-hand turn, she took notice.

The truck slowed, chugging along the two-lane road through a residential neighborhood—and she spotted Ian, racing up the street, arms bent, tight at his sides. Juanito lowered his windows and shouted, "Hey, amigo. It's me, Juanito. Manuel sent me. He's with Tess. C'mon, I'll give you a ride."

Ian's head turned, eyes wild, startled. He looked bad, she thought. His pallor, the way he gasped for breath, even the beads of sweat glistening on his face meant he would not be here much longer. She would be in a strong position to follow him back to his physical body.

He slowed and called, "Why should I trust you?"

"I'll call Tess. You talk to her."

Ian stopped, the truck pulled up to the curb, Dominica moved closer.

Juanito whipped out his cell, speaking softly to Ian as he punched out a number. Ian walked cautiously to the truck, frowning, sweatshirt tied at his waist, patches of perspiration darkening his shirt. His breath came in short bursts. He paused at the passenger window, watching Juanito warily. Then Juanito set a cell on the roof and Ian picked it up, pressed it to his ear and turned away. "Tess?"

With Ian's back to the truck, Dominica seized Juanito with such brutal swiftness that he didn't have a chance to react, much less fight. She grabbed control of his brain, limbs, lungs and heart, luxuriating in the flow of oxygen through her blood. *I have succumbed to convenience.* But for a male body, it was put together well. Esperanza's health and longevity benefits had been augmented by Juanito's care of his physical being—excellent nutrition, regular exercise. Even more important was that Juanito was emotionally and spiritually happy.

I like your body, Juanito.

Silence. She sensed he was busy burying information that he thought she might access, so she reached deep inside him and grabbed what she could. She only retrieved fragments, the linguistic equivalents of prepositions and conjunctions. *Come now, Juanito. Sooner or later your vigilance will slip and I'll find everything I need.*

As will I, Dominica.

I can kill you this second. A tiny bit of pressure at the base of your brain and you'll end up like Paco Faraday.

Juanito laughed. *Wayra always said the only way you know is death and destruction. You will not win this battle.*

It angered her that Wayra had spoken to this despicable little man about *her.* And in that moment of anger, her defenses were lowered and Juanito leaped into the basement of her mind. He flung out one memory after another from her centuries with Wayra, a movie of heartbreaking images so intimate and vivid and ultimately traitorous that an agonizing grief drove her out of Juanito.

Ian was still on the phone when Juanito suddenly shouted his name. He turned to see the man collapse across the roof of the truck, arms flopping like a fish out of water. Alarmed, Ian snapped the cell shut and ran over to him, caught him just as he began to slide off the truck, leaving behind streaks of blood.

Blood poured from his nostrils, rolled from the corners of his eyes, and left a warm, sticky trail from his mouth to his chin. Ian got him into the truck and Juanito slumped against the passenger window, chest heaving as he struggled for breath, mouth moving, trying to form words.

"It's okay, don't try to talk." Ian ran around to the driver's side, slipped behind the wheel. "I'm getting you to a hospital."

"No. I can . . . deal with this. Get to Manuel . . . the others."

"What happened, Juanito? Was it a *brujo?*"

". . . seized me . . . I drove her . . . out . . . But she managed . . . to injure me . . . as she left."

Ian started the truck and screeched away from the curb so fast he nearly plowed into an oncoming car. The cell rang, he grabbed it off the seat. "Tess?"

"It's Manuel. What happened? I heard Juanito shouting your name, then we lost the connection."

"He's bleeding." Ian repeated what Juanito had told him.

"Is he conscious?"

Ian looked over at Juanito. "Barely. Where's the nearest hospital?"

"We can treat him here. He knows what to do until you get him here, Ian. This has happened to him before. Stay on the same road for about ten miles, until you reach Calle Lima. Take a right, go six miles. You'll see Saint Francis Church on your left, on the corner. Go down the driveway, blaring the horn. Charge through any fog you encounter. That's important. Don't stop, don't slow down, keep the windows up. The door will rise, drive into the garage. Are you in Juanito's truck?"

"Yes."

"That's good. He has special seals on the windows, the vents."

"He's bleeding badly."

"Trust me. He knows what to do."

The line went dead, Ian floored the accelerator, and the truck shot forward. He drove like a maniac, tearing through stoplights, swerving in between other cars until he was outside of the city. Traffic thinned, the countryside opened up to hills and fields where banks of fog climbed toward the sky as if to swallow it. White and gray fog swirled around trees like cotton candy around a stick and rolled toward him from every direction. Somewhere behind him, sirens shrieked.

Juanito coughed, deep, wet, racking coughs. "They're trying . . . to intimidate you . . . they want you . . . to freak out . . . to . . . lose control, Ian."

"Fat chance."

He opened the truck up as wide as it would go. The speedometer needle swung past eighty and the old truck tore up the road, bouncing and clattering until it sounded as if it were falling apart. The needle climbed, the truck was running on empty, the gas light glowed red.

Shit.

Then the truck plunged into the fog. The stuff clung to the glass, pressing so tightly against it that Ian felt it was trying to merge with the glass, to pass through it. A tight, eerie silence claimed the air, a vacuum begging to be filled. Within seconds, the insidious whispering started and quickly escalated into that eerie chant: *find the body, fuel the body, fill the body, be the body.* He slapped a hand over one ear, gripped the steering wheel with his other hand, but it wasn't enough. He felt as if he were chewing on glass, as if red-hot pokers were being thrust through his eyes, his ears, down the back of his skull. The high-pitched chant nauseated him, he couldn't breathe, he started sweating, the world briefly blurred.

"Radio," Juanito rasped. "Turn it on. Music. Loud."

He hit the on button and spun the volume dial as high as it would go. In the cottage when this had happened, Tess had known instinctively to shriek, that it would drown out the keening. Now the music hammered through the truck, a Latin beat and a female singer whose shrill voice could shatter crystal. It drowned out the worst of the chanting. But the fog was so thick, visibility had shrunk to a foot.

"*Turn,*" Juanito shouted, gesturing wildly with his bloody hand. "Left. Fast."

Ian swung into a left turn, tires screeching against the pavement. The truck fishtailed and slammed down over roots, brush, rocks. He corrected slightly to the right and they raced on through the ever-thickening fog. He detected the vague shapes of buildings, but couldn't see any street signs, intersections, landmarks that might tell him where the church was. He glanced quickly at Juanito, but he had passed out.

Ian tapped the brake, struggled to see through the fog. His head ached in rhythm to the loud, pounding music. But he was terrified that if he turned down the volume, he would hear the chanting. That would be worse.

The cell vibrated against his leg and he swept it up and was forced to lower the radio's volume in order to hear Tess's voice, a lifeline.

"Ian, I'm about to pull out into the road, so you'll know where to turn for the church. Where are you?"

The chanting now sounded like a high-pitched electric saw that was slicing its way through his jaw, teeth, skull. "I made the turn half a mile ago. I'm slowing down, may run out of gas. I have to turn the music back up or I'm going to pass out. That chanting, Slim, that godawful chanting."

He dropped the cell on the seat, cranked up the radio's volume. He was now running on fumes, and leaned forward, desperately searching the fog directly in front of him, willing the truck to make it to the church before the tank went totally dry.

Inside the garage under the church, Tess readied herself. She felt like a Nascar driver, suited up, primed, with Manuel and Sara Wells and Illika Huicho snapping directions. *Do this, do that, bring them in.* Sara looked like a California girl, all blond and pretty and in charge of—well, something.

Illika seemed ancient, a century old, dark eyes trapped in a chaos of deep wrinkles, her face definitely that of the Quechuans she ruled.

"Wayra will be with you," Illika said, thrusting a headset into Tess's hands. "Follow his directions."

"Do whatever you must to bring in Ian and Juanito," said Sara Wells.

Manuel slipped his arms around Tess. That crushing sense of familiarity consumed her, that she knew him, that he was not just Manuel the inn employee, the man who had driven her and Ian and Nomad to Esperanza, that they were all *something else.* "Bring them in safely," Manuel whispered, his breath warm against the side of her face.

"I wouldn't be doing this if I thought I couldn't succeed," she said, and extricated herself from all of them and climbed into a Hummer, the behemoth that Manuel had referred to as their brujomobile. Wayra slid into the passenger seat. She still felt weird about him, about Nomad as a man, but was grateful for his company.

As the door of the church's underground garage clattered upward, the large fans that stood on either side blew away the swirling fog. Tess gunned the Hummer's accelerator and it roared up the ramp and out into the road, fast, powerful and sealed against the intrusion of fog. The flip of a switch on the dashboard activated an electromagnetic field around the vehicle that supposedly would repel any *brujo* that attempted to get inside.

She turned up the road, headlights burning a narrow path through the thick, darkening fog. The chanting rose now, a distant, menacing sound, and she slipped on a headpiece that blocked it entirely. Through her left ear, she listened to music from the CD player. Through her right, she heard Wayra's voice, directing her through the fog.

He sat slightly forward in the passenger seat, this tall, slender man with Nomad's tea-colored eyes that could see what she could not. *They're lurching about in the fog, we've thrown them off. On your right, a deer. A rhino at two o'clock. These things aren't real. They're conjuring; they're terrified, trying to throw you off.*

"Wayra, I need to know something."

"Drive. Slowly. Carefully."

"Why are you helping me and Ian?"

He looked at her—the face of an Olympian god, the eyes of a dog that were indescribably sad, tragic. "Because the two of you are our last, best hope."

"*Our.* Who?"

"The light chasers, the transitionals, Esperanza. There's—"

Static erupted in her headpiece. Where there had been music in her left ear there was now a menacing female voice. "Wayra, Wayra, so many lies. You want her help, but you tell her lies. You're in a coma, Tess Livingston. You were shot during a sting. Your friend Ian had a heart attack. You're the first transitional souls here in five centuries. That scar on your thigh? That's where you were shot. Everything you have experienced here is supplied by your imagination. Your soul is in flux, not here, not there, and you're being used by the chasers to—"

Wayra tore away her headpiece and hurled it into the back seat. Tess slammed on the brakes. "Who the hell was *that?*"

The fog closed in on them, a living, breathing mass of organic material that throbbed like a heart, spoke in tongues, pressed up against the Hummer's windows with a terrifying hunger. Wayra hurled open the passenger door, hopped out, kicked the door shut and yelled, "Show yourself, Nica."

But not to me. Tess drove on recklessly, too fast, unable to see, the horrifying chant rising again, *find the body, fuel the body* . . . Suddenly, inexplicably, a truck was in front of her. Real or conjured? She didn't know. She swerved violently to the right, but the truck veered in the same direction and they crashed head-on. The impact jarred her and crumpled the truck's front end like an accordion.

The Hummer's engine died, she slammed it into park, leaped out and ran over to the truck. *I can run, I'm breathing, I'm scared, I'm not in any coma.* But she felt as if she were trapped in a nightmare, the fog engulfing her, that high-pitched wailing piercing her to the bone. Ian was already out of the truck, hands pressed over his ears as he stumbled to the passenger side. "Help me get Juanito out," he shouted.

Juanito was unconscious, his face covered in dried blood. Ian pulled him out of the truck, Tess grabbed his feet, and they carried him to the Hummer, the sounds now so painful that she felt nauseated, weak, her breath trapped in her chest. Ian wasn't faring any better. By the time they got Juanito into the back seat, Ian's face was the color of day-old bread, he could barely stand. She grabbed the headset off the seat and shouted at him to put it on. As soon as they were inside the Hummer, she turned the radio to full blast and started shrieking and singing as she had done in the cottage.

Then the piercing sounds abruptly stopped, but the fog kept rolling over the Hummer, hugging the sides as if to carry it away. Ian whipped off the headset, Tess turned down the radio volume.

"Like before, Slim. The silence."

"We'll get out of here." She started the Hummer and backed away from the crumpled truck.

"I think we're in comas, you and I," he said, then a disconnected story spilled from him—what Paco Faraday had told him, what he had learned at the Incan Café, how he believed that Esperanza might already be a city of *brujos.*

It alarmed her—not because he sounded crazy or that she believed him, but because she suddenly understood why he was so flummoxed by his discoveries in the café.

"Ian, what's a DVD player?"

"A what?"

"What's Wi-Fi?"

"Wi-Fi. There was a sign at the café about Wi-Fi. But I don't know what it is."

"What's an iPod? BlackBerry? CD? Laptop? Windows? PC? MacBook?"

He looked terrified and shook his head.

"Bill Gates? Steve Jobs? Stephen King? George Lucas? Indiana Jones? E.T.?"

"Never heard of them."

Jesus. "What year is it?"

He thought a moment. "Nineteen sixty-eight."

"Dear God," she whispered.

"Is that the wrong answer or something?"

"No." She tightened her hands on the steering wheel, blinked back the hot sting of tears. "Has Nixon won the election yet? Have they assassinated Bobby Kennedy? He leaves the planet on June 5, 1968, the Ambassador Hotel, L.A. Or Martin Luther King? April 4, 1968. The Lorraine Hotel in Memphis. What about My Lai? You know about My Lai?"

"I . . . don't know what you're talking about, Slim."

She cited dates, events, situations, driven by a fierce urgency to get as much said as quickly as possible. Already, she felt her consciousness flickering, and once again, she thought she heard her mother calling to her. "Ian, for me, it's 2008. Forty years in your future."

He looked as if he'd been punched in the stomach, eyes bulging, his pallor so extreme now that she sensed their time here was nearly done. A kind of strange acceptance coursed through her. "*Palo* means stick, Ian. The Río Palo translates as Stick River or—"

"The river Styx," he whispered. "Slim, in the *Tibetan Book of the Dead*, the river Styx separates the world of the *dead* from the world of the *living*. It's the *bardo* where the soul takes inventory. *Hello, who the hell am I and what am I doing here?*"

From the back seat came coughing, that wet, hacking cough that could mean Juanito was drowning in his own blood. Tess drove faster, certain that if she stopped here, the thick, ubiquitous fog would enter the Hummer and consume them all.

Through an opening in the fog, she spotted the church just ahead and turned erratically toward it, horn squealing. The door started to rise, the fog thickened, a tsunami that just kept rising, higher and higher, until it covered the roof of the church. Tess raced into the garage, a bank of fog pursuing them.

He and Tess flung their doors open simultaneously and stumbled out of the vehicle. Ian felt weak, dizzy, used up, and made his way toward Tess by using the car for support. Confusion everywhere, people shouting, firing questions, a crowd tightening around them, no one in charge. Two men lifted Juanito onto a stretcher and carried him through double doors.

When Ian reached Tess, he slipped his arm around her shoulders and they leaned into each other like cripples. Her face looked ashen, her smile seemed weak, unfocused, as if she couldn't quite remember who he was.

"Let's get out of here, Slim," he whispered.

"Through those double doors. Into the bunker beneath the church. Can we make it?"

"If we hold on to each other."

"I feel like I'm two hundred years old, Ian."

"I think . . . we don't have much time left here. One way or another I'll find you again."

She threw her arms around him, holding him, burying her face in the curve of his neck, and he shut his eyes. The rest of the world went away.

The next thing he knew, he and Tess were sitting on a couch in a softly lit room with Manuel, an elderly Quechua woman, and a woman he recognized from the article he had read on Esperanza. "I know you," he burst out. "Sara Wells, cultural anthropologist from Berkeley. Won a Fulbright in the late sixties to study the *brujos* in Ecuador. Believed to have disappeared somewhere in the Andes. Presumed dead. What was the year, exactly?"

The astonishment on her face spoke tomes about the lengths people had gone to in order to keep him and Tess away from information. "My last contact with my old life was on May 16, 1969, Mr. Ritter. When I called my sister from Quito." She looked quickly at Manuel. "Will he remember that?"

She spoke as though Ian were no longer in the room. He resented it.

"Unknown," Manuel replied, and gestured at the bottles of water on the coffee table in front of them. "Keep drinking water. It'll buy us a few more minutes. If you both remember what has happened to you here and if you can make it back to Esperanza, you'll be able to be together despite your separation in time."

"How?" Tess asked.

Ian held tightly to her hand, but already it faded, flickered, brightened again.

"Because Esperanza exists both within and outside of time as we know it," the old woman said.

"Wayra got left outside," Tess said suddenly, her voice hoarse, thick.

"He's preventing the *brujos* from following you," Sara said. "We hope to keep them from following you back to your physical bodies."

"But if they find you," Manuel went on, "we won't be able to protect you as we have here. They still won't be able to seize you, but they can seize others and force them to kill you."

"But . . . this isn't our battle," Ian protested. "It isn't . . ."

Tess's body suddenly turned transparent, and for a single, horrifying moment, Ian could see the water she was drinking as it moved down her gullet, into her stomach. He wrenched back. "What . . . what's happening . . ."

She started choking. Ian leaped up and slapped her on the back, but his hands went through her. He could see his flesh inside hers, his hands inside her organs. Then Manuel thrust himself between them and wrapped his arms around Tess.

"What're you doing?" Ian shouted, stumbling back, his legs so weak that his knees buckled and he struck the floor.

Sara crouched in front of him, leaning in so close he caught the honeysuckle scent of her skin and hair. "Remember, Ian. Remember everything."

Red poured across his vision. He could still hear Tess choking, Manuel speaking to her, the words garbled, a thunderous roar echoing in his head. He lurched to his feet to get to Tess. But as he did so, Manuel's body shredded apart like Kleenex. An arm, a leg, gone. A shoulder struck the floor and disappeared. His head fell away. And then a man with white hair and Ben Franklin glasses held her in his arms. A huge smile lit up Tess's face.

"Dad?" she said. "Is it really you?"

Ian gaped. Was Manuel the virtual form of Tess's dead father, Charlie Livingston?

His vision went black and he felt himself falling, a meteorite hurtling toward earth, burning as it plunged through the atmosphere. Then there was only the soft, fading echo of a distant howling.

Dominica felt it, a tremendous shift in power and balance, as if tectonic plates were sliding apart beneath Esperanza. She shoved Wayra away from her. His sweet talk, his caresses, their lovemaking in the orchard beyond the fog: it had been a ploy to keep her from pursuing the transitionals as they fled back to their physical bodies.

"I will kill you for this," she hissed, straightening the clothes on her seductress body, the body he'd loved so well in Spain.

"I doubt it, *mi amor*. But I'm pleased to know you are so easily duped, Nica."

He combed his fingers back through his thick hair, his smile both joyous and tragic, this tall, beautiful, unattainable man who had betrayed her once again. "I'll find them, Wayra. You know that I will, I have resources . . ."

"As do I. As do others."

"Others?" Did he mean the liberation group? "What others?"

He smiled slyly. "We aren't alone in our battle against your kind."

Fear surged through her. *He knows. He knows about this group. Betrayer, I hate him.* "I'll order my tribe to sweep through Esperanza, to seize every man, woman, child."

"If you actually believed you could conquer in that way, you would've done it already. Face it, Nica. Your time is past. It's the dawn of a whole new age."

Then he turned away from her and ran toward the fog filled with *brujos* who would not be able to touch, seize, or harm him. He shifted as he moved, the man becoming the black dog with the golden eyes. Seconds before he plunged into the fog, his triumphant howls echoed across space and time.

Dominica stood there in her phony human form, sobbing uncontrollably.

Ian Ritter

1968

. . . .

We are in a time so strange that living equals dreaming, and this teaches me that man dreams his life, awake.

—Pedro Calderón, *Life Is a Dream*

Ten

Such stillness. He has never known anything like this. It's as if the universe has not yet taken its first breath, its heart has not yet begun to beat, all is unformed, unstructured, mere potential. He waits, an observer observing himself. He is consciousness, nothing more.

Then the stillness shatters with the universe's first shuddering breath, the first beat of its heart. He feels cold, stiff, uncomfortable. He aches all over, an undefined, nonspecific ache that extends to every part of his body, infecting his blood and bones, organs, cells. He's aware of everything that is wrong in his body, in his throat, lungs, heart. He tries to wiggle his fingers, but cannot. He struggles to move his mouth, head, toes, legs. Nothing works. His eyes beg to open, but the lids feel thick, cumbersome, like mud. He wonders if he has been buried alive.

A bubble of panic works its way up from his burning lungs, up through his aching throat, and spills into the air as a bead of spit on his lower lip. He can feel it, sitting there, perfect in shape, neither cold nor hot, just wet and indestructible.

Other details come to him, sounds and tastes, sensations that he knows he should recognize but does not. He has no labels, no categories, no names. I am . . . What? In pain. Uncomfortable. No, no, no. Go deeper. Remember, remember.

Who said that to him? Who told him to remember?

He fights his way back toward the stillness, but can no longer recall what it feels like. He can't block the sounds, the tastes, the sensations. The stillness is a flame that has been blown out like a birthday candle.

I am . . . A game. He knows this game. I am a bird.

What kind of bird?

Condor.

And for a moment he sees himself staring upward, watching a pair of condors cruising on the air currents, their tremendous wingspans casting shadows.

Then the image is gone and he wants to weep, to scream, please, come back, don't go away, please . . .

He hears a familiar voice. A man's voice.

"Mom," the man shouted. "Mom, get over here. I think he's conscious."

Warmth covered Ian's right hand, his cheeks.

"Dad? Can you hear me? Your fingers are twitching."

Luke. That's Luke. Fingers lifted his eyelid, light stabbed down like a dagger through his retina, into his brain. Ian turned his head away from it.

"Mom. Call the front desk. Where's the call button? Christ, Christ, he's back. He's conscious."

Now: a woman's voice that Ian recognized. Louise, his ex. *Please go away, Louise.* "Calm down, Luke." *Tap tap tap.* High heels against a floor. "It's probably just an involuntary reflex. We've seen this before. It doesn't mean anything. It . . . Oh my God. His eyes are opening." She leaned in close to him, the cloying scent of her perfume nearly choking him. "Ian? Blink if you can hear me."

Ian blinked.

"I'm getting the doctor. A nurse. Someone." Then Louise ran from the room, shouting, *"Nurse, nurse . . . He's awake, please get the doctor in here, my husband's awake . . ."*

"My God, Dad." Luke choked up. "I thought I'd lost you for good."

Ian turned his head again, muscles creaking like rusted hinges, his skull feeling as though it were being pierced by pitchforks. His eyes opened. A blur of gray. Noises. Beeps, pulses, his son's voice. His vision stabilized and Luke's face swam into view—shoulder length, curly hair pulled back in a ponytail, colorful hippie beads tight against his throat, T-shirt with the glaring peace symbol and the words PEACE NOW. Luke, who had his mother's mouth and skin, Ian's nose and dark eyes. Where did that dimple in the corner of his mouth come from? And his blond hair? Some recessive gene way back?

Ian squeezed Luke's hand, then pushed the oxygen mask off his face, a small act that took tremendous effort. "Not. A. Chance," he rasped. "Water." Cold water would make it easier to speak. He needed to tell Luke what had really happened, to explain, to describe. He needed to say all this before the memories slipped away.

Luke raised Ian's head and guided a straw between his parched lips. Ian sucked slowly and nearly wept as the cool liquid ran down his raw throat.

He sipped again, nodded, and Luke set the cup down. Ian's head sank into the pillow again. "How long?" he asked. "How long was I gone?"

"Three weeks, six days . . ." Luke glanced at the clock on the wall. "Nine hours and twelve minutes."

Ian couldn't help smiling. Since the time Luke was old enough to walk and talk, this sort of precision had marked him as surely as the color of his hair, that dimple at the corner of his mouth. "I died," Ian said.

Luke pulled a chair up next to the bed, sat down, and leaned in close to Ian. "You had a heart attack in your office, Dad. And right after you got to the hospital, you had a second heart attack and died for . . . I don't know . . . minutes, then slipped into a coma. I was on my way to the hospital when it happened. They thought there might be brain damage. For a while, you were on life support. You finally stabilized, but have been in a coma for the last several weeks."

"I . . . went somewhere." Ian closed his eyes, struggling to recapture Esperanza, his journey, Tess, everything he'd experienced. But already it seemed like a dream, some fictional world he'd built in his head, fading like an old photo. He talked fast, stumbling with words, desperate to communicate whatever he could.

But Luke interrupted him. "Dad, the doc will be in here in a minute. Just relax and . . ."

Ian's eyes opened, he grasped Luke's hand and held on so tightly that his son winced. "Remember these things. Cell phone. Internet. Google. Something called an iPod. Martin Luther King and Bobby Kennedy will be assassinated. Something about My Lai. A space station. DVDs. Laptops . . ."

Luke's expression of love, concern, and relief collapsed into incredulity and something darker, terror that his father had suffered brain damage.

"I'm not crazy, Luke." *I hope.* His voice: hoarse, uncertain. "Esperanza, Ecuador. That's where I was."

"Professor Ritter," boomed a voice from the doorway. "Back with us at last."

The man who entered the room, Louise hurrying alongside him, stood well over six feet and had a quick, engaging smile that could put anyone at ease. His stooped shoulders were testament to an adolescence locked in a self-conscious angst about his height. Early forties, Ian guessed, handsome in the way that most doctors seemed to be, a Dr. Kildare with black hair.

"I'm Dr. Andros, your cardiologist. How do you feel?"

"Better than I did fifteen minutes ago."

"Do you recall what happened?"

"An intense pain in my chest, while I was sitting at my desk. When it was happening . . . I think I knew what it was."

"Your secretary found you. You had a second coronary here at the hospital and—"

"It killed me."

"We, uh, had to revive you."

Andros looked down at the clipboard in his hands and Ian's gaze slipped to his ex-wife, who stood next to the doctor, as still and perfect as a brunette Barbie doll, her roiling blue eyes filled with utter fury at the inconvenience he'd caused her. His physical hiatus had taken her away from more important things—her charities, her new husband and extended family.

Louise said, "It's wonderful to have you back, Ian. We've been so worried."

"It's good to *be* back."

"If we could have some privacy, Mrs. Ritter?" the doctor asked.

"Of course," Louise said, moving away from the bed.

"Bell, Mrs. Bell," Luke said. "She remarried after the divorce."

Louise threw Luke a dirty look. Dr. Andros didn't seem to know how to respond to this, so he repeated his original request. Luke and Louise left the room, arguing in hushed voices, and Andros pulled the curtain shut. "I'd like to check you over, Professor. My goal is to get you out of here as quickly as possible."

"We definitely want the same thing."

Andros was personable throughout, chatting about this and that as he removed the heart monitor, catheter, IV, and turned off the oxygen. Ian tried to remain silent, to keep his experiences to himself. But he considered the possibility that he was mentally deranged, had hallucinated everything, that the anesthesia or whatever measures they had taken, whatever drugs they'd given him, had created a fantasy.

"How long was I dead?" Ian finally asked.

"Fortunately, you were in ER when your heart stopped the second time. I'm not sure how long you were actually dead."

"How long can the brain be deprived of oxygen before it's irreparably damaged?"

"Much longer than you were deprived," Andros reassured him.

"And what happened to me during that time?"

"I'm not sure I understand the question."

Ian pushed up straighter in the bed, sipped from a cup of water, and remembered how grateful he had been at the Bodega del Cielo when he'd tasted his first cup of hot coffee, bitten into that steaming empanada. "What happened to me while I was dead?"

Andros now stood at the sink, washing his hands, his back to Ian. "I don't have any idea, Mr. Ritter."

"You've never thought about it?"

"Of course I've thought about it." He snatched paper towels from the dispenser and turned, drying his hands. His handsome Dr. Kildare face revealed that he had given this very question a lot of thought over the years but had yet to arrive at any satisfying conclusion. "I spent two years in Nam as a medic. I lost a number of patients. But I also had patients who died and came back. Some of them asked me what you just did. I don't have an answer, just have a theory. Perhaps you can help me with that." He tossed the towels in the garbage can and approached the bed. "What did *you* experience?"

In 2008, Andros was either in his early eighties or dead. Ian knew if he had access to Google, he could type in Andros's name and something would come up, some starting point, some baseline. Ian wanted to tell him everything, to confess, confide, whisper, *I found my real life, my genuine self, I fell in love.* But if he did, he might be deemed a nutcase and find himself in a straitjacket. But maybe he deserved that straitjacket, maybe he *was* nuts. So he said, "Nothing. I don't remember anything at all."

Minutes after Andros left, Luke returned to the room. "He told Mom and me that we need to let you rest. I'll be back tomorrow, Dad."

"Wait. Luke." Ian grabbed his son's hand. "I need to get out of here. To Ecuador, to . . ." *I need to move forward forty years.* Oh, really? Forty years? Christ, he didn't know what the hell he needed.

"Dad, we'll talk later." Luke squeezed his hand. "I promise. And I'll tell Casey she can stop by now." He hugged Ian gently, as though he were afraid his father might break. "Every day I sat here, talking to you, begging you to come back. Now you're back." He straightened, but didn't release Ian's hand. "Mom's a problem. We need to talk about her, about you removing her as your power of attorney."

Louise had power of attorney? How had he let that slip since the divorce? "How's she a problem? She means well."

"Does she?"

Ian didn't want to go there. The hostility between Luke and his mother was *their* business. "I'll talk to the university attorney when I get out of here."

"I already got in touch with his office. He's out of town, but will be back next week."

"That's fine. Next week is soon enough."

"See you tomorrow, Dad."

Ian sat in a chair by the window in his hospital room, a Remington typewriter set up in front of him, and wished he had a computer like the one in the Incan Café. *If it exists.*

He'd started his adult life as a reporter back on that base in Stuttgart, when the military police had asked him to describe finding his father's bloated body hanging in the shower. He had stuck to the facts, as he perceived them. That was what he had done the last few days, filling more than thirty pages with notes and memories. The more he wrote, the more he remembered. Sometimes it seemed that the memories might provide him with a conduit through which he could move back into that world. But most of the time, he doubted any of it had happened and what he'd written seemed, at best, like colorful fiction and, at worst, the rantings of a madman.

Ian glanced out into the barren wilderness of a Minnesota March snow. The flakes silently touched the glass, shapes preserved for a perfect instant before melting into slush. His routine these past days hadn't varied much. He walked the halls incessantly, went down to the common room to watch television, ate solid foods, wrote, and hoped that the writing would prove he hadn't lost his mind when he had died.

In between, he could feel the structure of his former life coalescing around him. Work beckoned. Ian Ritter, professor of journalism at the University of Minnesota, winner of a Pulitzer when he was twenty-eight, had been on sick leave for four weeks and two days. Ian Ritter, columnist for the *Minneapolis Tribune*, hadn't written squat for five weeks. He needed to get back to work soon, to take one step and then another toward ordinary life, so that he could make plans for traveling to Ecuador.

He kept seeing her in his head, Tess on that bus, in the posada, Tess in the Hummer, in front of the fire in cottage 13. *Tess, fantasy woman, conjured from the depths of my unconscious while I was in a coma.* What was it about that number? He scribbled it on a sheet of paper, underlined it twice, then wrote: bus 13, cottage 13, 13 men, computer 13. Was he making it all up? And if not, what was the message with all those thirteens? Bad luck?

The PA suddenly burst with a woman's voice. "Code blue in room thirteen. I repeat, a code blue in room thirteen."

Goose bumps sped up his arms. *Thirteen.* It seized his attention. Ian didn't have any idea what "code blue" meant, but orderlies and nurses raced by, pushing gurneys and equipment. He got up and went over to the door. Across the hall, hospital personnel crowded into room 13, tending to some apparent emergency. On the cardiology ward, that usually meant a patient had suffered a heart attack.

"Poor Bill," said Gladys, the thin, elderly woman standing in the doorway of the next room. "He'd been complaining that he didn't feel well, but the nurse kept insisting his cardiac readings were fine and that he probably just had heartburn."

Ian had met her and Bill in the common room yesterday. Bill, a black man in his eighties, moved with a shuffle, his shoulders hunched over as if with an unbearable burden. "They'll save him. This hospital has one of the best cardiac units in the country."

The door to room 13 shut. Just as Ian was about to turn away, Bill stepped through the door—*the closed, wooden door*—and shuffled out into the hallway in his hospital gown and floppy slippers. He peered over the rims of his wire-framed glasses and scratched his nearly bald head, his expression troubled and confused. *Lock me up, throw away the key.* Ian glanced quickly at Gladys, but she gave no indication that she saw Bill.

But Bill saw her and hurried over. "Gladys, I'm really confused about something."

Gladys didn't hear him, couldn't see him, and walked back into her room and shut the door. Ian's instincts screamed at him to run up the hall and out the nearest exit. But his legs refused to move. When Bill's dark, damp eyes met his, Bill said, "You can see me. But Gladys can't. Why? What's happened to me?"

Not only could Ian see and hear him clearly, he caught the plaintiveness in Bill's voice, the confusion and fear. "I . . ."—*I've lost my mind, Bill*— "don't know exactly what's happened to you, Bill. But doctors and nurses poured into your room a few minutes ago, so I'm assuming you had a medical emergency." The answer to his other question, about why Ian could see him and Gladys could not, was suddenly simple. It was because Ian had been where Bill was now. Or because his mind had been left on the ER floor.

Bill looked at the closed door to his room, then back at Ian. "I think my heart gave out." He pulled out the sides of his hospital gown and started to laugh. "I hate this damn thing, leaves your butt out there for all of them pretty nurses to see."

"I know just what you mean."

"I'm so tired of being in this place."

"You don't have to stay, Bill. It's really your choice." *Why'd I say that? Is it true? Who am I to give advice to a nearly dead man?*

"Wife's been gone four years. Life's been real lonely without her. I got me six children and twenty-two grandchildren, but they all have lives of their own, you know what I'm saying?"

"I sure do."

"Dad?"

Ian spun around, startled that his son had come up behind him on feet of silk. "Luke."

"I thought I heard you talking to someone."

"Just to the ghost of the old man in that room." Ian stabbed his thumb toward Bill, but he'd evaporated. No surprise. Bill was a figment of his imagination.

"Yeah, right," Luke said with a laugh that came a beat too late, as if a part of him still believed that Ian's brush with death had left him brain-damaged. "Listen, I just ran into Dr. Andros. He's going to release you tomorrow. Mom's very much against it."

The door to room 13 opened, and doctors and nurses streamed out with their machines, their clipboards, their urgency gone. Through the open door, Ian saw two orderlies lift Bill's body onto a gurney, cover it, then they wheeled the gurney out into the hall.

"You weren't kidding," Luke said softly.

Shaken by the confirmation that he actually had seen and spoken to a ghost, Ian didn't respond.

"Jesus, Dad. Has this happened before?"

Nervous laughter bubbled through him. Happened before? Before when? Before he had died? Before his mind had been left on the floor of the ER? "No."

"Whatever you do, don't mention a word of this to Mom."

"I don't intend to." Ian wouldn't have said anything to Luke, either, if he hadn't been standing there while Ian was talking to Bill.

"She'll just use it as evidence that you're brain-damaged."

Maybe I am. "Any word from the attorney?"

"I'm still waiting for him to get back to me."

"How'd this ghost look, Dad?"

As they walked into the room, Ian described what had happened and Luke listened with rapt attention. "My sense was, uh, that Bill was ready to move on, but just didn't realize it." *Really? That was your goddamn sense? What's that mean? You're an expert now on mental derangement?*

"Wow, this is incredibly far out," Luke said. "Once, on an acid trip, I was walking around downtown Minneapolis and found myself surrounded by ghosts," Luke said. "They were all, like, talking at once, trying to get my attention, to give me messages for their families and friends, and some wanted to know if I was a helper who could get them someplace else."

"What'd you do?"

"Freaked out and ran back to the apartment and locked myself inside."

"Ghosts? Who's talking about ghosts?"

Louise sailed into the room without knocking, leading Ian to believe she'd been eavesdropping outside the door. She'd brought gifts—a huge bouquet of flowers. "Oh my, just look at you, standing up and all, with a typewriter and paper and everything," she gushed.

Luke rolled his eyes, but Ian smiled hello, then began gathering up the pages he'd written and handed them to Luke. "Keep these for me until I get out of here tomorrow."

"Tomorrow's way too soon," Louise said, setting the vase of flowers on the windowsill. "I just had a chat with Dr. Andros and pointed out that you had two major heart attacks."

"Andros is the cardiologist, Mom," Luke said. "I'm sure he doesn't need your input."

"I feel fine," Ian said. "I'm ready to check myself out."

"You can't do that," Louise snapped.

She faced Ian with her sprayed, bouffant hair, her unnaturally wide eyes, her blue skirt and jacket, matching shoes and handbag. Louise, fashion maven. He remembered her laughter in the early days of their marriage, when she was a whiz with numbers and worked as an accountant in a real estate firm, the only woman in an office of men. Her whole demeanor then had been softer, flowing, joyful. He remembered her as someone she no longer was, and sometimes he missed that old Louise, missed what they'd had in those early years.

"You're going to need care at home," she went on. "And we have to arrange for something, for someone to come in, for—"

"Thank you for the flowers, Louise, and for taking care of things while I was in a coma. I appreciate it. But I can make my own decisions," Ian said.

"Frankly, Ian, I'm not so sure that you're capable of making your own decisions. The oxygen loss to your brain was—"

"*Enough*, Mom!" Luke snapped. "Dad's fine."

Her eyes widened with umbrage, her bright red mouth pursed with disapproval, then anger. "Luke, this is between your father and me. And since I have power of attorney, I have a say in when he's released. Besides, I didn't see *you* paying for what his health insurance didn't cover. Not you or Casey or the university. *Me*, I paid for it."

"You're so transparent it's disgusting." Luke was practically shouting. "You don't give a shit about Dad. You're only interested in appearances. In your new role as the wife of a prominent business mogul and philanthropist, you want to be viewed in a sympathetic light. You're nothing but a goddamn social climber."

Louise's eyes brimmed with tears. "I . . . I can't believe you think that of me, Luke."

"Well, believe it," Luke shot back.

Ian's head started to ache. He realized Luke was using this opportunity to verbalize all the issues he had with his mother. "Please. Stop arguing." He spoke with such a strange calmness that they both abruptly fell silent and looked at him as if he were merely incidental to their disagreement.

Seconds ticked by, then Luke said, "You're right. There's no point in arguing. You're done here, Mom." He took her by the shoulders and walked her toward the door.

Louise wrenched free and turned on Luke as if he were a rabid dog. "Don't you *dare* presume to tell me what to do, young man."

"Later, Mom." Luke grasped her arm, led her into the hall, slammed the door. Then he leaned against it and in a softer voice added, "She's trying to convince Andros that a neurologist should check you out for brain damage. I'm telling you, Dad, this is all about getting even. She was humiliated by the divorce because you initiated it. She's conveniently forgotten that she was fucking what's-his-name while she was still married to you."

"Whatever." All this drama exhausted Ian. "There's money in that account with both our names on it, Luke. Pay her whatever I owe her. Hire a lawyer to get her name removed as my power of attorney. We're divorced. She shouldn't have any say about my life at this point."

A soft knock, then a pretty redhead stuck her head inside the room. "Hey, guys," she said. "Can I come in? It's hostile out here, what with the ex-Mrs. Ritter shooting daggers my way as we pass in the hall."

Luke laughed and hugged Casey O'Toole hello. "I'm on it, Dad," he called over his shoulder. "Be back later."

Luke shut the door on his way out and Casey came over, her smile bright enough to light up the dark side of the moon. "Hey, handsome."

"Casey O'Toole. I'm not at my best."

"You look wonderful to me." She set a box of chocolates on the table in front of him, then leaned forward and kissed him on the mouth.

He was intensely aware of how the shape of her mouth molded itself against his. But all he could think of was how the shape and texture of Tess's mouth differed. If Casey were still alive in 2008, she would be seventy-six. *And if any of it's true, I'd be eighty-four.* He didn't know what he felt for her now.

Casey pulled back, her beautiful hair falling along the sides of her face, her parrot-green eyes struggling to read him. "Luke called and said he'd gotten permission for me to visit. I was able to visit for a while when you were in a coma, but Louise got huffy about it and put a stop to it."

"It's great to see you," Ian said.

"Luke's been giving me updates." She pulled a chair close to his, sat down, crossed her lovely legs. Her eyes twinkled mischievously. "Are you allowed chocolate?"

He had a sudden memory of her eyes doing this when they had stood in front of Hiawatha Falls, in a park burning with autumn, and he had kissed her. "No one said that I *can't* have them."

She lifted the lid, revealing his greatest weakness, an exquisite display of Swiss chocolates, thick, nutty half-moons with light and dark swirls, heart-shaped chocolates filled with caramel, neat little squares topped with cherries, triangles sprinkled with gold slivers of dried fruit. Chocolate held special meaning in the lexicon of their relationship—chocolates on birthdays, Valentine's Day, Christmas, and sometimes, chocolate just because.

He chose one of the triangles, bit into it—and felt his throat closing up and nearly gagged on it. He grabbed a piece of Kleenex from a box on the table, spat into it, and dropped it into the trash. "I guess . . . it doesn't mix with my meds or something."

"It's probably too soon."

Ian immediately felt guilty because the stuff now revolted him. "Tell me what's happening on campus. And with you."

It was the right question. "The guy who's substituting for you doesn't seem to know squat about journalism and there've been complaints from some of your students that he's really prowar and . . ."

Something flickered over her right shoulder, and as Ian watched it, he lost track of what Casey was saying. An optical illusion, some trick of the light? He squinted slightly, looked to either side of it, whatever *it* was, hoping it would be clearer in his peripheral vision. It seemed to flit and dart, like a white moth, a ghost moth, and nearly disappeared when it entered the shafts of light coming through the window. It reappeared an instant later, on the other side of the room where the light didn't reach, and here it became a shadow that began to assume shape and substance. He knew, he *fucking knew*, what it was.

Ian leaped to his feet and lunged across the room, waving his arms, shouting, his heart hammering. He grabbed a lamp, hurled it, and it slammed into the wall, the base and bulb shattering. Then he saw it, a woman, a *bruja*, and knew it had followed him back from the dead. It was still there when two orderlies wrestled him to the floor and jabbed a syringe in his neck. The *bruja*'s laughter was the last thing he heard as he sank like a stone into darkness.

Eleven

He rushed toward Dominica like a crazy man, gesturing wildly, yelling, "I can see you, *bruja*, go fuck yourself, get away from me . . ." And when he hurled a lamp at her, aim perfect, she suddenly understood Ian didn't just *sense* her presence, didn't just detect movement in his peripheral vision, but actually *saw* her.

How? Outside of Esperanza, the only people who could perceive a *brujo* were those attuned to an inner consciousness—shamans, psychics, mediums. Ian was none of those. The reasonable explanation was that his near-death experience in Esperanza had blown open something inside of him. Did

Ian, like Consuelo, that young woman who managed the Incan Café, now have the gift of second sight?

As the orderlies sedated him and put him on a gurney, a kind of despair gripped Dominica. What now? If she seized one of the orderlies, she might be able to force the man to kill Ian. But maybe not. Her abilities in this era were untested. She never had gone back in time to kill anyone. Only to seize.

From her birth in 1408 to her death in 1444 to everything that had happened to her since, she always had moved *with* the flow of time, not against it. Even though it was possible for her kind to travel back in time, it wasn't easy. Just to get here, to find out where Ian was, had required days of surveillance, of eavesdropping on the likes of Ed, Sara, Illika, and the recovering hero, Juanito. She'd had to invade their computers, their security cameras, and then she'd used her own abilities to home in on the vibration that was uniquely Ian's. Then he'd seen her.

She had no plan B. But if nothing else, six hundred years had taught her adaptability. So she threw herself at the closest orderly, sank into him like a knife through butter—and was immediately hurled out. Incensed, she tried to seize the other orderly. When the same thing happened, she knew it was no anomaly. It had to be a restriction germane to this era—or specific to Ian and the people around him. After all, she had been able to seize Ben in 1914 without any problem. Did it mean she wouldn't be able to seize *anyone* here? Such a possibility terrified her as much as the apparent threat of the liberation movement.

She followed them up the hall and considered other alternatives. His son. His lover. His ex-wife. Could she seize any of them?

If she could, then his son, who wasn't even here right now, probably wasn't the best option. Even though Luke seemed to have doubts about Ian's mental stability, their relationship was probably too solid for her to be able to force him to murder his father. Besides, when he had been in the room earlier, she had sensed the toxins in his body, drugs popular in this era—pot, mescaline, acid, peyote, mind-altering poisons that would make it too easy for her to lose her way or that might allow him to determine her true intentions.

The pretty redhead tempted Dominica. She liked the woman's irreverence, her intelligence. But Casey O'Toole loved Ian, which discounted any possibility that Dominica might be able to force her to kill him.

So the last choice was the ex-wife. Dominica moved in closer to Louise as she hurried along behind the gurney, high heels clicking against the tile floor, her pretty little purse tight against her side, her dark hair so sprayed into place that it wasn't ruffled by tiny bursts of heat from the vents. Such a petite body. Wasp waist, a pleasing flare to her hips, a sassy sway to her walk. *Will I be able to seize you?*

Dominica moved up behind her and slipped into her as unobtrusively as a splinter sliding beneath skin. She rapidly dispersed her essence throughout Louise's body and wasn't hurled out. Louise didn't flinch or recoil, didn't even know she had been compromised. Perhaps that was the secret to finding a host body in this era. *Do it gently and lie hidden, like a cancer cell, awaiting the opportune moment.*

She took swift inventory of Louise's physical and psychological state. She was so attractive on the outside, but such a total mess inside. Her bitterness over her divorce from Ian already had created intestinal problems and stiffness in her knees and shoulder joints. She flourished on a diet of constant high drama that slowly ate away at her adrenal glands. Louise had been the unfaithful spouse when she and Ian were married, but saw herself as a victim because Ian had filed for divorce first, humiliating her deeply. Her foremost desire was revenge. She resented that her son was closer to his father, that Luke apparently regarded her as a kind of money-grubbing bitch who didn't have a clue about anything.

Aside from an occasional joint, she didn't do drugs, didn't smoke, drank only moderately. In other words, Dominica thought, Louise Ritter Bell would provide a fine, healthy body for the moment.

As the orderlies approached the double doors at the end of the hall, Dominica began to feel uneasy. Beyond those doors lay the psych ward. She could feel the collective malaise of the people inside, a tsunami of despair, depression, tragedy. Fortunately, Louise's body provided some protection, but it was painfully clear to Dominica that she couldn't seize anyone inside there to kill Ian unless her game plan changed.

The orderlies stopped outside the double doors. "No visitors are permitted inside," the taller, muscular man said.

"What ward is this?" asked Casey.

"The psychiatric unit, ma'am."

"He doesn't need to be in any psych unit," Casey snapped.

"Excuse me," Louise said, an arctic chill in her voice. Dominica felt the tension in Louise's body, the barely subdued rage, but didn't dare interfere. "This is a family matter, Ms. O'Toole."

Casey burst out laughing. "You haven't been a part of his family since he divorced you two years ago." She spoke forcefully to the orderly. "Mr. Ritter's son has legal authority."

Dominica felt embarrassed for Louise's mental confusion, the way she flipped through the files in her own head, seeking the legal document that had made Luke his father's legal guardian. When Louise concluded that Casey was bluffing, she told the orderly that she had power of attorney, but Casey butted in.

"You need to call Luke Ritter," Casey said.

"I'm sorry, ma'am," the orderly said. "Hospital policy dictates that any unruly patient goes to the psych unit for evaluation. We don't need anyone's permission to do that."

"Who's your supervisor?" Casey demanded.

"That would be Dr. Danforth, ma'am, the hospital administrator."

"Fine, I'll speak to him. And then *I'll* call Mr. Ritter's son."

Casey marched away, and Louise stared after her, fuming. Then her rage spilled over and she rushed after Casey, grabbed her arm, spun her around. "Let's get something straight." The words hissed through her teeth and she leaned in so close to Casey that Dominica could see the flecks of amber in her beautiful green eyes. "I don't want you anywhere near Ian, you understand me?"

"Get out of my face, lady." Casey shoved her away.

Louise staggered back in her high heels, one ankle twisted, she lost a shoe and her balance and fell to the floor on her pretty little ass. "That's assault. You'll be hearing from my attorney."

"Right." With a toss of her lustrous red hair, Casey turned, wiggling her fingers. "Ta-ta, Louise. I'm off to call Luke."

Louise had trouble getting up. Her skirt was too tight, the floor was slippery, and a clasp on her garter belt had popped so that one of her stockings sagged. She felt humiliated that the exchange had been witnessed by the orderlies and other personnel. But her wrath interested Dominica most, an emotion she could stoke and manipulate.

Once Louise was on her feet again, she picked up her spike heel, slipped it on, twisted around and looked at the run in her other stocking. "Goddamn bitch," she murmured, and moved up the hall in search of a pay phone.

She composed herself rapidly, Dominica noticed, rehearsing what she would say to her attorney, what he should say to the hospital administrator. But as soon as she began to travel along this line of thought, other options occurred to her that she explored in a depth that surprised Dominica. The woman was brighter than she appeared to be, able to extend a single thought outward in time, examining the possible ramifications, the various probabilities, weighing one against the other.

Dominica followed the twisted, devious path in Louise's mind: if the hospital shrink who evaluated Ian believed he'd suffered brain damage due to his deprivation of oxygen when he had died, then perhaps he could be persuaded to commit him for a period of time. For observation. Commitment, Louise knew, practically ensured that Ian's tenure at the university would be rescinded and he probably would lose his newspaper column as well. Unemployment would be the ultimate humiliation. He finally would suffer the depth of humiliation that *she* had when he had divorced her. Payback.

Despite Dominica's admiration for the way this woman thought, a loony bin would prove unspeakable for Dominica. Even though she usually couldn't feel the emotions of the people she possessed, a mental ward was different. The emotions inside of it were generally so extreme, so aberrant, that they penetrated whatever protection the host body offered. She wouldn't be able to endure more than fifteen or twenty minutes in such a place. However, if Louise was properly armed—like with a knife—Dominica probably wouldn't need much time to force Louise to stab Ian. But that might involve days or weeks and Dominica didn't want to spend that much time here.

A far simpler—and quicker—option would be to slip into a hospital employee, if she could, and force the employee to enter the psych unit and finish Ian off. An overdose of a drug would be best. Painless, quick.

While Louise was on the pay phone in the lobby with her attorney, Dominica slipped out of her and thought herself toward a plump young female nurse. She followed her into the elevator and, as soon as the doors whispered shut, melted into her. No reaction. It seemed that as long as she took bodies in this way—quietly, dispersing her essence throughout the host body—she wouldn't be thwarted. Perhaps that was the restriction—no violent seizures, no using up bodies for physical pleasures and discarding them. Fine. She could live with that.

The nurse—Edna—punched the button for the second floor, but the psych unit was on the third, the same floor as cardiology, so Dominica gently urged her to press three. She did. So far, so good. No resistance. But when the doors opened at cardiology, Edna hesitated, frowning, looking around with confusion, wondering what had happened. She started to punch the button that would close the door, forcing Dominica to exert more control. *Move. One foot in front of the other.*

Now that her essence was no longer so widely dispersed through Edna's body, Dominica needed to breathe, to feel the beat of the woman's heart, to use all of her senses fully. She was forced to seize the nurse's brain, lungs, heart, organs, to possess her completely. That first shuddering breath, that heart that now beat for Dominica, the beautiful and rhythmic flow of physical life: she nearly wept with joy.

But Edna spoiled it by screaming, *Who the fuck are you?*

Dominica scrambled to find the answer that would fit Edna's belief system. Not God, not traditional religious garbage, but an amalgam of paganism and New Age aphorisms. *Your higher self. You have a mission.*

I do?

A man in the psych ward is suffering. Dominica urged her through the double doors, bracing herself for the assault of emotions from the crazies. That first contact nearly crippled her, all those inner voices screaming for release, redemption, understanding, freedom. She imagined herself as water, a rapidly flowing river that carried that shrieking tsunami of despair beyond her. Then there was silence. Blissful. Healing.

Deeper into the ward they traveled, through a strange twilight, into the pharmaceutical area. *We want Ian Ritter to sleep,* Dominica whispered. *Phenobarbital would be best.*

Edna turned into a supply room, opened the fridge, withdrew a tiny bottle. She filled a syringe. *Slip it in your pocket.*

Out in the hallway again, Edna hesitated, Dominica nudged her forward, and she made a beeline toward the nursing station. No one questioned her presence. She picked up one of the clipboards, found Ian's name and a note: *Cardiac patient, violent episode, awaiting psych evaluation, straitjacket required. Room 13.*

That number captivated her. It seemed to recur consistently in Ian's life and she wondered if she should look for a deeper meaning. But what would that deeper meaning be? Bad luck? She nearly laughed. He was about to experience the ultimate in bad luck. Death.

Edna moved quickly through the twilight and slipped into room 13. *Oh, just look at him, that beautiful face.* Even in repose, trapped within a straitjacket, his physical appearance struck her as extraordinary. Ian Ritter, one of the first transitionals in five hundred years. Dominica had heard that a family had arrived in Esperanza shortly afterward, but they were dead, not in the between. That made Ian and Tess unique. Why had the chasers let *them* through? What was so special about them? About him?

Edna woke up enough to ask a question. *A transitional? What's that mean?*

One who walks among the dead.

But he's not dead. He's a sedated psycho.

Stop talking.

But—

Go away. Dominica shoved Edna's essence down into the metal room constructed weeks ago, when she had taken that tourist in Esperanza. She forced Edna to approach the bed, to bring out the syringe, to flick off the plastic tip that covered the end of the needle. *Stick it in his neck.*

Edna's hand started to shake. *That's wrong.*

He's suffering. You're an angel of mercy.

I'm no fucking angel, Edna screamed, and jammed the needle into her own neck, into the carotid, and pressed down on the plunger.

Dominica leaped out of her and watched as Edna crumpled to the floor, twitching, her bladder and bowels letting loose. Then Dominica shot through the roof, into the dusk of Minneapolis, circa March 1968, and screamed until self-disgust overwhelmed her. Then she went in search of Louise Ritter Bell, her best hope.

Twelve

One moment it was light, the next moment it was dark. In between Ian ate and slept and shuffled through a large room with a TV, Ping-Pong tables, board games. Dozens of men and women in pajamas and robes wandered freely, drooling and talking to themselves. People came and went. Light gave way to darkness and then to light once again. Several times a day, a nurse handed him a little white cup with pills in it and another white cup that held water and told him to take his medicine like a good little boy.

He resented being called a good little boy, as if he were four years old. He wanted to rebel, to refuse to take the meds. But a glacier had claimed his head and it just kept growing until it split open his skull and began to en-case his entire body. When he put food in his mouth, he couldn't taste it.

When people spoke to him, their voices sounded disembodied. When fresh flowers appeared in the large room, he couldn't smell them. So the next time the nurse handed him the two white cups and told him to take his pills like a good little boy, he slipped them under his tongue, pretended to swallow them. As she turned away, he brought his hand to his mouth and spat the pills into his palm. He buried them in a potted plant near the window.

He did the same thing for the next several pill cycles and the glacier that held him developed fissures, then cracks, then great chunks of it fell away. It became easier to taste his food, smell flowers, hear people when they spoke. In the next pill cycle, when the nurse addressed him as "professor," he didn't raise his eyes, couldn't bring himself to look at her. He was terrified she might see the truth, that he was no longer drugged.

"Here you go. Take your meds like a good boy."

She held out the first white cup and he emptied the contents into his mouth. Six pills. Next came the white cup with the water in it. He drank it down, she took the empty cups and patted his head as though he were an obedient dog. The name Ratched popped into his head, from Ken Kesey's novel, *One Flew Over the Cuckoo's Nest*. He was in a loony bin.

Jesus God. How's it going there in the shock therapy room? Who're you torturing today? Got any more happy pills for me?

"Very good, Professor. Be happy." Nurse Ratched gave a quick little wink, laughed, and wheeled her cart of happy pills on to the next patient.

Fuck you. As soon as her back was to him, he brought his hand to his mouth, spat out the pills, and stuffed them down in the crack between the cushion and the back of the chair. He resumed his paragon of vacancy. *Professor Ritter, dullard. Lights off. No one home.* After a few minutes, he went over to the window. Winter had fled. *How long? How long have I been here?* He nearly wept with frustration, with sorrow for the time he had lost.

The naked trees on the grounds just below showed early signs of spring, sprigs of green crawling out across the barren branches like a promise. The people out there wore sweaters or just shirts. Gone were the heavy jackets and coats, boots, scarves, knit caps. He choked back a sob.

Ian shuffled back to his room and stopped when he saw the number on the door: 13. Something about that number. What? Two images floated into his head—of a bus with a 13 on it and of another door bearing the same number. A door where? A second memory surfaced, of an elderly black man walking through a solid door, like some special effect in a horror movie. This image troubled him deeply. He sensed it might be connected to why he was here.

Ian went into the room to look for a pen, paper. Twin beds, identical wooden dressers, identical closets. He had a vague recollection of his roommate, a burned-out musician whose name escaped him. Ian's bed was under the window, clothes piled neatly on top it. He couldn't find a pen and the only available paper came from pages in the Bible in the nightstand drawer. He tore out one of them, ripped off a strip, went into the bathroom. He crouched to hide the strip behind the sink but found seventeen other strips there already. *Seventeen.* Had it been that long since he'd begun burying his meds? Seventeen pill cycles? Seventeen days? Weeks? Months? *What?*

Luke, where are you? Had his son been here at all? Had Casey? Now a clear memory surfaced, from when he had been in a regular hospital. He had freaked when he had seen a *brujo,* orderlies had wrestled him to the floor. He didn't have any recollection of what had happened immediately after that, of how he had ended up in Nurse Ratched's ward. Who had committed him? Louise? Luke? Some invisible authority? Had they fucked with his brain, given him electroshock treatments? He didn't know. His immediate past in this place was a tundra of nothingness.

He rubbed his hands over his face and returned to the large room, shuffling like the other patients did, eyes fixed on his moccasins. He sat in one of the chairs in front of the TV, his mind racing. What floor was he on? Where was this place located? In Minneapolis? Some other city? *Is it possible to escape?*

On the TV screen, a black dog barked. He suddenly remembered a black Lab—Nomad—who befriended him and . . . who? *Tess.* Memories flickered through him, but were they actual memories or fantasies his unconscious had weaved while he was in a coma? More importantly, how much time had he lost in this place?

He endured lunch, the crazies around him shoveling food into their mouths with their fingers or simply staring at their paper plates. Others turned their plastic spoons, the only utensil they were allowed, over and over again in their hands, studying them like alien artifacts. He finished eating, stood, picked up his paper plate and carried it over to the trash can. Nurse Ratched and her minions watched vigilantly, making sure the rules were followed. If a patient didn't pick up his dirty dishes, he was called back to the table to do so. If a patient spoke too loudly, if he resisted the rules or rebelled against them, he was reprimanded or given stronger drugs, isolation, more electroshock treatments.

Ian wandered back to the rec area and sat down again, facing the door. Where did it lead? Into a hall? A stairwell? He felt a powerful desire to step outside, to breathe the tenuous spring air, to stand alone beneath a sweeping blue sky, to see his shadow against concrete, grass, a field of flowers. If he made a break for it, how long would it take for Nurse Ratched or one of the orderlies to tackle him? *Seconds.*

He needed to get out of here, to Ecuador. He needed to know if what he remembered had actually happened, if any of it was real. At the very least, he should get back to work. What had happened to his column? Who was writing it in his absence? Who was teaching his classes? Was he officially on leave? Had he been fired from both jobs?

The door to the rec room opened and his son entered. *Luke.* Ian forced himself to remain seated, to stare vacantly. Luke was with a tall, thin man in a suit who stuck close to him, like a bodyguard. Ian vaguely recalled seeing this man before, but couldn't remember who he was. Doctor? Lawyer? Indian chief? They strode toward him and Ian sensed Nurse Ratched watching. If he didn't play this right, he might end up in this hellhole for another six weeks or six months or six years.

Luke strode over to him with the tall man. "Dad, good to see you." He spoke too loudly, as though he believed that Ian was hard of hearing. When Ian didn't react, didn't speak or blink, just kept staring vapidly ahead, Luke turned to his companion. "I'd like to take him outside for a walk, Dr. Parcell."

"I recommend doing it in a wheelchair initially, Luke."

"A wheelchair's fine. Could you get one for me?"

Parcell's expression said he didn't want to, that he usually left such tasks to the underlings, but he moved quickly away from them, long simian arms swinging at his sides.

"Dad, we're going for a walk." Luke kept speaking loudly. "Would you like that? The temperature outside is just perfect, in the high fifties." Then he leaned forward, whispering, "Our attorney had to file papers so that I could even get in here to see you. Do you understand what I'm saying?"

"Get me the fuck outta here, Luke. Please. Fast."

Luke drew back, eyes wide, apparently shocked to discover that his father wasn't a drooling idiot. "Let's get your sweater buttoned up . . ."

"Excuse me, sir."

Nurse Ratched had sneaked up behind Luke like some sort of secret agent, hands folded demurely in front of her, her implacable demeanor enough to intimidate heads of state. *Despot,* Ian thought. But Luke drew himself to his full height, towering over her by more than half a foot, and said, "And you are . . . ?"

"The head nurse. Frieda Bancroft."

"I'm his son. Luke Ritter. You any relation to Anne?"

"To who?"

Ian nearly burst out laughing.

"Anne Bancroft, the actress."

"Uh, no, Mr. Ritter, I'm not. And our visiting hours aren't until—"

"I'm with Dr. Parcell. I'm taking my father for a walk. With the permission of Dr. Parcell and on the advice of my attorney."

"I, uh, see. Well, I'm obligated to inform you that your father is heavily medicated, Mr. Ritter. I don't recommend taking him out of the building."

"With all due respect, ma'am, I really don't give a shit what you recommend."

Eyes widening, she fussed with stray hairs that had escaped the bun at the back of her head. "I'm afraid I'll have to speak to Dr. Parcell—"

"Good afternoon, Miss Bancroft," Parcell said, pushing a wheelchair over to them.

"Sir, may I speak to you privately for a moment?" she asked.

He nodded and parked the wheelchair in front of Luke. "Here you go. You may have to help him into it, Mr. Ritter."

You prick, I'm perfectly capable of getting into this goddamn chair by myself. I can tap-dance around you. But Ian stayed quiet and pretended he needed help standing, acting as though he were ninety-five years old and crippled from the inside out.

Parcell and Bancroft moved away and spoke in tense, urgent whispers, glancing frequently at Luke and Ian. Luke turned the wheelchair toward the door, so their backs were to the other two. "This is Mom's doing. She had you committed. Our attorney claims the divorce nullified her power of attorney and is threatening to sue the facility. You've got about fifteen grand left in your bank account and it's going to get you out of here and hidden. You understand?"

"I am—"

"My dad," Luke said quickly. "And I am—"

"My son," Ian whispered, and swallowed a sob of relief.

Luke pressed his hand against Ian's shoulder. "I'm here, Dad."

"I've been spitting out my meds, burying them."

"Good. Fuck them. Casey is driving the getaway car."

Ian talked fast. "Luke, when I died, I went to Esperanza and fell in love with a woman who is forty years in our future. I mean, I think that's what happened. I need to go to Ecuador, find out if any of it is true. If I told you this already, I apologize. I can't seem to remember a whole hell of a lot. But—"

"I believe you." Luke leaned forward, as if to adjust the collar of Ian's sweater, and kept whispering. "I believe that you experienced something, Dad. There's a doc doing research on what happens to people when they clinically die. I spoke to him, Raymond Moody. He hopes to publish his findings on these . . . these near-death experiences."

Near-death experiences: it was the same phrase that Tess had used.

"He's interested in your case, Dad. We'll get to the bottom of this."

Ian didn't need to *get to the bottom* of anything. He only had to prove to himself whether it was real or he was deranged. At the moment, he was just grateful that Luke had shown up and he wasn't still in his pajamas like most of the patients. He looked presentable enough to go outside—jeans, a pullover sweater, a pair of comfortable moccasins.

Parcell fell into step alongside Luke, accompanying them into the hall, to the elevators. "If you could stay on the grounds, Mr. Ritter, I would appreciate it. Nurse Bancroft apparently has some concerns about your father that—"

"She's a nurse. You're the doctor. And our attorney says—"

"Yes, well, I'm just looking at the bigger picture, Mr. Ritter. Your father has been here for seventeen days, on antipsychotic drugs, and he—"

"Needs to get some fresh air," Luke said.

Luke punched the elevator button, Parcell waited with them. "We encourage outings, visits from family members, anything that makes the patient more comfortable and secure."

Parcell sounded as though he were reciting from the facility's brochure, Ian thought, and wished he could slap duct tape across the man's mouth. When the elevator doors opened, Luke said, "I can take it from here, Doctor. Thank you so much for your time."

"Uh, right. Very good. If you could have him back in a couple of hours, for tea. We have afternoon tea and snacks. He's accustomed to that routine now."

"Not a problem," Luke said, and pushed the wheelchair into the elevator.

As the doors began to shut, Ian noticed that Parcell nervously shifted his weight from one foot to the other, scratched his chin, and seemed flummoxed about all of it. But he kept smiling. Then the doors clattered shut, the elevator lurched downward. "Where's Casey parked, Luke?"

"At the far end of the lot, where they can't see the van. She'll take us to my car."

"What's the date?"

"March twenty-seventh."

He had died in January. More than two months, gone. "Jesus. I've lost so much time."

"Can you walk?"

"Walk, talk, fart, joke, run fast." Ian felt a hard, painful throbbing at his temple, heard the muscles in his legs screaming. They were now outside, beneath the dome of a magnificent blue sky, and he sucked in the spring air. "What hospital is this?"

"The Minneapolis Mental Health Care Center. Daddy Warbucks is on the board here and also on the hospital board, so Mom was able to convince the hospital shrink that you should be placed under observation, then she pulled strings here to get you in. What do you remember?"

"Raving about *brujos*, two big guys slamming me to the floor, jabbing something into my neck, then there was a point where I came to and found myself in a straitjacket and nearly lost my mind. I think that was when it was easy for your mother to convince the hospital I should be put under observation."

"Casey called me and told me what had happened. By the time I got to the hospital, they'd committed you. A comatose nurse was discovered on the floor next to your bed, with a syringe sticking out of her neck that held traces of phenobarbital. They know you didn't do it because you were in a straitjacket. She recovered and the hospital fired her and filed charges against her for theft of the drug."

Alarm tore through Ian. Had the *bruja* he'd seen in his room followed him back to kill him? Were his memories real? If so, then the *bruja* couldn't kill him in her *bruja* form, and she'd taken the nurse, who resisted at the end and injected herself. "I need to speak to that nurse."

"Casey already did, Dad. The story's pretty weird. She claims she was possessed by a demon who wanted her to ease your suffering. That's an exact quote. She claims she fought back and injected herself."

So maybe he wasn't nuts, after all. And if he wasn't, his conclusions were real. "These *brujo* fucks intend to kill me. I need to get out of the country, Luke."

His son patted his shoulder. "I'm taking you someplace safe. To a cabin in lake country that a friend owns."

Luke didn't get it. He didn't understand that no place was safe from *brujos.* The pat on the shoulder was affection, not comprehension. "Where's your mother now?"

"The day after all this drama happened with you, she came down with a really bad case of the flu and has been laid up until last night."

Maybe that explained why the *bruja* hadn't taken Louise. "And you still think this is about revenge on your mother's part? Getting even?"

"Fuckin' A."

They moved swiftly along a curving path that followed the contours of a small pond, woods of denuded trees, farther and farther away from the main building. Now and then they passed other patients with nurses, friends, family members, all of them heavily drugged. Ian maintained the same blank stare when he and Luke weren't alone, but in between kept talking about Esperanza, what he'd experienced.

Now and then, Luke interrupted with a question or requested clarification. Then they rounded a curve in the lake, where tall, thick pines created a barrier between them and the main building. "Not much farther," Luke said, and picked up his pace until he was nearly running.

As the wheelchair clattered across the sidewalk, Ian glanced back. Through the branches of the pines, he saw part of the main building, and wondered if Parcell and his sadistic Nurse Ratched had been watching them through one of the barred windows.

Luke suddenly pushed the wheelchair into the trees and the sweet-smelling shadows of the pines, and stepped on the brake. "Here."

Ian was grateful that Luke didn't offer to help him up. As they left the safety of the trees, he felt a kind of wonder that he was walking on his own, out here in the free world, relatively drug-free, about to escape this hellhole. *I'm one step closer to Ecuador.*

They crossed an employee lot, moving as quickly as escaping thieves, and reached an old VW van parked at the end. A huge peace symbol was painted on its side, antiwar slogans covered the rear bumper, the side windows were blacked out. Luke slid open the side door, Ian scrambled in, then Luke climbed into the passenger seat. Casey, ensconced behind the wheel, her red hair tucked up under a baseball cap, glanced back and grinned. "We're busting you out, Ritter."

"I'm forever in your debt, O'Toole."

"You'd better get down low in the seat," she said. "We've got to drive right past the administration building to get out of here. We wanted to bust you out sooner, Ian. But Louise must've suspected we would because her attorney told Purcell that Luke and I were forbidden to visit you. Then when Luke got the new lawyer, it took him a week to work his way through the political machine that Louise's husband apparently rules."

The van backed up, its engine making noises that reminded Ian of that bus chugging up the Andes. "I'm just grateful for getting out at all."

"Okay, the cops are outside the building," Luke announced. "With dogs."

"Jesus, these people are nuts," Casey muttered. "You'd better duck down, Luke."

The van chugged on, turned, picked up speed. When Casey announced they were clear of the hospital, Ian rose up and leaned forward, between Casey and Luke. "As soon as Louise hears about this, she's going to press charges against you two."

"Hell, she already pressed charges against *me* for assault," Casey said. "But the bitch started it by sinking her finger into my boob, getting right in my face. I shoved her away."

"I hope you told her to go fuck herself," Ian said.

"Worse. I humiliated her."

"Then you're on the shit list for life, O'Toole. I'll pay for your attorney."

"No need. A friend's doing it for free. Says it's a pleasure to go up against any member of the Bell family."

"And she won't press charges against me," Luke said. "That would look bad to her friends, mom against son. And I'll just say I drove the car. Casey won't be implicated at all."

Casey reached back and patted Ian's arm. "Hey, don't worry about it. I'd love to have another excuse to take a swing at Louise."

Ian laughed and gave her hand a quick squeeze. Minutes later, she turned into a park and pulled up alongside Luke's 1967 Chevy. Luke got out quickly and Casey turned, her beautiful green eyes locking on his. She ran her hands along the sides of Ian's face. "I realize that something happened to you when you died, Ian, and that you're trying to sort things out. Luke told me about this Esperanza place."

I think I met someone there. I have to go to Ecuador to find her. He nearly blurted it, but couldn't stand the thought of hurting Casey. So he kissed her instead, acutely aware, again, of how her mouth differed from Tess's. "Thank you for all your help, Casey."

She immediately teared up. "If Louise doesn't have me tailed, I'll try getting up to the cabin where Luke's taking you."

He kissed her once more, then got out of the van and made a beeline for Luke's Chevy, the sensation of her mouth lingering against his. He hoped that she didn't come to the cabin. It would be better for Casey if he simply disappeared from her life.

Once they were headed north out of Minneapolis, Ian said, "I'm going to Ecuador. I need my passport. It's in my safe-deposit box at the bank. Since you're on the account, you shouldn't have trouble getting into it. And I'll need some of the cash. You keep the rest."

Luke's expression made it clear that while he believed his father had had some sort of experience when he was dead, he wasn't sold on the rest of Ian's story. A magical town high in the Andes. *Brujos.* A woman forty years in his future. Who could blame him? It sounded nuts to Ian, too.

"We can figure all this out later, Dad. Why don't you sack out? It's a couple of hours to the cabin. There's a pillow in the back seat."

Ian didn't feel tired, but a few minutes with his eyes closed sounded inviting. He reached into the back for the pillow, pressed it against the window, shut his eyes. When he came awake, long, thin shadows fell like stripes across the road. Late afternoon, he thought, rubbing at the crick in his neck. They were in the lake country, where everything seemed excessive—the towering pines, huge, naked oaks, vast expanses of emptiness. Through the trees, lakes glinted in the late afternoon light, surface ice breaking up as winter surrendered to spring. They appeared to be alone on a narrow dirt road.

"Where are we?" Ian asked, yawning.

"Close to the cabin. How're you feeling?"

"Sane."

"I stopped and got some food. Chicken, mashed potatoes, beans, everything cold now." He passed Ian a paper sack.

"It smells fantastic. Thanks, Luke." He opened the bag and went to work on the food.

"There's a thermos of hot coffee in the back seat."

Ian turned to retrieve the thermos—and laughed. The back seat was filled with groceries, bags of clothes, firewood, charcoal, pots and pans, quilts, sheets, pillows, camping gear. "Damn, you shopped."

"Yeah, I went overboard. The cabin doesn't have heat, so we're going to have to use the fireplace and the potbellied stove for that."

"Is there a television? Phone?" *Internet? Wi-Fi?*

"TV, but the rabbit ears rarely work right. Nearest phone is six miles south, in town. I went by your place before going to the hospital, so some of your clothes are in the trunk. And some books, your typewriter, paper and supplies, the pages you wrote while you were in the hospital. I, uh, read through them, Dad. I hope you don't mind. It's some pretty wild stuff."

"Wild and, I hope, true."

"For a few days, just lay low."

"You think I'm demented?"

"I think . . . something definitely happened when you died, Dad. But your story is so . . ."

"Outrageous? Ridiculous? Nuts?"

Luke rolled his lower lip between his teeth, something he'd done since he was very young, a sign that he was struggling to find a way to be tactful.

"Just say it, Luke."

"Dad, people don't fall in love when they die. And they don't fall in love with someone from forty years in the future, in some town way the fuck up in the Andes."

"Yeah? Says who, Luke?"

"People who know about such things."

"Ah, right. Theologians, priests, rabbis, preachers. You've had such vast exposure to organized religion."

They both burst out laughing. "Okay, you win. Maybe I just feel like I should play devil's advocate."

"C'mon, Luke. You've taken all kinds of consciousness-altering drugs, and you still feel a need to play that role? Tell me again about that mushroom trip you took where you talked to gnomes."

"Okay. So death is like a mushroom trip."

"Maybe it is. I wouldn't know. I'm probably the least hip professor on campus."

"You make death sound like an adventure."

"Honestly, I don't know if everything I remember actually happened. That's why I need to go to Ecuador." Ian pressed the heels of his hands against his eyes and forced himself to recall that conversation with Tess in which they had realized they were comatose or dead and separated by forty years in time. It came back with shocking ease—dates, incidents, names. "But if it *is* true, then remember this. On March sixteenth of this year, there supposedly was an incident in Nam that will come to be known as the massacre at My Lai. In September of next year, men will be charged with the massacre of hundreds of Vietnamese men, women, and children at My Lai and it won't come to the attention of the American public until November of next year, when Seymour Hersh breaks the story. On April 6, Martin Luther King supposedly will be assassinated at the Lorraine Hotel in Memphis. Jessie Jackson will be standing on the balcony with him when it happens. On June 6, Robert Kennedy supposedly will be assassinated at the Ambassador Hotel in L.A."

"You said this before, right after you regained consciousness. I . . . thought you were raving. Can we stop it?"

"If my memories are true, I don't have any idea if any of it can be stopped."

"I know this reporter who interviewed King recently. I'll warn him . . ."

"The most you can tell him is to keep King away from the Lorraine Hotel in Memphis. I don't know if that will change the outcome. Besides, if you tell him anything else, we'll have the Feds at the cabin door."

"We may anyway, if Mom figures out where you are."

Luke turned up a side road as narrow as a footpath. In the dusk, the trees seemed to hug the car, the encroaching darkness felt intimate, dangerous. The headlights struck a tiny wooden structure that looked as if it were held together with glue and tape. The chimney was large, though, and firewood was stacked to the right of the front door. Frost covered the tiny windows, icicles hung from the shingled roof. Ian hoped he had not traded one prison for another.

The car stopped. Luke turned off the engine, the headlights. Darkness closed around them, tight as a fist. It scared Ian. A part of him still equated darkness with the fog, *brujos*.

It apparently occurred to Luke that it would be difficult to carry supplies to the cabin without some light, so he turned the headlights back on, and they started unloading the car. The cold, sweet air of the Minnesota woods invigorated Ian. He peered up into the underbelly of an ink-black sky burning with stars. Somewhere in time, Tess was appreciating this same sky.

When they finally were settled in front of the fire with a couple of beers,

Luke said, "Okay, let's say your memories are true. What else should I know?"

Ian thought about it. "Nixon wins the election this year, and later, under threat of impeachment for something called Watergate, resigns. Gerald Ford becomes prez. After him comes some guy named Carter, Southern man, Georgia, I think, a peanut farmer. Gas becomes a big problem, three-hour waiting lines. In her time, gas is more than four bucks a gallon."

"Look, as a favor to me, would you please just spend a few days here, laying low until I get the money stuff squared away?" Luke asked. "And finish writing out everything you remember. Everything. I mean, c'mon, if this stuff really happened to you, Dad, then we're getting a chance to look forty years into the future. Maybe I can learn to play the stock market and walk away with a couple of million. Or I can invent something that will change the world."

"Google," Ian said. "It changes the world. It's a search engine for the Internet."

"Put that in the notes," Luke said.

They laughed again and in that moment of complete communion, a form took shape over Luke's right shoulder—an elderly man with thick gray hair who wore Ben Franklin glasses. Ian recognized him, Charlie Livingston, Tess's dead father. He flashed a peace sign. "Welcome to the mad hatter's tea party, Ian. You aren't out of the woods yet. They can't take you, but they can seize people around you and try to force them to kill you. Your ex is going to pull out all the stops. Dominica has taken her. Compile your notes, lay low, leave when you feel it's time. San Francisco, Sara Wells at Berkeley, should vanquish any doubts you have."

Ian pushed to his feet, his doubts gone. Charlie looked solid and, as Ian moved toward him, he didn't evaporate or fade away. "Tell me about the nurse, Charlie."

"Dad?" Luke sounded worried.

"Do you see him, Luke? The gray-haired guy?" Ian didn't take his eyes off Charlie.

"Uh, no, Dad. We're alone here."

"No, we're not alone. The nurse, Charlie. Tell me what happened."

"Dominica seized her, just as you thought, and tried to force her to kill you."

Outside, the wind whined through the trees, branches slapped the windows. The flames in the fireplace leaped and danced, the logs crackled and hissed, plumes of smoke drifted upward. His throat felt parched, he was hungry, tired.

"She used Louise once and will use her again," Charlie continued. "Louise won a reprieve because she was sick. Your son is not fully convinced of your sanity, Ian. And because you need his support, you have to convince him that you're fine, but changed."

"Yeah? How the hell do I do that?"

"Uh, Dad, you're talking to the wall," Luke said.

Ian ignored Luke, listened to Charlie. "Ask Luke about Casey. About what happened that night they were both in your room, when you were in a coma. Go there, Ian. He'll never again doubt your sanity."

He wasn't sure he wanted to *go there*. Wasn't sure that he needed to *go there*. But because Luke was directly behind Ian, gripping his shoulders, speaking to him as though he were a demented old man—*c'mon, Dad, sit down, it's warmer by the fire, I'll fix us something to eat, you're talking to the fucking wall*—Ian knew that he had to *go there*.

"Charlie's saying I should ask what happened between you and Casey while I was in a coma, Luke." Ian pulled free of his son's hands, turned, and saw the truth in Luke's face—incredulity that his crazy old man had figured it out.

And Luke, God bless him, didn't deny it, protest, lie, or make excuses. He pressed his fists against his eyes and emitted a single, heartbreaking sob. "We were there, by your bedside, day after day, waiting, hoping, and I don't know what happened. Our . . . love for you . . . brought us together, Dad. I . . . I can't explain it in any other terms. I . . . Jesus, I'm so sorry, I'm so ashamed . . . it only happened once, it . . . it . . ."

Ian understood his son's visceral attraction to Casey and why she would gravitate toward Luke during the time that he himself was in a coma. He got it. He knew he should feel anger, disappointment, indignation, something other than what he actually felt—relief and gratitude that his son and his former lover had discovered something profound in each other.

"I'm pleased for you, Luke. For both of you."

Luke looked astonished, shocked, and then skeptical, as if he had expected Ian to damn him from one side of the universe to the other. "I . . . Jesus, Dad, I . . ." Luke shook his head and threw up his hands, patting the air and backing away from Ian as if he couldn't quite understand what had happened.

"I'm happy for you, Luke. For both of you."

"I . . . need some air." Luke snatched his jacket off the back of a chair and headed for the door, the woods, the sanctuary of darkness beyond the cabin.

Ian went to the window, staring out into the moonlit woods. Luke sat out there, legs pulled against his chest, head resting against his knees. Ian was still standing there an hour later when Luke's car peeled away from the cabin.

Thirteen

Dominica was just about to slip into Louise Ritter Bell when Ben joined her.

For him to seek her out in the past meant that the news was very good—or treacherously bad. *It's bad,* he said, reading her thoughts. *We haven't been able to track down Tess Livingston. It's like she slipped into a black hole, Nica.*

Or the chasers were protecting her, camouflaging her in some way. But she doubted it. Chasers were powerful, but not omniscient. They weren't gods. And *brujos* were limited in their ability to find the living across the vast spectrum of physical life, spread through space and time. *Just keep looking.*

There's something else. We believe the liberation group is getting help from churches around Ecuador and that they have spies within the local populace in Ecuador. Pearl and some others slipped into priests in Punta, Guayaquil, Quito, and Puyo and learned they are amassing flamethrowers for some big battle with brujos. But apparently the priests aren't privy to all the information. We couldn't find out dates and details.

The church. The goddamn church had more money and resources than the government and its network was vast and intricate. *Put the tribe on alert. Tell them to have bodies picked out that can be seized at a moment's notice, to locate trucks and supplies that can be moved into a defensive position quickly, and to begin adding to our stash of weapons.*

And you'll stay here to kill Ian?

Yes. Isn't his ex-wife pretty?

They watched Louise hurry down the sidewalk to her shiny Mercedes, a gift from her new, rich husband. *You're prettier,* Ben thought, and briefly melted into her, the only way they could connect outside of Esperanza. *Love you, Nica, see you soon.* Then he was gone and Dominica felt his absence acutely.

She wondered if she should rush back to Esperanza to help prepare the city for an assault by this liberation group. But Ian's death seemed equally pressing. She quickly slipped into Louise and dispersed herself through the woman's cells, just like she had done ten days ago, before Louise had gotten sick. Louise gave no indication that she was aware anything unusual had happened.

Louise, the paragon of cluelessness.

The virus that had made her body uninhabitable was still present, although in a much weakened state. But because Dominica had stayed away from Louise precisely because she had been so ill, she went to work on killing the damn virus. Since Louise's appetite for high drama, revenge, and her turmoil about Ian had lowered her resistance, Dominica also bolstered her immune system, then prompted her pituitary gland and her hypothalamus to release endorphins, so she wouldn't be in such an agitated state. Dominica understood her anxiety—Ian had escaped from the mental hospital two days ago—but only a cool head would prevail now.

By the time Louise pulled into a parking lot, the virus was dead, her congestion was cleared up, her energy had surged. Dominica also had taken care of some other impending health problems—like the stiffness in Louise's knees and shoulders, the precursors to arthritis, and the irritations in her digestive system. She figured Louise now owed her a favor.

Louise swung her slender legs out of the car, smoothed her hands over her tight blue skirt and the matching jacket. Apparently her humiliating fall in the hospital corridor had convinced her to shelve the ridiculous spike heels. Today she wore plain black flats. She shut the door and started toward the ugly brick buildings that constituted the Minneapolis Mental Health Care Center.

"Hey, Louise," someone called.

A tall, Ichabod Crane of a man unfolded himself from a shiny BMW, briefcase in hand. Ray Garthe, Louise's attorney and financial advisor, was impeccably dressed in a tailored coat and trousers and moved with long, restless strides.

"Ray, I thought you were already inside," she said.

"Up until five minutes ago I was on the phone with Dr. Parcell, letting him know we're going to sue their goddamn ass."

"They had strict orders not to let Luke or Casey in to see him."

"Yeah, and we're packing up his stuff and payment stopped yesterday."

Inside the building, the stink of mold, darkness, and pockets of madness threatened to overpower Dominica. She barely resisted the urge to press her hand over her mouth and nose. They stopped at the front desk, where a bamboo-thin woman fussed with papers. Ray said, "We're here to see Dr. Parcell."

"I'm sorry. He's busy right now and—"

"*Busy?*" Dominica slapped her hand down so hard against the counter that the woman wrenched back. "You tell him to get down here now or there will be a lawsuit against this facility in his mailbox by tonight."

"Uh, yes, ma'am. Your names?"

"Louise Bell and Attorney Ray Garthe."

The clerk quickly picked up the receiver. Ray nudged Louise's elbow and his brows shot up. *Impressive,* he mouthed. *You should be a lawyer.*

In the Kansas life, Dominica thought, she and Ben had been attorneys.

"He's on his way down," the woman announced.

They didn't have to wait long. Dr. Parcell showed up minutes later, his ruddy cheeks pink with exertion. "So sorry to keep you both waiting." He extended his hand first toward Ray, who shook it, and then toward Louise, who wanted to, but Dominica prevented it.

"We're here to pick up my ex-husband's belongings, Dr. Parcell."

"Certainly. They're being brought down now."

"No. We'll pick them up from his room," Ray said. "Immediately."

Dominica rather liked this Ray. Demanding. Cocky. Sure of himself.

"Oh, I'm sorry," Dr. Parcell said. "Visitors aren't permitted in the living quarters."

"Dr. Parcell, I don't know how to make this any clearer," Ray said. "Your facility is guilty of a serious infraction. You allowed the professor's son to come in here against the written instructions of Mrs. Bell, who holds power of attorney. Then Mr. Ritter pulled a knife on his son and forced him to drive to a train station. He's been missing for forty-eight hours, is now considered armed and dangerous, and is being sought by the state police."

"Our patients don't have access to knives." Parcell's eyes flicked nervously from Ray to Louise and back to Ray. "And your son, Mrs. Bell. How do you know he's telling the truth? He could have made up the story about the knife."

"You're missing the point, Dr. Parcell." Ray sounded pissed now. "The young man wasn't allowed in here in the first place. Now, shall we proceed upstairs?"

Parcell cleared his throat. He looked embarrassed—and mighty uncomfortable. "It's a rather long walk. Our elevator broke down this morning."

The building was massive, deeper than it was wide, and during the long walk through it, Dominica felt compelled to take over Louise completely, but knew that small increments were safer, one organ or limb at a time. Louise seemed oblivious until Dominica claimed her heart and her lungs, possessing her completely. Then she screamed, *Hey, get outta here,* as though Dominica were the hired help, the inconvenient intruder.

Go to sleep, Dominica told her, sucking at the air that flowed through Louise's mouth, into her lungs.

But Louise refused to shut up, so Dominica shoved her down inside that metal prison and specifically looked for anything useful on Luke. Where might he have taken his father? Who were Luke's friends? Did any of them have a house outside the city? Perhaps in the woods, the countryside, in another town? Where did Ian bank? Did he have a passport already? How much money was in his accounts?

Her digging around in Louise's psyche yielded more information than she needed—how Louise had hired a private detective to follow Ian, to search for something she could use to tarnish his reputation. It gave her insight into Louise's dysfunctional relationship with her son, the child she never had wanted and hoped to abort.

That's a goddamn lie, Louise screamed. *I wanted kids, Ian didn't.*

Dominica muted her voice and she and Ray followed Parcell into a long, dingy hallway that smelled strongly of cleansers. Beneath that odor lurked the stink of urine, unwashed bodies, madness.

"Here we go. Room thirteen," said Dr. Parcell.

How many thirteens did that make?

A large room, with a bed under the barred window and another against the east wall. Pale gray walls. A single ceiling light. Depressing didn't begin to describe it. A man sat at the edge of a bed next to the window, staring through the bars with utter dejection and misery. Unshaven jaw, graying hair cropped close to his skull, right hand beating out a monotonous rhythm against his left thigh.

"Hi, Keith," boomed the doctor, as though Keith were deaf. In a quiet, confidential tone, he added, "Keith is a paranoid schizophrenic. He has been with us for three years. He used to be a musician. That's why he moves his hand that way. It's as if he's hearing an internal rhythm."

Yeah, thanks for that insight, Doc. Dominica went over to the stuff piled on the other bed. Not much here, just a few clothes, a backpack with a pair of running shoes inside, shampoo, Ian's electric razor, everything Louise had brought from the house the day after his commitment. She shoved the clothes into the pack, zipped it shut, slung it over her shoulder. She opened the nightstand drawer, picked up the Bible, flipped through it.

Some pages were heavily marked, but probably not by Ian. According to what she learned from Louise, Ian wasn't religious. On other pages, strips had been torn from the top or bottom. For what? Louise opened the drawer all the way, found a soft bristle hairbrush, but no books other than the Bible. Dominica, now in full control of Louise's body, aimed her toward the bathroom. She didn't resist.

Dominica looked around slowly, hoping that whatever she sensed would leap out at her. She checked the contents of the medicine cabinet—a container of Band-Aids, squares of gauze, bars of soap, folded washcloths, but nothing that could be used as a weapon. She popped open the lid on the Band-Aid container. It was stuffed with slips of paper. Dominica picked out one of them. Scrawled on it was: *I remember condors.*

"Shit." She selected another strip. *I remember brujos, greenhouses, Ed, Manuel, Illika, Juanito. I remember Tess.*

She read another and another. Some slips held only a single word. Others held several sentences. All were snapshots of what Ian had been remembering while he'd been here. She admired his fierce tenacity, true to the lightning-bolt shape of his body as he'd slept.

She shoved the Band-Aid container down inside her bag and turned to join Ray and the doctor. Keith stood in the doorway, hands planted firmly against the frame, blocking her way.

"What're you doing?" He cocked his head to the left and the left corner of his mouth swung upward. "It looks to me like you're snooping. Ian told me about you. About what you're like. You're his ex. Except that's not really who you are, is it."

Dominica craned her neck, trying to see into the room beyond him. But Keith was tall, with broad shoulders, and blocked most of her view. "Hey, Ray," she called.

"Oh, they stepped out into the hall. To talk privately. Dr. Parcell is concerned because your friend is a lawyer. The doc hates lawyers. I hate doctors, lawyers, just about everyone. I especially hate phonies. I think you're a phony. You're not Ian's ex-wife. You're"—his bright blue eyes narrowed—"something else."

So. A crazy could sense her.

He took a step toward her, his right hand now balled into a fist that he ground against the palm of his left hand. "I think you're one of those hungry ghosts he told me about. The Hungry Ghosts of Hope, that's what he called you." He slapped his fist against his palm now and took another step toward her. "You're Dominica. He told me that, too."

Don't fuck with me, Keith the paranoid schizoid.

"Those pieces of paper you found in the Band-Aid can? He forgot to take them. Didn't find a chance to come back to his room for his things, I guess." *Slap, grind,* went his fist. He moved closer. "I saw you reading them. That's wrong, to read what's private."

Dominica moved left, trying to get past him, but his right arm shot out, blocking her way. "Do not pass go. Do not collect two hundred bucks, Hungry Ghost of Hope." Keith grinned.

"You're not being very polite, Keith. Let me by."

"You're not being very forthright, ma'am, so stay the fuck back."

He was pissing her off. "You know about Tess?"

"Sure, I know about her." He pointed at the back of the toilet, where it fit into the floor. "I know about those, too. There's seventeen of them."

Her eyes followed his finger to the targeted spot, where she saw something stuck to the back of the toilet. "What're they for?"

"He used strips to count the days or pill cycles when he pretended to swallow his meds and didn't. I started doing that, too." His grin widened, the most singularly horrid smile she had ever seen, revealing teeth screaming for a good dentist, a smile that said, *Gotcha, you're fucked.*

Then he lunged for her, swinging his fists. Dominica sprang out of Louise and into Keith the wacko. The abruptness of it shocked her more than it did him. Compared to Louise, Keith's body was a garbage dump, a heaving, stinking mass of confusion, sickness, addictions. The drugs he had been fed the last three years acted on her like concrete poured over a leaf. She couldn't figure out how his body worked, so she couldn't fit herself into it in such a way that enabled her to breathe. His heart beat, but not for her. The body jerked and fought and tripped over its own feet and then it was falling and Dominica fell with it, fell as Louise Ritter Bell screamed and shrieked and stumbled back into the room and out of sight.

She was moments away from dying inside of Keith, dying the way only a *brujo* could die within a body it had seized. Annihilation, extinction, obliteration. *Gone*, no matter how you looked at it. She thrust an imaginary fist deeply into Keith's brain, and in the few seconds before he began to bleed out, she leaped again, back into Louise.

This time Louise fought and Dominica was weak and couldn't gain control of Louise's body. She rolled across the floor of the room, Dominica jumped out of her, then Louise slammed into the wall and went still. Dominica thrust her essence into Louise's motionless body, the ultimate invasion. She was lifting up on her elbows when Ray and Dr. Parcell ran into the room. Ray took one look at all the blood pooling under Keith's body, running across the floor, and slapped his hands over his nose and mouth.

"He . . . he attacked me," she stammered.

Ray made a beeline toward her. Louise was one of his best clients, so he did all the right things, arrived at all the right conclusions, and when the local cops showed up, he made it clear that Dr. Parcell was at fault for allowing her to be alone in the room of a mental patient. And that was what made it into the Minneapolis newspapers the next day, compassionate activist attacked by mental patient, who suffered a cerebral hemorrhage and died.

As one day melted into the next, Ian chopped wood and took long walks in the woods. He ate simple foods and drank gallons of water to flush the drugs from his body. He began to reclaim his spirit.

But in his darker hours, he obsessed about everything—his sanity, the career he was forfeiting, the life he would be leaving behind. The only thing he didn't obsess about was Luke and Casey. He continued to feel only relief and gratitude that they had found each other.

Luke had returned several days ago with supplies and news that the cops had visited him twice, questioning him about where he'd taken Ian. Luke had stuck to his story, that his father, armed with a knife, had forced him to drive him to the train station. Casey's name had not come up. Apparently the matter was as closed for Luke as it was for Ian. He just wanted to move forward, to Berkeley, where he would look for Sara Wells, his final confirmation.

From what he recalled, her last contact with family would be a call to her sister on May 16, 1969. He needed to see her, to know she was real—and, therefore, that all the rest of it was real, too, that he wasn't in a psych unit somewhere, hallucinating all of this.

Which was why he now was en route to town in the cabin's rusted old Renault. He intended to buy his ticket to California, via Duluth. Luke was due back to the cabin this evening and could drive him to the airport.

Ian turned onto yet another bumpy dirt road. The afternoon light feathered through the pines, creating strange, erratic shadow patterns in front of him. He felt a sudden urgency to get into town and back to the cabin before dark. It would be too easy to lose his way in these woods once the sun went down.

He emerged from the final stretch of pines, onto pavement and the main road through Hibbing. Named after its founder, a German iron ore prospector, the town was built on the rich iron ore of the Mesabi Iron Range. At its height in the early 1900s, it had a population of more than twenty thousand. Today, it hardly qualified as a bustling metropolis, but had a comfortable, friendly feel to it. Maybe a bit too friendly and comfortable, he thought, and was glad he looked like no one his ex-wife or anyone else would recognize. He had lost fifteen pounds in the last few months, was bearded, and wore a baseball cap, jeans, and a denim jacket and boots, not the kind of clothing that Louise associated with him. If anything, he looked like some backwoods Paul Bunyan.

He drove slowly up the main street, scanning the buildings for the travel agency he remembered. The glorious weather had lured people outside. They strolled the wide sidewalks, shopped, enjoyed late lunches beneath the trees. Ordinary life, he thought, and wasn't surprised that it no longer appealed to him. All he wanted to do was get the hell out of here to the next leg of his journey.

He nosed the Renault into a small parking lot and joined the flow of pedestrians. He felt uneasy among people, though, and was grateful to step inside the travel agency. Colorful posters of far-flung locales covered the walls. Rio, London, Istanbul. Only one woman was inside, a redhead in her early forties, he guessed, with a sprinkling of freckles across her pale cheeks. She reminded him of Casey.

She sat behind a desk strewn with travel brochures and booklets of flight schedules. "Afternoon," she said cheerfully. "What can I help you with, sir?"

He claimed a chair in front of her desk. "I'd like to book a flight for tomorrow from Duluth to San Francisco."

"We can certainly do that." She picked up one of the booklets, paged through it. "Ah, let's see here." She ran her fingernail up and down pages.

Ian remembered Tess telling him that in 2008, you could book your own flights through the Internet. Had that made travel agents and their agencies obsolete?

"There's a flight at eleven tomorrow morning from Duluth to San Francisco by way of Chicago."

"Perfect."

"How will you be paying for this, sir?"

"Cash."

"And your name?"

He used his mother's maiden name. "Ian Hawk."

According to Tess, air travel in 2008 was a bureaucratic nightmare. To even board a flight, the name on your ticket had to match the name on your I.D., you could be pulled out of line at random and body-searched, you couldn't have more than three ounces of certain kinds of liquids in your carry-on luggage. You also had to take off your shoes for some reason, but maybe she was kidding about that. He hoped so. From the little she had told him about air travel—and life—in her time, it sounded like the Bill of Rights had been shredded. He knew there were other rules and regulations, all of which had come about as a result of something that occurred in September 2001, but those rules were the only ones he remembered. So even though his time lacked the Internet, cell phones, laptops, Wi-Fi, and all the other technological wonders of the world forty years from now, some aspects about 1968 were vastly preferable.

As the travel agent booked his flight, a *feeling* burned across the pit of his stomach like a tongue of fire. He stood suddenly and strode over to the picture window. Outside, shadows lengthened against the road, there seemed to be more pedestrian and vehicular traffic. Commuters headed home, couples on their way to movies.

On the other side of the road, a large group gathered outside a television repair shop. Even as he stood there, the group swelled until it spilled off the curb and spread to the store windows on either side. People began to break off from the group, some of them shouting and waving others over.

"What's going on out there?" the travel agent asked.

"I don't know. They seem to be watching something on television. Do you have a TV?"

"Not in here. But I've got your ticket ready, Mr. Hawk."

"Great." He returned to the desk, she handed him the ticket and his change. "Thanks so much."

"You bet. Happy flying."

The burning sensation in his stomach abruptly worsened, he gasped, his vision blurred, and he nearly doubled over in pain. It didn't last long, twenty seconds at the most. But when his vision cleared, he saw Charlie Livingston in the back hallway, where the restrooms were. He gestured urgently toward the rear exit. "Get out of here now, Ian. King is dead."

King. What king? What the hell was Charlie talking about?

He hurried over to the picture window, where a black BMW pulled up to the curb across the street, slightly behind the gathering crowd on the other side of the road. Louise and her attorney, Ray Garthe, got out.

Except it wasn't Louise. Ian sensed the *bruja* inside of her, and if *he* could sense *her*, then she might be able to sense him, too. A state police car drew up behind them, a cop got out and joined them.

Louise gestured toward the crowd now gathered around the window, Garthe threw his arms out at his sides, as if in exasperation, and Ian turned to ask the travel agent if he could use the restroom. Just then, a teenage girl hurried in.

"Hey, you know what happened, Mom?" The girl rubbed her hands together to warm them. "Martin Luther King was assassinated."

It's true, it's all true. King, dead.

There was no hysteria in the girl's voice, no sadness, no regret, zero grasp of the implications. But, then, why should there be? Hibbing was predominately white, blue-collar. To them, King was just one of those rabble-rousing black dudes. He figured the reaction of his ex-wife would be pretty much the same—if she was cognizant of anything.

When mother and daughter went over to the window, Ian hastened away from them, to the back of the store where he'd seen Charlie, and out a rear door into an alley. He broke into a run, shoes slapping the cobblestones, and at the end of the alley turned right toward the main street, head down, mind racing, seizing and discarding options.

He paused at the end of the block, noting that the number of the curious and the puzzled had swelled. No blacks in the crowd, no one sobbing or protesting, but no one cheering, either. Just curiosity. Ian turned away from them and headed quickly toward the parking lot where he'd left the Renault.

Fortunately, the crowd was concentrated much farther down the main street, so he was able to drive out of the lot without running into an obstacle of cars or people. He took the first side street he reached and wended his way through several blue-collar neighborhoods, struggling to maintain the speed limit. His fear ratcheted upward another notch. Since a *brujo* had gotten to Louise, had one taken Luke, too? He had to be sure. But how?

The same way you were sure about Louise.

He made it back to the cabin by dusk, ran inside and gathered up his belongings—clothes, toiletries, Polaroid camera, extra film, the pages he'd written. He had made a carbon copy of his recollections and left that on the kitchen table. He put the typewriter into its carrying case, but the damn thing was so heavy he decided to leave it here, in the cabin. He wouldn't need it in Esperanza.

Ian left the lights on, so the spill of illumination through the windows would enable him to see the driveway and porch. He grabbed his pack and the shotgun, and raced back outside to the Renault. He tossed everything into the passenger seat and drove the Renault as deeply into the trees as he could take it. Headlights off. The engine ticked like an alien heart straining against the heavy tug of gravity.

Have to be sure. He got out and moved swiftly to the edge of the thicket, where he had an unobstructed view of the cabin.

Darkness settled in, the night came alive with the hum of animal life. Something large thrashed through the underbrush nearby, an alarming sound. Black bear? He stretched out on his stomach, shotgun tight in his hand, and seriously considered retreating to the Renault and fleeing. But the thrashing noises moved away from him. Pretty soon, he heard a car, moving toward him. Luke? Or someone else? Until he knew the truth about Luke, neither choice was good.

His son's Chevy roared into view, kicking up clouds of dust that drifted in the wash of the headlights, and behind it came Casey's VW Bug. Both cars screeched to a stop in front of the cabin. Luke leaped out of his car, shouting, "Dad, Dad, turn on the news! You were *right*, they offed King. But he was at the Artisan Hotel, not the Lorraine!"

Luke burst into the cabin, still shouting, and Casey scrambled out of her VW, racing after Luke.

Luke and Casey: possessed by *brujos*?

Ian remained motionless, clutching the shotgun, his mouth desert dry. And then it hit him. The Artisan Hotel, not the Lorraine. Had history been changed because Luke had warned the journalist who knew King? He might never know for sure, but it seemed to be a reasonable assumption. Did that mean Robert Kennedy's assassination couldn't be prevented, either?

"Dad?" Luke and Casey ran back outside and stood in the circle of light streaming through the windows, holding hands. Ian studied them, didn't feel anything unusual, and finally called, "Yeah, I'm here." He emerged from the trees, the shotgun cradled in the crook of his arm.

"Thank God," Casey burst out, but it was Luke who rushed over. "We thought . . . we didn't know what to think."

Ian held him tightly. "They got your mother, Luke. We need to leave. Immediately."

"*They?* Who?" The eerie light cast part of his face in shadow. "The *brujos?*"

"One *bruja*. Dominica."

"Jesus. How do you know?"

"I was in town. I saw Louise and sensed the thing inside of her. Louise arrived with that lawyer prick."

"Garthe, that makes sense. But how . . . how did she know you were near Hibbing?"

"I think that when a *brujo* seizes someone, it has access to that person's knowledge. Your mother must know you have a friend who owns a cabin near town."

"But—"

"It doesn't matter *how* she knows, Luke," Casey said. "It's enough that the *bruja* is six miles from here."

Casey got it, Ian thought. "Can you drive me to Duluth, Luke?"

"Now? Tonight?"

"We need to get out of here. I'm booked on a flight to San Francisco to-morrow."

"Okay, sure, Dad. Of course. Let me just grab my stuff." Then he frowned and gestured toward the shotgun. "Why're you clutching the shotgun?"

"Because . . . I thought they may have gotten to you, too." He looked at Casey. "And you."

Luke came over to them, slung one arm around Ian, the other around Casey, hugging them both fiercely, tightly. "Never," he whispered.

"Let's get a move on, guys," Casey said.

And only then did Ian truly believe that neither of them had been taken, and he wondered just what the hell he would have done if the opposite had been true. Would he have shot them? Luke pressed the Chevy's keys into Ian's hand. "Five minutes, Dad. Get the car going. Casey, you can leave your wheels here."

"Grab the carbon of the manuscript," Ian called after him, and tossed the shotgun into the front seat of the Chevy.

He backed up to the side of the car, the heels of his hands pressed over his eyes.

"Hey, Ritter." Casey ran her hand across the back of his neck. "It's okay. We'll get you to where you need to be. But don't be surprised if Luke and I follow you at some point."

Ian wrapped his arms around her, familiar Casey, his redemption and his salvation these last few years, both as a peer and a lover. "Casey, you and Luke, take care of each other."

Casey rocked back, nodding, tears glistening in her eyes. "We will." The lights in the cabin went off one by one, then Luke ran back outside. "Let's hit it."

Ian gave Casey's hand a final squeeze.

Ɗ𝗈𝗆𝗂𝗇𝗂𝖼𝖺 saw the crowd down the street, clustered outside one of the shops. She figured they were watching the coverage of King's assassination, which she'd heard about on the radio on her way up here. That meant today was April 6, 1968. Where had King gone? He definitely wasn't among the *brujos*. Anytime someone famous was headed their way, they knew about it. So where, then? The fact that she didn't have any definitive answer to that troubled her. She'd been asking the same question for centuries.

So where were the chasers? Why weren't they here, screwing up her plans, pushing against her like a force of nature? Maybe some higher power had seized the chasers. Ha. Wouldn't that be ironic? In the event she ever ran into a chaser, she had plenty of questions to ask and foremost among them was, *Who's pulling the strings? If not you guys, then who or what? And is this liberation group part of the chaser army?*

More to the point, though, was that she had overlooked the importance of today's date. But living the life of Louise Ritter Bell qualified as a major distraction. The woman had more dramas than Shakespeare, her appetites required full attention. Yet, when Dominica commanded her to shut up and crawl into her cave, she did. She understood the rules. And when Dominica had narrowed her information down to three towns, Louise had recommended that she go to Hibbing first. The family of Luke's best friend owned a cabin outside of town.

She checked out a restaurant and a bar, asking if anyone knew where the Trebelle family cabin was located. But if anyone did, they weren't saying.

Her third stop was a travel agency where two women, mother and daughter by the looks of them, appeared to have been arguing before she came in. As soon as the mother opened her mouth, Dominica knew Ian had been here, that he'd bought a ticket to somewhere. It was as if he had left an imprint in the air, like an odor, triggered by this woman's brief association with him.

She moved in close to the older woman, the mom. "I'd like to know if an Ian Ritter bought a ticket from you today."

"What?" The woman slipped off the desk where she had been sitting.

"Ian Ritter," Dominica repeated.

"I had an Ian, but not a Ritter. I think he was . . . wait a minute. Who're you?"

"His wife."

"Ian Ritter's wife?"

"Yes. But he may be traveling under another last name."

The teenage girl looked warily at Louise, perhaps sensing that she wasn't what she appeared to be, and whispered something to her mother. The mother nodded and said, "I'm not permitted to give out that kind of information."

"I would rather not bring my attorney or the police in on this, ma'am. Mr. Ritter is a fugitive." She gestured outside at the cop. "All I need is his destination."

"I'd like you to leave," the woman said.

"You give me no choice," Dominica said, and turned to open the door and call to Ray.

"Duluth to San Francisco," the woman said quickly. "Now get the hell out of here."

Dominica leaped out of Louise, back into the grayness of her own world. Louise stumbled, her hands flew to her face, and she started clawing at her skin and screaming, *"Help me, someone help me."*

She thought that Louise should be grateful that she hadn't been left bleeding out. But maybe gratitude was what Louise was here to figure out.

Dominica wished she knew what *she* was here to figure out. She took one last glance at Louise and drifted away.

Fourteen
BERKELEY, CALIFORNIA

The bus dropped Ian off at the south side of the Berkeley campus. He slung the strap of his small bag over his shoulder and stood in the bright, cool air, orienting himself to the map Luke had given him. Then he started walking up Telegraph Avenue, headed for the administration building six blocks north. If Sara Wells existed and was teaching here this semester, then he would find her.

After twenty-four hours of traveling, it felt wonderful to walk, to know that he was about to prove conclusively one way or another whether he was demented or sane. He needed just this final piece of evidence, to actually see someone from Esperanza. He didn't even have to talk to her. In fact, it probably was best if he didn't. If he meddled, if he introduced himself and tried to explain who he was, it might change something up the line. He couldn't risk that. Look what had changed just because Luke had spoken to the journalist who knew King—the location of the assassination had been changed. There might be some events so intrinsic to the unfolding history of the world that they couldn't be altered.

As he worked his way deeper onto campus, he passed throngs of students—those holding vigils for King, others who were war protesters, members of SDS posting signs about demonstrations this weekend against the war, Black Panthers with raised fists, shouting, "Black power." King's assassination might not have made any significant impact on life in Hibbing, Minnesota, he thought, but here in Berkeley it was part of the battle cry for ending the war.

He passed the student union building, music blasting from the open doors. The Beatles, a cut from their *Sergeant Pepper* album. Numerous posters were plastered to the windows, announcing events—an antiwar demonstration, a Janis Joplin concert, a poetry reading by James Dickey, an SDS rally. One poster featured Robert F. Kennedy and read: KEEP THE LEGACY ALIVE.

Have they assassinated Bobby yet? Bobby Kennedy? He leaves the planet on June 5, 1968, the Ambassador Hotel, L.A. Tess's words now haunted him.

Since she'd been right about King, she undoubtedly was right about RFK, too.

The lobby of the administration building was dominated by a round information booth manned by four students. No waiting lines. He went over and a pretty young woman asked what he needed.

"I've got an appointment with Professor Sara Wells. But she forgot to tell me her office number. She teaches cultural anthropology."

The woman flipped through pages on a clipboard, ran her finger down lists of names, shook her head. "I can't seem to find her, sir."

It stunned him. Deep down, he'd been convinced she was real, that she would be here. "Can you check again? W-e-l-l-s."

"She's social sciences," said a young man behind the desk. "But they've got some of those profs in the humanities building while they're renovating."

More flipping of pages, more lists, then: "Here she is." The young woman made a red *X* on a campus map, slipped it toward him. "Second floor, office thirteen."

Thirteen. He nearly laughed out loud. "Thanks very much."

Ian flew out of the building. He convinced himself that he would just knock on her door and ask if he could speak to her about the *brujos* of Ecuador. He would say he was a freelance journalist doing a travel piece on that country, and while he had been down there, he had heard about the legends of the *brujos*, had talked to locals who believed they were ghosts—hungry ghosts. Something along those lines.

But when he finally climbed the stairs to the second floor of the humanities building and was within seconds of knocking at her door, he suffered a crisis of confidence that nearly sent him screaming for the nearest exit. He flopped forward at the waist, so that blood flowed into his head, and just hung there, eyes squeezed shut, fingertips brushing the floor.

"Hey, are you all right?"

"Uh, yes, I just felt a little dizzy."

He rose up—and astonishment ripped through him. *Real, all of it real, it happened.* Sara Wells looked exactly as she would look forty years from now, a tall blonde, slender, pale and lovely, certainly not a day over thirty-five. So what Paco Faraday had told him was true—people in Esperanza didn't age. Her thick blond hair was cut shorter, in an attractive style that showed off the bold line of her jaw. She wore a touch of makeup, earrings and a matching necklace made of some lovely dark stone flecked with amber. Gone were the jeans and black turtleneck sweater he recalled; her blue print spring dress matched her eyes.

"You look really pale. My office is right here." She gestured toward her open office. "Why don't you sit inside and I'll get you some water."

"Thanks very much."

Ian shuffled inside, his bag bumping against his hip, trying to play the part of a man who moments ago had been on the verge of passing out. He sank into the nearest chair, set his bag on the floor. He felt the burning across the pit of his stomach and suddenly *knew* she was puzzled by how easily and readily she had invited him into her office and that on some level she sensed he was familiar to her.

While she filled a paper cup with water from the cooler, he noticed how she had decorated the office. Hanging on the wall across from him were framed posters from a Joan Baez concert and the Monterey Festival. Her framed degrees filled space in the middle of them, as though they were of secondary importance. A tall bookcase occupied the east wall, books neatly arranged. To his right were photographs of Ecuador—the shaded, labyrinthine mystery of Quito's streets, a Quechuan woman wrapped up in colorful blankets, cooking outdoors, and the volcano that overshadowed Esperanza. His heart seized up just looking at them.

"Were you up here looking for someone?" Sara handed him the cup of water.

Nodding, he emptied the cup. "For Professor Wells. I'm doing a travel article on Ecuador and I understand that she's one of the foremost experts on Ecuadorian mythology."

"I'm, uh, Professor Wells."

He acted surprised. "Fantastic. What a stroke of luck. I'm Ian Ritter."

Despite his certainty that he was familiar to her, her expression revealed nothing. "I'm only an expert in one small piece of Ecuadorian mythology, Mr. Ritter. But the entire culture and country fascinate me."

"What can you tell me about the widespread belief in mysterious *brujos* that travel in fog? Some people refer to them as *mala sangres*. During my travels there, I heard locals talking about them, about how they can possess people, but no one would discuss them with me. What can you tell me?"

Something shifted in her expression. "The *brujos* you're talking about, at least to my understanding, seem to be the Ecuadorian version of the bogeyman." She frowned and shook her index finger. "You've been a bad boy and the *brujos* are going to hear about it. Like that."

"Do you think there's any truth to the myth? That they might actually exist?"

"I don't know. In Esperanza, where the myth is most pervasive, the locals profess to believe in them. So I think it's fair to say the myth is alive for them. But I never saw any hard evidence that these creatures exist. As a cultural anthropologist, I'm more interested in the mythology."

"Suppose the myth is real? Suppose these *brujos* really *do* exist?"

She sort of smiled and cocked her head, eyes narrowing as if she were really seeing him for the first time. "It sounds as if you had an experience of some sort while you were there, Mr. Ritter."

He didn't know how much he should say, what he should admit. "Tell me. In your research, did you find any information about the mythology of the town itself?"

She sat behind her desk now, elbows propped on the surface, chin resting against her clasped fingers. "I'm not sure what you mean."

"Centuries ago, according to the myths I heard, Esperanza was a nonphysical place where transitional souls went to discover that death wasn't the annihilation of consciousness. The *brujos* loved it, because it meant they had a huge pool of souls they could seize. There was a great battle between a group of evolved souls and the *brujos,* who lost. That was when Esperanza became a physical place."

"What was this group of evolved souls who won the battle?"

"I heard them called *cazadores de luz.*"

"Light hunters. Or light chasers." Her smile softened her mouth. "Forgive me, Mr. Ritter. But it all sounds like the Ecuadorian version of *Paradise Lost.*" Her eyes searched his face for a moment, then she frowned. "You seem so familiar to me. Where do I know you from? I have this . . . this kind of half memory, of being in a room, crouched in front of you and telling you to *remember.* And there was a tall, blond woman with you." She laughed quickly, softly, as if with embarrassment. "And yet, I know I've never seen either of you before. Does any of that make sense to you?"

How could she remember events that lay forty years in their future? Einstein had stated that time was an illusion, that man perceived it as past, present, and future because it was the only way human beings could function. But Einstein hadn't addressed soul, that part of man that survived death, that seemed to be eternal. Suppose that soul consciousness, once it had experienced an event, was able to transcend the boundaries of time? To recall snippets of what, on a mundane level, hadn't happened yet?

"Do you have some free time?" he asked. "For brunch?"

She glanced at the clock on the wall. "Three hours until my next class. I know just the place."

"By the way, if you apply for a Fulbright, to study the *brujo* myth, you'll get it."

She was on her feet then, purse in one hand, keys in the other, and her eyes widened. "How . . . I mean, yes, I, uh, *have* applied. But I won't hear for months."

"In May of next year, you call your sister from Quito. It's the last time anyone hears from you. Because you won the Fulbright, left for Ecuador, and took up residence permanently in Esperanza."

Her eyes held his for a long, uncomfortable moment. "How do you know I have a sister?"

"I read about you on the Internet, in the Incan Café in Esperanza, in 2008, when I was in a coma in 1968."

Her expression was as inscrutable as a fortune cookie. It wouldn't surprise him if she suddenly picked up the phone and called security. Instead, she threw her head back and laughed. "You know what's weird? I believe you, Mr. Ritter."

Over lunch at a waterside café in a beautiful and scenic spot on the bay, he told her everything, A to Z. He even showed her copies of his medical records that Luke had obtained before he'd left Minnesota, records from the hospital, the nuthouse. She combed through them, mostly silent, occasionally commenting or asking a question.

"Do you know the way to Esperanza?" she asked finally.

"Take a plane to Quito. Beyond that, I don't have a clue. What about you?"

"I've been there only once, two years ago. And I don't know how I got there. I had taken what I thought was a bus headed to Otavalo. But the bus ended up at—"

"The Bodega del Cielo?"

Stunned, she stammered, "This is . . . beyond weird."

"Were you alive? Conscious?"

"Alive and kicking."

"Who drove your bus?" he asked.

She stared out over the sunlit water of the bay, Alcatraz a vague shape in the distance. "A tall man with thick black hair. His name was odd. Wayra, I think that was it."

He recalled the name, but no face or person was connected to it. Still, it smacked of deliberate design. But whose design?

"Tell me about this Ed Granger," she said. "He was an Aussie?"

"Who ran the posada." Ian described what he recalled about the place and the people, naming names that included the animals. Nomad, Kali, Whiskers.

For the longest time, she didn't say anything. She stabbed at the bits of salad on her plate, dipped her spoon into her soup. Finally, she said, "I think you and I should head to Esperanza as soon as possible, Ian."

Where was Charlie when Ian needed him? "No. It has to remain like it would have been if we'd never met."

Her mouth went as flat as a dash. "I can't wait that long."

"Look, two weeks ago, I told my son that Martin Luther King would be assassinated on April 6, at the Lorraine Hotel in Memphis. He knows a guy who interviewed King and told him to make sure King wasn't anywhere near the Lorraine on that date. I think that as a result of that warning, King moved his operation to the Artisan Hotel. That warning changed some small part of history. It'd be a mistake for us to change the timelines of events. Neither of us can risk it."

She leaned across the table, eyes darkening with some powerful emotion. "I'm the captain of my own ship, Ian. If I choose to go now, then I will. If I choose to go later, then I'll do that. I don't need you or anyone else to tell me when or how."

"You're right." He dropped a five on the table to cover lunch, then picked up his bag and pushed to his feet. "I had no right to say any of this. I appreciate your time, Sara. I'll grab a cab back to my hotel."

"Wait, where're you staying?" she asked.

"In San Francisco." He moved quickly past her and was getting into one of the waiting cabs outside the restaurant when she barreled through the front door, shouting his name.

"Step on it," he said to the driver.

"Where to?"

"Hotel Drisco."

Half an hour later, the driver let him out in front of a two-story hotel high on a hill at the corner of Pacific Avenue and Broderick Street. He had gotten the name from a magazine article on one of his flights. Breathtaking views of the bay fell away on either side of him, sky and water melting seamlessly together on his right, Alcatraz Island visible on his left, but not for long. A fog moved toward the island. He suddenly wondered if *brujos* could travel in *this* fog. A cold tongue licked its way up his spine. Ian shivered and hurried into the hotel.

His room faced the bay and he threw open the windows to the glorious view. He could see Alcatraz from here, the fog rising, rolling, starting to wrap around the base of the island. It probably was regular fog, not *brujo* fog, but it spooked him nonetheless.

Ian backed away from the window and sat down at the edge of the bed. He rummaged through his suitcase, appalled that he had fled with such a small bag and only two changes of clothes. He would have to shop before he left here. But first . . . He got out his BankAmericard, dialed for an outside line, then 0 for operator, and got the numbers he needed. His first call was to Pan Am to book the next available flight from San Francisco to Quito. There was a flight at nine this evening, which would get him into Quito at eight tomorrow morning. Two stops, Houston and Caracas. He booked it and could pick up the ticket at the airport.

His next calls were to the *Miami Herald*, *Fort Lauderdale Sun Sentinel*, and the *Palm Beach Post*, where he placed ads in large bold type, in the classified personals, that were to run daily for the next two weeks. *Slim, it's real. Am leaving 4/8/1968, Frisco—Quito. Love, Ian Ritter from Minneapolis.*

The ads cost him a small fortune, but he'd left money in his account at home for Luke to pay off any outstanding bills. Ian would call him later and let him know. For now, he needed to buy a larger bag, more clothes, good hiking shoes, and then settle his bill here.

As he got up, he took another look out the window. The advancing fog had completely obscured Alcatraz and seemed to be moving toward the mainland now. *Doesn't mean anything.* But he quickly shut and locked the windows, his mouth bone-dry.

D o m i n i c a loved San Francisco in any era, any time. Aside from the obvious beauty of the city, it was the fog that spoke to her most deeply.

The fog here was the loveliest and most complex she'd ever encountered outside of Ecuador. It was easily manipulated, sculpted and molded, and could be used in the same way they used it at home. Since it was so common in San Francisco and not associated with anything dangerous or evil, as it was in Esperanza, people wouldn't think to take shelter from it until it was too late.

She knew that Ian Ritter was here, but couldn't get a precise fix on him, so she thrust her arms upward, like Moses parting the Red Sea, and summoned a legion of her kind. *Come and feast! Ben, you're needed. Lead them here.*

She didn't know if the restrictions she'd encountered about seizing people violently would hold for a mass of *brujos* descending on the city, but suspected she was about to find out. Who or what had imposed these rules? In the years she'd commanded this tribe, the only time she had summoned them like this was when she and Ben had returned to the Esperanza area twenty years ago to erect their home base in the twin peaks. Within minutes, the dark fog began to gather well off the mainland, growing larger and thicker as the *brujos* congregated, as if they had been waiting to be summoned.

Then the fog tumbled across the surface of the water, gathering speed and mass, and quickly enveloped Alcatraz Island. The place was closed, it wasn't a tourist site yet, but there were many bodies to choose from—National Park employees, construction workers, the crew of a boat that ferried employees back and forth between the island and the mainland. The *brujos* seized and feasted, proving that en masse, her kind could negate the stupid restrictions. Others, like Dominica and Ben, didn't take bodies. They fed on the stark terror and horror of those who were seized.

I like it here, Ben thought. *But we're powerless outside Esperanza.*

No. Even if we can't assume forms, we can certainly create terror. And maybe find and kill Ian Ritter in the process. Any news yet?

We have a lead on Tess. And Pearl and Rafael are working on a couple of priests who seem to be on the inside loop of the liberation group.

Progress. A sign the tide was turning.

Suppose we don't find him, Nica? Or kill him? There's growing sentiment in the tribe that we need to act defensively now, against the liberation group. They're our biggest threat. Not the chasers.

She bristled. *As long as I lead this tribe, Ben, we do it my way. We kill the transitionals first.*

She felt the intensity of his scrutiny, then he turned away from her, toward the fog, now advancing onto the mainland. Dominica suddenly felt that Ben was no longer her ally. It frightened her. She wanted to rush after him, to insist they seize bodies, use them up in a wild frenzy of sex and desire. But already, he was too distant from her, and the madness of the *brujo* frenzy was washing over her.

Am I wrong? Were her priorities misplaced?

Her people seized fishermen, tourists, waiters and waitresses, cops, businessmen, hippies, teachers, students. Up the hills the dark fog rolled, thickening, expanding in width and height until it swallowed cars, cafés, shops, restaurants, and climbed high into the trees. Her tribe was drawn by the promise of bedlam just ahead, where crowds of war protesters shouted and pounded their fists against the air, their voices ringing out through the streets.

With any luck, Ian Ritter would be trampled and killed in this attack.

Ian started downhill on foot, headed for a clothing store where he could buttress his meager wardrobe and buy a new suitcase. Every building he passed boasted ceramic flower pots exploding with colorful flowers— bougainvilleas, pansies, roses, daffodils. Like outside the posada, he thought. Music drifted from open windows. The Presidio stretched before him, a military base that looked like a vast, verdant park stretching all the way to the shores of the bay. Even from here, he could see several hundred war protesters marching and chanting outside the gates, their voices echoing through the clear afternoon air. *Bring 'em home, bring 'em home.*

As he neared the bottom of the hill, thousands more protesters spilled down Presidio Avenue, block after block, wave after wave, clear to the bay. Cops in riot gear stood on either side of the road, ready to move in if the swelling group became violent. The sidewalk was still open, pedestrians hurrying along behind the line of cops. Ian hesitated, reluctant to get caught in the crossfire.

He studied the map of Pacific Heights that the hotel employee had given him. The store was just four blocks from here, on California Street. He debated turning back to take Divisadero Street to California, but the protesters might occupy that road, too. So he hurried forward, hands in the pockets of his jacket, measuring the mood of the crowd. At the first sign of hostility, he would dart into one of the shops.

He walked fast, the chants and shouts rising and falling around him, each wave louder, angrier, more hostile. Then the mob surged toward the cops, pelting them with eggs and rocks and screaming, *Death to the pigs!*

The cops retaliated, a crushing tsunami of swinging batons that cracked heads, faces, arms, and drove protestors to the ground. Tear gas thickened in the air. Ian tore up the sidewalk, but hordes of people suddenly scrambled for safety and shoved their way toward the shops, diving for cover under the tables and benches, hurling chairs at the cops. The injured stumbled through the throngs, sobbing for help, blood streaming down their faces. Two women got knocked to the ground and were trampled by the mob behind them. Ian helped one man to his feet and jerked him toward the door of a coffee shop where a woman gestured frantically for people to take refuge inside. They lurched inside the building, the woman slammed the door, and urged them all to the back, where people were streaming out the rear exit, into an alley.

Ian hurried toward the promise of sunlight and escape and stumbled into the alley with several dozen frantic, terrified people. He tore right, racing along with the crowd, and abruptly stopped at the end of the alley. He knew what he was seeing, and his brain kept yelling, *Run, run,* but he couldn't run. The fog hadn't just rolled inland. It now climbed the hills, moving toward them with shocking swiftness, thick, dark, at least half a mile wide. Already, he could hear an eerie chant rising from the fog, *Find the body, fuel the body, fill the body, be the body,* and he was suddenly back in Esperanza, the chant crashing over him.

He tore in the opposite direction, pounding the pavement, arms tucked in tightly at his sides. The fog tumbled through the alley behind him, chants rising and falling. *Find the body, fuel the body* . . . Tear gas now mixed with the fog and people ran with their arms covering their mouths and noses. Some of them now twitched, bodies jerking this way and that, as *brujos* seized them. Ian had no idea how this nightmare had found him, but he wasn't about to be seized. He ran faster, faster, breath exploding from his mouth, and burst out of the alley.

Sirens sundered the air. Police wearing gas masks seemed to be everywhere, leaping out of patrol cars, swinging batons, galloping into the crowd on horses, herding curious spectators to stay back, move aside. He tore up the hill with crowds fleeing the pandemonium on Presidio. His lungs strained, sweat poured down his face.

The fog moved uphill, but at a slower pace, as if the *brujos* were so busy feeding off the bedlam around them they didn't wanted to stray too far from the mob. *Fill the body, be the body* . . . He didn't slow, didn't look back again. At the top of the hill, Ian nearly doubled over from pain, gasped for breath. The hotel doorman trotted down the steps and helped him into the lobby, to a chair.

"Sir, sit tight. I'll get you something cold to drink."

Ian couldn't speak, his chest heaved. The doorman returned with a tall glass of ice-cold water. Ian raised it to his mouth, hands shaking violently. He sipped, eyes darting toward the door, terrified he would see the fog pressing up against it, tendrils clawing at the glass like some rabid dog that wanted in. Instead, people ran past, cop cars raced down Pacific.

"What's happening down there?" the doorman asked. "We heard the cops moved in on the protestors and it's a bloodbath. And the fog . . . never seen nothing like it."

"Thank you for the water. I'd like to settle my bill, get to the airport. I'll need a cab."

"Yes, sir. I'll take care of it."

He didn't know how many minutes passed. He finished the water and glanced anxiously toward the door again. Then the doorman brought over the bill and his puny bag. His clothes buying would have to wait until he got to Ecuador. Ian dug out his wallet and gave the doorman cash for the room and a generous tip.

"Your cab's on the way, sir. There's some weird stuff going on down there, that's what we're hearing now," the doorman said in a soft, confidential tone. "Like, people acting really strangely, having seizures or something. Fires have been set. Ambulances and fire trucks are on the way. Some of the roads are blocked off."

"Will I be able to get to the airport?"

"For now, the road to the airport is clear."

Fifteen minutes later, Ian stood at the hotel door, watching fire trucks and ambulances roar past, sirens shrieking. Crowds continued to pour across the sidewalks, desperate to put distance between themselves and the mayhem at the bottom of the hill. Several times, people tried to enter the hotel, but the doors were locked.

The fog's advance appeared to have slowed or maybe even stopped somewhere below. When a taxi parked at the curb, Ian swept up his bag, the doorman opened the door, and he hastened out. As the cab pulled away from the curb, the driver, a slightly built Asian man, said, "War protesters are setting buildings on fire down there, people are having convulsions, dozens injured and killed."

"Can we get to the airport?"

"Don't worry." He shook his head. "This is about the war. People know it's wrong, they want it to end. The war's to blame."

The war for souls. Ian leaned forward, vigilant, alert for any sign of fog. As they reached the top of a hill, fog climbed toward them from a hill to his left, and people were racing away from it, hollering, terrified. The cabbie hit the left blinker. "Go right," Ian said urgently. "Do whatever you have to do to stay away from the fog."

"But the airport is to the left and—"

"Go right," Ian shouted. "Fast."

The cabbie hung a right, stepped on it, and the cab sped forward, careened onto another street, tore down another hill, screeched into yet another turn, weaving back and forth on one-way streets until they seemed to have broken free of the area the fog covered. Minutes later, signs for the airport appeared.

Would the fog turn toward the airport, socking it in so that flights were delayed or canceled? He didn't know. But he hoped the *brujos* were like ticks bloated with blood, rendered useless once their appetites were sated.

The cab drew up in front of the airport and Ian handed the cabbie a huge tip. "For your own safety, avoid the fog on your way back."

Ian scrambled out of the cab with his pack and sprinted into the terminal.

Tess Livingston

2008

. . . .

We will first understand how simple the universe is when we recognize how strange it is.

—John Wheeler

Fifteen

The wind chimes that hung in the trees outside her mother's kitchen were made of pipes and seashells, aluminum, copper, glass. They sang and gonged in the sunrise breeze like high mass rituals in the Sistine Chapel, calling birds to the feeders. Flocks of crows and blue jays, wrens, blackbirds and doves, even wild green parrots fluttered and squawked and jockeyed for spots at the feeders. They brushed the wind chimes, changing the tempo until the yard sounded like an amateur band tuning up. Tess didn't see a single hummingbird among them and felt immeasurably depressed by their absence.

Ridiculous. Tess couldn't recall ever seeing a hummingbird in the Florida Keys or anywhere in South Florida.

Her own reflection in the window stared back at her. *I'm still me.* Eyes a smoky blue. Hair long, blond, wavy. A mouth that could yet smile. When she had died five months ago today, her inner landscape had changed dramatically, but she didn't see it yet in the way she looked. This seemed important.

Pipes clattered somewhere. Her mother or niece were up and she wished she could have an hour more alone. She immediately felt guilty about thinking that way. Her mother had been at the hospital constantly since Tess had been shot back in January. While she'd been in a coma, her mother had moved her to the hospital here in Key Largo where she was director of nursing. The move probably had saved Tess's life. When she'd awakened from the coma, the faces of her mother and eighteen-year-old niece, Madison, were the first she saw.

In the six weeks since Tess's release from the hospital, her mother and Maddie had been her most intimate support group. They had cared for her, driven her to physical therapy, cooked and shopped for her, been there when no one else was. Since the house sat on concrete pilings that elevated it twenty feet off the ground, they had had a wooden ramp built that had enabled her to navigate her wheelchair into and out of the house. Her mom and Maddie even sorted the mounting tally of medical bills, now into seven figures. If Tess's health insurance covered sixty percent of that, she would still owe enough to make her an indentured servant to the FBI for the next twenty years.

She slid the window open and the June humidity, thick with the scent of ocean and earth, enveloped her. On either side of the window, the edges of the aluminum hurricane shutters were visible. The entire house could be shuttered in about ten minutes, but there were two skylights—one here in the kitchen and another in the living room—without protection. Tess shut the window and turned, staring up at the kitchen skylight, suddenly worried that *something* would get into the house through there.

Absurd. Even though hurricane season had started June 1, the National Hurricane Center had declared that the Atlantic basin was quiet. Besides, the skylights were built to Hurricane Andrew standards, able to withstand category five winds. But could they withstand—*what*? She felt the weight of the word at the tip of her tongue, then it slipped away. This kind of thing had been happening to her often since she'd regained consciousness. She wouldn't be sharing that detail with the Bureau shrink she was supposed to meet with today, who would determine whether she was mentally healthy enough to return to work.

The bullet that had turned her life inside out had pierced an artery in her right thigh and she nearly had bled to death before she made it to ER. During emergency surgery, she had flatlined. She still didn't know how long she'd been dead. Not that it mattered. Nothing had happened—no tunnel of light, no celestial choirs, no reunions with the departed.

The femur bone in her right thigh had required steel pins and rods to restore. She now had so much metal in her leg that in an airport screening she probably would trigger alarms. Her limp remained noticeable, but improved daily. In fact, she felt better today than she had in weeks, and was sure that daily yoga helped, her compensation for physical therapy since her insurance coverage had run out. All she needed to return to work was a clean bill of *mental* health.

She wasn't entirely sure that she wanted to return to the Bureau, but her leave was nearly used up and she needed the income. Her boss had assured her she was first in line for any Bureau position that opened in the Keys, but such openings were rare. The Keys were a coveted location, more laid-back, less bureaucratic bullshit. But until or if it happened, she would commute to Miami, two hours round trip if she didn't drive at peak hours. Even though the prospect didn't thrill her, what with the price of gas as high as it was, she had no great desire to move back to Miami. Couldn't afford it, given all her bills. The town house she'd rented for seven years was now occupied by someone else and her mother had moved most of her belongings to storage.

"Hey, Tesso. What's up?" Maddie strode into the kitchen dressed in her tank top and running shorts, carrying her shoes in her hand.

"Too early for much to be up. Where're you running?"

"The beach. Two miles round trip. Want to come?"

Maddie reminded Tess of a frisky colt, all legs, with a lovely mane of thick red hair that came from her father's side of the family. The rest of her was pure Livingston—dancing blue eyes, a mouth that perfectly reflected her moods, high cheekbones. Her pale complexion wasn't genetic, she worked at it. No sunbathing. Many creams and sunblocks. A Nicole Kidman in the making. She was a fussy eater, too, a true vegan who ate only raw fruits, vegetables, tofu. A ruby stud flashed from her left nostril.

"You'd lose me after three yards," Tess said.

"You're underestimating yourself." Maddie dropped her shoes, popped open the fridge, poured herself a tall glass of OJ. "You know how I was a year ago. I could barely walk thirty yards without getting winded. I was just your local fat girl, headed toward diabetes, reviled by fellow students, a laughingstock. If I can do it, so can you."

A year ago, Madison wasn't just the local fat girl. She had been living in North Carolina with her mother, Tess's older sister, and her new husband, a man Maddie detested. She was nearly flunking out of school, had been arrested twice, was on a fast track to nowhere. So when Tess's sister had called and asked their mother if she would take Madison for a few months, as though she were a stray desperately in need of a home, Lauren Livingston had driven to North Carolina and picked her up.

Madison took to the Keys the way a frog took to insects. Hungry for change, she had turned her life around and graduated from high school in December, six months earlier than her peers. She recently finished her first semester at the junior college and had been accepted to the University of Florida for the fall. The software company she and a friend had developed would be paying her bills. She wanted to be a vet.

"Okay, get Lauren and I'll give it a shot."

"I appreciate the fact that no one referred to me as 'Nana,' a word I've always detested." Tess's mother stood in the doorway, already decked out in her running clothes, her short, thick hair brushed back dramatically, a salt-and-pepper lion's mane. Her sinewy body, as slender and compact as a shoot of bamboo, looked like that of a woman of forty. Daily runs, yoga, a moderate diet. She probably would outlive them all. She threw her arms out dramatically. "Now, I ask you, does Lauren Livingston look sixty-three?"

The chorus was unanimous. "No way!"

"You both will live to see another day. Now let's get on with this run, ladies."

The beach on which Tess's mother lived was not really a beach in the way most people thought of Florida beaches. No endless white sands, just endless mounds of rocks, shells, seaweed. They ran at the water's edge and every quarter of a mile crossed a dock that thrust out into the water, a boat of some kind tethered to it. After crossing one too many docks, Tess slowed to a walk and her mother fell into step beside her.

"You want company today, Slim?"

Slim. How odd that her mother would refer to her by the nickname her dad always had used. Slim, from one of her favorite Bogie and Bacall movies, *Dark Passage.* The nickname made her uncomfortable, as though it carried an association that Tess couldn't recall.

The question was a tactful way for her mother to ask if Tess needed emotional support for her appointment with the shrink. Oddly, it hadn't occurred to her. Most of the time, she felt emotionally absent, as though her heart had been carved up and tossed to wolves. She didn't say that to her mother, though. Lauren Livingston, ex-hippie, connoisseur of the best of the mind-altering drugs of the sixties, acid-tripping companion of Terrence McKenna in the summer of love, was now a mainstream nurse and might read something into those words. *Emotionally absent.* It sounded dangerous, like the description for a serial killer. But Tess knew something was missing inside. It was as if huge chunks of herself had gotten lost when she had flatlined.

"I'm fine, Mom. I've been driving for two weeks."

"To and from yoga and the grocery store is a little different than a drive to Miami."

"My leg took a hit, not my head."

"You know what I mean."

"I'm good, Mom. Really. Everyone treats me like I suffered brain trauma."

"Well, you *did* flatline. I was talking to Doc about the kinds of questions the shrink might ask, and he felt pretty certain the flatline would come up."

Tess disliked the idea of her mother discussing her with Doc Brian, her mother's intermittent lover. "How would he know?"

"His background is psychiatric ER, that's how. Possible brain trauma enters the equation. Do you remember anything from when you were in a coma or dead?"

Tess had lost count of how many times her mother had asked this question. Her answer never changed. "Nope. There isn't anything, Mom. I died, that's it. Then I started breathing again and my molecules swam back together and here I am." Tess stooped down and swept up a piece of driftwood. She ran her fingers over the smooth bark, studying the swirls of patterns, spirals within spirals. The driftwood was more interesting than death, she thought.

"That sounds cynical, hon."

"Yeah, I guess it is. But death isn't an acid trip, Mom."

"I'll be sure to include that in my book about McKenna and Kesey and the gang."

Her mother's wild youth in the sixties.

Ahead of them, Madison stopped, hands on her hips. "Cheaters," she shouted. "No walking allowed."

"I can't believe my own granddaughter is calling me a cheater," Lauren said.

Tess smiled as her mother jogged on.

Tess's Mazda 3 purred north on U.S. 1, headed toward the campus where Maddie and her software partner would be testing their newest product on a student focus group. Maddie fiddled with her hair, put on peace symbol earrings. "Lauren's convinced something happened to you when you died, Tesso."

"Why?"

"Probably because she's been reading all these books about near-death experiences, Buddhism, reincarnation. Why does Lauren ask any of these questions? It's just how she is."

"Nothing happened to me. Or if it did, I can't remember it."

"You're different now. You know that, right?"

"I am? How?"

"You really listen."

"I didn't before?"

"Not like now. When I say something to you now, I know you're really hearing me. And there're other things, like what you eat. You used to eat red meat, a lot of junk food, and drank tons of soda. You haven't touched any of that since you woke up. You never took vitamins or practiced yoga. Then there's Dan. Before you got shot, you were talking about moving in with him. Now you avoid his calls. You're not the same person. And I think I like this Tess better."

"So before I was Cruella De Vil. Now I'm Mother Teresa?"

Maddie snickered.

"Okay, scratch the Mother Teresa reference."

"You're just different, Tesso. From the instant you came out of that coma, there was something in your eyes that said everything had changed."

Really? From the moment she had returned to the world, her dominant emotion was deep appreciation that she was alive.

She pulled up in front of the main building on campus and her niece swung her long legs out the door and pointed her index finger and thumb at Tess, like a gun. "Go show that shrink how Tesso rocks. I'll get a ride home."

The drive to Miami was fine for the first forty minutes, relaxing, slow, minimal traffic. Not many tourists in June. She stopped twice to snap pictures of wading birds that filled the shoals where the waves had receded. She counted six osprey nests, better than she expected, and caught sight of a pod of dolphins working their way out to sea.

A part of her desperately craved to lie low here in the Keys, to find a simpler, more satisfying life—tour guide, clerk, lifeguard, fisherwoman, dolphin trainer. The pay would suck, but so what? Let the hospital sue her. Let the insurance bastards come after her. Let the IRS garnish her wages. She didn't own anything that could possibly make a dent in her medical bills.

But she couldn't just shirk all responsibility. Even if she didn't want to continue investigating homicides and drug deals and partnering with Dan Hernandez, her other options were limited. Private practice as a defense attorney with a firm in Miami or working for the Florida state attorney's office. Neither appealed to her.

As U.S. 1 melted into the turnpike, traffic swelled and moved more quickly. She sat up straighter, both hands gripping the wheel as though she were some decrepit old woman with vision and reflex issues. Cars cut her off, whizzed past her, squeezed her out. Suddenly, it all came to a grinding, screeching conflagration of metal against metal, tires shrieking against hot pavement, glass shattering.

Tess swerved to the shoulder to avoid crashing into the car in front of her. She slammed on the brakes, the engine died, ticking impotently in the silence. For moments she gripped the steering wheel, heart hammering, eyes glued to the sunlit chaos in front of her. Three cars lay on their sides in a twisted, smoking heap of metal and broken glass, a fourth car lay on its roof in the grassy gulley that separated the north and south lanes. An SUV stood in the middle of the road, the driver's door smashed in, windows shattered, tires flat, gnarled front fender on the ground in front of it.

Tess scrambled from her car, punched out 911 on her cell, spat out her approximate location to the emergency operator. "Five car pileup, north-bound lane, definite injuries."

Even as she said this, a teenage girl stumbled from the SUV, shrieking and sobbing, *"My mom, someone help my mom, please, oh God, help my mom . . . "* Blood streamed down her face, she clutched her bloody left arm, and weaved toward the driver's door and struggled to open it.

"I'll get your mom," Tess said gently, touching the girl's shoulder. "But I'd like you to go sit down by the side of the road. An ambulance is on the way."

"I'm a doctor," said a man who hurried over, medical bag hanging from his shoulder, and immediately took charge of the girl.

Other people came forward to help and Tess suddenly found herself in charge. Two off-duty firemen with paramedical experience helped remove a child from the overturned car in the gulley, several women rescued injured children wandering around, a skinny guy in stained coveralls had tools to pry open crumpled doors and went to work on the SUV.

As soon as the door fell off, Tess got a close look at the woman inside, trapped against the seat by the airbag. She nearly vomited, the man beside her wrenched back. Large pieces of glass and metal protruded from the woman's shoulder, arrows of glass stuck out of her right eyebrow, the left side of her face was torn open from her chin to her ear. Barely conscious, she somehow turned her head slightly, terrified eyes begging Tess to help her.

"Can't . . . feel my legs," she murmured. "My . . . daughter . . . where?"

"She's fine," Tess told her. "She got out. And we're going to get you out of here." To the man, she said, "You have a knife that will puncture the airbag?"

"Right here."

Tess slipped her arm around the woman's chest so she wouldn't flop forward as the air rushed from the bag. The pressure eased, the woman sobbed, then passed out. The man said he'd get the doctor and sprinted off.

The airbag puddled in a bloody heap across the woman's thighs, Tess's hands and arms were slick with her blood, her clothes were stained with it. The stink of impending death suffused her nostrils. "You hold on, okay? The doc's on the way, your daughter is fine, the—"

Suddenly, the woman was standing next to Tess, khaki Capri pants and turquoise blouse no longer torn and bloody, her pretty face clean, dark hair brushed back behind her ears. "It looks bad," she said with strange detachment. "Do you think I'll make it?"

Jesus, she's a ghost. Yet, Tess felt the woman's heart beating beneath her hands. So she wasn't dead, just . . . out of her body. "Do you want to make it?"

The woman stared at her bleeding body. "I think my back is broken," the woman said finally. "That's why I can't feel my legs. I don't want to be a burden to my husband and daughter. But . . . I'm . . . afraid to die."

It's real. She hears me, I hear her. "Is that fear greater than your fear of pain?"

"I don't know. But suppose there isn't anything after death?"

Something stirred within Tess that she knew she should explore. She sensed it was connected to her disappointment about the lack of hummingbirds in her mother's yard, her ambivalence about the Bureau, to the emotional vacuum she'd experienced since emerging from a coma six weeks ago. "Death might be even grander than any of us imagine," Tess said. "But I think the decision about staying or moving on is up to each of us."

The doctor appeared, Tess moved aside. The woman's spirit was gone. Tess glanced quickly around, but didn't see her anywhere. She heard sirens now, closing in, and ran toward the three tangled cars.

Several men struggled to open doors crushed like tin cans. The off-duty firemen turned fire extinguishers on the thickening gray smoke that rose from the hoods of the cars. The air stank of fire, scorched metal, blood, death. The hot sunlight that beat down against the pavement exacerbated the stench. Tess's growing nausea prompted her to move to the shoulder of the road, where she could breathe more easily. Here, the injured were being tended to by the doctor or his surrogates, who had set up a makeshift first-aid center that looked to be well supplied now with bottled water, blankets, rudimentary treatments.

Tess's cell rang, and when she answered it, the woman on the other end said, "This is Dr. Yates's office. May I speak to Tess Livingston, please?"

Yates, who the hell was Yates? "Speaking."

"You had an appointment with Dr. Yates today at noon?"

Shit. Her ticket back to work. "There was a five-car pileup on the turnpike and traffic is blocked for miles. May I reschedule for later today?"

She was transferred to the netherworld of hold. Tess squeezed the bridge of her nose and turned toward the tall, lovely pines that blanketed the land beyond the road. A young boy and a dog stood in the shadows, watching the chaos. The boy was eight or nine, his hand rested on the back of a collie Neither the boy nor the dog showed any obvious signs of blood or trauma, but their bodies vacillated between solidity and a transparency that allowed her to see through them, into the woods.

Christ. Tess moved toward them with the cell still pressed to her ear. The receptionist returned. "Ms. Livingston, the doctor said she'll be here till six this evening and we'll get you in whenever you arrive."

"Thanks, I appreciate it." Tess slipped her cell down into the back pocket of her jeans, her gaze never straying from the boy and dog. When she reached them, the kid regarded her with a kind of implacable interest, like an employer sizing her up for a job.

"Wow, I love collies," Tess said, and held out her hand so the dog could sniff it. She felt the warmth of the dog's breath. If she tried to stroke the collie, would her hand slip through the dog's body? "What's her name?"

"Jessie. And I'm Josh. Do you know where my mom is?"

"Which car were you in?"

"That . . . silver VW."

One of the three in the tangled heap. "I'm sure she's okay. How do you and Jessie feel?"

"We're okay now. But before, when we were in the car, I was hurting a lot right here." He brought his hand to his chest. "And I think Jess was hurting all over."

A woman ran toward Josh and the dog, flung her arms around them. Then she looked at Tess, eyes bright with tears. "What happens now?"

I'm not sure. "I, uh, think you have a choice. You can return to your bodies or you can move on."

The woman gestured out at the road, where paramedics now removed bodies from the wrecked cars. "Our bodies are beyond repair."

"We just want to be together," Josh said.

Tess had no idea what to say, what to advise. It wasn't like she could call someone to ask what these three spirits should do to get to wherever they were going. "If I were you, I'd walk down into the trees, away from this ugliness out here, and ask for help from anyone you know who has passed on."

The woman tightened her hold on her son's hand, combed her fingers through Jessie's fur. "That sounds like a really good idea. Thank you so much. Ready, gang?"

They turned away from Tess and moved swiftly toward the trees, Josh's voice echoing. *"Dad, hey Dad, we need some help."*

Tess watched until they faded into the shadows, then sat in a patch of sunlight, hugging her thighs to her chest, and wondered what the hell was happening to her.

"Ma'am, are you hurt?"

She looked up at a cop. "No." But it wasn't surprising that he mistook her for one of the accident victims. Her clothes and body were covered in blood. She would have to stop at a gas station to clean up and change before seeing the shrink. She always carried a set of clothing in her trunk, a habit she'd learned from Dan. Tess got to her feet, dug out her Bureau badge, held it up. "How many fatalities?"

"At least five, Agent Livingston." He handed her a bottle of water and an old towel. "Here, use this to wash off the blood."

"Thanks." She poured the water over her hands and arms and rubbed with the towel. "What about the woman from the SUV?"

"Gone. But her daughter made it out okay. A woman and boy from the mangled VW died before they were freed and their dog was already dead. And two elderly men from the other cars."

So it's true, I spoke to the dying and the dead.

"I'm trying to clear this area of people so we can direct traffic out along the shoulder."

"I'd better get moving then."

Her mother had advised her to just tell the shrink the truth. But Tess suspected the truth might result in unemployment and a straitjacket.

Here's how it is, Doc. I see ghosts now. I talk to them, they talk to me, and they apparently think I know how they're supposed to get to wherever they're going.

She desperately wanted to turn around and go home, but if she didn't get this over with today, she might never show up for her mental health review. That would mean she couldn't return to work. No paycheck. So at five on the nose, she swung into an old residential neighborhood in Coral Gables, where tremendous banyan trees loomed on either side of the road, branches braiding together overhead to create a tunnel of green.

She parked and followed a shaded mulch path through an explosive jungle of tropical plants to a charming wooden porch where a pair of cats sunned themselves on the banister. A black and white tuxedo cat regarded her with such cool detachment that she was surprised when he jumped down and rubbed up against her legs, purring. As Tess stroked his soft, thick fur, he gazed up at her with beautiful celery-green eyes, meowed, then darted past her to the door. He slipped into the waiting room with her. No one chased him out. The receptionist leaned over the counter and snapped her fingers. "C'mon, Whiskers, up here, boy."

Whiskers. I know that name. But she'd never had a pet named Whiskers. As the cat leaped gracefully onto the counter and preened himself, an image popped into her head of a tuxedo cat curled up on a hotel desk, purring as she petted it. *What hotel? Where? When?*

She signed the patient sheet and Whiskers nudged her hand with his head, then licked the back of her hand, his sandpaper tongue warm and moist.

"That's amazing," the receptionist said. "I've never seen Whiskers do that with anyone. He likes you."

"The kitty seal of approval. I'm Tess Livingston."

"I heard about that accident. Five fatalities. Sounds just awful." The woman handed her a clipboard. "Fill out the top three boxes, then we'll get you right in to see Dr. Yates."

Tess carried the clipboard over to a chair and the cat followed her, jumped into a chair beside her, and curled up. "You're my familiar now?" she asked.

Whiskers turned those gorgeous eyes on her, yawned, and curled up. When she was admitted to the inner sanctum, the cat accompanied her down the hall, into the office, and claimed one of the two vacant chairs in front of the desk. Valerie Yates, an attractive brunette in her early forties, greeted Tess, then told Whiskers he wasn't on her schedule today.

"He seems to have adopted me," Tess remarked, sitting in the other chair.

"He's our mascot. Back in early January, I was coming into work one morning and saw him lying in the middle of the road. He'd been hit by a car. He was still breathing, so I rushed him over to the vet. During surgery, he died. They resuscitated him, but the prognosis wasn't good. A couple weeks later, he really started to rally, so I brought him home and he has been with me ever since."

A strange feeling swept over Tess, as though she were sinking into quicksand and had only seconds to pull herself free before it covered her face and head and suffocated her. Another image popped into her head, of a tuxedo cat following her, a man, and a black dog through a beautiful courtyard somewhere, a place she was sure she had never been.

"So Whiskers and I have something in common," Tess said. "We both died and came back."

"I was struck by that coincidence while I was reading through your file. You two were injured and died just a day apart—January third for Whiskers, the fourth for you."

Tess knew enough about Jung and synchronicities so that the information troubled her. Throughout her years in the Bureau, she had learned that if you didn't pay attention to seemingly random coincidences—synchronicities—you often missed the very thing that cracked the case. What were the odds, after all, that the Bureau shrink—an independent contractor—would have a cat that she, Tess, seemed to recall?

Dr. Yates sat forward, hands folded on top of the file. "What's your last memory from the day you were shot, Ms. Livingston?"

"My partner and I were in the middle of a counterfeiting bust in a neighborhood in west Miami. We had just gone into the warehouse with six other agents and . . . and someone opened fire. I remember a blazing agony in my leg, saw blood spurting out of it, and then . . . nothing."

"It says in your file that you were clinically dead for six minutes and you slipped into a coma three days later."

"*Six minutes?* I didn't realize it was that long."

"Any time an agent is clinically dead, there's a mental health review before you can return to work." Yates scribbled some notes. "Do you feel you're ready to go back to work?"

"I've used up most of my leave. I need my paycheck. Physically, I feel fine, just a few twinges in my leg now and then."

"And emotionally?"

"Not going back to work would be more stressful than the alternative."

"I understand completely." She slipped a scrap of paper from Tess's file. "I'm not sure how this got in here, but it was stapled to some other papers. It appears to be a dream you had on March nineteenth." She started reading: "'. . . am in mountains with Ian and Nomad. Humming-birds everywhere. We're looking for way out of Esperanza. Scene switches to underground bunker of some kind. *Brujos* outside, trying to get in.'" Yates paused. "Do you have any idea who Ian and Nomad are? What Esperanza is? What *brujos* are?"

That strange and unsettling feeling rushed through Tess again, but this time it was like standing at the precipice of a high cliff, staring down hundreds of feet to juts of sharp rocks and a raging ocean. If she took another step forward, she would be in a freefall, an Acapulco diver plunging head-first into a cosmic river. Her head started pounding, she felt nauseated, and wanted nothing more than to leave.

"I . . . don't remember having that dream. Or writing it down."

"In mid-March you were still on heavy-duty meds, so it's not surprising you don't remember."

"May I see the piece of paper?"

Dr. Yates passed it to her.

Definitely her handwriting. But the names—Ian, Nomad, Esperanza—meant nothing to her. Yet, as she read the words, an overwhelming grief welled up inside of her, and to her utter horror, she began to cry, then sob. Dr. Yates handed her pieces of tissue and Tess pressed them against her eyes and struggled to regain control of herself. *What's happening to me?* The waves of heartbreak just kept rolling over her, unaccompanied by any images that might explain why she felt so bereft. Whiskers climbed into her lap and settled down, purring loudly as if to comfort her. Tess's fingers slid through his fur, her sobs started to subside, she blew her nose.

"I'm sorry . . . I . . . don't know why I'm crying."

"You've been through a lot and this dream apparently triggered something in you. Look, I'm going to recommend that you're ready to return to work. But I think this dream is key to understanding some internal shift you're experiencing."

"I . . . think something happened to me when I died." *And that's why I can see and talk to ghosts.* "But I . . . can't remember what it was."

"It's possible. There's been considerable research done on near-death experiences. You might want to pick up Dr. Raymond Moody's book, *Life After Life*. He was one of the early pioneers into NDEs . . ."

The pounding in her head now roared, drowning the doctor's voice. The room turned a vivid blue, she didn't have any idea what she said. She only wanted to get back to her mother's place and crawl into bed. Whatever her response, it was functional enough for Dr. Yates to complete their interview because now Tess was outside, on the front porch, crouched in front of Whiskers, clutching the scrap of paper on which she had recorded the dream. "I remember you," she whispered, petting him. "I remember you curled up on the front desk of a hotel and that you tagged after me, a man, and a dog. I just don't understand what the hell any of it means."

He meowed, as if concurring, rubbed up against her legs once more, then bounded off into the lengthening shadows, chasing a lizard.

As Tess drove out of Coral Gables, she smoothed the scrap of paper against the steering wheel. Ian, Nomad, Esperanza, *brujos*, mountains, hummingbirds. She would start with those six words, like a storyboard she might put together for an investigation.

Ian. Nothing. She didn't know anyone by that name, had never known anyone by that name. She had read all of Ian Fleming's books, but that probably didn't count. Could this Ian be the man with whom she, a dog, and a tuxedo cat were walking?

Nomad. Zero. But she designated him as the dog.

Esperanza. Other than the fact that the word translated as hope, she was clueless. But it felt familiar somehow, like the name of a childhood friend.

Brujos. Witches. So?

Mountains. What kind of mountains? Like the Catskills? Rockies? Alps? An image popped into her head of a snow-capped volcano. Hawaii? No snow on those volcanoes.

Hummingbirds. Given her recent thoughts about hummingbirds, this word seemed important.

Tess turned into a shopping center where one of the cafés had Wi-Fi and went inside with her laptop. She ordered broccoli cheese soup, a cappuccino, and found a vacant table at the window. She brought a notepad and pen out of her purse, Googled Esperanza.

The links ranged from a resort in Cabo San Lucas to an organization that promoted Hispanic education to an organic clothing company. She clicked around randomly, but none of the articles seemed relevant. She finally clicked a link from an academic journal on world mythology:

In Esperanza, Ecuador, it's impossible to separate the mythology about the *brujos* from the mythology about the town itself. Among the Quechua Indians, the largest indigenous population in Ecuador, it's believed the town was once a nonphysical place, a kind of virtual construct where souls in transition went to explore the afterlife. Here, these transitional souls could decide whether to release their hold on physical life or return to their bodies.

Go to paypal to read the rest

Excited, Tess returned to Google and typed in *Esperanza, Ecuador*. Dozens of links came up. From a bird-watcher's site, she learned that the hummingbirds of Esperanza were among the most beautiful and rare in the world, capable of living at such a high altitude—13,200 feet—because of the profusion of flowers in and around Esperanza. Another Web site, for an Ecuadorian tour company in Quito, offered guided tours of Esperanza, but it was booked three years in advance. Photographs of the city filled another site—ancient stone buildings, labyrinthine streets, a park shaded by monkey-puzzle trees, rolling pastures where alpacas and llamas grazed.

Something about the alpacas and llamas struck a visceral cord, but she couldn't summon the particulars. She ran her fingers over the laptop's screen, as if to feel the texture of the stones, the cool shade of those buildings, the softness of an alpaca's fur. *I've been there. I've walked those streets.* Either that or she really had lost her mind and become a functioning crazy, capable of fooling most of the people most of the time. *And now I talk to ghosts, too.*

But suppose the first possibility was true? Suppose she actually had gone to this place when she'd died or been in a coma and something profound had happened to her? The best argument against that possibility was that she would have been just consciousness without a physical body. Yet, she clearly remembered *walking* through a courtyard with a man and a dog, a cat trotting along with them, a bird—parrot?—sweeping along beside them. They all had been physical. Besides, if that had been the afterlife, wouldn't her dad have been there? Dead ten years, Charlie Livingston would have been her tour guide.

But maybe not. Josh, his mother, and their beautiful dog probably had been dead when she had spoken to them. No one had been there for *them*— except her, a stranger who through some fluke had been able to interact with them. They didn't have any idea what to do or where to go until she had suggested they head into the trees and ask for help from someone they knew who had passed on. Had Josh's father shown up?

Her head ached with questions she couldn't answer. She'd been to Ecuador twice, had traveled extensively around the country, but had never heard of Esperanza. It supposedly was a real place, a real location. She would check it out on her next trip to Ecuador which, given her medical bills, might happen in twenty years.

In the immediate future, she decided to stop by the local video store on her way home and rent a couple of movies. She had no idea what was new, so she Googled *Netflix new movies.* One of the first to appear was the new George Clooney film, *Michael Clayton.*

You look like George Clooney.

Who?

Tears flooded her eyes. She stared at Clooney, fists clenched against her thighs. *I know you.* Maybe not Clooney, but a man who could be his twin. Tess clearly recalled this conversation, but was it some dream snippet from the hospital, a drug-induced fantasy? It had come down, finally, to a fantasy world.

Disgusted, she packed up her laptop and headed back out to the car. She turned on her iPhone, which immediately jingled, a text message from Maddie. A friend was giving her a ride, the focus group loved the new software, she wouldn't be home for dinner. Tess sent her a recorded message, much easier than texting: "Hope the friend is male."

Ordinary life pinched the vein of Tess's theories, cutting off its blood supply. She had died, been resuscitated, survived, and could now interact with ghosts. End of story.

Palms loomed against the sky, their silhouettes in the dusk larger and more magnificent than they actually were. Everything she looked at seemed excessive in the day's last light—the tomatoes and broccoli plants growing in the garden at the side of her mother's house, the lush bushes of night-blooming jasmine, the acacia trees blazing with reddish-orange flowers.

As she pulled into the empty driveway, the outside security lights blinked on. She retrieved her laptop and the *Michael Clayton* DVD from the passenger seat and slung her purse over her shoulder. The underside of her wrist itched and burned fiercely. She scratched at it, wondering what had bitten her. She hoped she could find Benadryl somewhere in her mother's bathroom cabinet.

Tess inserted her key into the lock but the door swung open before she turned the knob. No one in this household ever forgot to lock the door.

She set the laptop down, reached into her bag, slipped out her weapon, a Glock model 26, palm-sized, that weighed 21.75 ounces. It held eleven rounds of nine-millimeter parabellum bullets, and was unencumbered by any safety latch. The safety features were built in; the gun wouldn't fire unless you pulled the trigger. *Draw, aim, fire:* simple and clean.

With her pulse throbbing in her throat, Tess slipped into the shadowed room, the security light's glow spilling through the open door. Her mother's living room had been trashed—furniture overturned, a floor lamp smashed, pictures and art torn from the walls, couch pillows sliced open, stuffing strewn around the room. A bookcase lay on its side, books littered the floor. Tess stepped over and around the fallen objects.

The skin on the underside of her wrist burned fiercely now, as if she had held a hot iron against it. She strained, listening for unusual noises, but heard only the hum of the fridge, the ice maker churning, the ticking of the clock on the kitchen wall. Tess moved forward slowly, cautiously, into her mother's bedroom—and heard something behind her, a whisper of air, and spun around. A figure darted for the open door. "FBI!" she shouted. "Stop or I'll shoot!"

The person didn't stop. She fired low, aiming for the leg.

A man shrieked, crashed forward, and rolled, clutching his leg. Tess hit the nearest wall switch and ran over to the intruder. A thin Hispanic, bearded, wearing jeans, a work shirt. He breathed through clenched teeth, hands already slick with his own blood, words spilling out in Spanish. "My calf . . . you . . . shot away . . . my calf."

Tess answered in Spanish. "I'll be glad to call nine-one-one as soon as you tell me what the hell you're doing in my house."

The tendons in his neck strained, threatening to pop through the skin. "I . . . help me," he pleaded, his voice soft, desperate. ". . . It is inside me, forcing me . . ." Then his head jerked from one side to the other, his body bucked, he gasped—and spoke in English, his voice hard, tight, distinctly different. "It appears that I cannot seize you, Tess Livingston, that you are shielded. But I can seize your mother, niece, and partner just as I have seized this man. And I *will* seize them, one after another, if you try to find Esperanza."

What the fuck. "Sit up. Back against the wall. C'mon, do it, fast."

He laughed, slapped his bloody hands against the floor, pushed up. "I will show you what your loved ones will suffer if you defy me."

The man's head suddenly snapped back and he screeched and crashed back to the floor, thrashing as if with convulsions, his agonized screams echoing. Then he began to bleed from his eyes and ears, nostrils and mouth, the pores of his skin. Blood seeped from under his fingernails, ran down his chin, and he started to choke, to gag. Blood rapidly pooled around his body and streamed across the floor, into the cracks of the tile, so much blood that the stink nauseated her.

Horrified, unable to wrench her eyes away from him, Tess scrambled back toward the counter, groping blindly behind her for the phone. Something emerged from his head and nostrils, a dark mist, and drifted upward, forming what appeared to be a small, dark cloud of smoke. It hovered for a moment in the circles of light, then moved swiftly toward a window and passed right through the glass. The man went still, silent. Tess whipped around, hands shaking violently as she punched out 911.

"What's the nature of your emergency?" asked the operator.

"There's . . . a dead man. On my living room floor." She spat out her name, address, and the operator assured her someone would be there shortly.

Tess dropped the receiver into the cradle and backed out of the room, eyes flicking here, there, seeking the dark mist, the cloud of smoke, whatever the hell she had seen. She backed through the door, then pounded down the ramp, the man's final words ringing in her skull. *I will show you what your loved ones will suffer if you defy me.*

Sixteen

Dominica soared through the window of the house on stilts, stunned that Tess had been able to see her, even more shocked that she didn't seem to have any idea what was going on. Was it possible that she'd returned from the dead with no memory about what had happened to her? If so, then the joke was on the chasers, now wasn't it? Ian apparently returned with his memories mostly intact, had somehow retained them while he was in the nuthouse—and the other transitional had returned with amnesia. Ian would head for Ecuador forty years in Tess's past and Tess would stay right here. Payback.

She thought herself back to Esperanza and immediately noticed how many locals were compromised. Apparently Ben had implemented their defense plans, which included seizing locals so that weapons could be gathered and stored, fuel trucks could be moved, so they would be prepared for any incursion into the city by this liberation group.

Dominica dipped into the posada looking for Nomad, but didn't sense the dog's presence. Business at the inn appeared to be slow—the lobby with the inviting fireplace was practically deserted, the front desk was empty, tables in the restaurant were set, but only one couple dined. A quick circuit of the cottages revealed that only one was occupied. *One.*

Apparently word had gotten around through the Internet that Esperanza was dangerous for tourists. While bulletins were issued for other South American cities because of political situations, drug runners, terrorist groups, Esperanza was deemed risky because of its homicide rate. Good. Maybe that would be enough to keep this liberation group away.

Dominica moved quickly out of the city, toward Gigante. Windmills covered the countryside, supplementing the power of the hydroelectric plants along the rivers that kept the cities and towns in these mountains lit, the Internet functioning, that maintained a quality of life despite anything the *brujos* did. Kill the source of the power, she thought, and Esperanza and every miserable hovel north of Río Palo would be isolated and vulnerable, unable to communicate. Everything was being put into place so that when an attack was imminent, the power grid could be brought down within minutes. That was how they would ultimately triumph and create a city of *brujos.*

On the street where Manuel Ortega lived, she assumed the form of a simple Quechua woman. She had used this humble, nonthreatening form many times to move through Ecuadorian cities. She hoped she would find Nomad with Manuel. She'd last seen them together the day that the dog and Tess, as a transitional, had traveled to Gigante to find Manuel.

But the driveway was empty, the windows dark, and the door swung open into utter emptiness. Everything was gone. *Everything.* No furniture, nothing on the walls, nothing anywhere. The hollow shell seemed to laugh at her, mock her. She left the house and moved quickly into the woods, shouting, "Wayra, I know you can hear me. Show yourself."

But he didn't appear in either of his forms. She shed her human form and thought of him, of the shape-shifter she had loved, and willed herself to find him. It took a while to locate his unique frequency, but when she homed in on it, she ended up in the bar of an inn in Otavalo.

Wayra was playing pool with a European tourist. He sensed her presence the moment she appeared—his shoulders tensed, his eyes darted around the room. "You've got it," he said to his opponent, and laid down the pool stick and went over to the bar to settle his bill.

Wayra, barfly. It would be funny if it weren't so out of character. Dominica looked quickly around for a suitable host, and slipped into one of the waitresses. No fight from her. Dominica told her to follow the tall, handsome man and she did so, right outside to his truck. When he turned, she said, "Pool? In a bar? Oh, Wayra, you really have descended into mud."

He leaned against the truck, arms folded across his chest, and laughed. "Hey, I've gotten really good at pool. What do you want, Nica?"

"The truth."

"Right. Which truth? The one you hope to hear or the one you refuse to hear?"

"In 1968, I couldn't seize anyone. I had to melt into them, gently, and the only time that restriction could be overcome was with a legion of my people."

"That's not a question, Nica."

"What kind of war is this?" she demanded. "What are the rules? Who is this Manuel Ortega? Who is Charlie?"

"Your real question is why are you having trouble meeting your agenda? Why should I help you answer that?"

She wished she could hate him. "Because you have to."

"Really? Who says I do, Nica? You? Your arrogance is stunning."

"I learned it from you."

He burst out laughing. "I'm afraid I can't take credit for that."

"Why're you in Otavalo?"

"It's where I choose to be."

"You're waiting for Ian. Or Tess."

"I'm waiting for Godot, for garlic and sapphires, Seth, the Dalai Lama, Nelson Mandela, Jerry Garcia. Leave me alone. Go play with Ben."

"You'll regret this. I promise you. I don't know what you and the chasers think you're going to accomplish with just two transitionals, but I'll make sure they never get to Esperanza."

"Do what you must." With that, he got into his truck and sped off into the darkness.

Dominica ran after the truck, hollering, *"Coward, you're a coward."* Her voice echoed, rising and falling in the stillness. He didn't return.

Enraged that he had shunned her like this, she slipped out of the waitress and thought herself back to her town house. Ben paced the living room, a cell phone pressed to his ear. He sounded agitated and signaled he would be off the call shortly.

She realized the retriever pup hadn't bounded into the room to greet her. He wasn't on the porch, either, where the animals usually sunned themselves. The Persian looked up at her with those sad amber eyes and meowed. The conure, perched on the railing, whistled and said, "Pup, pup." Shit. The retriever had left.

"I didn't expect you back so soon." Ben stepped out onto the porch. "The pup left during the night," he added, reading her thoughts. "The cat and bird have been sitting out here for hours, like they're waiting for the pup to show up again."

She drew her phony fingers through the cat's phony fur. Soft, but not like in the physical world. "Where did it go, Ben?"

He shrugged. "No one knows."

"We need to know. We need to find the answers to those kinds of questions."

"Yes, but not right this second. That was Pearl. Rafael has been cleared by the counselor and they're helping the group that's readying the defensive perimeter. As of right now, three thousand locals have been seized and are being used to implement our defensive measures."

"Do we know any more details about the liberation group?"

"We will shortly. *Brujos* who have seized priests are returning soon with a report."

"Then why did you sound so agitated?"

"Because they're still pushing this idea about launching a massive attack on everything north of Río Palo. They feel we'd be in a stronger position by launching an attack rather than by just fortifying the city. They seem to be gathering support."

In other words, Pearl and Rafael were stoking the fires of insurrection. "What did you tell them?"

"That you haven't issued orders about attacking, so we stick to the plan."

Was he lying or was she paranoid? He could be hiding information from her in the same way that she hid her encounters with Wayra from him, by locking the information away so deeply that no other *brujo* had access to it. Even *brujos* had a right to privacy.

"You're not telling me everything," she said.

He gazed off into the distance, at the lakes and volcanoes beyond the porch, rolled his lower lip between his teeth. "Pearl said they've gathered support from nearly half the tribe, Nica. They're already planning how to launch the attack."

I knew it. "Shortsighted assholes."

"Look, I told her we need three days to find the transitionals and eliminate them. I asked her to give us at least that long."

Three days? With the way things had been going, she would be lucky to accomplish anything in three months. "You don't have to ask *her* anything. She's not in charge. *I* am."

"Then maybe you need to speak to the tribe. Explain to them what's going on, why the death of the transitionals is so important."

"I don't know why because I don't know why they were allowed in to begin with. Diversion? Distraction? What? But since the chasers have gone to extraordinary lengths to protect them—as transitionals and now that they're back in the physical—I have to assume that some significant shift will occur if they're able to return to Esperanza. So it's imperative that they die. Their deaths will end whatever plan the chasers have. Then we can attack Esperanza. But until their deaths our defensive measures have to be our priority."

"It didn't work in San Francisco. We descended on the city by the thousands, in the fog, and Ian still escaped."

"We were working against restrictions and rules in 1968 that we don't have in 2008. This time, Ben, it will be just you and me. We'll seize two morally compromised individuals and use them to kill Tess. Then we wait for Ian to return here, do the same thing, and kill him."

"If you're assuming he'll be in 2008 by then, how's he going to move forty years forward in time?"

She didn't know. Even *brujos* had trouble moving back and forth in time. "When Esperanza was still a nonphysical place, transitionals came here from many different times. It wasn't a problem. Perhaps that's what the chasers are banking on now."

Ben stood there for long, uncomfortable moments, uncharacteristically contemplative, his thoughts hidden from her. Then he flashed that smile that had won her over from the first time she'd seen it nearly a century ago. "I'll ask Marla next door to come in and look in on the critters, then we can leave."

As though the animals were alive, in need of cat litter, fresh food, water. Ben's primary concern—and hers—was the love part of the equation, the reason these animals had found their way to them to begin with. So while he went next door to talk to Marla, Dominica remained on the porch with the cat and the bird. They usually didn't name their animals. That made it easier not to become emotionally attached, not to mourn them when they mysteriously moved on. But she'd secretly named the cat Shelley and the bird, Shriek. So she addressed them by name and asked them to please stick around for a while, that she and Ben loved them too much to lose them. She promised that the retriever pup—whom she had named Mole, for her ability to burrow deeply into the heart of a *brujo*—would be back.

When Ben returned, happy that Marla would look in on the animals, he slipped his phony arms around her phony virtual form. His warm breath against her neck felt nearly real. "We'll conquer because that's what we do," he whispered, and then she thought them to South Miami Beach, the best place to find killers.

Seventeen

Too uneasy to wait in the dark, Tess moved to the front of the house and paced beneath the glow of the security lights. She called her mother, but Lauren didn't answer, so Tess left a voice mail. She felt fragmented and strange, and as soon as she disconnected, couldn't remember exactly what her voice mail had said. She kept hearing that cold, wretched voice: . . . *you are shielded somehow . . . I can seize any of them . . . if you try to find Esperanza.*

A pleasant breeze kicked off the water, stars popped out against the black skin of the sky. Everything out here looked normal, ordinary. But inside her mother's house a man lying in a pool of his own blood had been possessed by something that had known her name and threatened to kill her mother, niece, and Dan. If she divulged this fact to anyone, she would find herself locked up in a padded cell.

She replayed what had happened, slowing the events down, examining them more closely. She remembered how the underside of her wrist had burned in the moments before she had entered the house and until the mist or smoke or whatever the hell it was had left the man. She rubbed her fingers across the skin there. It felt warm and tingled slightly, but the burning sensation was gone. In the glow of the security lights, it looked as if a bruise had formed.

That's some nasty bruise on your arm.

Some guy outside grabbed my wrist and told me I was an intruder here.

Tess struggled to follow whatever this was—memory, auditory hallucination, derangement—and suddenly recalled being outside a building, in fog, and stumbling over a dead man, a Quechuan, covered in blood. He looked exactly like the man on the floor, as if he had bled out. The memory seemed no stranger than what she had experienced inside the house or earlier today with the ghosts at the turnpike wreckage. But it couldn't be her memory. She was certain she'd never seen a dead Quechuan.

The shriek of sirens intruded and within moments two county cop cars sped into the driveway. Tess recognized one of the three men, Frank Cerlane—burly weight lifter, father of two young boys, wife was a teacher. They'd worked together on a case a couple of years ago.

"Tess," Frank said, shaking her hand. "It's great to see you. When that call came through . . . I mean, the last I heard, you were still on leave."

"Got my clearance today, came home, and found the house trashed and the perp still inside. He tried to run, I shot him in the leg, and then he . . . I don't know, Frank. He went into convulsions and started bleeding out."

"You sure he's dead?"

"Yes." *Something drifted out of him.*

He gave her arm a reassuring squeeze. "Stay right here, we'll take a look. The medical examiner is on the way. Send him up when he gets here."

He and the other cops moved past her. Tess sank to the lowest step on the stairs and was still sitting there when two more cars arrived—her mother's Prius and Doc Brian's VW Jetta. Lauren bounded out of her car as though she were being pursued and threw her arms around Tess. "Christ, Slim," she whispered. "Are you all right?" She stepped back, eyes searching Tess's face the way only a mother could. She looked as if she had aged fifteen years since this morning. "Did he hurt you?"

"I'm fine, Mom. Just rattled." *And you called me "Slim," again. You channeling Dad?*

"My cell didn't work in the restaurant where Brian and I were having dinner. I didn't get your message until we were getting ready to leave. Who *is* he?"

"Was. He's dead. And I've never seen him before. He trashed your house."

Doc Brian stood behind Lauren, a thin man whose body hummed with excessive energy. He paced like a caged animal and stabbed his fingers through his thick, gray hair. "If you're hurt, Tess, we can get you over to ER ASAP."

"I'm fine, Brian, thanks."

He eyed her skeptically, as though she were a life-form he'd never encountered before. Hell, maybe she was.

"I called Dan." Her mother. "He's on his way."

"Dan? Why'd you call *him*?"

"It was the only thing I could think of doing. Brian and I will find out what's going on." They slipped past her, up the ramp.

Tess was reluctant to follow, to enter the house again, but terrified that if she didn't, the *thing* that had spoken through the man might seize her mother. How could she protect Lauren and Maddie when they slept?

None of them would be staying *here* tonight. She went up the ramp, her thigh no longer aching, the burning itch in her wrist now gone. Inside, in the blaze of lights, the floor glistened with the dead man's blood and everyone stood well clear of it and the body. Her mother was saying, ". . . he's part of the lawn maintenance crew that works in this neighborhood."

"No ID on him," said Frank. "Do you know his name, Mrs. Livingston?"

"No. But the woman who lives across the street will know. He does her lawn."

"Do you think my shot killed him, Frank?" Tess could barely bring herself to look at the man. "It hit him in the left calf. That was the leg he was clutching."

Frank, now wearing a pair of latex gloves and rubber boots, moved closer to the body and rolled up the left leg of the man's jeans, turned it slightly. "What do you think, Doc?"

Brian inspected the injury without touching it. "The shot took out a chunk of skin. But it looks like a clean shot. It didn't penetrate into the leg. And it certainly didn't cause all *this*." He opened his hands, indicating the unspeakable damage to the man's body.

The forensics team arrived shortly afterward and Tess and Frank moved outside, onto the back patio where an outside light shot a bright beam from the patio to the beach. Moths and June bugs fluttered and flitted through the air, the breeze rustled through the tall sea oats. She didn't sense anything threatening out here.

Tess typed up her formal statement on Frank's laptop, sent a copy to her own e-mail. When she returned to the front of the house, Maddie was standing in the driveway, talking to Dan Hernandez. The three people that *thing* had named were now all gathered in one place. Tess looked around uneasily, and wondered how she could protect anyone from something that could possess another person.

Brujos are ghosts who are stuck . . . they are able to seize us, our bodies, to step into us with impunity and use us. Few have survived this possession. It is too violent, too alien . . .

Had that conversation happened? And if it had, why were these memories coming to her in sound bites? Why not in images, complete with characters, names, a plot?

Hungry ghosts. Possession. Was that what she had seen leaving the dead man? A *brujo*?

"Tess?"

Dan Hernandez stood there in the spill of light from the house, a Cuban anomaly with blond hair and blue eyes, some recessive gene that dated back centuries to his European roots. Before she had died, she thought she'd loved this man. Right now, she felt only fear that a *brujo* would enter him, possess him, kill him.

"Dan. Mom shouldn't have called you, but I appreciate your making the drive."

"Hey, I was in Homestead. It's not that far."

He hugged her a bit too closely. She breathed in the familiar smells of Dan, the mint of his aftershave, the summery scent of the detergent he used for his clothes, and then the deeper, more complex odors that led her quickly into the memories of the intimacy of their relationship.

"I'm sorry you had to go through this, Tess, on top of everything else," he said.

She quickly disengaged herself. Yes, she feared for him. But that fear wasn't inviting him back into her life as a lover. "This afternoon, I got my clearance to go back to work, but that may change now."

"Look, I just talked to the ME and to Brian. Yeah, you shot this guy, but both docs are ninety-nine percent sure that your shot didn't kill him. They concur that the guy had, at the very least, a cerebral hemorrhage. But the autopsy will tell us for sure. Regardless, you shot him in self-defense."

"I shot him because he was about to run out the door."

"*After* he broke into your home. By the day after tomorrow, you'll be cleared. Forensics will be here for hours yet, then they'll bring in a cleaning crew. So I got the three of you a suite over on the beach at the Key Largo Resort."

"Thanks, Dan, but that'll cost you a fortune."

"The owner's a friend. I'm getting it for next to nothing."

Of course. Dan rarely paid full price for anything. He took advantage of the fed, state, and county perks. The thought immediately made her feel guilty and ungrateful. "Then let us buy you dinner."

"You're on."

The way he said it, so quickly and enthusiastically, caused her to regret the invitation. He might get the wrong idea. On the other hand, she didn't want any of them to stay here tonight and she at least owed Dan a dinner for facilitating their accommodations elsewhere.

Her iPhone jingled, and when she slipped it from her pocket, the message read: *Your recorder is full.* She either had forgotten to turn it off after she'd sent her voice message to Maddie or the recorder button had gotten pressed when it was inside her pocket. Did that mean that the voice of that *thing,* the *brujo,* was on here? "I need to get some clothes and stuff, Dan. And drag my mother out of there." She pointed at Maddie, who paced back and forth in front of her car, talking on her cell. "Could you let Maddie know she should pack a bag?"

"Sure thing."

Tess slipped the iPhone into her purse and went upstairs again. Her mother, Brian, and the medical examiner had moved away from the body and blood and were debating the possible causes of a bleed-out this massive. Lauren noticed Tess gesturing at her and excused herself. They moved into the hall. "What is it, hon?"

"Mom, Dan got us a suite at the Key Largo Resort. Let's pack and get out of here."

"You go along. I'll join you and Maddie later."

"*No.* We go together. I asked Dan to have dinner with us. I know you guys just ate, so how about coffee and dessert? Invite Brian, too."

Her mother seemed surprised by the forcefulness with which Tess had uttered that one word, "no." "Uh, okay. Brian and I just ate, so he doesn't need to come along."

In other words, her dinner with Brian hadn't gone well. "I'd like you and Maddie to hear a recording. Pack whatever you need for a trip." Just in case the *brujo* returned and they had to leave for a few days. "Laptop, notes, passport, whatever."

"Done."

"*We're* off to pack." Maddie came up between them, slung her arms around their shoulders, walked them into one of the bedrooms, kicked the door shut. "Can someone tell me what's going on? Please?"

Tess's unease spiked to a new level. "At the hotel. We'll talk there."

The resort sprawled across ten acres on the Atlantic side of the islands, a make-believe world that tourists took as the true representation of life in the Florida Keys. Tennis courts, swimming pools, beaches, saunas, hot tubs, 24/7 restaurants and cafés, shops and a tourist office, high-speed Internet, satellite TV. Tess wished she could find a closet and duck into it with her mother and niece and Dan and play the iPhone recording for them. But first she had to make sure it was audible. The phone had been in her slacks pocket, she had no idea what the recorder's range might be.

At her earliest opportunity during dinner, she excused herself and crossed the massive lobby to reach the ladies' room. She locked herself in a stall, plugged in the iPhone's earplugs, clicked to recordings, scrolled until she found music from the car radio. Apparently, the recorder had come on during the drive back to her mother's place. She fast-forwarded to the slamming of the car door. Moments later, her voice rang out as she shouted for the intruder to stop or she would shoot. Then the shots sounded and she fast-forwarded the recording to the point after the intruder had pleaded for help. *It is inside me, forcing me . . .*

It. The recording captured his thrashing, the hard strangeness of his voice, the stilted formality of his English. *It appears that I cannot seize you, Tess Livingston, that you are shielded. But I can seize your mother, niece, and partner. I can seize any of them, just as I have seized this man, and will seize them, one after another, if you try to find Esperanza.*

Tess turned off the recorder, unable to listen to the last part, about how they would suffer. Suppose her mom, Maddie, and Dan couldn't hear the voice? At the accident scene earlier, she was apparently the only person who had seen and spoken with ghosts. But this was *recorded.* Even if they could hear it, how could they be protected? It wasn't as if they could arm themselves against whatever had spoken through the lawn man.

And it knew my name.

Dominica and Ben wandered through a crowd of tourists on Miami's South Beach. People spilled off the sidewalks, music pumped from open doorways, the night scene in SoBe was a people-watcher's wet dream. Dominica sought evidence of *brujos* inhabiting bodies around them, but didn't see their kind anywhere. After a certain point, it didn't matter. The beautiful bodies, the sensual promises, the possibilities enticed them even though they existed as nothing more than wisps of smoke, a blur of peripheral movement, a trick of light. That was only when they were perceived at all. Here, they were merely shadows hungry for form. At every turn, she was reminded of how paltry they were, how low in the scheme of things, how truly powerless.

This place, after all, was not Esperanza—no residual power here to help them assume virtual forms, no fog, no place to hide, nothing within which they could move rapidly from place to place. The air was like glass, the clear summer sky brilliant with stars. They were out of their element and knew it.

"Well?" he asked. "Have you seen anyone who fits the bill?"

"No." Forcing someone to commit murder wasn't easy. The individual had to be prone to such violence. America in 2008 had no shortage of violent, neurotic, gun-loving people, but finding exactly the right individuals for this job would be a challenge. Tess's partner? To even be in his line of work, he needed a violent streak, just as Tess did. But if he was still in love with her, it would rule him out unless his body's chemistry could be extensively manipulated. The ideal was to find someone without emotional ties to Tess, a complete stranger who was prone to violence and knew how to use a gun.

When she said as much, Ben nodded. "We're surrounded by hip couples in search of the next high, the next thrill. What's a bigger thrill than murder?"

"No thrill seekers."

"Then what?"

"I'm not sure yet." They moved on for another few blocks before Dominica gestured at a neon blue sign that read: CLUB MARTINIQUE. "Let's try here."

A private club. They drifted past the bouncer checking membership cards at the door. Secluded booths tucked away in shadows, behind large billowing potted plants, were occupied by upscale couples, the urban cool crowd. She and Ben moved through the main room, checking out the customers, searching for a pair who appealed to them. What delicious choices. Black, white, brown, Indian, Latino, Asian, Canadian, European. A banquet.

Ben indicated a booth next to a window, where a handsome couple sat alone, two wrestler types standing nearby. Bodyguards. "What do you think?" Ben asked.

An Asian woman, a man who looked European. "Intriguing possibilities."

He said he'd check them out and drifted away, a shadow merging with darker shadows. Dominica remained close to the beautiful oak bar, shaped in a sweeping half-moon that crossed the width of the room. Now and then people walked through her, but only one young man seemed to feel it. He shuddered and rubbed his hands over his arms, as if to warm himself against an inexplicable chill.

When Ben reappeared, she sensed he was pleased. "She's a model, he's her photographer. Both bodyguards are armed, one of them drives the car."

"Can they kill?"

"We'll test them." He explained his plan, she liked it, and they drifted over to the booth.

The bodyguards had been poured from the same physical mold, large, muscular men with biceps the size of tree trunks. One was bald, the other had thick dark hair and an intricate tattoo of naked women on the inside of his left arm. Dominica and Ben moved past them and regarded the model and the photographer.

The woman was pretty but not stunning, not the way Dominica imagined a model would be. Her companion had a cute, friendly face. They held hands, sipped from tall glasses of red wine, spoke in hushed, intimate voices. Ben stood behind the man, Dominica came up behind the model. Dominica wanted to tell Ben that the photographer appealed to her. But if she did, he would tell her how much the Asian woman intrigued him, and then as soon as she and Ben took them, they would lose themselves in sensuality and lust.

Ben stepped into the photographer, Dominica entered the woman. No resistance. It was as if this woman already had lost her soul to the countless photographs that had been taken of her, to the strange adulation that had made her a commodity. She believed her own PR, her self-concept defined by *People* magazine.

Since she wasn't going to be in this body long, Dominica didn't need to take stock of it, but it was difficult not to notice how fine it was. Excellent lungs and heart, all the internal organs worked well. However, her internal chemistry was a bit screwy, too much sugar, too many salads, not enough nutrients. Dominica felt she might be in the early stages of diabetes.

Other than a few twitches and an unnatural movement here and there, Ben didn't seem to have any trouble with the photographer. No battles. Nothing to indicate the photographer knew he had been compromised. He reached for Dominica's hand and brought it to his mouth, kissing each knuckle, his eyes holding hers. It stirred all those human desires and passions and such deep hunger for his body that she nearly lost track of why they were here.

Ready? he mouthed.

Dominica slung her designer bag over her shoulder, stood. The bald driver seemed surprised that they were leaving so soon. Dominica found the man's name. "Jim, could you bring the car around back?"

"Sure thing." Jim looked at Tattoo Man. "Lew, get the bill, okay?"

After Jim left, Lew signaled for the bill, paid it, then guided them around the dance floor, through the pounding music and the stink of booze, sweat, and hormones to the rear of the club. As they stepped outside into the alley, the dark Ford Expedition drove up, Jim behind the wheel.

Ben opened the door. "I'll drive, Jim."

"You're sure?"

"Yeah, man, it's cool."

Dominica leaped out of the woman, into Lew with his snake tattoo, and instantly was immersed in the violent undercurrents of the man's personality. Ex-gang member, ex-con, ex-employee of a private security company in the Mideast, loved his guns. She zipped herself up inside him, seized control of him so swiftly and smoothly that he never even flinched. His essence shouted and swore but she shoved him down into that metal room and that was it.

The model sort of stumbled forward, as if startled awake. "Holy shit, *that* was weird. I felt, like, I don't know, like . . ."

"Something just left you?" Dominica asked in Lew's voice.

"Yes. That's it exactly, Lew."

Dominica summoned all the violence inside this man and slammed his elbow into the bridge of the woman's nose. Shrieking, she wrenched back in shock and agony. Her hands flew to her face, blood poured through her fingers. Dominica grabbed the sides of her head with Lew's large, powerful hands, and snapped her neck. She crumpled to the ground.

Dominica urged Lew to pull the body into the darker shadows in the alley. She was aware of music hammering against the walls and hoped no one stumbled out the rear door. She couldn't deal with anyone else right this second. But the only person who appeared was Ben as Jim the driver, pulling the photographer's body along behind him, the man's legs thumping across the old cobblestones in the alley. No question they had chosen the right two men for murder.

They deposited the model and her photographer between garbage cans heaped with trash, relieved them of their wallets, phones, iPods, Black-Berrys, and ran to the Expedition. The SUV peeled out of the alley, Ben at the wheel. "Where to, Nica? Where is she? Tess has that mark on her arm, so that should make it easier for you to pick up her signal, right?"

"It may take a little while. It's harder to hear when I'm in a body. But head south to Key Largo, to her mother's house. The closer we are to where she has been, the more likely it is that I'll be able to pick up something."

"We need a map," he said.

Dominica opened the glove compartment. No map, just an odd gizmo with a little screen and a plug for the cigarette lighter at the end of it. "Do you have any idea what this is?" she asked, removing the object.

Ben glanced at it, shook his head, then: "According to Jim, it's called Magellan."

"Magellan? What's that mean? Magellan was an explorer."

"I don't know. Jim shut down. He's laughing at us."

Dominica stuck one end into the cigarette lighter, pleased that she at least knew how to do this. She and Ben had taken enough tourists in Esperanza to have quite a bit of knowledge of the twenty-first century. But some of the finer nuances escaped them.

She turned on the Magellan and a pretty blue screen came up with three symbols on it. She pressed *menu*, then *calculate route*, and suddenly understood how this little marvel functioned. "Ben, it's pegged to satellites. It knows exactly where we are."

"Satellites? Satellites are watching us? What, like Sputnik?"

Sputnik. He was stuck back in that Kansas life and didn't seem to be quite as knowledgeable as she'd assumed. "Ben, Sputnik was launched in 1957. A Soviet satellite. It was maybe the size of a goddamn beach ball. It's fallen out of the sky since then and bounced down on some beach."

"Very funny. I know there's a space station, that there're spy satellites, that in January of this year, a disabled spy satellite was shot down. Some people are saying the military shot it down so the enemy wouldn't be able to nab its secrets. Others say it was shot down because it got photos of genuine UFOs and an alien base on the fucking moon. Don't talk to me like I'm a moron. We have access to high-speed Internet, you know."

His recitation shocked her. She always had believed that longevity meant you knew more. Her six hundred years made her his elder, a revered one, practically a *fossil*. "Well, hey, you make this stupid remark about Sputnik, what am I supposed to think?"

"Think what you want," he said. "Enter Tess's address."

She glared at him.

"What?" he said. "What the hell's the problem now?"

"Whenever we take bodies of the same gender or bodies that don't appeal to us physically, we end up talking instead of having sex and this is what happens. We argue about the stupidest things."

He gripped the steering wheel harder.

"Did you hear me?" she snapped.

"I'm not deaf. Check out one of the BlackBerrys. Find out if there are any more entries on that liberation blogspot."

How quickly he changed the subject, she thought, and brought out a BlackBerry, one of her favorite twenty-first-century toys. It was the equivalent of carrying a world of information in the palm of your hand. She quickly navigated to the liberation blogspot, clicked on the top entry.

"Read it out loud," Ben said.

" 'It has come to our attention that the parasites may be on to us. We've gotten reports of priests being taken in at least four different cities. They weren't killed, merely used, scanned for information about our organization. The parasites are trying to determine our plans. For the sake of safety, further entries will be posted only on our mirror site. Group A will inform B about our URL. B will inform C and on down the line. We must, from this point forward, be vigilant and exercise great caution.' " She paused. "That's it. The *brujos* should've killed the goddamn priests, Ben."

"As soon as we're done here, I'll return to Esperanza and talk to Rafael and Pearl. They're debriefing the *brujos* who seized those priests."

"One of us could enter the Internet, Ben, and find that mirror site."

Horror filled his eyes. "The last time we attempted that, we lost five *brujos*."

Yes, they had. The relentless assault of a digital stream had fried them, consumed them, or taken them into itself forever. But those *brujos* had been relative newcomers. She felt certain that if she or Ben attempted it, or even Rafael or Pearl, they wouldn't succumb to what had taken the other *brujos*.

"First things first," she said. "Tess."

Eighteen

After dinner, they moved out onto the wide veranda behind the restaurant. Tess could see the moonlit beach, wind whipping the sand into tiny dervishes that spun furiously along the water's edge. Waves crashed rhythmically against the sand, the tall, graceful sea oats that grew on the nearby dunes swayed like hula dancers. Oddly peaceful. And they weren't alone out here. Families and couples strolled the beach, swam in the tremendous pool off to their far right, the laughter of children rang out. Tess felt the spot was sheltered and safe enough to play the recording. If she lost her job over this, so be it. She could always bag groceries at the local Publix.

Dan ordered a platter of desserts and a round of cappuccinos. Once everything was on the table, Maddie got right to the point. "So, Tess, what's this recording you want us to hear?"

"It explains what killed that man. I didn't realize my phone recorder was on. Listen to what the lawn guy said after I shot him." She pressed a button on her iPhone and Dan, Lauren, and Maddie leaned forward simultaneously, as if they were controlled by the same brain.

While the recording played, she watched their faces—her mother frowning, Maddie growing paler by the second, and Dan listening intently but obviously baffled. She tuned out the words, the voice, the horrid reality of what had happened in her mother's living room, but the images ran in an endless loop in her mind. Inescapable evidence. Something had followed her back from the dead.

When it was done, Tess turned off the recording, started to delete it, then decided to save it as proof that she was threatened. In the subsequent silence, the crashing of the waves and the mournful whistles of the wind seemed disturbingly loud. Maddie broke the silence first.

"Why is it coming after *me*? What the hell did *I* do?"

"What's Esperanza?" her mother asked.

And from Dan: "What's he talking about? Shielded from what? And why does his voice sound so different when he's pleading for help? It sounds like two different people."

"Don't you get it?" Maddie looked pointedly at Dan. "Something happened to Tess when she died and some sort of . . . ghost or demon followed

her back, killed that lawn man, and now . . . *we're* targets. All of us. Right, Tess? Isn't that what it's about?"

"I think so. I'm starting to remember events that happened when I flat-lined or from when I was in a coma. I went somewhere, to a town called Esperanza. For the last ten years, the people there have been battling these . . . ghosts, hungry ghosts that they call *brujos*—"

"*Witches?*" Dan choked back a laugh and shook his head, making it clear he found the entire conversation a joke. "C'mon, Tess. Demons, ghosts, and now witches? Which is it?"

She ignored his derision. "That's just what they're called. But they're spirits who're stuck, dead but unable to move on. They've existed for centuries and seemed to have evolved into beings that are much more than what we think of as ghosts. They're able to possess people, to manipulate them, force them to—"

"Possession." Her mother looked ill. "Are we talking *The Exorcist* sort of possession?"

"Not by devils," Tess said. "At least not the way we think of the word. But they seem to be able to move into a body and take it over. They do it to experience physical existence. But the lawn guy was used to show me what would happen to you all if I try to get to Esperanza. His personality, his essence, broke free of the *brujo's* control long enough to plead for help, and then it tightened its control over him again. That's why there was such a marked change in his voice. Then this *brujo* killed him."

"Aw, for crissake," Dan muttered. "This is such bullshit."

Lauren shot Dan a dirty look. "Enough with the commentary, Dan." Her voice was uncharacteristically sharp. "Tess experienced something, and even if you don't agree with her interpretation of what happened, you can be courteous enough to let her talk."

Chastised, Dan held up his hands. "Right. You're right, Lauren. Sorry, Tess."

His voice smacked of irritation, not apology. Tess let it pass, she couldn't blame him. She knew how this sounded.

"What stuff do you remember?" Lauren asked.

"Being outside a bus terminal, thick fog. A man grabbed my arm and told me I was an intruder. Later, I saw the same man on the ground by a row of outhouses. He'd bled out, just like the guy in your living room, Mom." She turned her arm, displaying the purple bruise, clearly visible on the underside of her wrist. "This is where the man grabbed me—"

"Wait," Dan said. "A guy in this afterworld place grabbed your arm? And that's what caused the bruise?"

"That's what I just said, Dan. And as I neared Mom's place earlier, the bruise started itching and burning."

Dan, clearly agitated now, just rolled his eyes. "I'm sorry, but this whole story is ridiculous. When you die, you don't go to someplace called Esperanza, there're no witches in the afterlife, and it's physically impossible for an injury you supposedly sustained when you were dead to show up while you're alive. It's—"

"How the hell would *you* know?" Tess snapped. "Have you died and come back?"

"He's Catholic. Their afterlife beliefs are complicated," Maddie said.

Dan looked disgusted. "I'm not getting into a religious discussion with an eighteen-year-old."

"How about a religious discussion with a thirty-three-year-old, Dan?" she shot back.

"Yeah, right. You're the least religious person I know. There's a perfectly plausible explanation for why that man died and it doesn't have squat to do with possession or *brujos*."

"Then how do you explain the change in his voice?" Tess snapped. "And the fact that he threatened the three of you? How do you explain that, Dan?"

"He was a psycho."

"Hold on, just hold on," Lauren said angrily. "Look, whatever happened to Tess when she died or was in a coma is *her* experience. We can't say it happened or didn't happen. But one thing we can all agree on is that the threat on that recording is *real*."

"Yeah, fine." Dan nodded. "And the guy who made that threat is dead."

Such hard finality in his voice, Tess thought, and knew it was useless to pursue this. "Believe whatever the hell you want. I know what I experienced."

In the uneasy silence that followed, his cell bleated. He got up to answer it.

"What a dickhead," Maddie mumbled.

Lauren flicked her hand through the air, dismissing Dan. "Forget him. Let's backtrack. Start with Esperanza. What is it?"

"And talk fast," Maddie added. "Before he comes back and has to have a religious discussion with an eighteen-year-old."

Tess picked her way carefully through the day's events. The story sounded demented, but neither Lauren nor Maddie gave any indication they thought she'd lost her mind.

"You *helped* them," Lauren said. "*That's* what it's about. You were able to make them understand they had a choice. My God, this is phenomenal."

Tess wasn't so sure she'd go *that* far. "Mom, I'm the last person anyone should ask for insight or answers about what happens after death. Until today, I was pretty sure that when I died, I just went into a black hole of nothingness."

"Maybe that's exactly why you returned from the dead with this ability."

Maddie immediately powered up her skinny MacBook and went online. She interrupted periodically with some piece of information about Esperanza, the *brujos,* the myth and legend versus the reality, filling in gaps in their knowledge. Her mother asked about Ian. But about him, Tess could offer hardly anything at all, even though he seemed to be pivotal to the story. Ian who? From where? What did he do? Nothing specific came to mind. "I remember walking somewhere with a man, a dog, and a cat. He may be the guy."

"Do you think he was dead, too?" Maddie asked. "Or in a coma?"

"That feels right. But I haven't found those memories yet."

"What's his last name?" her mother asked. "Where's he from? What's he look like?"

Tess remembered her reaction to George Clooney's picture on the cover of the *Michael Clayton* DVD. "I think he looks like George Clooney, but I can't remember anything else."

"Shit, he looks like *Clooney?*" Maddie exclaimed. "Wow, Tesso. You're making death sound better and better." She glanced at her screen. "Okay, I just shot off an e-mail to someone who's going to help us figure everything out."

"Yeah, who's that?" Tess asked.

"A psychic. I asked if you could get in to see her tomorrow. She's really good. I met her and her daughter at one of those college fairs last year and had a reading with her. That's what convinced me to move down here with you guys."

"A *psychic?*" Tess wiggled her fingers. "As I come into your vibration . . . shit, that kind of psychic? No, thanks."

"She works with your people," Maddie said. "The Feds. Her name's Mira Morales."

"Never heard of her."

"Ever heard of Agent Sheppard?"

"*Wayne Sheppard?*"

Maddie nodded, her sly little smile hinting that she was fully aware of Sheppard's reputation. He was practically legendary in the Bureau's southeast division for cracking serial cases—murders, abductions, rapes. "They *work* together?"

"And live together," Maddie added.

"Okay, I'm game."

Lauren sat forward, her voice softer, as if she thought someone—or something—might be listening. "How do we protect ourselves from something we can't see or hear, Tess?"

"I *did* see it. As it left the lawn man's body. It looked . . . like smoke. And I think that when one of them gets close to me, my arm starts to burn and itch. So if that happens, we'll know."

"And then what?" Maddie asked. "That voice said it can't take you, that you're shielded, but it can take me, Lauren, Dan, all of us."

"Maybe you two should stay in Key West for the night. Or in a different room. Or . . ."

"We're staying together." Lauren pressed her palms together, fingertips touching her chin. "And if they come, you'll know it and Maddie and I will leave. Don't bother trying to convert Dan, Tess. His mind is made up. The three of us will figure this out together. We'll go back to the house tomorrow and get the mess cleaned up. I'll take the day off from work and—"

Dan interrupted as he returned to the table and announced he had to shove off. "Double homicide over on Miami Beach."

"Where on Miami Beach?" Tess asked. Before she was shot, Miami Beach was an area she and Dan covered together.

"Outside Club Martinique. Celebrity murders. The local guys are trying to keep it under wraps, but already the press smells a story. The woman was on the cover of *Vogue* a month ago, the guy was her photographer. There were security cameras in the alley where the bodies were found and the owner is sending me the video stream. He claims it shows their bodyguards attacking them."

"May I see it?" Tess asked.

"Sure, if he sent it already." Dan flipped open the lid of his laptop and went online.

"Wait a minute," Maddie said. "*Vogue?* I read *Vogue*. And last month's issue had Barbara DeLinno on the cover. Is *that* who got murdered?"

"I don't know her name. Okay, here's the stream." He motioned for them to take a look. "Is this her?"

They all gathered around, watching the images—a striking Asian woman and two men stepping out of a rear door into an alley. The light wasn't good, so Dan brightened the images.

"That's her," Maddie exclaimed. "The bald guy looks like a bodyguard, so the other guy must be the photographer."

On the video, a dark Expedition pulled up in front of them and the photographer opened the door, said something to the driver, and he got out. Behind them, the model suddenly stumbled and Tess leaned in closer. "Pause it, Dan." She could hardly speak around the pulse pounding in her throat. "There. See it?"

"See what?" Dan asked.

Tess tapped the screen, pinpointing a thin, almost watery discoloration, similar to the mist or smoke she'd seen drifting out of the lawn man just before he died. "That. Right there."

"I don't see anything," Dan said.

"Me, either," said Maddie.

"What about you, Mom? Do you see it? Like thin puffs of smoke?"

"Nope, I don't see it," her mother replied.

"It's probably a flaw in the video," Dan said.

As he put the stream in motion again, the mist disappeared into the top of the bodyguard's skull. Seconds later, the bodyguard slammed his elbow into the bridge of the model's nose and she fell back, blood pouring from her nostrils. The streaming images lacked sound, but Tess knew the woman was screaming. The bodyguard snapped her head from one side to the other and she dropped to the ground. Simultaneously, the man who had been driving the Expedition punched the photographer in the jaw, then sank a knife into his side.

Jesus God, the brujos were in the model and photographer, jumped into the driver and bodyguard, and . . . Bile flooded the inside of her mouth. She barely made it to the railing before she vomited.

Dan's hand, cool, certain, and gentle, touched the back of her neck. His knees cracked as he crouched beside her on the edge of the porch where she now sat. Her stomach kept bubbling like a witch's cauldron, her head spun. He pressed a sweating can into her hand. "Sip slowly. It's ginger ale. My *abuelita* used to give me this when I was a kid with an upset stomach."

She tilted the can to her mouth, sipped, rolled the can across her forehead and cheeks. The wind that kicked in off the Atlantic smelled of salt and distant places, of mystery and unexplored depths. "Dan, whatever I brought back from the dead was inside the model and the photographer and jumped into the bodyguard and the driver. I *saw* it happen. It was the same stuff that drifted out of the lawn man as he died. That essence, whatever it is, now possesses the bodies of the bodyguard and the driver. If you find them, it'll seize you, too."

He didn't laugh, but he exhaled loudly, as if to mask his exasperation. "Look, Tess. I believe that something happened to you while you were dead or in a coma. But possession is a real stretch for me."

She looked over at him, Dan the blond, blue-eyed Cuban. Curious, that he came from a family where his grandmother and father were both practitioners of Santería, a Cuban mystery religion that involved trance states and possession by guardian spirits. "Every time your dad and *abuelita* see clients they're possessed by their *santos*. Why is this any different?"

He rolled his eyes. "C'mon. There's a huge difference. Santería is a religion. You're talking about devils, demons, *brujos, mala sangre.* Crazy shit."

That phrase, *mala sangre,* blew open yet another door in her memory. A bus. A man making the sign of the cross on his forehead and murmuring *mala sangre.* And Ian Ritter from Minneapolis was saying, *There were other Americans out there. Why did he target us?*

Tess went completely still inside. She felt as if she had broken out of a prison of utter barrenness into a place lovely and rich with color and life. *Ian Ritter.* A breathtaking memory surfaced—and it was a *full* memory, complete with audio, visuals, emotions, textures, mood—of herself and a man who resembled George Clooney making love by a fireplace. A black dog was curled up nearby, she heard logs crackling, smelled the pine-scented smoke.

It happened.

Dan regarded her as if she were an alien who had suddenly appeared in front of him. She desperately wanted him to go away so that she could mull over this breakthrough in her memory. But he seemed to be waiting for her to say something. "Someone who has never heard of Santería could watch your *abuelita* working with a client, Dan, and think she's bat shit."

He thought about it for about five seconds, then shook his head, hard, vigorously. "It's not the same thing."

"Oh, *please.* Your grandmother's eyes roll back in their sockets, she froths at the mouth, she twitches and jerks, and then she might as well be speaking in tongues."

"That's a goddamn exaggeration."

Bottom line: Dan Hernandez couldn't move beyond his cultural conditioning. Fine. She got it. "Whatever, Dan. I've warned you, that's all I can do. And thanks again for getting us the suite here."

He seemed surprised that she backed down and sat with her a few minutes longer, hands grasping the lower railing, feet swinging like those of a kid fishing at the edge of a pond. "I don't understand what happened to us, Tess."

She'd been expecting this remark for weeks. The topic of their relationship had come up several times, but not as a genuine plea that begged for an honest answer. Tess gazed out over the crashing waves, the white foam visible in the spill of lights from the pool area.

"What happened was that I died and fell in love with someone else."

Everything today had shocked her, but not like this, not with the same certainty she felt now, that the man she had met when she died was the man with whom she would spend the rest of her life.

Dan's face, usually so easy to read, now looked closed, hard, like metal. "You mean, someone you met while you were dead?"

"Yes."

His expression cracked open, his incredulity shone through. "This is real to you, isn't it. Like, you know, *real* in the sense that you believe it happened."

Nuance. He hadn't said that it was real to her because it had *happened* but that she *believed it had happened,* suggesting she was delusional, that dying had broken her mind. Her mother was right. No point in trying to convince him of anything. She suspected she would be hearing from her boss tomorrow, informing her that she had been reassigned to a desk job or fired.

Tess touched his arm. "Be careful, Dan." Then she pushed to her feet and walked back to the table where her mother and niece were huddled around the MacBook. "I'm whipped. Let's call it a night."

"I call first on the shower," Maddie said, and bounded ahead of them like some creature corralled too long.

"Maybe you should go to Esperanza," Lauren said. "To resolve this."

"That's exactly what I was warned not to do, Mom. It would put you and Maddie at risk."

"We'll go with you."

"You've got a job, Maddie's in college."

222... Trish J. MacGregor

"Hey, I've got eight months of leave. Maddie's free for the summer. That aside, I'm sixty-three years old, healthy, reasonably happy. I did acid and DMT with Terrence McKenna. I smoked pot with Ken Kesey and Jerry Garcia. I rode around on that silly bus of Kesey's for months. And you know what I discovered, Tess? That fear of death is what drives us. Now McKenna, Kesey, and Garcia are dead. I'm not. And I'm not afraid to die. Whatever we are, it's more than this." She flung her arms out. "I need some time to work on my book and Ecuador may be exactly the right place at the right time. So when you're ready to return to Esperanza, I'm with you all the way."

She clearly remembered reading a text message from her mother when she had been in a bus climbing through the Andes. "You texted me when I was dead, Mom. You said you were ready for some great adventure—not for fifteen more years at the hospital, working alongside Doc and his issues. Something to that effect."

Lauren's eyes teared up, she slipped an arm around Tess's shoulders. "You want to hear something really weird? While you were in a coma, I spent hours by your bed talking to you, texting you, e-mailing you, begging you to come back. You're not slipping away from us again, Tess. One way or another, we're going with you."

Tess wrapped her arms around her mother, neither of them speaking or moving until Maddie called, "Hey, ladies, we should pick up a bag of groceries in the store here."

Tess didn't know if the *brujos* would arrive in the bodies of the two bodyguards they'd seen on the security video or if they would arrive in their natural forms, as whiffs of smoke. They had to be ready for either eventuality. So once they were inside their suite, they sealed the cracks under the doors with towels, taped the edges of the windows and the sliding glass doors. Tess felt like she had done this before, against the same enemy. The feeling didn't come with images or sound bites, but she accepted the emotion as a different kind of memory, every bit as valid.

Lauren made a pot of Cuban coffee in the suite's tiny kitchen. They sat around the butcher block table for hours, talking quietly, and came up with a plan. But it was predicated on Tess's belief that the bruise was a kind of alarm that would itch and burn if a *brujo* was nearby. "It'll buy us a little time," she said. "As soon as I feel anything, you two get out of here. Go to Tango Key. I'll meet you there."

"Nope." Lauren shook her head. "Maddie and I agree we're not going anywhere without you."

"Mom, it can't take me. The only way it can hurt me is by seizing either of you. So let *me* be the decoy. We'll stay in touch by cell phone."

Maddie pressed her hands between her knees and looked around uneasily. She whispered, "They could be here now, Tesso. Listening to what we're saying."

"I don't think so."

Her mother pushed back from the table and went over to the coffeepot. "Refills. We're all staying up. I'm going to make omelets."

She went to work, browning mushrooms, whipping up eggs, folding in cheese and diced tomatoes. Watching her, Tess found another memory, of Ian creating culinary delights that had reminded her of her dad, not of her mother.

"Mom, when I was growing up, who cooked dinner most of the time?"

"Your dad. He was a fantastic cook. Since Charlie died, I've gotten better. But nothing I cook will ever equal the kind of stuff he could concoct."

"I remember Ian cooking meals." *And I fell in love with him.* "Ian Ritter. He's from Minneapolis."

"Fantastic, hon. It's a start. With Google, anyone can be found."

By two, her mother's eyes were pinched with fatigue and Maddie kept nodding off, chin dropping toward her chest. Tess convinced them to move into the bedroom and promised she would wake them if her wrist acted up. Once Tess was alone in the kitchen, with fresh coffee in her mug, she used Maddie's laptop and went online.

She brought up the reverse phone book for Minneapolis. A query for Ian Ritter produced numerous links at the University of Minnesota and the *Minneapolis Tribune*. She clicked that link first, a piece from 1978 about the inauguration ceremony for the Ian Ritter School of Journalism Award. One paragraph in particular seized her attention:

The award, named after journalism professor and Tribune columnist Ian Ritter, brings a $10,000 prize to a journalism student for investigative skills. Named after the professor and Pulitzer-prize-winning columnist who vanished under mysterious circumstances in April 1968, the prize is funded by a special trust established by Ritter's ex-wife, Louise Ritter Bell, and their son, Luke Ritter, and his wife, Casey O'Toole Ritter, the Minneapolis Tribune, and the Department of Journalism.

"What the fuck," Tess whispered. *1968?*

And did *her* Ian have a son?

How old is your son?

Twenty-one. He's a senior at the University of Minnesota.

This conversation took place outside a store, in the fog, while she and Ian waited for a bus. Which bus?

Thirteen.

Apparently the key to unlocking her memories was to ask the right question. She clicked the link and it led her to Professor Luke Ritter's university Web site in 2008. It provided mundane info, like the classes he would be teaching in the fall. Tess clicked on his bio.

Born in 1947. She pressed her fists against her eyes, struggling against the dreadful possibility—the likelihood—that if Luke Ritter was *her* Ian's son, it meant that she and Ian were separated by forty years in time. Luke would be in his early sixties now, nearly Lauren's age, and Ian might be dead. Tess clicked his campus e-mail address:

Dear Professor Ritter,

My name is Tess Livingston. I met your dad under unusual circumstances and would be most grateful to know what, if anything, you can tell me about his location now. Did he return to Esperanza? Thank you in advance for anything you can provide.

She included her cell number and two e-mail addresses, but by three, Luke Ritter had not responded, her eyes ached and throbbed with fatigue. She slipped Maddie's computer into its pretty fabric case and set it next to her bulging pack in the bedroom. As she headed for the door, her niece whispered, "Tesso?"

In the spill of light from the hallway, she could see Maddie sitting up, hugging a pillow against her chest, dark hair wild. "I put your MacBook against your pack."

"We have to get out of the country," Maddie said. "You know that, right?"

"Right now, we just need to get through tonight."

But it was as if she hadn't spoken. Focused on her bottom line, Maddie rushed on. "Lauren and I have our passports with us. Do you have yours?"

"Yes. Go to sleep, Maddie."

"What time does the sun rise?"

"A few hours. Don't worry. I'll wake you if there's trouble."

Tess left the bedroom before Maddie could ask any more questions. The couch in the living room sure looked inviting and she propped up the pillows, grabbed one of the throws, and sank into the comfortable cushions with the Glock pressed to her chest.

Her heart beat frantically for a long time.

Tess. Wake up now, you're in danger . . .

She bolted upright, blinking hard and fast against the dark, certain she had heard her dead father's voice. "Dad?" she whispered, and realized she was clawing at the mark on the underside of her wrist. It itched like crazy. She leaped off the couch, ran into the bedroom, turned on the lamp, and woke her mom and Maddie. "They're close. You two have to get out now."

Maddie knuckled her eyes like a sleepy three-year-old, took hold of Tess's arm, looked at the mark. "Oh my God," she whispered. "The bruise is getting darker." With that, she vaulted out of bed.

Lauren had gone to bed in jeans and a T-shirt, and now hurried around the bedroom, jamming stuff in her pack. "How much time do we have? How close are they?"

Time. Tess didn't know, it was all too new. Even though the bruise itched and had turned a deeper plum color, it didn't burn yet. Yesterday when this happened, the burning had started right after she had pulled into her mother's driveway. So perhaps they had a little time.

Tess raced back into the living room, jammed her arms into the sleeves of a lightweight jacket. Ridiculous. A jacket in June. But its multiple pockets held two guns and four clips. When Lauren and Maddie joined her, she handed her mother one of the weapons and two clips "Mom, take this. Twenty-two rounds. You'll be carrying it illegally, but use it if you have to."

"Lauren doesn't know how to shoot a gun," Maddie said.

"Ha," Lauren said, "Tess taught me long before you arrived."

Tess tore the towels away from the cracks under the door, swept up her room card. As they entered the quiet hall, she noted her room's distance from the elevator and the exit sign that led to the stairs. The latter was closest, but she suspected these *brujo* bastards would arrive in human form, as the bodyguards, and would use the elevator. Would she hear the elevator doors opening if she was inside her suite? Probably not. But she had her own alert system. The bruise looked nearly black and itched terribly, but it still didn't burn. They had time. *Please let me be right.* She pushed open the door to the stairs, hugged her mother and Maddie.

Her mother whispered, "We'll check into—"

"No, don't tell me. The less I know, the better. I'll call when I'm on my way."

She waited by the railing, watching them descend through the stairwell, footfalls echoing. Many flights down, her mother leaned out over the railing and blew Tess a kiss. Tess choked back a sob and hoped that sending them away was the right thing to do. The door below clattered open and shut.

Plan, what's my plan? She muted the iPhone's ringer, ripped away the tape on the sliding glass doors, opened them a foot, closed the slats on the wooden Levalors. She swept up all the towels, and in the room her mother and Maddie had shared, stuffed pillows and some of the towels under the covers, the oldest trick in the adolescent playbook. She hoped these *brujos* had been dead too long to know it. She left some clothes on the chair, turned out the lights, went into the smaller bedroom, and threw the covers back. She draped towels over the back of the chair to make the room look inhabited, turned on the lamp.

Her wrist began to burn. Badly. *Shit, not much time.* Bathroom. Shower on. She spun the faucet to hot, tossed a beach towel over the upper edge of the door. It was large enough so that it fell halfway down the glass. It would make it difficult to see inside. She stepped out, shut the door. *Where to hide?*

Linen closet. It stood between the bathroom and the bedrooms. The wooden slats in the door would enable her to see them once they crossed the living room and entered the hall. She slipped inside quickly, testing the range of her vision. Not as wide as she'd hoped, but it would do. The skin at her wrist now radiated heat. *They're close.* She turned on the phone's recorder.

The fridge hummed, the shower drummed, the breeze kept knocking the Levalors together, *clickety-clack.* Then she heard something else, a popping sound, and the bruise suddenly felt as though it were on fire, burning from the inside out. They had arrived.

Tess peered through the door slats, heart thundering so loudly she was terrified they might hear it. One of them entered her view—dark hair, a muscular man. As he moved toward the bathroom, she saw his face. One of the bodyguards. His companion, just now coming into view, was the bald-headed clone of Vic Mackey from *The Shield.* He veered toward the bedrooms and Tess suddenly had no idea how she was going to do this. She couldn't shoot them simultaneously and didn't know which one to aim at first. The dark-haired guy solved the problem. He slipped into the bathroom and shut the door. Tess opened the linen closet quietly, grateful that it didn't squeak, and slid across the tile floor in her stocking feet, toward the bedroom where baldie had disappeared. She heard popping sounds in the bathroom, the shattering of glass, and the bald guy spun around, clutching his weapon, and saw her.

For the briefest second, their eyes locked, and Tess sensed the *brujo* inside, a male energy shocked to see her here, armed. Tess fired. The bullet struck him square in the forehead, an explosion of blood and bone marking the entry point. His eyes widened with astonishment—then he simply fell back onto the bed. Nothing emerged from him, no dark wisps. Tess dived for the floor and rolled away from the door as the other man charged in, shouting, *"Ben, get out, it's a setup, the shower's empty."* And Tess opened up.

Her shots hit the man in the legs and he went down so hard that she heard his knees cracking. He shrieked in pain, fell forward onto his chest, lost his grip on his weapon. Tess leaped to her feet and moved toward him. "Don't move." She swept up his weapon.

"Ben," the man hollered.

"He's dead," Tess said. "Ben is dead."

Nineteen

Dead?

Ben?

Dominica looked up and saw the body on the bed in front of her, a bullet through the head. Fire or the instantaneous death of the host body were the only ways to obliterate a *brujo*. Ben, gone. And *she,* this terrible, wretched bitch, had done it.

Grief nearly crushed her, a sorrow so deep she hadn't even known these emotions existed. She started sobbing and, in between sobs, tried to speak. But this horrible woman was snapping questions at her, threatening to shoot *her* in the head if she didn't start talking. Her fierce, sudden rage stole the life from her grief.

"I promise you this, Tess Livingston. I will take everyone you love as much as I loved Ben and will make sure their deaths are excruciatingly painful. Worse than the lawn man's."

"What are you called?"

"Dominica."

"What do you want from me, Dominica?"

"Your death."

"Why?"

"You're important to the survival of Esperanza. And to the chasers. They've gone to great lengths to protect you."

"Chasers? I don't know what you mean."

"You will."

"Get up," Tess barked.

"I can't. You shot this body in the knees."

"Roll onto your back."

Dominica severed the connection to Lew's pain centers, forced his body to roll, then to vault forward and lunge for the horrible woman. Tess leaped back, but too slowly, and Lew fell onto her, all two hundred and twelve pounds of him. He knocked her sideways into the bureau, air rushed from her lungs, her gun skittered across the room, and Lew crashed to the floor.

Dominica seized control of Lew's limbs, forcing him to his feet again, forcing him to grab the lamp. The cord jerked from the socket and he staggered toward Tess on his injured knees, swinging the lamp like a baseball bat. But Lew's legs were in such bad shape that he lurched like a cripple, the lamp whistled past Tess, and she dived for the gun and squeezed off a shot that ripped into Lew's thigh. Dominica didn't feel it, but Lew did, and he shrieked and went down, crushing the lamp with his body.

"Tess Livingston, you'll wish you had stayed dead!" Dominica shouted.

Because Lew's body was beginning to lose consciousness, Dominica leaped out of him and through the roof, into the darkness. Wind swept her through the night. She called repeatedly for Ben, called just in case she was wrong that instantaneous death of the host body could obliterate a *brujo*. Where had she heard that? Who had told her? She didn't know. Among her kind, there were certain things that you just knew. But because you *knew* them, did that mean they were true? She kept calling to him, but he never answered.

Distraught, directionless, she wandered aimlessly, struggling to come to terms with Ben's annihilation, with the gaping dark hole it had left inside of her. She didn't understand how she, dead for nearly six hundred years, could feel this kind of despair and loss or why she had felt it for most of her life as a *bruja*. Despair over Wayra, Ben, the animals that came and went through her town house. Wasn't death supposed to be the end of suffering?

Awhile later—minutes, hours, she didn't know—she found herself back inside Tess's mother's house. The rooms were empty, someone had cleaned up the crime scene, a dreadful silence suffused the air. She listened to this silence, hoping she might hear Ben whispering to her, laughing, urging her to follow him to wherever he had gone. The silence, so vast and deep, mocked her. She screamed and shrieked, but because she was formless, the noises she made didn't register in the physical world. Only the silence remained, the air shaking with its soundless laughter.

Enraged, she tried to turn on a stove burner so the gas would seep into the air and she could strike a match and blow up the goddamn house. In Esperanza, it wouldn't be a problem. Here, it was impossible. She couldn't make her hand solid enough to touch the knob, to pick up a match. Here, she was nothing, powerless.

Unable to retaliate against the bitch for what she had done to Ben, unable to get even with her, to make her suffer, Dominica left the house, uncertain about where to go, what to do. Should she mobilize her tribe? She imagined it, thousands of her own kind descending on the Florida Keys, sweeping across this miserable string of islands, seizing every person in sight. Another San Francisco feast, but larger and minus the fog.

A car pulled into the driveway and she paused, hopeful that it would be Tess, whom she could follow to wherever her mother and niece were. But Dan Hernandez got out. Good. She could take him, injure him, kill him. She could use him to extract her revenge, to make Tess suffer.

He stood outside his car for a few moments, looking around furtively, checking out the dark street behind him, the yards to either side of him. There were no people around, no other cars, windows were dark. He climbed the stairs quickly and walked right through her. No reaction. Dan tore away the crime tape, turned the knob, flicked on a light switch and only then did he enter. *Afraid of the dark, Agent Hernandez?* Curious about why he was here now, in the hours before dawn, Dominica followed him into the house.

He turned on an overhead light, studied the floor where the lawn man had fallen, looked around the room, obviously inspecting the cleaning job. He proceeded into the kitchen, opened a door under the sink, brought out a bottle of Pine Sol. He wet a hand towel, wrapped it around the bottom of a sponge mop. In the living room, he splashed Pine Sol all over the floor and started mopping, long, vigorous strokes that threatened to scrub away the color of the tile.

Intrigued, Dominica just watched him. The house had been cleaned professionally, so he wasn't here for that. She had the distinct impression that the cleaning symbolized something he hoped to eradicate within himself.

Dan tossed the dirty towel into the washing machine in the utility room, reached under the sink again, removed more rags and bottles of cleansers. Then he went to work in earnest, cleaning counters and windows, tabletops, even the ceiling-fan paddles. He stacked dishes in the washer, started it. He scrubbed the double kitchen sinks, ran the garbage disposal. A one-man cleaning service.

The whole episode was so strange that Dominica decided against taking him right now. Better to accompany him for the time being, to observe, allow her grief to take her in some new direction. So when he finally shut the front door and went downstairs to his car, she was beside him, settling into the passenger seat.

Right now, she didn't give a shit what happened to Esperanza. It could fall, collapse, be conquered. It didn't matter. The only thing she cared about was revenge. *You were her lover before Esperanza. And now you're mine, Dan, whenever I choose to seize you.* He would be her conduit and her ultimate retribution against Tess for what she had done to Ben.

One man dead, the other a raving maniac, and the local cops didn't have a clue what was going on. Until they wised up, Tess's federal badge was all that stood between her and an arrest warrant.

The cops and forensics team finally left her suite just before dawn and she checked out of the resort shortly afterward. Tess drove her mother's Prius south, her exhaustion extreme, her mind blank. But in the back of her head, that eerie voice looped through her thoughts. *I promise you this, Tess Livingston. I will take everyone you love as much as I loved Ben and will make sure their deaths are excruciating.*

Tess lowered the windows and the warm air that blew through the car smelled thickly of summer, ocean, salt. But she felt vulnerable with the windows down, worried that the *bruja* who had threatened her might come through the windows, might . . . *Stop it.* The mark on her wrist didn't burn, the discoloration had nearly faded. That meant there weren't any *brujos* nearby. She would be sure to share that little tidbit with Dan, the Bureau shrink, and her boss.

She called her mother's cell and didn't even reach the voice mail, a sure sign her phone was dead. When she tried Maddie's cell number, her niece answered on the first ring.

"Tesso. Are you all right?"

"I am now. Where're you and Mom staying?"

"Tango Fritter Inn, northwest part of the island, about half a mile out-side the town of Pirate's Cove." She ticked off the address. "Enter it into the GPS. It's tricky finding this place. We're in room thirteen."

Bus 13. Cottage 13 . . . fear of the number 13 is called triskaidekaphobia . . .

The number 13, the wrist mark an alarm system, talking to ghosts, at-tacks by spirits. It was as if her life had collapsed into a whole new para-digm and she didn't have any idea what the rules were. She braked for a stoplight just short of the Tango Key bridge, rubbed her eyes. "Unlock the door. I'm nearly there."

"Unlocking door now, Tesso. See you in a few minutes."

Tess plugged the GPS into the cigarette lighter and typed in the address for the Tango Fritter Inn. The light turned green, she continued on toward the bridge. By any standard, it was an engineering feat, crossing the twelve miles between Key West and Tango. It had been badly damaged in the cat-egory five storm that had devastated the island several years ago. For months, residents had come and gone only by plane or boat. The bridge fi-nally had reopened last July 4 to great fanfare. She remembered because she and Dan had attended the massive celebratory street fair and fireworks display.

She fully expected that in a few hours she would be unemployed and perhaps sought by the police for the man she had killed in the suite. Then there was the other guy with his shattered kneecaps, and the man she had killed in her mother's house. She knew how guilty it made her look.

As she crossed the bridge, the copper sun punched a hole in the horizon. Light touched the trees on the opposite shore, setting them on fire, and the flames burned across the placid silver waters of the Gulf of Mexico. She turned right onto the perimeter road that led around the island, the old road with its rich history, its landmarks, its meandering course that rose steadily from sea level to hundreds of feet above the gulf, along the peri-meter of cliffs.

Cliffs, in Florida.

Tango Key was like no other island in the Florida straits. Even the geo-logical structure was different—no limestone, few flat surfaces except to the south in the town of Tango, where the hurricane devastation had been extreme. Up here in the hills, nature appeared to have restored itself, with farms flourishing, wooded areas thickening, fruit groves bursting with new life. As she approached the outskirts of Pirate's Cove, she felt a glimmer of hope and optimism for the first time in months. Every time she came to this island, it was like that. If she arrived in a depressed mood, that darkness lifted within minutes.

As if to emphasize just how different Tango was from the rest of Florida, Tess suddenly spotted what looked like a flock of low-flying humming-birds. The morning light washed over them and seemed to fill them until they were luminous, celestial. The flock angled east, toward Key West, and she lost sight of them Humming bird. Here. One more impossible thing. But it felt like a sign that she was doing the right thing.

Just beyond the town, the GPS directed her to take a series of quick turns. She finally followed a sparsely populated dirt road to the edge of a cliff. The hotel stood there like a crane with one foot anchored on land and the other tucked out of sight. Part of it jutted out over the cliff, some fancy architectural thing that would crumble away whenever the cliff did. But Florida didn't experience earthquakes and the hard stone that comprised the island seemed capable of withstanding nearly anything. The hotel had not been taken out by the category five hurricane. It hadn't suffered any damage at all.

Her mother opened the door, took one look at Tess, and slid her fingers through Tess's hair. "My God, what happened to your hair?"

Her hair? "Windblown, Mom."

"Never mind." Lauren pointed at the bed. "If you don't fall into this bed immediately, I'm going to knock you out with a punch to the jaw."

"I'm thirty-three, Mom, not fifteen. But the bed sure looks inviting." She crawled into it and the last thing that registered was her mother drawing the covers up to her chin.

As he slept, Dominica pulled up an imaginary chair and watched him—the REM movements of his eyelids, the constant shifting of his body, the way he ground his teeth. She drifted into him slightly. *Brujos* weren't supposed to taste; they had to *take*. But she had traveled well beyond rules and re-strictions. Dominica enjoyed what she tasted in Dan. She appreciated that he could come home from a really bad day, curl up like this and sleep. She liked his connection to Cuban mysticism through his father and grand-mother, that his left brain fought it every inch of the way. It was why he made a good agent. Could she love this man? Maybe. She needed to love someone, anyone. It seemed to be her fate and the reason she suffered so deeply when the one she loved was gone. So be it. *Love the one you're with.*

Dan tasted a lot like Ben. But to love him, she could not take him. Another *brujo* would have to take him and there were no other men in her tribe whom she loved or to whom she was remotely attracted. Could the rules be bent so you could seize the one you loved?

His cell belted out a Latino song and Dominica rapidly withdrew from him. Dan groaned and rolled over. Groggy, groping around on the nightstand like a drunk, he scooped up the cell, pressed the speaker button. "Hernandez."

"It's Lieutenant Frank Cerlane with the Monroe County Sheriff's Department. I answered the call Tess Livingston made yesterday about the dead man at her mother's place."

"Right." Dan sat up in bed, combed his fingers through his disheveled hair, turned on the lamp. "What is it, Lieutenant? What's going on?"

"I, uh, understand that you investigated a double homicide last night in Miami Beach."

"Yes, that's right. A model and her photographer, Barbara De—"

"Yeah, I know who they were, Agent Hernandez. I know who the suspects are. I saw the security video from Club Martinique. And I'm calling to tell you we have one suspect in custody and he's a complete nutcase, and Tess shot and killed the other man. They apparently broke into the suite where she and her mother and niece were staying."

Shit hits the fan, Dominica thought. *Here we go.*

Dan swung his legs over the side of the bed, reached for his clothes. "Talk to me, Lieutenant. Give me some details here. I've got you on speakerphone so I can get dressed. Talk loudly."

The lieutenant's voice followed Dan around the room as he thrust his legs into jeans, jerked a clean shirt off a hanger, swept up his holster, his gun, and pulled on socks and running shoes. Dan fired back with questions, requested details, and at every step of the way Dominica sensed his worldview stretching to accommodate the details.

"I tried to get hold of Tess, but her cell either isn't working or she isn't answering it. Do you have any other numbers for her?"

"Let me see what I can do, Frank. I'll get back to you as soon I have some info."

"Thanks, Dan, I appreciate it."

Frank and Dan. Down to first names. Dan sat at the edge of his bed and punched out one number, waited, punched out another number, waited some more, and finally got through to someone. Since his cell was no longer on speakerphone and Dominica hadn't taken him, she could gauge the situation only through what he said.

". . . what're you doing *there*? . . . I need to talk to her . . . I want to know exactly what happened in that suite last night . . . What? Excuse me, Maddie, but this is a goddamn homicide investigation and—" He slammed his cell phone down against the mattress and squeezed the bridge of his nose. "Fuck. Fuck this shit."

Dominica mustered all her skills and slipped into him as unobtrusively as possible. She was not disappointed. His body felt strong, solid, healthy. He took care of himself. The gym, a vegan diet, exotic juices loaded with nutrients and antioxidants. He loved his work, which bolstered his immune system. But the deep bitterness he harbored about his loss of Tess had canceled out some of the benefits of that vegan diet. He'd quit smoking six years ago and his lungs had recovered, their oxygen capacity boosted by his daily three-mile runs. He would do well in the thin air of Esperanza, she thought.

He didn't realize she had slipped inside of him, that he was now compromised. He didn't seem aware of her at all. No screaming or internal dialogues, no struggle. Tense, she waited for him to shout, fight. Nothing. Yes, she had been cautious before when seizing someone, but never *this* cautious, *this* determined to remain hidden, disguised, allowing her essence to be dispersed, scattered among his molecules and cells. She was now liquid to his earth, spread everywhere but concentrated nowhere. It diluted her strength, but served her purpose.

Once he was in his car, he drove south to Tango Key. Morning now. His body was in such excellent health that using his senses was sheer joy. The sun blazed, the sky was gloriously blue, and the air smelled of salt, heat. He stopped for a cup of café con leche at his favorite Cuban eatery. She wanted a croissant with a dripping fried egg inside, but Dan the vegan hadn't eaten eggs in years, and bought a container of granola mixed with soy yogurt. She could live with it, for now. She didn't dare rock this strange and wondrous vessel she had borrowed.

She thought, briefly, of Ben—Ben and his Mercedes, Ben and his hunger for physical life—and wondered where he was now, where annihilated souls went. Maybe he was with Mole, the retriever pup. This question had nagged at her for centuries, and even after nearly six hundred years she didn't have an answer.

As they neared Tango Key, Dan started feeling sick, a malaise so powerful that he pulled to the side of the road, stumbled out, and puked. Dominica gently urged him to get back into his car and return to Key West. He made a hasty U-turn in the middle of the bridge and, almost immediately, his nausea ebbed.

For a while, he drove the narrow, tangled streets of old town Key West, mulling things over. Dominica remained silent, observant, made small adjustments in his blood sugar levels. She thought that might be why he had gotten sick. He finally parked, went into a restaurant, and ordered a salad, veggie burger, cold iced tea, no sugar. Afterward, he felt much better and decided stress was the culprit—over the breakup with Tess, work, high gas prices, life in general.

As he approached the bridge again, something took shape in his peripheral vision, in the passenger seat, but Dominica realized only she could see it. Whatever it was didn't register for Dan. Then she saw it clearly—a hummingbird, white, luminous, wings beating fast. The shape slowly solidified into a man with thick white hair, Ben Franklin glasses, broad shoulders. He wore jeans, sandals, a pale guayabera shirt. Not a *brujo*. This man was some other sort of spirit—a chaser?—and he shook his finger at her as though she were a naughty child. *I don't think so, Dominica. You won't be getting anywhere near them. Not on this island.*

Who the hell are you?

The man laughed. *You'd better make your host turn around or he's going to get really sick this time.*

As soon as he said this, she felt the sickness bubbling up through Dan's body. Before she could convince him to turn around, he vomited violently all over himself. He swerved to the side of the bridge, slammed on the brakes, got sick again. The car reeked, he was sweating, clumps of his undigested lunch clung to his jeans and shirt, to the seat and console.

The man with the white hair said, *I told you. Get him off the bridge. Tango Key is off-limits to your kind.*

Dan started to open the door, but Dominica seized control of him completely. She forced him to start the car, check for traffic, then to make a U-turn. He sped away from Tango Key.

Very wise, Dominica, the white-haired ghost said.

What are you?

Your worst nightmare.

That doesn't mean anything to me.

Then this will, and the white-haired ghost became Manuel Ortega, companion of Tess, Ian, and Nomad. Then the image faded and the luminous hummingbird flew up through the roof and away. A mounting horror flooded through her. Tess Livingston was being protected by the same man who had driven her bus to Esperanza, the bastard who had turned the flamethrower on her. A light chaser. His real form, she guessed, was that of the white-haired man, but when he was in and around Esperanza, his virtual form was Manuel Ortega. Or a hummingbird. He wasn't allowing her to enter Tango Key, and as long as she was inside of Dan, he wouldn't be able to get on the island, either.

Twenty

When Tess woke at noon, her eyes felt like they were filled with sand, her stomach rumbled with hunger, she was alone in the room. She looked around uneasily for any sign that the *brujo* had pursued her here. But the shadows pooled in the corners were only shadows. Motes of dust drifted in the ribbons of light that slipped through the curtains, the air conditioner wheezed. On the nightstand, she found a note from her mother that she and Maddie had gone shopping. They would be back around twelve-thirty to take her to lunch and then to her reading with the psychic at two.

Tess had been to only one psychic, at the South Florida Fair shortly after she and Dan had gotten involved, a Gypsy lady in a tent, five bucks for a five-minute reading. *Long life, happiness, true love, good health.* Yeah, right. *And you win the 30-million-dollar lottery.* So, in spite of the fact that Mira Morales had worked with the legendary Sheppard, Tess harbored doubts about how useful this would be. But she had nothing to lose.

She turned on her iPhone and found a dozen text messages from Dan and nearly as many voice mails. It amounted to one long litany about why she should call him. *We need to talk about what happened last night. Local cops have serious questions. Got thru to Maddie, she said you're on Tango, then hung up on me. Call me. Let's talk.*

Call? And tell him what? That she no longer lived in a world of reason and left-brain logic? He already suspected as much. He had ridiculed her once, she wouldn't invite it again. Tess turned off the phone, selected clean clothes and toiletries from her pack, and went into the bathroom to shower. She caught sight of herself in the mirror and just stood there, staring. No wonder her mother had asked what had happened to her hair. It had turned completely white.

On**e** World Books reminded Tess of a house in a fairy tale, all crooked corners, a sloping front porch with a hammock at one end, two stories painted blue and yellow. Dozens of wind chimes hung from the mango and banyan trees that shaded the building. As the breeze blew, the chimes danced and sang, filling the air with music.

Inside, walls had been removed to create a vast, open area filled with bookshelves, wide aisles, a coffee shop. Dozens of customers browsed in the aisles, where sunlight from the many tall windows streaked the cherrywood floors.

"I'll find out where we're supposed to go," Maddie said, and hurried off.

Lauren touched Tess's arm. "I'm going to browse. And stop fretting about your hair. I think you look terrific."

"You're my mother. You'd say that even if I was covered with warts. And c'mon, how many thirty-three-year-olds do you know who are totally gray?"

Her mother pretended to think about it. "Dozens. There's always Clairol."

Sure. Better living through chemicals. "I'll order us cappuccinos, Mom."

Once she had ordered, she claimed a table by the window, opened her laptop, and went online to check her e-mail. She ignored the dozens of e-mails from Dan and clicked on the only one that mattered, from Professor Luke Ritter.

Dear Ms. Livingston,

My inclination is to believe this is some sort of joke. I last saw my dad 40 years ago, when I drove him to the Duluth airport. But if you're who you say you are, then you should be able to answer a couple of simple questions. What was my dad's nickname for you & why? Who was Nomad?

In which cottage did you stay? Who drove the bus to Esperanza?

Luke Ritter

She read the e-mail several times, dread and excitement thrashing around inside her. A separation of forty years meant that Ian was either very old by now or dead. But this e-mail was confirmation that he'd existed, that what she was remembering had happened. A kind of Zen stillness claimed her, then memories poured into her like sunlight through darkness.

Dear Luke,

He called me Slim, from the movie Dark Passage. Nomad was a black Lab. We stayed in cottage 13. Haven't recovered the memory about the bus driver's name. But I remember *brujos*, being on bus 13, Ian cooking, hummingbirds, a black & white cat named Whiskers. I remember sealing doors and/or windows with duct tape to keep out *brujos* during an attack. I remember falling in love w/yr dad. Memories continue to surface, but those are the ones about which I'm certain.

Six months ago, I was shot during a federal counterfeiting sting, died during surgery, was revived & spent weeks in a coma. Only recently have these memories started returning. If Ian told you about *brujos*, then you'll understand why I ask if he was threatened by them once he regained consciousness.

Thank you again.

As she sent it off, a slender, diminutive woman stopped at her table. "Excuse me, are you Tess?"

She looked to be in her early seventies, her salt-and-pepper hair pulled back into a braid that snaked down her left shoulder. She wore loose black pants, a T-shirt with a ceiba tree on it, hemp sandals. There was such presence about her that for a moment Tess wondered if she might be another ghost. "Yes, I'm Tess."

"I'm Nadine."

The name didn't mean anything, but Tess felt compelled to honor this woman in some way, so she brought her palms together. "Namaste."

Nadine looked astonished, pulled out the chair on the other side of the table, and sat down. "How long have you been practicing yoga?"

"A few months. My downward facing dog stinks, I still can't get my heels flat, and in class I feel like the turd the dog dragged in."

Nadine laughed. "Even the masters have trouble with certain postures. Some of them can tie their ankles behind their heads, but they can't lie flat in a forward bend, with their chests flush with the floor. Some of them can't do a lotus because their hips are too tight. You do what you can and honor that part of yourself that tries. The divine light in me recognizes the divine light in you. That's what 'Namaste' means. That's what our yoga practice is about." Then: "My granddaughter is ready for you."

"Your granddaughter?"

"Mira Morales. You have a reading with her?"

The psychic of Tango Key. "Should I pay you or her, Nadine?"

"She said the reading's free."

"*Free?* Why?"

"Usually when she does that, it means she's picking up something so unusual about you or your situation, it will give her a chance to expand her
ability."

It sounded incredibly idealistic, but what the hell. She slipped the laptop
in its bag, and she and Nadine picked up the coffees, and headed toward the
back of the store. "Nadine, is it true that Mira lives with Wayne Sheppard?"

Nadine emitted a derisive laugh. "Today she does. Tomorrow, who
knows? I've given up trying to figure out their relationship. Why?"

"Just curious."

"*You're* FBI?"

"No longer."

"I wish Shep would say the same thing."

"But I hear he's phenomenal at what he does."

"He is. But when you're in that kind of profession, you attract experiences
you might not attract otherwise. You're better off doing something else,
Tess."

That remained to be seen. Right now, "something else" might be the inside of a prison cell.

A cat snoozed in a chair at the end of a bookcase. In a reading area,
a clutch of teenage girls huddled together, laughing, whispering, text-
messaging. Photographs covered a wall on Tess's right that captured the ineffable essence of the island's mystery, moodiness, majesty. They entered a
comfortable room with a huge picture window that overlooked an exquisite
Japanese garden bathed in early afternoon light. Beneath the window stood
a stone coffee table with couches and chairs arranged in a half-moon around
it. Lauren and Maddie sat there, talking with a slender, attractive woman.

Mira Morales. Her dark hair was pulled back from her face with mother-
of-pearl combs and tumbled to her shoulders. She wore gray Capri pants
and a black T-shirt with TANGO FRITTER written across it in a luminous
blue. No carnival Gypsy, Tess thought. No dumpy frump in a muumuu
whose voice was husky from too many cigarettes. She didn't wear a million
rings and probably wouldn't say, *As I come into your vibration.*

"Tess, it's wonderful to meet you. Maddie and I have just been catching
up on her move to Florida."

Tess and Nadine set the cappuccinos on the table. "I understand you were instrumental in convincing her to move. Mom and I appreciate it. We love having her with us."

Lauren pushed up from her chair. "We'll wait outside, hon."

"I've got nothing to hide," Tess said. "You're involved. You *should* stay."

"Is that okay with you, Mira?" Lauren asked.

"Absolutely."

Tess settled into the chair between her mother and niece. She didn't see any tarot cards or other divination tools on the table. Mira didn't look like the type who would pull some Santería bullshit from her bag of tricks, like a reading that first required an offering to the *orishas*, the saints—coins, chocolates covered in honey, a piece of jewelry, or a hefty check. She had seen Dan's grandmother and father at work in that regard.

For a few moments, Mira said nothing. It seemed to Tess that her breathing altered slightly. The room felt thick and sluggish with silence.

"Tess, a man came into the room with you," Mira said suddenly.

She glanced behind her, but only Nadine was there, standing by the door. "She means a spirit," Maddie whispered. "A ghost."

Not another one. A legion of the dead followed her. "Is he . . . hostile?"

"Not at all. He's smiling. He's got a broad chest, thick white hair, large blue eyes. Ben Franklin glasses. Right now, he's standing between you and your mother and I believe his name starts with a *C*."

Tess and her mother glanced at each other. *Holy crap,* her mother's eyes screamed, and she said, "Charlie? He's here?"

"He's nodding," Mira said. "That's his name."

Tess considered it ironic that she could interact with strangers who were dying or dead, but couldn't see her dead father.

"Tess, Charlie's insisting that you can see him," Mira said. "That you can talk to him, interact with him. He says you have that ability now. He's mentioning something about hummingbirds. That's how you'll see him sometimes."

The flock of hummingbirds this morning.

Mira sat forward, her intense gaze pinning Tess. "Charlie's saying that you saw spirits at an accident scene yesterday."

"The accident on the turnpike?" Lauren asked.

Tess nodded. "But that happened spontaneously."

"Charlie suggests that when you're consciously trying to see a spirit, you should use your peripheral vision. Or roll your eyes upward, toward a spot between your brows, and try alternate nostril breathing, like what you do in yoga."

"Is that what *you* do?" Maddie asked Mira.

"I don't seem to have much of a choice," Mira said. "I've been seeing spirits since I was a kid. Fortunately, Nadine was my teacher. Lauren, Charlie apologizes for leaving when he did. But he says it was necessary for certain events to unfold. He hopes that you'll forgive him and that by the end of this reading you'll have a better understanding of why he had to leave."

Lauren looked on the verge of tears. "I forgave him a long time ago. But his reasons better be damned good."

Tess felt a breath of cold air on her left, between her and her mother, but didn't see anything in her peripheral vision.

"Charlie is telling me that you died, Tess. That you were in a coma for a while."

Tess wondered if Lauren and Maddie had given Mira this bit of information.

"He wants you to know that he didn't meet you then because you were supposed to experience something, so that you could return with this ability you now have. This place you went. He's trying to tell me the name, but I'm only hearing the sound *esp*. Does that mean anything to you?"

This woman was definitely not some wacko carnival Gypsy. "Esperanza. In Ecuador."

Mira's eyes glazed over. "All right, he's confirming that. He says that when you were on the first bus, you and an American family were booted off at a store. One of the kids, a young girl, got sick. You gave the mother something to alleviate the girl's nausea and, later on, the girl thanked you and said something about her bear. Do you remember that?"

Sweet Christ. The memories came fast and furiously now. Tess felt the blood drain from her face. "Yes."

"He was the girl. Your father assumed her shape."

"How could he do that?" Maddie asked. "Assume a shape?"

"That family was dead and Charlie knew how to assume the child's shape." Mira paused and cocked her head, as if listening to something Tess couldn't hear. "He's telling me, Lauren, there's a key on your key ring that has puzzled you since his death. You found it among his things. It fits a safe-deposit box here on Tango. Box thirteen. He left money in an account to pay for the annual fee for a dozen years. You need to get to the safe-deposit box as soon as possible. You'll find enough cash to get the three of you to Ecuador and do whatever else needs to be done. He's been waiting a long time to tell you this. And he knows you're going to be pissed about it, about how he managed to tuck away so much money."

"Fuck," Lauren said.

"Charlie's laughing. He knew you'd say that," Mira said.

"What bank?" Lauren asked. "It would be helpful to know that."

"He's not sure. It has changed hands several times and the hurricane altered the landscape so that he seems confused about the location. I think it's in the northern part of the island." Mira's eyes darted to Tess. "Has the number thirteen recurred for you since you died, Tess?"

Where'd she get that? "Numerous times."

"Esoterically, the number thirteen represents someone who is reborn into a higher level of consciousness and has reached a state of transmutation," Mira said. "It's one of the patterns, the synchronicities, that will continue to be important for you. Charlie says it's vital to keep the police confused, so you may have to book several flights to Quito. Also, Lauren and Maddie will be vulnerable to—" She stopped, gasped, her eyes bulged, and she suddenly doubled over, arms clutched to her waist.

Nadine hurried over to Mira, whispered something. Mira shook her head. "It'll pass."

Tess and her mother exchanged a glance, no one spoke. Minutes ticked by, then Mira said, "I sometimes pick up . . . physical stuff. And right then I was hooked into a man whose name starts with *D*—Don, Dick, Dan, Drake, something like that. One syllable. He's sick. There's something inside him that's . . . making him do things." Another pause. "Does any of this make sense to you?"

Tess couldn't speak around the rising tsunami in her throat. She wanted to leap to her feet and shout, *Who the hell are you that you know these things?* "Dan. His name's Dan. And what's *in* him? What *is* it?" She already had figured it out, knew that the *brujo* who had threatened her was making good on her promise. *I will take everyone you love as much as I loved Ben and will make sure their deaths are excruciating.*

"It's a . . . a hungry ghost, that's the phrase Charlie is asking me to use. My understanding is that it's a spirit, a lower astral being that stays close to our physical level of existence. These kinds of souls cause hauntings and poltergeist activity, and can sometimes attach themselves to the human energy field and create all kinds of problems. There're different reasons for their inability to move on—a traumatic or sudden death, a lack of belief in an afterlife, a refusal to accept guidance from other spirits. Those are the most common reasons. But these beings seem to have developed in an unusual way."

"They . . . invade people," Tess said. "Possess them. Take over their bodies, use them as hosts and force them to do things."

"Not unheard of. Charlie's telling me these entities have a name for themselves and they number in the millions."

Millions? "They call themselves *brujos*."

"The spirit that has taken Dan intends to kill you, Tess, and needs Dan's body to do that. He's trying to come to Tango. But Charlie and his group are preventing Dan from coming here because of this entity inside him. They make him sick every time he tries to get on the island."

"A group," Tess said. "What's that mean? What kind of group?"

"Of energy. Of souls. Charlie is part of this group."

"Good and evil?" Lauren asked. "That's what it sounds like."

"These *brujos* don't see themselves as evil any more than Hitler saw himself as evil. This battle between the *brujos* and Charlie's group has gone on for centuries. It's about control of Esperanza and other places like it. You and a man figure prominently in this battle and the *brujos* intend to stop you any way they can. Does the word *wayra* mean anything to you?"

Wayra was the name of an independent record label that specialized in Incan music. But as she repeated it to herself, the word became a magical abracadabra that hurled open yet another door to buried memories. *A greenhouse. Two men. One of them begins to change, body transmuting, shifting from human to dog. Wayra/Nomad, shape-shifter.*

"Charlie's telling me Wayra is a part of his group. They call themselves . . . light chasers, yes, I think that's the phrase. Wow, this stuff is . . . incredibly strange. Powerful." She brought her fingers to her right temple. "Over here, there's a channel about the chasers. And over here . . ." Her fingers slipped to her left temple. "There's other stuff. Which do you want?"

Panic. What did she want? AM or FM? "Other."

"A man whose name starts with a *T* or an *I*. Do you have any idea who he is?"

"Ian. I met him when I was . . ." *Dead.* "In Esperanza."

"This man is like . . . your other half. Charlie seems to have a deeper agenda for the two of you, but I can't interpret what he's trying to communicate about that. He and his group can help to manipulate events, to shield you and Ian, but they're as limited in their way as the *brujos* are in theirs. They can't physically fight this battle."

Mira paused again, shut her eyes, and was silent for so long that Tess thought the reading was finished. Tess realized she was sitting forward, her body rigid, muscles tight, and finally forced herself to sit back. She felt that cold breath of air intensely on her left side, and when she turned her head, her dad took shape between her and her mother. Charlie, poking his glasses back up onto the bridge of his nose.

Hey, Slim.

You're freaking me out, Dad.

C'mon, hon. I've been talking to you since the day I left. Now listen real well. You need to get off the island with your mother and Maddie. It won't be safe here much longer.

His form flickered, then disappeared. Tess thought it likely that she was now in complete mental meltdown.

"Maddie and Lauren," said Mira. "The two of you will be going to Ecuador with Tess."

Maddie frowned. "I'd like to go. But is there some particular reason to do so?"

"Because you're young and see what they can't, because they're your family. And I think your ultimate destiny lies there, Maddie."

"My ultimate destiny as what? To do what?"

"I don't know. Tess, Charlie is insisting that Ian contacted you, but there seems to be . . ." She frowned, her hands in front of her, as though she were holding something. Then her hands moved away from each other, as if the object were growing. "A space like this between you. I have absolutely no idea what that means."

"I think I do. Ian lived in 1968, died, ended up in Esperanza in 2008, and . . . and . . ." *And then he vanished mysteriously in April 1968 and now his son is sixty-one years old.*

"Wow," Maddie breathed. "This is so unbelievably awesome."

"*Awesome?*" Lauren balked. "This is confusing. Even if you both make it back, Tess, how will you end up being together if you're from different times?"

Tess felt small, miserable, uncertain. "I don't know."

"Uh, Charlie's assuring me there's a way."

A breath of cool air brushed the back of Tess's neck, goose bumps sped up her arms. *The three of you need to be gone by tomorrow, Slim.*

"Charlie just left," Mira announced.

Lock me up. Her dad had just *left,* Mira said, but he actually had left ten years ago, left her mother in the lurch—single mom, one daughter in law school, the other not doing well financially. Her dad's death had reduced them to statistics. But now she was supposed to believe it had happened for a reason.

Fuck this.

"Give me a call in the next day or so," Mira said. "Let me know what you decide, Tess. If I pick up anything else, I'll call you."

They exchanged cell numbers and e-mail addresses, and a few minutes later, the three of them went into the café. They claimed a table, and once they were seated, Lauren spoke in a soft, conspiratorial tone. "Reality check. What we've just heard is so far out there that we need to reach a consensus here. Are we nuts? Is Mira a wacko? Was Charlie really talking to Mira? Did Tess see Charlie? Hello, I'm losing it here."

"My vote," Maddie said, "is that we move forward according to the information she gave us."

"Tess?" Lauren looked at her.

"I'm not sure what I want to do."

"Wait a minute." Maddie's face turned to stone. "You'd actually stay *here,* Tesso? And do what? Resume your work as a field agent with a partner who's possessed? Hope that whatever weirdness seized Dan will get bored and move on? What kind of solution is that?"

"I need a café con leche," Tess said.

"This isn't a Cuban bakery," Lauren pointed out. "I'll get us cappuccinos. Then I need to check three banks before five this afternoon."

"I'm hungry," Maddie said.

They both got up and left Tess alone at the table. She quickly went online. There were two e-mails from Luke.

Wow. I am so sorry I was such a presumptuous shit. So many of Dad's predictions came true thru the years, beginning with King's assassination, then RFK's, then Nixon & Watergate & everything else. The Internet, Yahoo, cell phones etc. He seemed to have incredible recall of what he'd experienced while in a coma, but admitted that his time in a mental facility had wiped some memories clean. He knew, for instance, that he wasn't remembering some vital detail about Nomad. He couldn't recall yr line of work. That made it tough for me to find u the several times I tried to track u down. Yr phone # was never listed. I figured you'd left the Miami area.

Yes, the *brujos* did try to attack him—and couldn't get near him. But one of them took my mother—an experience from which she never really recovered. The *brujo* used her until Dad fled to San Francisco to search for Sara Wells, a cultural anthropologist who went to E in 1969. I think he needed her as a validation. He also seemed to return from the dead with the ability to see the dead.

The last time I heard from him, he was @ the ExPat Inn, Otavalo. I told him I would be there in a few days, but when I arrived, he was gone. I spent months traveling around Ecuador, looking for him, but never saw him again.

Just in case you're going thru the same kinds of doubts he did, I'm sending an attachment that should put your doubts to rest. Start yr search in Otavalo, Tess. Kim Eckart used to be the ExPat owner. My contact info is at the end of this e. Please stay in touch & and when u find Dad, ask him to call. He'll be thrilled to know he has a 31-year-old granddaughter!

Best,
Luke

Tess eagerly clicked the attachment. The first image was of credit card receipts dated April 6, 1968, and appeared to be for ads Ian had taken out in three South Florida newspapers. The second image was a photo of the man she remembered—the same warm smile, those eyes like dark pools, a beard sprinkled with gray. Not exactly a dead ringer for Clooney, but close enough so when she'd seen Clooney's face on the cover of the DVD for *Michael Clayton,* it had resonated. The third attachment was from the personal ads of the *Miami Herald,* dated April 8, 1968. In the middle of the page, in large, bold letters, was an ad that read:

Slim, it's real. Am leaving 4/8/1968, Frisco-Quito.
Love, Ian Ritter from Minneapolis

Tess pressed her fists against her eyes.

Twenty-one

Dominica refused to release him. If she couldn't get onto Tango Key in Dan Hernandez's body, then she would use his body to force Tess, her mother, and niece off the island.

She spoke to him through his limbic brain, associated with pleasure, sexual arousal, rage, a hunger for revenge. Atavistic urges, that was her understanding. It seemed to work. Dan Hernandez drove much too fast to Tess's mother's house.

It was early evening when he pulled into an empty lot half a mile from Lauren Livingston's place. He retrieved his bike from the rack on the back of the car and pedaled through long, narrow shadows, a man on a mission. He rode into the deserted cul-de-sac, then into an overgrown field, and dismounted. Gun. Cell. His needs were simple. He took his time, walking up the road, enjoying the smells of early summer in the Keys. Night-blooming jasmine, the ocean, the day's warmth trapped in the asphalt. He felt happier as the day surrendered to twilight. He was less visible now.

The half-dozen snowbirds who lived on this street had departed after Easter and the other residents wouldn't pay any attention to a guy out for his evening constitutional. No one would remember him. She kept working on his limbic brain, stoking the fires, conjuring images of how he had been used by Tess, victimized, wronged. *Revenge, revenge* became his mantra.

Before he crossed the street, he picked up a large branch, tore off the leaves, swung it through the air. He wasn't sure yet how it would serve him, but sensed he might need it. *For what?* his conscience asked. He didn't know yet, but the question caused him to hesitate. Dominica felt his sudden uncertainty, the doubts that seeped through him. He looked at the house on the other side of the road, down at the branch he clutched. "What the . . . ?"

Dominica quickly ramped up her own efforts—*revenge, revenge*—and his anger roared back. "Goddamn bitch." He trotted across the street.

At the top of the steps, he set the branch against the wall, unlocked the door, took one last furtive glance around, and slipped inside. Dan went directly into the kitchen, turned on the gas oven and the four burners, just as she had tried to do. She urged him to open the cabinet doors under the sink, to remove rags and two cans of lighter fluid. But he knew what to do now and didn't need prompting from her.

Dan twisted off the top of one can and backed into the living room, saturating the couches, chairs, throw rugs. He moved through the bedrooms, bathrooms, utility room, squirted the lighter fluid on bed, clothes and shoes, towels and bath mats. When he'd emptied the first can, he opened the second and went through the rooms again. He made a deliberate trail of fluid to the front door, stepped out on the porch, and wrapped rags around the end of the stick. He soaked the fabric, held a lit match to it.

The rags burst into flames and Dan hurled the burning branch into the house, certain it would ignite the gas escaping from the stove. He slammed the door and made it down the stairs and out of the cul-de-sac before two convulsive explosions lit up the dusky sky, catapulting burning debris that cast the street and houses in an eerie orange light. He didn't hesitate, didn't stop. He hopped on his bike and pedaled madly for the lot where he'd left his car, threw himself inside, and took off. The distant squeal of sirens sent his blood pressure soaring, he drove like a madman.

Eighty-nine minutes to his parents' place in Little Havana. Some sort of festivity was going on—an engagement party, families and friends, couples and singles, coworkers and bosses, barbecue grills set up behind the house, people stoned, drunk, gone. No one would remember when he arrived.

When the first reports about the fire began coming in on his BlackBerry, anxiety gripped him. Dominica adjusted the dopamine levels in his brain. As he calmed down, she convinced him to find a spare bed and take a nap. He was wonderfully suggestible and collapsed on a couch in one of the back rooms, an office.

Once he was asleep, Dominica went to work on him, reinforcing his conviction that Tess's near-death experience had snapped her mind, she was desperately in need of psychiatric help, that her breakdown had caused her to kill two men and gravely injure a third man. Self-defense had nothing to do with it. Dominica planted the suggestion that Tess was a flight risk who would attempt to leave the country for Ecuador, searching for the place she claimed she had visited when she was in a coma. Armed and dangerous, that was Tess. A modern-day Bonnie without her Clyde.

Dominica blocked any memory he had of destroying Lauren Livingston's house. This last part was possible only because she had been inside of him when he'd done it and knew exactly which parts of his brain to manipulate. Then she waited for him to awaken.

When Tess's cell rang at eleven that evening, she, her mother, and Maddie were tallying their totals for the money Lauren had removed from Charlie Livingston's safe-deposit box. She was surprised to see Mira's name and number in her cell's ID window.

"Hey, Mira," Tess said.

"Are you alone?"

"No."

"Pretend your reception isn't good and come outside."

"You're breaking up, Mira. Let me step outside."

Lauren and Maddie continued running their tallies and Tess quickly stepped out into the breezy darkness of the motel parking lot. The scent of ocean here was much stronger than it ever was in the Upper Keys, as if Tango were its own continent, with its own rules and parameters. It reminded her that nothing in the world she occupied now was what it appeared to be.

"Okay, I'm outside," Tess said. "What's up?"

"I'm in the VW on the other side of the lot. Flashing my headlights."

Tess trotted over to the VW and slipped inside. Mira had changed clothes—jeans, sandals, a black tank top. She looked tense. "Sorry to be so cloak-and-dagger, Tess. But I wanted to speak to you separately from your mom and Maddie."

"They're counting the money Mom removed from that safe-deposit box. That was a definite hit, Mira."

"Not my hit. I just repeat what the ghosties are saying. I hope it's substantial. You're going to need it."

Tess didn't like the sound of that.

"I don't know if Maddie told you, but the man I live with—Shep—is an FBI agent. A little while ago, he got a call from an Agent Hernandez, requesting that he bring you in to the Miami office for questioning in the deaths of two men and an assault on a third man. And Hernandez apparently called the Tango County cops to find you and turn you over to Shep. The only reason you haven't been picked up is because the local boys don't know where you are." She paused. "My instincts tell me that the thing inside Dan is making him do this. That's why I'm here."

Mira seemed to be waiting for her to offer her version of events. But there wasn't any *version*, just the truth. All her life, she had been like this. Black or white, good or bad, right or wrong. Tess's world consisted of contrasts, opposites, absolutes. Nuances were rare. It was why she'd been attracted to law enforcement rather than to the practice of law. Too many nuances in the law, hardly any in law enforcement. It probably explained why most of her relationships had ended up in the recycling heap.

"Look, I shot both men in self-defense. One of them trashed my mom's place, the other one tried to kill me, and the third one has shattered kneecaps. I killed one of these *brujos,* but I don't have a clue how that can even be possible because my understanding of *brujos* is that they're already dead. I don't know what else to say."

Mira's expression didn't change. "There's more. Apparently your mother's house was torched earlier this evening. Burned to the ground. Nothing left. Shep says that's how Hernandez described it to him."

Torched. Tess pressed the heels of her hands against her eyes. *Everything gone.* And it was her fault. Because of her, her mother and niece were now on the run, her mother's house had been destroyed, years of memories and irreplaceable memorabilia gone in a flash. *Mom, I'm so sorry.* She felt certain that the *bruja* inside Dan had made him do it, but didn't say it. Even though Mira grasped the situation, Tess's conclusion might be too big a stretch even for Mira.

"Mom's going to insist on driving up to Key Largo."

"It'll put her at risk, Tess. Whoever did this may be trying to draw all of you off the island."

The bruja's *promise.* Tess raked her fingers back through her white hair and exhaled slowly. "What do you think we should do?"

"Get out of the country as soon as you can. I spoke to a friend, a pilot who runs an air charter and cargo business here on Tango. He's got a cargo flight leaving for the Dominican Republic in about an hour. From there, you can book a flight to Quito. He'll charge you a couple hundred apiece. But there won't be any record that the three of you were on the flight."

"He can bypass TSA? Homeland Security? The State Department?"

"He operates on a whole other level, Tess."

"Yeah? And what level is that?"

"The level of the very wealthy and the well connected. He's a close friend. I trust him."

"We'll do it. We've got two cars, though, both paid for. Can we leave them with you?"

"You bet. I'll put them in my garage."

"I'll give you the name of a doc my mother works with. He'll help out with the cars, come and get them." Doc Brian would do a favor for her mother.

"How fast can you get your stuff together?" Mira asked.

"Ten minutes. We'll follow you to your place."

"I imagine there'll be insurance questions about your mom's house. We can deal with that through e-mail."

"I can't thank you enough, Mira." Tess started to get out of her car, but paused. "Do you do this for all your clients? Is this normal? For you?"

"Normal?" Mira's brows shot up, forming little peaks. "No way. This situation is so *not* normal that I'm going to have to visit Esperanza."

"Ten minutes." Tess got out of the car, wondering how to break it to her mother that her house was a pile of smoldering ashes.

When she entered the room, Maddie announced that the grand total in cash at their disposal was $497,000. Lauren said she had no idea where the money had come from. But Tess did. Her dad had squirreled it away, a bonus here, a stock sale there, money tucked away every year he had spent on the planet. He always told stories about how his grandparents had hidden money in their mattresses during the Depression.

"What'd she want?" her mother asked.

"We need to leave." Tess told them what was going on, then added: "There's something else, Mom. Your house has, uh, burned to the ground."

Lauren's expression shifted rapidly from incredulity to grief to shock to rage and then her face collapsed and she stood rapidly and walked into the bathroom. Tess and Maddie just looked at each other.

"Jesus, Tesso," Maddie whispered.

"It's the *bruja* inside him," Tess whispered back. "It's revenge against me."

"So Dan wouldn't realize what he was doing?"

"Probably not."

After a few minutes, she and Maddie both got up and went to the bathroom door. Tess heard running water, her mother blowing her nose, then the water went off, Lauren opened the door, and Tess and Maddie wrapped their arms around her. Tess couldn't grasp what this meant to her mother. She didn't know what treasures the house had held, didn't have any idea how emotionally vested her mother was in her home. She had not shared the house with Charlie, but the presence of Tess's father had been everywhere.

She was surprised when her mother stepped back from them, her eyes still red from crying, and said, "Okay. I had my good cry. But here's the deal. Anything Maddie and I owned that was of real value is in a storage unit in Miami, along with your stuff, in preparation for hurricane season. So the goddamn *brujos* are welcome to the ashes. That's who's responsible, right?"

"Probably."

She waved her hand. "Clothes, dishes, furniture, shoes, even the house, that's all replaceable. I've got you two, my passport, laptop, and everything I need to write my book. Let's get this show on the road."

Lauren Livingston, a study in resilience, Tess thought.

"How're we going to carry all this money?" Maddie asked.

"Divide it among our packs," Tess said. "Then we'll have to tape the bulk of it to our bodies until we've gone through customs. We'll borrow some masking tape from Mira. She's going to keep our cars for us. Maybe you should call Brian, Mom, and ask him to phone Mira in a few days. Maybe he can handle the insurance claim on your house."

"Good idea," Lauren said. "But what about the thousands you owe in medical bills?"

"It'll have to wait." Sooner or later the bills would be sent to a collection agency and then to the police. One more addition to the list of her transgressions. Tess tossed the Prius keys to her mother, scooped up the keys to the Mazda 3. "Mira's waiting outside. We're going to follow her to her house." Since the room was paid for through tomorrow morning, she left the key on the dresser, swept part of the money into her bag, and opened the door.

They were halfway across the parking lot when a cop car turned into the motel. Tess immediately did a one-eighty and walked faster to catch up with her mother and Maddie. It meant the Mazda wouldn't make it to Mira's and there was a good chance it would be impounded and towed off at some point in the next day or two. But if her mother could move forward after her home burned down, then Tess could walk away from her car.

Minutes later, Tess drove the Prius out of the lot, and followed Mira through the Tango hills. Mira called her en route to tell her that someone at the motel had reported seeing her. "I just heard it on the police radio."

A tense urgency seized Tess—and a profound fear that something would go wrong at the eleventh hour. If the *bruja* inside of Dan put out the call to her minions—*millions*, Mira had said—they would descend on Tango Key in such great numbers, with such numbing power, that even the chasers wouldn't be able to stop them. The feelings didn't leave her even when she pulled into Mira's open garage. Tess parked next to a dark SUV, Mira left her VW behind the Prius, and the garage door clattered shut behind them.

Mira threw open the doors of the SUV. "Get down on the floor and into the back between the boxes of books and pull the quilts over you," she instructed them. "I have the police radio on, so we'll know what they know."

Lauren wedged her body into the space on the floor behind the front seat, pulled a quilt over herself. Tess and Maddie climbed into the back well, pressed their bodies between boxes. Mira drew quilts over them. "Okay, five minutes or so and we'll be at the airport."

The engine hummed to life, the garage door clanked as it rose, the car sped off into the dark. It didn't take long for the police radio to crackle.

". . . this is Sergeant Travers. The suspect's room is empty, but her car is in the motel parking lot. What would you like us to do with it, Agent Hernandez?"

"Impound it," Dan replied. "Have it towed to the station and a truck will be out there tomorrow to bring it to Miami."

"Do you want us to join the roadblock on the bridge? To help check cars leaving the island?"

"No, we've got enough men there already and we have men at the major marinas. You three should head to the airport."

"No commercial flights fly in or out after dusk, Agent Hernandez."

"What about private planes?"

"Uh, yes, sir, private planes do. We're headed over there now. Over and out."

"Shit," Mira said.

The SUV picked up speed, turned abruptly to the right, slammed down over potholes. Branches slapped the sides of the vehicle. The boxes of books shifted as Mira took an abrupt left turn.

"We have a slight lead on them," Mira said. "I'm calling the pilot now."

What followed was a rapid exchange in Spanish that Tess couldn't follow.

"The plane's on the runway," Mira said as she disconnected. "I can see it ahead. I'll come up as close as possible to the plane, so when I stop, you guys flat-out run. I've got a pack for you to take with you. Clothes, snacks, makeup, shampoo, stuff to make life easier."

Tess, now free of the quilts, sat up. She saw the airport at the bottom of the road, the runway lights, a Learjet idling on the tarmac. "The *jet?*" she exclaimed. "That's your friend's plane?"

"Yeah. And if he likes you, he'll take you all the way to Quito."

"He'll like us," Lauren said. "Count on it."

"What's his name?" Maddie asked.

"Ross Blake. Like I said, a trusted friend. Maybe I can talk him into taking me down there for a visit."

Mira swerved into the airport's charter area and stopped just short of the tarmac. Everyone scrambled out, hugged Mira good-bye, and she passed the extra pack to Tess.

"I owe you, Mira. That means we haven't seen the last of you."

"You're right about that. Get out of here, fast!"

Tess raced after her mother and niece toward the waiting Learjet. As they flew up the stairs, sirens screeched, closing in. An attractive woman greeted them at the door, urged them to take their seats. Moments later, the Learjet lifted into the starlit sky.

Journey
1968/2008

· · · · · · ·

The intellect has little to do on the road to discovery. There comes a leap in consciousness, call it intuition or what you will, the solution comes to you and you don't know how or why.

—Albert Einstein

Twenty-two
MAY 1968

Thanks to an upcoming election, Quito was a city under siege. Soldiers stood on every corner, gunfire echoed around the clock, a dusk-to-dawn curfew was in effect.

Ian had spent two weeks here, talking to travel agents, bartenders, hotel clerks, tourists, anyone and everyone who might be able to direct him to Esperanza. Apparently, no buses traveled there, no planes flew into the city, and even people who had heard of the place seemed clueless about exactly where it was located. It was inconceivable that a city could get lost in the Andes, but that appeared to be the case with Esperanza. His best advice had come from a hotel clerk, who told him to go to the ExPat Inn in Otavalo and hire a driver to take him to Esperanza.

Great plan. But the government-imposed sanctions on travel within Ecuador meant he needed a visa from the Ministry of Travel. So for the last five days, he'd stood in line at the ministry with hundreds of other tourists and Ecuadorians. Today was no different.

It was now one P.M. and Ian had been waiting six hours. A dozen people stood between him and the front door, giving him a shot at getting inside the building before the sun went down and the curfew went into effect. Three soldiers stood guard at the door, blocking it with their bodies. Every time people inside were ready to leave, one of the soldiers unlocked the door, another counted how many people exited, and a third waved an equal number into the building.

At one-thirty, when Ian was just eight people from the door and could actually see inside the building, the blinds were lowered and one of the soldiers announced the ministry would be closed until three for lunch. A roar of protest went up from the hundreds in line behind him and suddenly the crowd surged forward, toward the building.

Ian moved fast in the opposite direction, against the tide, shouldering his way through throngs of enraged people. As the hordes converged on the building, soldiers fired tear gas into the crowd. The air quickly filled with the stuff and the panicked flew out in every direction, hundreds stampeding through the streets, diving behind cars, into open doorways. Then they started hurling rocks at the soldiers, the buildings. Windows shattered, cars were torched, tires set on fire, and clouds of dark, oily smoke quickly poured through the street. A full-blown riot had erupted.

He pressed his arm across his nose and mouth and pushed his way through the crowd, eyes watering, lungs on fire. As soldiers started shooting, staccato bursts echoed through the street, screams and cries pierced the air, people fell into Ian, knocking him forward. He struggled to maintain his balance, but someone slammed into him from the left, an injured woman sobbing and shrieking in pain, blood pouring from a gash in her head. He crashed into the wall, the woman collapsed. He tried to get to her, to help her, but she was quickly trampled. More shots rang out, sirens squealed.

Ian broke through the crowd and raced around the corner of the building, where several hundred protesters fled the pandemonium. He kept expecting fog to roll up the street, to hear the loud insidious chants, *Find the body, fuel the body.* But the threat seemed to be entirely human—more police cars roaring toward them, a pair of tanks thundering behind them.

Tanks. He looked around frantically for a store he could dart into, an open doorway, a window. But shops were locked up tight, wooden shutters closed, people barricaded inside. He didn't see any side streets, alleys, no way out except to turn back toward the riot.

The crowd split open, giving the cops and the tanks room to move, and people hugged the walls on either side of the street, shouting, shoving, stumbling. The cop cars sped past, sirens at full tilt, tanks rumbling after them. As soon as they were past, the crowd spread through the street again, racing for an intersection just ahead. Ian ran with them.

At the intersection, the crowd suddenly grew larger as people from the center of the riot poured toward them, a pulsing, rushing river of color and terror. Ian pushed his way past the intersection, where the road sloped steeply downward, past more ancient stone buildings. Police now streamed into the intersection, more gunfire shredded the air, more people fell.

Then he saw it, a space between two stone buildings that was so narrow he had to slip into it sideways. Light at the end. He moved toward it crablike, fast, the gunfire closer, echoing, bullets slamming into the corners of the buildings.

He finally stopped to catch his breath and fell into a crouch, breathing hard, perspiration rolling off him. He clutched his knees to his chest, pressed his forehead against them. His heart raced. Even though he had been here for two weeks, his body still wasn't accustomed to the altitude. It hurt to breathe.

When he raised his head, a man, woman, teenage girl, and a young boy huddled in the alley with him. "*Señor, por favor, puedes ayudarnos?*" the man asked.

After two weeks in Ecuador, his Spanish was improved and he at least understood the man was asking for help. He also understood the man was dying or already dead and so was his family. Ian could see through them to the old stone walls against which they stood.

"*Claro, señor.*" He groped through his tiny mental dictionary for the word "stay," then in awkward, hesitant Spanish told the man it was safest if all of them stayed in the alley for now.

"My English no good," said the man. Short and thin, he was gripping his teenage daughter's hand and looked just as frightened as his companions. "*Los soldados,* my son he be pushed, he fell—"

"A soldier . . . shot my father," said the girl in a soft, halting voice, her English heavily accented. She looked maybe sixteen. "Another soldier hit my mother. I try . . . to find my brother when I . . . something hit me in the back. I . . . I think we be dying. Or . . . we be dead. We want . . . to stay together . . ."

"Then you will." Ian hoped that much was true. "It's important that you all hold hands and that we stay here in the alley until the shooting stops."

She spoke rapidly in Spanish to the others. The mother moved closer to her husband, who took her hand, but the young boy remained huddled against the wall.

"*Jorge, ven acá,*" the girl said to her young brother.

Jorge shook his head adamantly, his eyes wide with terror.

"My brother . . . he too afraid," the girl said.

Ian moved toward the boy, crouched in front of him. In Spanish, he told Jorge that everything was okay. But the boy's lower lip trembled, tears now coursed down his cheeks, and he pressed his head against his arms, and started sobbing.

Ian rubbed his hand over the boy's back. "Ask him if he'll walk with me," Ian said to the girl.

She did and Jorge raised his head, nodding fast. Ian adjusted his pack and gestured for the boy to get on his back. Jorge climbed on quickly and Ian stood, shocked that he could feel the boy's skinny little arms around his neck, that he could feel his weight—all forty or fifty pounds of him—and that he could even smell Jorge's fear.

"*Es mejor así?*" Ian asked him. *Is it better like this?*

Jorge's arms tightened around Ian's neck. "*Sí, sí, gracias, señor.*"

Ian groped around in his mental dictionary for a few more words and, in Spanish, said, "I'm your horse."

The boy actually laughed.

The five of them moved single file up the alley, their clasped hands connecting them like paper cutout dolls. The gunfire, screams, and shouts echoed loudly and seemed uncomfortably close again. Now and then, they spoke quickly among themselves, then the father glanced back at Ian. "You are dead, señor?"

Ian shook his head. "Not yet."

"My mother says you must be shaman," the teenager remarked. "Is that why you can see us, talk to us?"

"I'm not a shaman. I can talk to you because months ago, I died and came back. While I was dead, I ended up in a place called Esperanza. Have you heard of it?"

She rapidly translated what he said and all of them nodded. But it was the boy, Jorge, who replied in broken English. "Esperanza. Májica."

"Sí, sí," the girl said. "There are many stories among Quechuans about Esperanza, that it is magical place, once a place for souls. We learned—"

The rest of whatever she was going to say was truncated by the appearance of a brilliant ball of light that bounced soundlessly toward them, like something from the TV show *The Prisoner*. It expanded as it moved, looming over them, taller than the buildings on either side, as wide as the alley, then it started to glow and pulsate. Before they had a chance to react, it swept over them. For the briefest moment, an overpowering sense of love and well-being filled him. Then the luminous ball of light was gone and he was alone in the alley again. Ian spun around, but didn't see the light or the family.

Freaked out, he ran to the end of the alley and it emptied into a wide, deeply shadowed street. No cops or fleeing rioters. This area looked and felt like a very old part of the city, where Quito turned labyrinthine, strange, infinitely mysterious. It was as if the alley connected the new and old section of Quito.

He moved forward hesitantly, passing families of Quechuans living where they sat. Most were bundled up in layers of clothing and had small fires for cooking. The food odors permeated the air. Quechua children ran through the street, laughing, tossing a red ball back and forth. Skinny dogs and cats skulked through shadows, noses to the ground. Now and then kids came up to him, hawking native jewelry that dripped from their arms. The blunt contrast between this and what he had just experienced astonished him. It was as if that narrow slit between the colonial buildings had been a portal to another world.

As the street widened, the areas the Quechuans had carved out for themselves grew proportionately larger. Here and there stood makeshift huts of tin and wood, donkeys, wagons piled high with hay, baskets filled with vegetables, fruits. His hotel bordered El Ejido Park, but he had no idea where it was in relation to his location now. He'd been lost since the day he arrived, a gringo adrift, Heinlein's stranger in a strange land.

But he had his pack, had been paying by the week, didn't have to return to his hotel. *"Permiso,"* he said to an elderly Quechuan woman, who stirred the contents of her iron cauldron with infinite patience.

"Sí?" Her eyes met his.

Ian didn't know how to ask his question in Spanish, so he pointed at his stomach, at the cauldron, and pulled out a dollar.

"Ah, tienes hambre." Her smile threw her face into a chaos of wrinkles, and she reached back and brought out a metal bowl. She spooned stuff into it, dropped a tarnished metal spoon into it, held it out.

The dollar Ian handed her disappeared into the folds of her clothing. The bowl was warm enough to take the chill from his hands. He didn't have any idea what he was eating, but it tasted delicious and filled the gaping hole in his stomach. *"Es bueno?"* she asked.

"Delicioso."

The old woman looked pleased and patted the ground beside her. Ian held out his bowl, raised his brows, and she laughed and scooped out more of the delicious stew. He handed her a couple more dollars, sat down. In fairly decent English, the woman said, "You run from guns?"

Ian nodded. "I was trying to get a travel visa. The office was going to close for lunch and people didn't like it."

"Ah." She tipped a bottle of Ecuadorian beer to her mouth, then passed it to Ian. The stuff was slightly warmer than the air, but tasted great.

"You want to go where? U.S.?"

"To Esperanza."

She threw her head back, laughing. "No, no, *guapo*. Esperanza is, how do you say?" Her hand moved through the air, searching for the right word. "*Leyenda.*"

Legend. Ian shook his head, set his empty bowl on the ground between them. "No, I went there. It's not just a legend."

Maybe it was the shadows in the street, his imagination, or something else altogether. But Ian thought her expression changed. "*Tu nombre, señor?*"

"Ian Ritter."

For long, uneasy moments, her dark eyes held his. Then, in a mixture of Spanish and English, she said, "The story is ancient. It is not a story in which you should become involved."

"I'm already involved."

"You have my sympathy." The old woman touched his arm. "How may I help you?"

"Tell me how to get out of the city. To Otavalo. I can pay."

"How much?"

"What can you offer?"

Twenty bucks bought him a ride deep in the hay on a donkey-drawn wagon bound for Otavalo, no travel papers necessary. Potholes riddled the dirt road, the hay made him sneeze, but the sky above him was a perfect liquid blue. Once they were outside of Quito, the sky looked almost incandescent and contrasted sharply with the lush green countryside and the spectacular mountains. He wished that Luke were with him. He wished for the company of people he knew. But he finally was out of the city.

The journey took three days over rough, mostly unpaved roads. They ate at local restaurants—huts made of tin and wood with a few tables outside and pots simmering on open fires. At night, they camped wherever they happened to be when dusk fell, and slept in the back of the wagon, beneath a sky strewn with more stars than Ian had ever seen. Every night, he dreamed of Tess and woke wondering if she had found his message in any of the South Florida newspapers. He worried that she might not remember him or Esperanza. Or that she'd returned and married her picky lover. Or that he would arrive in Esperanza and discover she hadn't made it back. Or that the place didn't exist at all, that it really was a myth. Sometimes, he despaired. But always, he kept moving forward a step at a time, one mile after another.

On the afternoon of the fourth day, they entered the town of Otavalo, home to the Otavalon Indians, among the wealthiest and most self-sustaining indigenous tribes in Ecuador. Everywhere he looked, he saw men and woman in traditional Otavalon clothing. The men wore white calf-length knickers, blue ponchos, fedora hats, and sported *shimbas,* long braids that fell nearly to their waists. The women dressed in white blouses, blue skirts and shawls, gold beads, and red coral bracelets. A festival of color.

The scenery was the sort of thing poets idealized—mountains rising on every side, Imbabura volcano visible in the distance, colonial buildings lining the narrow streets. The driver dropped him off at the ExPat Inn, a beautiful three-story colonial structure owned, he said, by two Europeans.

Inside, arched doors and window frames were made of hardwood, the floors terra-cotta. Light streamed across a dining room large enough to seat fifty, glass doors overlooked a courtyard filled with lush, exotic plants and trees.

The attractive brunette at the front desk looked to be about thirty and greeted him in French. He shook his head and she switched to Spanish, then English, equally fluent in all three. She didn't ask to see his travel visa or passport, just his cash payment for the room, a bargain at fifteen bucks a night, with one meal a day included. She didn't even ask his name.

"I hear things in Quito are very bad," she remarked.

"It's like an armed camp."

"Until the elections are over next month, you should stay out of large cities."

"I intend to."

"I'll show you your room. It faces the garden."

"Is it possible to call the States from here?"

"I can place the call for you and have it ring in your room. But it's not cheap."

She pushed through a pair of double doors and they stepped out into the stunning courtyard and garden around which the inn was built. Tremendous flowers bloomed, colorful faces turned toward the sun and the blue dome of sky. Birds flitted through the branches of the tall trees, vines with leaves the size of house cats twisted around the trunks.

"How long have you lived in Ecuador?" he asked.

"Ten years. I came from Nice when I finished at university, met my husband here and we borrowed to buy the inn."

"Then you've been here long enough to tell me how to get to Esperanza."

"Esperanza? I've never heard of it. But there are so many towns and villages in Ecuador that I could live here for decades more and not know them all."

The depth of his disappointment probably showed on his face. "Is there anyone in town who might know?"

"Possibly. Ask around in the shops. By the way, I'm Kim Eckert."

"Ian Ritter."

Something flickered in her eyes, but he couldn't read it.

"Ian from the cold country?"

Huh? "Well, I'm from Minneapolis and it's plenty cold. But—"

"You are, well, almost famous among some Quechuans."

"I am?"

"Months ago, the Quechuans alerted everyone in the expatriate community throughout Ecuador about the possible arrival of an Ian Ritter who would be looking for Esperanza. We were asked to put you in touch with a man who lives just outside of Otavalo."

"So you've heard of Esperanza."

She looked a little guilty. "Sorry, Mr. Ritter. Most people who know about the town are careful about divulging the information."

"Why?"

"Because it's considered to be a sacred place to the Quechuans. They don't want it overrun with tourists, smugglers, and drug dealers."

"Have you been there?"

"No. And I don't know how to get there and you won't find it on maps, either. That will change eventually, but for now, the city remains well hidden."

She unlocked the door to his room. He eyed the large bed covered in colorful native quilts, the handwoven red and blue throw rug on the tiled floor, the tasteful decorations, the pair of windows, without screens or glass, thrown open to the garden. Off to the right was a bathroom.

"You should be comfortable in here, Mr. Ritter. Let me see if I can get in touch with the Quechuans' contact person. I'll need the number in the States and will ring it through."

"Great." He scribbled down Luke's number. "Thank you. Tell me, Mrs. Eckert. Do you get fog here? In Otavalo?" *Should I keep the windows shut?*

"Occasionally. It always burns off fast, though."

As soon as she left, Ian made a beeline for the shower. His clothes were ripe after three days in the back of a wagon, his hair smelled like the inside of a barn, his beard felt gritty with dirt and bits of hay. The water pressure was fantastic, the hot water plentiful. But as the steam rose up around him, it made him uneasy. Too similar to fog. He quickly got out.

The phone rang, he grabbed the receiver. The connection wasn't the best, but he heard Luke's string of invectives clearly enough. The call, after all, was four days later than the date they had agreed on. Ian let him rant, then finally said, "Grab a pen. I've got a lead." Ian gave him Kim's name and the name of the inn.

"Fantastic, Dad. I've got a flight to Quito the day after tomorrow."

"What? When did you decide to come here?"

"I'm done with classes. I feel . . . guilty about what happened. I'd just like us to spend some time together."

Guilty, about Casey. "There's nothing to feel guilty about, Luke. Come because you want to. Whatever you do, get out of Quito fast. The political situation is too explosive. Just make arrangements to come straight to Otavalo. If I'm not here, tell Kim Eckert who you are."

The connection burst with static, the phone died. He would ask Kim to try again later, he thought, and stretched out on the deliciously soft bed. A nap, that was all he needed. But when he woke, it was the next morning. He had slept twelve hours.

He brushed his teeth, dressed, and wended through the exquisite garden to the main building. He worried about Luke coming here, now, when so much was in flux. He didn't know from one moment to the next where he would end up, what would happen. No guarantees.

He selected a table next to the front window that overlooked the dusty street and the plaza beyond it. A young Indian woman came over with a menu and a pretty smile and he ordered the vegetarian omelet. It arrived with a basket of hot, homemade rolls, coffee, and slices of chilled papaya and mango. His first good meal in days. He forced himself to eat slowly, savoring every bite.

Across the street, kids in uniforms poured from a school bus. Employees unloaded donkey-pulled carts filled with fresh fruits and vegetables, Otavalons were busy in the plaza, setting up the stands for their handicraft market tomorrow, and a black dog loped across the plaza with swift determination. It wasn't distracted by people, smells, children, not even traffic. It just kept heading toward the ExPat, panting, tail straight up in the air. It vanished behind one of the wooden wagons, reappeared, then he lost sight of it behind the school bus.

Ian dropped a couple of dollars on the table to cover breakfast, pushed back from the table. The bus pulled away from the curb. No sign of the black dog. But a man in jeans and a blue work shirt crossed the street, his thick, black hair pulled back in a ponytail. He didn't look like a Quechuan or an Otavalon.

Where's the dog? He felt sure it had been Nomad. Impossible. But since the day of his heart attack months ago, his life had become a testament to impossibility.

His gaze swept through the street, across the plaza, pausing at trees, patches of grass, in front of shops, and returned to the man. He glanced at Ian, who looked away, pretending that he was waiting for someone. But as the man walked past him, an overpowering sense of familiarity seized Ian and he turned—only to find the man staring back at him.

Tall, a broad forehead, neatly trimmed beard, tea-colored eyes. Ian nearly said, *Nomad?* But couldn't bring himself to do so because of what it would imply. *Yeah? And what's that implication?*

A dog that had changed into a man. Shape-shifter. Sure. And it would mean he might still be in the nuthouse.

"Are you Mr. Ritter?" the man asked with barely a trace of an accent.

"Yes."

"It's a pleasure to meet you." The man extended his hand. "I'm Wayra. Kim called me. Should we talk inside?"

Wayra? Who had driven Sara Wells to Esperanza two years ago? Maybe he wasn't nuts. "Before we talk about anything, I'd like to know if you can show me the way to Esperanza."

"Perhaps."

"That sounds cagey. It's either yes or no, Wayra."

"In the world you've stumbled into, *muchacho,* nothing is that black or white. What do you remember about your time there?"

The question both disturbed and intrigued Ian. It suggested that Wayra understood things he had no way of knowing. "I remember a lot, including the *brujos.*"

"Do you remember me?"

"Your name, that's all."

"Well, now that you and I have made contact, the *brujos* will be out in full force." He gestured down the street, where a light fog had begun to form.

Ian thought of what had happened in San Francisco, how quickly that fog had rolled up from the bay, consuming everything, and opened the door. "Will we be safe in here?"

"For a time. It would be foolish for them to upset the delicate balance they have with the people here. Otavaleños are world travelers, so when *brujos* take them, they do so to learn about the larger world, about the making of leather, their art, their business sense. They don't wear out the bodies. There's a kind of strange cooperation. In return, the Otavaleños are often healed of physical ailments and disease. The *brujos* are not entirely evil, Mr. Ritter."

"I hate to sound selfish, but I'm more concerned about one of them seizing me."

"They won't do it here. They risk losing too much. But once we move beyond Otavalo . . ." He shrugged. "Then the rules change."

Wayra greeted Kim Eckert. While they chatted, Ian ordered two coffees from the young woman who had brought him breakfast and said he and Wayra would be out on the back porch. He rushed back to his room for his pack, then joined Wayra on the porch that faced the beautiful garden. His coffee steamed in the cool air. "Do you know about Tess?" he asked.

"Yes. She survived."

Ian shut his eyes, stunned that Wayra had said the one thing that mattered. *She survived.* He had a million questions, but didn't know where to start. Wayra spoke first.

"Look, I know you've got a lot of questions. I'll try to answer them. Let me give you some basics first. Among *brujos* and people associated with them, there's a kind of information network that extends through time and space. Like most systems, it's imperfect and, unfortunately for us, they can access it the same way that those on our side can."

"So they know what we're doing?"

"They have a general picture, as do we. For instance, I know you were under a great threat in San Francisco, that Dominica seized someone close to Tess, and also seized someone close to you. I know Dominica's longtime partner, Ben, is dead. Tess killed the body he was using and Ben couldn't escape before the host body died. Most of what I know, they know. But the specifics escape me. If I try to figure out all of the angles, I get lost. I have to concentrate on the present. And right now, my job is to get you to Esperanza, any way I can."

This was sounding like an updated version of *Paradise Lost,* just as Sara had remarked. "How could she *kill* Ben? Aren't the *brujos* already dead?"

"Dead but stuck. My friend Paco used to refer to certain Tibetan doctrines, where it's believed there are six possible realms into which a soul can be born—the realms of Hell, Hungry Ghost, Animal, Human, Demi-God, and God. He felt that the souls who become *brujos* are actually born into the Hungry Ghost realm, a place entrenched in greed, where desires can never be satisfied. That pretty much describes the world of *brujos,* from what I know of them."

"Paco Faraday? I remember him. He stitched me up. And told me people in Esperanza don't age. I saw the evidence of that in Sara Wells."

"All very true."

"So how old are you, Wayra?"

"That discussion is for another time, *muchacho*. The—"

The doors burst open and Kim Eckert ran out, her face bone white. She rattled away in French, Wayra shot to his feet, translating aloud almost as quickly as she spoke. The fog was thickening, rolling up the main road through town, swallowing all in its path. "Get your husband, your employees," he told her. "Take them to the highest room where there aren't any windows. A closet, a storage shed. It doesn't matter as long as it's high, above the fog. It isn't after you. Once we're gone, the fog will leave, too. Where's the nearest rear exit, Kim?"

She stabbed her hand toward the rear left corner of the property. "That way. Toward Imbabura. Go quickly." She hugged them both. *"Con Dios."* She rushed back into the building.

Ian grabbed his pack and raced after Wayra, tearing through the garden toward the rear gate. Already, ribbons of fog swirled under the fence, and when Ian waved his pack back and forth, they broke apart. He and Wayra threw their bodies against the gate simultaneously and it broke open, tearing away screws, hinges, pieces of wood. They fled into the road, but the ubiquitous fog tumbled toward them from every direction, not just ground swirls, but great, thickening clouds. Wayra said, "Forgive me, Ian. There's no other way." Then he grabbed Ian's shoulders.

Agony exploded from the depths of his being and flashed outward to every other part of his anatomy. His bones cracked, his spine snapped inward, his skull hammered.

But suddenly his sense of smell was sharper than it ever had been. The entire genesis and history of a pebble, leaf, bush, lay within its scent, a universe that yielded information. Incredible power filled his legs. He felt that he could run forever. His vision exceeded twenty/twenty. He could see the bump on the back of an ant, the bending of light. Only then did Ian realize that he was running on four legs, that he was a dog or a wolf or some mix of the two, racing alongside a similar creature that carried his pack between its teeth. Only then was he totally certain that he was still locked up in the Minneapolis Mental Health Clinic, in a straitjacket, in a padded cell.

They plunged into the thick, dark fog. He discovered he could see through it—to the sunlit buildings and cars on the other side—and that he could see the *brujos* traveling within it. They looked like fragmented mosaics, sadly incomplete, as if parts of their souls had been left behind when they died. Most of them were dark, angry colors—bloodred, violent purple, burning orange. The fog remained close to them, but didn't touch them. Chanting filled his skull, rising and falling, hideous, painful. *Find the body, fuel the body, fill the body, be the body.* But he ran effortlessly. His lungs didn't strain, his heart didn't pound. The wind bit into his eyes, but it didn't burn. In the air, he tasted the *brujo* history and knowledge about them poured into him. Then they were on the other side of the fog, the sun shone, life continued normally.

They kept running until they reached a black truck parked on an empty street. Wayra dropped Ian's pack on the ground and in the blink of an eye changed from canine to man, then touched Ian's shoulder. "You're gonna be really pissed."

The pain this time was minimal. But nothing else was. Robbed of his exquisite senses, vaguely aware of what had just happened, of what it meant, Ian threw himself into Wayra, shouting, *"You prick, you lousy prick, you didn't tell the truth!"* They crashed to the ground, rolled, and Wayra pinned Ian's hands behind him. "It was the only way to get you through it."

"Get the fuck off me before I bite your arm or something," Ian snapped, and Wayra moved away from him. Ian sat up, brushed off his shirt. "I liked you better as Nomad."

He stood, grabbed his pack, got into the truck. Ian didn't know what angered him more—the fact that Nomad wasn't just a lovable dog or that he had been deprived of such an exquisite sensory experience.

Twenty-three

From the moment the plane landed in Quito, Dominica pushed Dan Hernandez hard. She ramped up his adrenaline to counteract the effects of the altitude, worked on his pituitary and hypothalamus so they released endorphins that made him more receptive and compliant, convinced him to keep drinking enormous amounts of water.

After he got through immigration and customs and hailed a cab into the city, she offered the name of a small hotel in Quito's new town that was close to restaurants, Internet cafés, bookstores, all that was familiar to him. When he gave the name to the cab driver, she allowed herself to relax and reached out, searching for Tess.

Nothing. Since Tess and her group had a two-week head start, it was possible they were already en route to Esperanza. The more she thought about this, though, the less likely it seemed. No local tour agency offered trips to Esperanza. It had been crossed off the tourist list years ago, after three busloads of international tourists had been attacked by *brujos* on a lonely stretch of road well south of Río Palo. All eighty-two of them had bled out.

The government, naturally, blamed it on an unidentified virus. But the Ecuadorian people knew the real reason. From time to time, some entrepreneurial tour operator dismissed the urban legend about *brujos* and launched a tour to Esperanza. It usually took only one or two trips to convince the operator it was a stupid idea—hazardous roads, roving groups of *banditos,* and drug smugglers looking for easy marks. Tourists who found their way there tended to arrive in vans, cars, or on local buses—the Bodega del Cielo was a hub for local transportation to spots all over Ecuador. They were young, in their twenties and thirties, traveled in pairs or small groups. Since they were generally healthy, the *brujos* welcomed them as part of the growing pool of humans on which to feast. But generally, the route to Esperanza remained a well-kept secret, so she felt that Tess and her little group would still be in Quito, trying to find their way to the city.

As soon as Dan checked into the pretty hotel, Dominica pushed him to walk over to the bus station and buy a ticket to Otavalo. From there, he would be able to get to Ibarra and then to Esperanza. But the endorphin high was wearing off, he was sliding into adrenal exhaustion, the altitude was winning. He refused to acknowledge the suggestion. He collapsed on the bed beneath the open window and immediately dropped into a deep sleep. Dominica made some minor adjustments in his brain chemistry that would keep him asleep longer than usual, thus giving her a chance to slip away and return before he woke.

When his brain waves slowed sufficiently, she slipped out of him and immediately mourned the loss of color, physicality, of those wonderful human senses. But it was easier to tap into the information she needed, call to her own kind, see the people on the busy Quito streets who were being used by *brujos*. Not many. Maybe a dozen in this part of the city. Usually, in the larger Ecuadorian cities, it was many times that. It meant members of the various *brujo* tribes who lived outside Esperanza had been summoned home—by Rafael? Pearl?

She sent out a call to Rafael and Pearl, then moved restlessly through Quito, trying to zero in on Tess's signal. Even though the signal wasn't supposed to be affected by distance, she couldn't get a fix on it. Had Tess found some way to diminish or mute it? Perhaps the chaser who had prevented Dominica from entering Tango Key was shielding Tess's signal in some way.

Dominica finally picked up a faint trace and headed north out of Quito, following the four-lane highway toward Otavalo. It led her to the center of the city, where people filled the plaza, browsing through the endless displays of wools and textiles, handicrafts, artwork, jewelry, leather goods. She felt wary about Otavaleños, about the camaraderie her kind had shared with them over the centuries. Consent and cooperation were not hallmarks of the *brujos* and in recent years, the camaraderie had begun to fray, break apart, as tribes of *brujos* expanded their hunting grounds farther south. She must exercise caution here. While Otavaleños were peaceful people, they didn't live in fear of *brujos* as so many Ecuadorians did.

She finally pinpointed the signal, coming from inside a colonial structure, the ExPat Inn. Eager to see Tess, she drifted closer—and was instantly repelled. It shocked her. How could this building be protected? By what?

"Extremely low frequency waves," Rafael said, manifesting himself to her right.

"It's the newest defense against us," added Pearl, who appeared on her left.

"But how long has it been in place here?"

"Unknown," Rafael replied. "We haven't been down here in a while. We heard about Ben, Nica. We're really sorry."

She appreciated the condolence, even though it was disingenuous. Neither of them had liked Ben much. "I'm pleased you're doing better, Rafael."

"I just had to understand my limits. I hear you failed to find the man?"

You failed. He didn't emphasize the word, but she knew that was the implication. "No one has *failed*, Rafael. We'll get him. And her."

"Explain to me, Nica, why killing them before we seize the city is so important?"

Dominica felt Pearl's tension and suddenly understood Rafael wasn't here to back her up. He hoped to evaluate her strength, resolve, motives, and then manipulate this information to make her look too weak and indecisive to lead the tribe. He wasn't just seeking a *brujo* takeover of Esperanza. He intended to overthrow her as the leader and install himself as the king of a city of *brujos,* a country or continent of *their kind.* Dominica threw herself at him, a real joke since neither of them was physical or even inhabiting a virtual human form. But he felt it energetically, as only a *brujo* could, the full brunt of her disappointment and rage. "I rescued you and Pearl, nurtured you, trusted you, brought you up through the ranks, Rafael. Now you presume to depose me? What kind of gratitude is that?"

Rafael somehow disentangled his energy from hers, a maneuver so swift and certain that she suspected he'd learned it in counseling, which meant that the insurrection in her tribe went deep. "You represent the old way, Dominica. We're sick of the old way of doing things. But know that the city is ready for an incursion by this liberation group or anyone else. We have done our part."

With that, he thought himself away. "Do you agree with him, Pearl?"

"No. His counseling was a disaster. He can't seize to kill, can't seize for sex because it might mean that the host will bleed out, can't function the way *brujos* must. He's weak. I voted to have him banished. I was overruled. We, he and I, don't . . . agree on anything anymore. But there are many who believe in him, who believe that he symbolizes change."

"How many?"

"A majority. But you have loyal followers, those who believe the chasers are up to no good, that you and only you grasp the larger picture. Your followers believe that Rafael is just a rabble-rouser. Right now, your followers are stronger, but not in numbers."

"And what do you believe, Pearl?"

They regarded each other like sisters whose passions were divided, but whose inviolate connection, a kind of spiritual DNA, they both acknowledged. "What is it that the physical beings say? Men are from Mars? Women are from Venus? Living or dead, it's true. Let's go do what we're here to do."

Just like that, Pearl turned her attention to the people on the street and Dominica sent out a call to her followers, to surround the building with fog. "How about them?" Pearl asked, gesturing at a couple of tourists. "They seem to be part of a tour. They look nonthreatening."

And overweight. That meant clogged arteries, diabetes, arthritis. But she would be borrowing the body, not inhabiting it forever. "Let's do it."

Dominica and Pearl came up behind the women, slipped into them.

"Did y'all feel that?" drawled the woman Dominica had taken. "Lordy, it felt like someone was strollin 'cross my grave."

"A chill jus' went up mah spine," said the other woman.

Lily and Cecilia, sisters from Virginia. They had never been to South America before, considered it a wild adventure, and were ready for just about anything. Lily's body was in bad shape—arthritis settling into her joints, early stages of diverticulitis, and she might soon be facing heart surgery for two arteries that were eighty percent clogged. She took so many meds that her blood chemistry was completely screwed up.

"I really gotta pee." Lily gestured toward the inn. "Let's see if we can use the restroom."

Dominica sensed that Pearl was doing the same thing she was, screening herself by dispersing her essence through the woman's cells. But she felt uneasy as Lily approached the front door. She braced herself for a sudden and violent physical reaction from Lily—nausea, vomiting, bleeding, no telling what. But Lily waddled through the front door and into the building and Dominica experienced only the slightest twinge of discomfort. Lily's fat protected her.

In the hotel lobby, Bob Dylan sang from a hidden speaker. War, change, heartache, all the sixties themes that were still relevant today. All hail Dylan. She hoped that when he passed on, he would end up in her tribe. But she wasn't holding her breath on that one.

"Morning, ladies, may I help you?" asked a young woman at the front desk.

"Sweetie, may we use yo' restroom?" Lily asked in her thick drawl.

"Of course. Straight across the dining room and into that corridor. It'll be on your right."

"Hold it," said an older woman who stepped up to the desk. Slender, short, gray hair, early seventies, eyes like ice. "I'm sorry, but the restrooms are only for guests."

Lily's smile shrank. "And if you don't mind my askin', sweetie, who might *you* be?"

"Kim Eckert. The owner."

The younger woman said, "Mom, it's okay. Really. They're just tourists."

"You don't know that," Kim snapped.

Lily leaned against the edge of the counter. "Mrs. Eckert, I don't mean to presume, but how would our being guests assure you that we aren't . . . well, whatever it is you're afraid of?"

Dominica decided she liked Lily from Virginia. Plenty of spunk and good old-fashioned balls. Dominica didn't have to prompt her at all.

"I . . . well, I don't know."

"Fine. We'll pay for a room. And then use the restroom."

"Ridiculous," muttered Cecilia. "I am *not* paying sixty bucks to use a bathroom."

"That's right. You're only paying thirty," Lily said, and slapped three twenties on the counter. "You can repay me later, Cecilia. Or not. I just know I am *not* going to pee in a disgusting Jiffy John or some bathroom where the toilet bowl is black. Now, Mrs. Eckert, may we use your restroom?"

"I guess it's okay."

"Wonderful." Lily gestured at her sister. "To the restroom."

As the sisters waddled off, Dominica felt strangely magnanimous toward Lily, toward both of them. She went to work on the plaque buildup in Lily's heart arteries, the arthritis in her joints, the wicked pockets in her intestines. Then she tweaked her brain chemistry so that she wouldn't stuff her face every time she sat down to eat.

"Now *what* is that woman's problem?" Lily griped as she and her sister were in the restroom.

"No tellin', Lil. Bitterness, who's to say? You know, mah feet don't hurt anymore. And that migraine I told you was comin' on? Gone. Totally gone."

"My joints don't ache. I can breathe nice and easy. I think this country suits both of us."

When they exited the restroom a while later, they were still discussing how much better they both felt. They were oblivious to the fact that they'd been compromised. Oblivious until Dominica suddenly noticed a white-haired woman sitting at a table next to the window. Tess Livingston. But when had she gone gray? The night she killed Ben? Life's little shockeroos.

No mother, no niece, just her, the horrible woman who had threatened and hurt her and killed Ben in that resort on Key Largo. Tess was scanning a menu and kept rubbing at her forearm. Dominica suspected the mark on her arm was activated when a *brujo* was nearby. No wonder she'd been ready for her and Ben that night in Key Largo.

Dominica forced Lily to walk over to the table, to say, "Hello, so nice to see you again."

Lily sucked in her breath as soon as she uttered the words and started to scream. Dominica seized control of her, preventing her from saying anything at all. But apparently Tess didn't need to hear what she already knew, what her burning arm had told her, that a *brujo* was right in front of her. She shot to her feet, towering over Lily, then grabbed the front of the woman's shirt, jerking her forward. Face-to-face, eye to eye, she hissed, "You don't scare me, you can't take me, so it's time you just went away, Dominica." Then she screamed, *"She's one of them, Kim, she's one of them!"*

Dominica jerked Lily's body back, but too late. The old woman—Kim—vaulted over the front desk and tore toward Lily swinging a goddamn bat. It slammed down against the corner of the table, tipping it so that glasses and plates slid off, shattering against the floor. Lily wrenched away, but Dominica forced her to jerk the bat from Kim's hands and swing it at the closest window. The glass exploded, shards of glass flying off into the sunlight and triggering an alarm that shrieked like a wounded animal.

Then Lily with her new, improved joints and her new, improved heart and lungs leaped through the broken window, with Cecilia right behind her, shouting, *"Go fast, oh God, run . . ."*

As Tess and Kim swept up the shards of glass and broken dishes, Tess kept an eye on the two women across the street. Their plump hands moved through the air, gesturing at the inn, as they attempted to explain to the local police what had happened. Spectators gathered like crows along a fence.

"What're you going to tell the cops?" Tess asked Kim.

"The truth. They know about the *brujos*. In the last ten years, *brujo* attacks have soared."

Following Luke's advice about starting their search in Otavalo, Tess, Lauren, and Maddie had arrived here yesterday afternoon on a bus, a two-hour trip on a fast four-lane highway. Before that, they'd spent a week in the Dominican Republic, and another week in Quito. This was the first incident with any *brujos.* "Did you know what they were when the two women came in?" Tess asked.

"I felt something wasn't right. I mean, they paid sixty dollars to use the restroom. How many tourists do that? But honestly, ever since you and I talked last night about the *brujos,* I've been uneasy." Kim's dark eyes filled with worry. "If your mother and niece had been in the room and they aren't protected like you are, they would've been seized." She gestured at Tess's arm. "It alerted you. That bruise or whatever it is."

Yeah, whatever it was. Tess plucked her bag off a nearby table, thrust her hand inside. "Could you take a look at this, Kim?" She withdrew the photo of Ian that Luke had sent her, now printed on photography paper that vastly improved the quality. "Have you ever seen this man? I believe he came through Otavalo a very long time ago."

Kim stared at it for the longest time, then finally raised her eyes. She looked deeply shaken, but tried to disguise it with a quick smile. "George Clooney. If he visited Otavalo, he never stopped here. Too bad. I love his movies." She passed the photo to Tess.

Stunned, Tess pressed on. "His name's Ian Ritter. According to his son, Luke, Ian stayed here forty years ago. He called Luke from here. Luke told me to begin my search for Ian here. He gave me your name. In 1968, Luke came to the ExPat to look for his dad, but Ian had left. Can you tell me where he went? How long he was here?"

Kim emptied the dust pan into a large trash bin, then looked at Tess, her face torn with conflicting emotions. "Why? Why do you want to know?"

Tess gave it to her straight. "Because six months ago I died and fell in love with Ian when both of us ended up in Esperanza. I know how nuts that sounds, but—"

Kim made a small, startled sound, sank into the nearest chair. Her small, delicate hands clasped the armrests. "Dear God," she whispered.

Tess brushed glass off the table, sat across from her. "Please, tell me what you know."

"I've struggled for forty years to understand all this." She threaded her fingers together, stared at her white knuckles. "Ian arrived in May 1968, after fleeing the political chaos in Quito. One of the first questions he asked was if I knew how he could get to Esperanza. Back then, the city was considered a sacred place to the Quechuans and was well hidden. They had sent out word to the expat community that if an Ian Ritter from the cold country showed up, we should contact Wayra, one of the Quechuans' trusted friends, who lived just outside Otavalo. I didn't have any idea why they had put out the word on this man, but my husband and I were guests here and were always respectful of the Quechua beliefs and requests."

Wayra, shape-shifter.

As Kim talked, a man emerged from the kitchen and came over to the table. He wore khaki pants and a black T-shirt that read, *Joaquin here. Tell Kim she's got at least another 20 years. Or she can find her way to Esperanza and we can spend infinity together.*

Uh-oh, Tess thought, and drew her attention back to Kim, who was talking about the fog that had rolled up the streets of Otavalo shortly after Wayra had arrived. She and her husband had had some experience with the fog, she said, so when Wayra instructed her to get everyone upstairs to a windowless room, she had done so. "But for a few minutes, I stood on the roof, on the balcony where I could see in every direction, and watched the fog's approach. Watched Ian and Wayra race through the garden, out into the road. The fog came at them from every direction—low to the ground, so they were still visible. I saw Wayra grab Ian and . . . then there were two dogs racing into the fog. Or two wolves. Or a mix, I don't know. But they *shape-shifted*. As soon as I saw that happen, I realized I . . . had to rethink everything I believed to be true about the world. So I've spent the last forty years doing that."

Get a grip, it's no weirder than any of the rest of it. But what the hell did it mean? That Ian was now like Wayra? "Have you seen either man since?"

"No. And Esperanza has opened up to tourism and the Quechuans I know rarely speak of the city as a sacred place anymore."

Now Joaquin stood behind Kim's chair, waving his arms like an umpire calling time-out. The words on his T-shirt had changed. *Tell her the police chief is about to cross the street. She should draw his attention to the mark on your arm. He's got one, too.*

"Uh, was your husband's name Joaquin?"

Kim looked startled. "Yes, but how . . ."

"He's standing behind you."

No quick backward glances from Kim. No freak-out. No tears. Instead, she leaned forward, eyes bright and hopeful. "He was Portuguese, mystical. He didn't see what I did that day, but he didn't have any problem believing it. Eight years ago, he left for Esperanza. Never came back. His body was found in the mountains. Ask him what happened."

Tess looked at Joaquin. *Okay, my friend, you heard her. What happened?*

Joaquin brought his hands to his wife's shoulders. She flinched, as if she felt his touch. A new message appeared on his T-shirt. *Ambushed by* brujos *south of Tulcán. I escaped, got lost, killed later by Colombian druggies. When I passed, Wayra was waiting. I joined the chasers.*

Tess read the message aloud. Kim's hands were pressed together in an attitude of prayer, the tips of her fingers touched her chin, eyes bright with tears. "We need to get all of you out of here. And fast."

Two cops came in and Kim hurried over to the front desk to speak with them. Tess went over to her mother, who was sweeping up glass in another area of the room. "Let's get our stuff. We're leaving."

"How? There's fog rolling up the street, Tess."

"I don't know how, but we are." Tess tilted her head toward Maddie, also sweeping up glass, iPod buds in her ears. Music as refuge. "If you two get our stuff, I'll settle our bill."

"Done."

Kim strode over with one of the two cops, an Otavaleño, an older man, his *shimba* almost completely gray. "Tess, this is Enrique Vicente, Otavalo's chief of police. He can get you and your family safely out of town."

"We can pay," Tess told him. "But how can you do this?"

"The *brujos* generally do not take the people of Otavalo unless we consent to it. And we have not consented today. That is why they took two American tourists." His smile was thin, nervous. "My son and I can drive the three of you out of town. It would be best if you wore hats that cover your faces. And perhaps shawls, like the women of Otavalo wear."

"I appreciate any help you can provide," Tess said.

"Understand, please, that we do not do this out of compassion. We do this because the sooner you are gone, the sooner peace and tranquility will return to Otavalo."

Fair enough, Tess thought.

Kim said, "Enrique, if you can bring your car around to the back gate, they can leave through the garden. I'll get hats and shawls."

As Kim left, Enrique's gaze fixed on Tess's arm. "That mark on your arm, señorita. May I ask how you got it?"

Like the mark of Cain. "A, uh, *brujo* grabbed my arm."

Enrique frowned. "But *brujos* do not leave such marks in the physical world."

She thought of Joaquin's message about this man's mark. "How do you know that?"

He rolled up his left sleeve and showed her a similar, smaller mark on his upper arm. "When I was a young man, my horse threw me. I hit my head and found myself in thick fog, outside a bodega. A man grabbed my arm and told me to leave, that I was not welcome. It shocked me so deeply that I woke up on my back, in the field where my horse had thrown me. I have had the mark ever since."

"Was it Bodega del Cielo?"

He made a hasty sign of the cross on his forehead. "*Sí, Dios mío.* You are the first I have met with such a mark."

"Does your mark ever itch and burn?" she asked.

He shook his head. "No. But I was told that it protects me from the *brujos,* that they will not—or perhaps cannot—seize a person with this mark."

"But they can seize the people you love." She nearly choked on the words.

"My son and I will not let anything happen to you and your family, señorita. It is an honor to help one who carries this mark."

Fifteen minutes later, the three of them were dressed in the traditional clothing of Otavalo's women—white blouses, blue skirts, and shawls. Even though the women usually didn't wear hats, Kim gave them three fedoras to put on.

"I feel like Indiana Jones." Maddie tugged the brim of the hat low over her forehead. "All I need is a whip."

"Even Indiana Jones might have trouble with *brujos,*" Enrique said, his smile tense. "The fog has not yet come up the street as far as the inn. It seems to be . . . waiting."

"This is creeping me out," Lauren murmured.

"Don't let it, Mom. They can sense our fear."

Her mother swallowed hard and tightened her grip on her pack. "Okay, let's get moving so I don't have to think about this too much."

They fled the inn in single file, racing through the garden with Enrique in the lead, Kim bringing up the rear. Except for the whisper of their footfalls against the grass, the sweet-smelling air was eerily silent, as if the entire town held its breath. Tess's arm itched, but didn't burn yet. At the gate, they hugged Kim, then Enrique raised the latch and they ran out to the car, a silver Mustang with a monstrous engine that roared even as it idled. Tess,

Lauren, and Maddie piled into the back seat, Enrique scrambled into the passenger seat. Before he shut his door, the kid behind the wheel gunned the accelerator and the Mustang shot forward.

"This is my son, Camilo," Enrique called. "He drives like Mario Andretti. *Vamonos! hijo, por allá. Rápido, más rápido.*"

The Mustang tore up the road, swerved into a right turn, tires kicking up gravel and dust, and hit the four-lane highway. Through the rear window, Tess saw the fog racing along behind them, thickening, darkening. Was it possible to outrun this shit? She had no idea. But Camilo was trying. The speedometer needle swung past a hundred.

"It's still coming." Camilo sounded terrified. "What do you want me to do, *papá?*"

"Go faster." Enrique gestured frantically with his hands. "In four miles, turn left. They will not go near Wayra's old place."

Four miles later, the Mustang took the turn on two wheels, onto a dirt road with open fields on either side and thick woods beyond.

The fog made the turn as well. But it didn't seem to be moving as rapidly as before, Tess thought. Enrique was on his cell now, chattering in Spanish, listening, then snapped the cell shut and gestured wildly again, snapping instructions in Spanish.

Camilo veered right, the Mustang crashed through the wire mesh fence that separated the field from the road, took out several wooden posts, and raced across the field, frightening a herd of horses and half a dozen llamas grazing in the tall grass. It turned sharply behind a barn, slammed down into a ditch, sped up a steep footpath that angled into a thicket. Branches slapped the sides of the car, clawed at the windshield, then the trees ended and they reached a flat area at the top of the hill. A chopper stood in the center of it, blades turning slowly.

Camilo slammed on the brakes, the doors flew open, and they all stumbled out, coughing from the clouds of dust that settled around them. The pilot motioned them aboard and all five of them raced toward the chopper. Once they were inside, Enrique shut the door and the pilot turned around in his seat, headphones covering his bald head, shades hiding his eyes. Tess suddenly remembered him. Tattoo Man, Ed Granger.

"Tess, almost didn't recognize you with that white hair." He shouted above the din of the rotors. "Great to see you again. Now buckle up, mates. It's going to be bumpy."

Then the rotors spun faster, the engine hummed, the chopper started to rise.

Just before Dominica slipped back into Dan Hernandez, Pearl brought information that filled Dominica with dread. Tess and her companions had been rescued by Ed Granger, who had whisked them away by helicopter. Dominica doubted that Ed would fly them into Esperanza—the topography made it challenging, the winds aloft were usually a deterrent. But even if he did, her tribe would be all over them as soon as they landed. He probably would fly them into Ibarra, the largest town in the region north of Otavalo, or into Tulcán, Ecuador's northern border town. From there, they would drive as far as the Río Palo, to the town of Dorado, or even to the Bodega del Cielo.

Then what? She wasn't sure. She doubted that a rickety bus driven by Manuel Ortega would be an option this time, didn't think they would risk any sort of vehicle on that isolated road. Too many opportunities for ambush. Perhaps when they neared the Río Palo, the people of Esperanza would venture forth, guarding them as they made the trek toward the city. Cell phones, when they worked at the higher altitudes, made life much easier.

Yet, people who lived in Esperanza rarely left it, they aged too quickly. And when they did leave, it was a quick trip to buy supplies, gather information, visit family in other countries, or for rescues, like Ed Granger's little trip. Stupid idiot. *The city is ours. The hell with the chasers and this liberation group and Rafael. Fuck all of them.* But even as she thought this, a profound terror gripped her that it was all too late, that the *brujos* might not only lose Esperanza, but would be annihilated as well.

"Pearl, instruct our most reliable to seize any available bodies," she said. "Our plan has changed. We've got our defenses in place against an attack, so now we're going to seize the city. This should delight Rafael."

"Are you sure you want to do this, Nica? You don't think the chasers will retaliate?"

"They might. But I don't think there're enough of them to fight us. So we cut off all power to the city, isolate them. Seize whoever we can. It's time to take Esperanza back. Has Ian, in his time, reached Esperanza yet?"

"No. I heard he was helped by someone and our people lost him."

"Help from whom?"

"From Wayra."

Of all the names she might have uttered, this one shocked Dominica. Wayra? Again? Back then? Since when had the shifter been able to travel in time? When had he gained the ability? "That's impossible. Where did you get that name?"

"It was reported by the *brujos* who followed Ian Ritter."

"Pearl, tell Rafael my new instructions. Then take a group to 1968. Find Wayra and the American. They're to be brought to me, just two men. Surely we can capture two men."

Then she slipped into Dan and tweaked his brain chemistry so that he began to emerge from his deep, Snow White sleep. His eyes opened, enabling her to look around. She sensed that Pearl was gone. *You're now going to rent a car, Dan, and you're going to drive very fast for a very long time. Pack your things.*

"Damn, how long did I sleep?" He rubbed his hands over his face.

Do you want to find Tess or not?

He scrambled to his feet and spun around the room, certain that someone was here with him. Dominica decided she liked him much better when he just went along with her suggestions. She hoped she would not have to demonstrate what would happen to him if he misbehaved.

Well? she asked.

Dan stumbled into the bathroom, certain he was losing his mind. He splashed water on his face, leaned close to the mirror, staring at himself. "Must be coming down with something."

Other than the effects of the altitude, your body is quite healthy.

He staggered back from the sink, genuinely scared now, waves of panic crashing over him. Dominica quickly adjusted his pituitary, releasing a flood of endorphins, and within minutes he began to calm down and talked quietly to himself. "Hey, man, it's okay. You're just zapped by the altitude. Got to drink a lot of water, have a bite to eat."

Excellent suggestions. Buy something on the way. We need to rent the car fast, so we have at least four hours of driving before the sun goes down. Once we're on the road, you'll call Tess's cell and we'll try to get a fix on her.

He returned to the bedroom, packed, checked to make sure his cell was powered up, then punched out Tess's number. He reached her voice mail, left a message, and checked out of the hotel. Dominica directed him to a car rental agency, and thirty minutes later they were on the road. He stopped once at a roadside store to buy water, a vegetarian sandwich. By the time they reached Ibarra, it was two-thirty in the afternoon. It would be dark by six, and because they were practically on the equator, the sun wouldn't rise for twelve hours. Too long. She had to get him into the higher mountains before then.

She instructed him to enter a general store in Ibarra and buy a host of items that would enable him to cook and eat by the side of the road and to sleep in the car. Pleased with her own planning, she dispersed herself throughout his cells, where she could think about Wayra, and how deeply he had betrayed her this time.

Twenty-four
MAY 1968/JUNE 2008

The truck climbed steadily into the mountains outside Otavalo. Ian's ears popped every few hundred feet, but otherwise the increase in altitude didn't bother him. The road did, though. Pitted with holes, mostly dirt and stones, it was hardly fit for the donkeys and wooden carts they passed. He worried that the next hole they slammed across might take out the exhaust pipe, an axle, a tire.

He poured water onto a towel and dabbed at his hands. They were badly scraped, the result of stones and branches and thorns and Christ knew what else that he had run across as a dog. *A dog.* Yeah, like he could put that into any kind of perspective.

The cool, sweet-smelling mountain air blew through the open windows. The radio was on, music fading in and out because the mountains interfered with the reception. Wayra sometimes hummed along or tapped his fingers and thumbs against the steering wheel. They had said only a few words to each other since they'd left Otavalo hours ago. Ian finally broke the impasse.

"Ed Granger or Juanito or someone told me you used to run with the *brujos*. Is that true?"

"You remember *that*? You remember *them*?" He looked over at Ian, his eyes intense, a pale amber, like Nomad's eyes.

"Yeah, I remember them."

"Interesting. Tess remembered nothing for months."

"You've *seen* her?"

"No. That's what I heard from others."

"What else have you heard?" *Does she remember me?* "Is she trying to return?"

"She's on her way, with her mother and niece, but the *brujos* know it and are after her just as they are after us."

"How can you even be here? We first saw you outside the bodega in 2008."

"I have a limited ability to move around in time."

"As Nomad?"

"In both forms. But I prefer my Nomad form. It's cleaner, simpler, and a much richer sensory existence."

"So are you a dog or a wolf?"

"Both. The shifter that bit me was half wolf, so I guess that makes me a quarter wolf. Or something. Whatever. I'm a hybrid."

Lock me up. "Am I still locked up in the psych ward?"

Wayra laughed. "You're quite sane. You've just stumbled into a very old story and are now intimately connected to how that story continues or detours or ends."

"You didn't answer my question. About whether you ran with the *brujos.*"

"Once, many years ago."

"How many years ago?"

"Hundreds. I'm the last of my kind."

Ian heard the loneliness and resignation that echoed in his voice, and decided he didn't really need to go there. "Were you born a man?"

Wayra looked amused. "How's your history, Ian? I was born the same year that Thomas à Becket was appointed archbishop of Canterbury."

Becket? Ian nearly choked on that one. "Late eleven hundreds."

"Eleven sixty-two. When I was eighteen years old, I was bitten by a shape-shifter in the English countryside, a creature that was part wolf, part dog, part myth. In Spain, in the fourteen hundreds, I was killed because the father of the woman I loved hated me. I arrived in Esperanza when it was still a nonphysical place. But because I was a shape-shifter, different from anything Esperanza knew, I became part of its knowledge and helped to bring about its expansion into the physical world. Because of what I am, I became physical again when Esperanza did."

"A kind of Lazarus," Ian remarked.

"Lazarus minus the religion. Right now, Esperanza straddles many times and dimensions of consciousness. Even though it's a physical place, it retains attributes from when it wasn't. That's part of its magic—and also its curse. It's why the *brujos* are able to wreak so much havoc in Esperanza, but also why the people of Esperanza were able to interact with you and Tess when you weren't physical. It's why I continue to flourish. Then there's the slow-aging factor."

Never mind that what he said smacked of mental derangement so severe that even electroshock and massive doses of Thorazine wouldn't help this guy. Ian believed him. He'd seen the slow-aging evidence in Sara. "And that's why most people in Esperanza haven't fled."

"Exactly. The choice for them is stark—fight the *brujos* or risk accelerated aging or death if they flee."

"From what I remember, they don't do much fighting. Mostly, they seem to hide."

"They don't know *how* to fight the *brujos*. Everything they've done these past seven or eight years is defensive. So the *brujos* have become bolder. They seize people in other towns, they terrorize communities. There are many in 2008 who believe the appearance of the first transitionals in five centuries is a sign that a nationwide revolt against the *brujos* is imminent, led by a group whose members lost loved ones to them. They number in the tens of thousands. We need numbers. We need an army. So when the revolt happens, the role of physical helpers will become extremely important."

"What's a physical helper?"

"Do you remember anything about the light chasers?"

"Just the phrase. What are they?"

"Evolved souls. The chasers set events in motion. But they can only do so much. They aren't gods, Ian, and they aren't physical. Right now, the only physical helpers the chasers have are me, Ed Granger, Sara Wells, Juanito Cardenas, and a few others in and around Esperanza. It's not enough. Every day, somewhere in the world of 2008—and in the latter part of the twentieth century—there are disasters, war, genocide, torture, populations ravaged by disease and bigotry and hunger. Every day, thousands of transitional souls need guidance, insight, direction. The chasers are spread so thinly that they can't deal effectively with the *brujos*. They're outnumbered. And none of their physical helpers can do what you can now, interact with the dying and the dead to offer what chasers typically do. To win this war against the *brujos*, we need more physical helpers like you, Ian, who can deal with transitionals. You've been one, you understand the landscape."

"*Understand?*" Ian laughed, but even to him the laughter sounded scared, desperate. "I haven't *understood* a damn thing that's happened to me since I came to in a hospital room. And, just to set the record straight, my interaction with the dead has been pretty pathetic. An elderly black man who was a cardiac patient, and a family of four in Quito. They asked me questions I didn't have answers to, Wayra. And in both instances, they disappeared. Moved on. In Quito, some sort of weird light bubble swallowed them."

"Weird light bubble." He smiled at that. "I'll have to pass on the description. It was a group of chasers. And, *just for the record,* Ian, that elderly black guy you spoke to at the hospital? He's now working in Rwanda, 1994, during a genocide in which more than eight hundred thousand people, mainly Tutsi, are killed by extremist Hutu militias, and countless thousands more are maimed and injured. And the family of four you spoke to? They'll soon be dispatched to December 26, 2004, when a 9.3 earthquake in Indonesia creates a tsunami with fifty-foot waves that will sweep across eleven countries and kill nearly three hundred thousand. The little boy is a gifted empath. In Tess's time, two accident victims that she helped are now working in Darfur in 2006, where drought, desertification, and overpopulation have resulted in a humanitarian crisis in which half a million have died from disease and hunger, and more than a hundred thousand a year are dying from hunger. But we need physical people in these areas who can immediately help transitionals, who—"

"Stop," Ian said. "Please." He suddenly felt weak, nauseated, just as he had in those final hours in Esperanza. He understood the implications of what Wayra was saying, but couldn't process anything. "I'm gonna be sick."

Wayra swerved to the side of the road, slammed on the brakes. Ian stumbled out and made it as far as the line of trees before his knees buckled and he doubled over and puked. He dug his fingers into the soft earth, breathed in its fecund scent, and sensed the emergence of the larger picture, the plan the chasers had set in motion.

Behind him, Wayra said, "Your nausea is probably the result of your brief jaunt as a, uh, hybrid."

Ian rose up, rocked back on his heels. "Or it could be my body's reaction to the way you people used Tess and me. You allowed us into Esperanza as transitional souls in the hopes that if we survived the journey back to our physical bodies and returned to Esperanza, it would embolden the masses to revolt against *brujo* tyranny. You did this to *start a war* between the living and the dead. And the subplot is that you hoped our near-death experiences would enable Tess and me to interact with . . . transitional souls, and then we would become the first of the new human helpers who would begin to assume some of the chaser chores. Clever, Wayra." He pushed to his feet. "Did it ever occur to you that your war against these *brujos* is not *our* battle? Did you ever think that maybe we wouldn't want the job? That maybe you shouldn't have interfered in our lives? I had a life. A profession. Relationships. You and these chasers fucked it up big-time."

Wayra didn't deny any of it. He just said, "You never would have met Tess."

It infuriated Ian that Wayra's voice remained calm, even. "Since we're separated by forty years, maybe I wasn't meant to meet her."

"We didn't expect the two of you to fall in love, Ian. That was a bonus. It gave both of you a powerful incentive to survive your physical injuries and to remember what had happened."

The gall, Ian thought. "You're talking about Tess and me like we're some sort of metaphysical experiment. So forget it, *muchacho*."

Wayra now looked exasperated. "Look, Tess's father, Charlie, knew there was a strong probability that she would be shot in the line of duty, so he made it possible for her to enter Esperanza, the only place where she might find the will to return to the physical. He also knew she had the qualities we look for in helpers—a strong sense of right and wrong defined by conscience rather than religious beliefs or dogma, a need to serve a cause larger than the self, a great capacity for love and compassion. Charlie wanted a second person with similar attributes, and I suggested you."

"How the hell could you know anything about me?"

Wayra hesitated. Sunlight and shadows ebbed and flowed across his face, changing its contours. He ran his fingers through his hair, started to pace. "I was with a group of chasers who helped your father after he died. Suicides always deserve extra attention. I was curious how his suicide would sculpt the man you would become, so I kept an eye on you through the years. Your need to prove your father wrong about what kind of person you are drove you to write about social and cultural issues. It helped to develop your social conscience and landed you a Pulitzer prize at the age of twenty-eight, for your investigation into the rape and murder of a black woman. It drove you to—"

"I know my own history. Just because you've been alive for centuries doesn't give you the right to try to psychoanalyze me. You've got a lot of goddamn nerve, Wayra, and where the hell does Charlie get off, trying to mold his daughter's destiny from the afterlife?"

Wayra's expression suddenly changed. "Move quickly, *muchacho*." He spoke softly. "Fog. In the woods behind you."

Ian glanced back. Ribbons of fog snaked along the ground through the trees, wrapped around trunks, brush, and drifted into the lower branches, where it seemed to flutter like a flock of white birds. Already, Ian could hear a soft, insidious sound, like palm fronds dragging against pavement. Then a kind of lewd whispering suffused the air and a bank of the stuff rolled out of the trees, twice as tall as he was, perhaps a quarter of a mile wide, and the chanting exploded through the air. *Find the body, fuel the body, fill the body, be the body.*

Ian whipped around and tore after Wayra, heart hammering, blood pounding in his ears, memories of the chaos in San Francisco vivid. He threw himself into the passenger seat and Wayra careened onto the road, tires kicking up stones, clouds of dust. The fog rolled on through the dust, gathering speed, growing in size until it filled the side mirror.

"Jesus, Wayra. We're not going to be able to outrun it."

Wayra eyed the speedometer, barreled into a curve, then tapped the brake, slowing the truck as the road dropped into a steep descent. "Grab your pack, Ian."

Ian didn't like the sound of that. "Why?"

"Just do it!"

The tires shrieked, the engine roared, and Wayra swerved sharply to the right. The truck crashed through a flimsy wood railing, splinters flying like spears in every direction, then the tires left the road and they suddenly were airborne. The engine conked out, air whistled past the windows, sunlight exploded through a field way below. For moments, they seemed to ride the currents, suspended between heaven and earth like one of the giant condors Ian had seen in Esperanza. Then the truck's nose dipped forward, the field below rushed toward them, and Ian knew he was about to die.

Wayra threw his arms around him, hugging him so hard he couldn't breathe. His body felt as if it were collapsing, skin and organs turning to mush, bones and cells compressing, eyeballs popping from their sockets. He went blind, deaf, and dumb. Then there was nothing.

When he could see again, he was flat on his back in a field, a chilly wind blowing over him. He stared into the belly of a twilit sky, heard distant strains of music, smelled smoke and food from a barbecue. *What just happened?* Ian pushed himself up. Across the field lay a paved road crowded with traffic—buses, vans, trucks, a line of tidy, colorful concrete buildings.

Somewhere nearby, a church bell tolled, its sonorous chords echoing through the moonlight.

He leaped to his feet, looking around for Wayra, and saw him curled on his side a hundred yards away, his body caught between wolf and man, a kind of chimera. The sight fascinated him in a bizarre kind of way, the compression and extension of bones, snout and head rearranging themselves until the skull and face were human. The fur vanished in a flash, human skin and hair appeared, limbs and paws gave way to two legs, two arms and hands, tail pulled into the body. It happened between one heartbeat and the next. When Wayra peered up at him, the tea-colored eyes were Nomad's.

"Explain," Ian burst out. "Please. Where's the truck?"

Wayra sat up with considerable effort, exhaustion apparent in the circles beneath his eyes, the twitch at the corner of his mouth, the soft popping of his joints. "Calm down. You're making my head hurt." He rocked slowly onto his knees, brought a cell phone from his back pocket. "Shit. No signal. Let's go. We need to find a phone, car, weapons."

As they strode through the field, Ian said, "Where are we?"

"The village of Punta in, uh, 2008."

"*What?*" Ian stopped. "You . . . can *do* that? All this time you could've brought me *forward*? What the hell were you waiting for?"

Wayra kept moving down the hill toward town. Ian loped after him, caught his arm. *"Talk to me."*

"Okay, okay." He wrenched his arm free of Ian's grasp. "I've never tried it before. I didn't know if it was possible to take someone else forward or backward or anywhere in time. It was our only option." Then he grinned. "But hey, it *worked!*" Wayra flung his arm around Ian's shoulders. "And getting here was half the battle."

Ian wasn't feeling quite as magnanimous as Wayra. He shook off the other man's arm. "Hold on. My son is back in 1968. How am I supposed to get in touch with him? The last time I talked to him, he was on his way to Quito."

Wayra paused. In the starlight, his features looked more wolflike than human, his teeth seemed pearl white, sharper. Ian instinctively stepped back, putting a little more distance between them. *Shit, suppose he bites me? Will it turn me into a shifter?*

"I wouldn't," Wayra said, as if reading Ian's mind. "I never have. That's why I'm the last of my kind. We'll figure something out about your son. I'll know more when we get into town. But you must do everything I tell you, follow my instructions to the letter. I know Dominica. I know what she's capable of, and she'll find us."

With that, he walked on ahead, quickly, as if he couldn't get away from Ian fast enough. Ian stared after him, mortified and ashamed that he had hurt Wayra's feelings.

Dan drove through the twilight with a CD playing, fingers tapping against the steering wheel. He kept worrying about the voice in his head that he'd heard earlier, so Dominica urged him to sip more water and eat some of the snacks he'd bought. She made minor adjustments in his blood chemistry that calmed him. She wished she could do the same for herself.

She felt increasingly anxious and wasn't sure why. Perhaps she had to get out of Dan to explore the feeling. But she didn't dare do it while he was conscious. She couldn't risk that he might recover all his memories and take off.

When they reached a lonely stretch of road, she put pressure on his bladder, released more endorphins, and Dan pulled to the side of the road. Yawning, he got out and relieved himself by the side of the car, taking in the glorious moonlit landscape around him. The majestic volcanic peaks, the steep slope covered with trees, the silver ribbon of a river meandering way below him. He glanced at his watch, frowning, and wondered what he was doing out here, miles from any town or village. Dominica quickly censored these doubts by tweaking his pituitary gland again. Now he could barely keep his eyes open.

She urged him to remove the keys from the ignition and toss them off to the side of the road. Now, in the event that he awakened, he wouldn't be able to flee in the car. Dominica erased his memory about the keys. She would remember, that was all that mattered. She coaxed him to the trunk.

He removed the sleeping bag, and spread it out on the back seat. Then he climbed into it, zipped himself inside, a caterpillar in a cocoon, and fell asleep. Dominica quickly went to work on him, making sure he would sleep soundly and deeply for several hours. Then she slipped out of him and immediately heard Pearl calling to her. Dominica located her at the edge of a nearby village.

"Nica, I wasn't sure if you could hear me," Pearl said. "We found Wayra and Ian. They were arguing and . . . Ian seemed to be ill. We pursued them as they drove away from us and something . . . unprecedented happened. Wayra drove their truck over the side of a cliff and it crashed into a field a hundred feet below. We searched through the debris, but found no sign of either of them."

"That's impossible. You must not have checked the area thoroughly."

"We checked a five-square-mile area." Her voice turned to steel. *"They are gone."*

Even Wayra couldn't take a human being through time. He certainly couldn't do it while the car he drove plunged over the side of a cliff. "Then we shall go to Tulcán to find Tess and her group."

"What about Dan?"

"He'll sleep for hours yet. What does Rafael report?"

"By dawn, the entire city and the surrounding villages will be completely shut down. No power, total isolation. We believe the liberation group may make their move on the solstice, during the nationwide celebration in honor of Inti."

The ancient Incan sun god, Dominica thought.

"Much of the tribe now believes that the insurrection is in full force," Pearl went on, "that Rafael has overthrown you. He hasn't told them otherwise. To maintain your position as tribal leader, Nica, you'll have to address the tribe and do something impressive that really fires their hunger and passions, that shows your strength."

"I appreciate your honesty. What sort of impressive feat do you suggest?"

Pearl told her and Dominica smiled.

Twenty-five
JUNE 2008

They dropped off the Otavalo cop and his son in Ibarra, where they also refueled, and landed in Tulcán just after dusk, as the moon pushed up from the horizon. It was the northernmost city in the country, a popular border crossing between Ecuador and Colombia, located at just over three thousand feet. Tess didn't know how far it was from Esperanza, but in the Andes, distance was less important than topography.

The Andes—nearly 23,000 feet above sea level at their highest point—ran like a spine down the middle of this country, with Esperanza folded somewhere within those impossible peaks at 13,200 feet. They would have to ascend more than ten thousand feet. Even if Esperanza was seventy miles from here, the trip could take hours. It would depend on the weather, the treachery and general condition of the roads, whether there were landslides, fog.

Ed Granger already had said they would go the rest of the way by car. Although it was possible to fly into Esperanza, darkness and the crosscurrents right now created too much risk for a chopper. But Tess wanted to know who was driving what kind of car, how far it was, and what sort of weapons he had to protect Lauren and Maddie from *brujos*. So as they crossed the tarmac, she said, "How about some details on all this, Ed?" And enumerated her questions.

He seemed astonished that she asked. "Don't you worry about it, mate. Ed Granger knows what he's doing."

It troubled her that Granger spoke of himself in the third person. "I appreciate everything you've done. But you didn't answer my questions."

"We're renting a four-wheel drive at the hotel. We can trade off on driving. It'll take seven hours and we can't do it at night. We'll start at first light. It's three hundred and ten miles."

The minicalculator in her brain did some quick division. "That means we'll average about forty-five miles an hour, Ed."

"On these roads, with switchbacks, landslides, iffy weather, that sounds about right." In the waning light, the tattoo that climbed from his hand up his arm seemed to be dancing, laughing. "Hey, mate, trust me. Even if we could fly closer, we can't do it in the dark and the roads are impossible at night."

"Manuel Ortega drove from the bodega to Esperanza at night."

"Manuel's a goddamn nutcase."

Manuel is the form my dead father uses in Esperanza, you jerk. She didn't like being herded and that was how this felt—Granger calling the shots, controlling where, how, when.

"If you knew we were in Otavalo," said Maddie, "why didn't you just pick us up there?"

"I didn't know where you were until I got a call from Kim Eckert." He glanced at Maddie, as if really noticing her for the first time. "And no one told me you and your grandmother were along for the ride."

"We're not along for any ride," said Lauren. "We're here because we're family."

"I didn't mean that in any sort of demeaning way, ma'am."

"You could've flown into town," Tess said. "And saved us a harrowing escape."

"I'm all for the cause, but I don't do Otavalo. I don't like leaving Esperanza. But Illika Huicho asked if I'd help, so here I am." A big PR smile from Granger. "Do you remember her?"

The leader of the Quechuans. "Yes. So what's the plan after we get to Esperanza?"

"The plan?" He blinked rapidly, as if he didn't understand the question. "What do you mean?"

"The plan. You've gone to all this trouble—but for what? Why?"

"I'm not the guy to ask." He strode on ahead of her, swinging his long arms.

Lauren and Maddie fell into step beside her. "Thoughts?" Lauren asked.

"He makes me uneasy," Tess said.

"I don't trust him," Maddie said. "He has a chopper, for crissake. He could've picked us up in Quito and flown us to Esperanza when the winds were calmer. Or something."

"I just don't like him," Lauren said. "Do you think he has a *brujo* inside him?"

Her mother's question spoke tomes about how far they had come in terms of accepting what was possible. "My wrist doesn't burn, so I don't think it's that. Maybe it's just how he is. He's got an agenda. I think he and his agenda have bothered me since the beginning."

"What do you want to do?" her mother asked.

"We're going to get Granger roaring drunk and pump him for information."

Maddie snickered. "And then what?"

"We'll find our own way to Esperanza."

Lauren rubbed her hands together like a gleeful kid. "Now you're talking my language."

Inside the terminal, Granger filed paperwork with airport security about the chopper, paid the tie-down fees, then they took a cab to Hotel Inca, Tulcán's equivalent of upscale. Not a Hilton or a Radisson, for sure. But the property featured a restaurant, wireless Internet, a swimming pool, a thermal spring. It seemed that the comforts of home were intended to lull them into a complacency they might not feel otherwise.

Once they were in their room, Tess took a quick shower, put on clean clothes, then counted out cash from their reserves, money they'd carried hidden on their bodies and in their packs. She went downstairs and bought supplies in the hotel store—bottled water, fresh fruit, canned goods, flashlights, matches—and a bag to put everything in. Then she approached the young Asian man at the desk and asked about the rental car reservation under Ed's name.

The man found it readily enough, a Ford Expedition, four hundred a week, to be returned in Tulcán. Bad gas mileage, Tess thought, and counted out the cash. "I'll need a map, too. We're headed to Esperanza first thing in the morning."

He brought out a map, drew a red *X* on Tulcán, another *X* on Esperanza, then drew a line into the mountains, an erratic zigzag that looked like a two-dimensional roller-coaster track. "Carry extra gas with you. Even though there're stations, the pumps are often dry because the *campesinos* hoard gas for their generators. I can include a ten-gallon container in the price."

"I appreciate it."

"There's a GPS in the car, so you can recheck the mileage and the route I've drawn. There may be a lot of traffic. In the last two days, I've rented twelve four-wheel-drive vehicles—what we usually rent in a week. All of them seem to be headed to Dorado, the last town before Esperanza."

"Why? What's going on?"

"The summer solstice, the Festival of the Sun, when the Quechuans and the Incas honored the sun god Inti. There'll be free concerts, free food, that kind of thing. A hotel guest gave me a blog address where more information is available." He handed her a slip of paper. "Here, you can check it out in the computer room. The Ford's silver and it's parked at the right side of the building. The gas container will be inside. Here's the key, I just need to see your driver's license and passport."

She set both on the counter, picked up her bag of supplies, and hurried toward the computer room. "Be right back."

The blog, liberationblogspot.com, appeared to have been started by a woman named Vivian Ortiz, whose parents had bled out simultaneously on a beach in Guayaquil in 2003. Once the coroner had ruled out a virus or bacteria and determined that her parents had died of cerebral hemorrhages, she'd started the blog to find out if anyone else had experienced something similar. When reports had started pouring in from all over South America, her blog had expanded to a website, where readers posted their own stories.

Tess clicked around on the site, noting the map of red dots where every bleed-out had occurred, a running tab on the number since 2003: 22,272. The latest blog entry had been made two days ago.

As longtime readers of this site know, we intentionally avoid words & phrases that would enable our enemies to discover this site by doing a Google search. We have used codes for those buzzwords. That said, you'll understand the following announcement.

The time has come. We will be gathering in Dorado on June 21. We encourage you to arrive a day early as turnout is expected to be high. Dorado has only 2 hotels.

A campground will be available in a pasture at the south end of town. General parking will be in the high school football field NW of downtown. Signs will be posted. For subscribers, I'm posting a list of necessities **here**. Feel free to pass this info on to everyone on your list whom you trust. Bus transportation is listed **here**. If you're driving your own vehicle, we encourage you to follow buses. Safety in numbers. We've waited a long time for this moment, people. Let's make it count. Now isn't the time to be afraid or intimidated. It's up to us to do what is right, to end the tyranny that has torn apart so many lives. *Sí, se puede.*

Viv

It sounded like a call for grassroots war against the *brujos*. But in what sense? To fight them? With flamethrowers? Even if their army numbered in the tens of thousands, where would they get enough flamethrowers?

Tess printed the latest blog entry, clicked to a map of Ecuador. She located Dorado, a town of 21,000 located at 7,200 feet, with the Río Palo less than a quarter of a mile to its north, Esperanza fifty miles beyond that— and six thousand feet up.

She clicked the link for bus transportation. Fourteen Ecuadorian cities were listed, with at least two buses leaving from each city. All buses were identified as Dorado 13. The synchronicity of that number prompted her to scroll down the page of cities to check for Tulcán. Sure enough, two Dorado 13s had left Tulcán at seven this morning and another two were scheduled to leave at ten tonight. She scrolled up the list again, clicking cities at random. All buses traveled in pairs. *Safety in numbers.* And a greater choice of host bodies for *brujos.*

Her cell rang. It had been so long since she'd had any cell service that she'd nearly forgotten about the phone. The message in the window read: *You have 10 new voice mails*. All were from Dan, pleading for her to turn herself in, her status as a fugitive could add another fifteen years to any sentence she received, she couldn't stay on the run forever. He was in Quito and would help her cut a deal.

"Yada, yada," she said, and deleted all the messages.

She picked up her printed sheets and returned to the front desk, where the clerk returned her passport and driver's license. Tess called Ed's room from the lobby and invited him to dinner. Then she called her room, and when her mother answered, Tess told her she'd rented a car and they should load up before dinner with Granger. "Look for a silver Expedition on the north side of the building."

Ed didn't get drunk easily: a bottle of wine with dinner, most of which he drank; a couple of beers, then several shots, one after another. By the time he was into the shots, his tongue had loosened considerably. He ranted about the stupid chaser plan to enlist human beings to do what chasers did, guiding transitionals into the afterlife. "I mean, mates, are you kiddin' me? How many people can see transitionals, much less talk to them and have the knowledge to guide them?"

"No one in Esperanza whom Ian and I encountered had any problem interacting with us," Tess remarked.

"Only because you were in Esperanza." His words slurred now, so the sentence actually sounded more like, *Oncause yuh speranza*. "Woulda been a lot different if you'd ended up somewhere else, I can tell you that. But see, someone got the bright idea that if you and Ian survived your near-death experiences, you'd be able to see and talk to these souls, and could take over some of what chasers do, then more transitionals could be recruited and pretty soon there would be hundreds or thousands of helpers worldwide who would be offering guidance to transitionals at the scenes of disasters, wars . . ." He threw back another shot. "That would free the chasers to tend to the *brujo* bastards. Me, I don't see how it's going to work. Right now, Dominica's tribe is the largest we know of and it's pretty clear that *brujos* worldwide outnumber chasers."

"In other words, you're saying that evil is winning," Maddie said.

"You got that right," Granger murmured.

Lauren piped up. "Then why don't you amass an army and fight them?"

"Fight them?" He threw out his beefy arms. "How?"

Tess couldn't let that pass. "I seem to remember you and your gang racing down from the posada with shovels and rakes and flamethrowers, Ed."

"Sure, we can do that. A small group of *brujos,* no problem. But there're tens of thousands of them around Esperanza. We aren't equipped to deal with *that.*"

"Excuse me, Ed, but it seems to me that most of the people in Esperanza who have stayed now live defensively, in fear of the *brujos,* terrorized by them, deluding themselves that they can live their lives around them. Why not come up with some comprehensive plan to take them out?" Tess asked.

"For crissake." For the first time, Granger's voice held a sharp edge of irritation. "You can't *take out* what's dead."

"Sure you can," Maddie said. "Head to head, toe to toe, one to one. Your flamethrowers are the weapon of choice? Great, supply flamethrowers to every Ecuadorian who has lost a loved one to a *brujo.* Galvanize them, organize them, get them all to Esperanza at the same time and wipe them out. But that takes too much work, doesn't it, Mr. Granger. Just like flying us into Esperanza would take too much work. You can do it, I know you can. But the status quo is easier, isn't it. I frankly think you assholes enjoy being victimized by the *brujos.* You're more united in your struggle *against* a common enemy—the commies in the fifties, the establishment in the sixties, Nixon in the seventies, the Muslims and gays in the twenty-first century. There always has to be some amorphous enemy, doesn't there. Jesus, you disgust me. I wouldn't ride to the mall with you and I sure as hell won't endure three hundred miles in a car where you think you're in charge. You're pathetic."

Maddie punctuated her soliloquy by shoving her chair away from the table, grabbing her bag, stalking off. Tess felt like cheering, Granger looked to be on the verge of a stroke, and Lauren tried not to explode with laughter. Neither Maddie nor Lauren had seen the blog yet.

"*That* young woman," Ed said, stabbing a stubby finger after Maddie, "has some serious issues."

"She has an excellent grasp of history." Lauren tapped the back of Granger's hand. "And if we're going to talk about issues, let's start with your alcohol problem, Mr. Granger. Ten years of *brujo* attacks have reduced you to a caricature. We'll find our own transportation to Esperanza. Thanks so much for the chopper ride. It was my first and thoroughly enjoyable." Then she, too, pushed away from the table and walked off.

Granger picked up his last shot, turned it slowly in his hand, sipped at it rather than downing it like a man dying of thirst. "I knew this wouldn't work. But when Charlie cleared the way for you to come through, I figured we had to do our part. The first transitionals in five centuries and one of them is Charlie's kid. That symbolism was just too great to ignore."

"Why?" Tess asked.

"Because we recruited him when he was still alive, when he took up meditation during the final two years of his life. Major stress levels for him then. The meditation helped. He entered fully into the chaser world when he died. He understood what was at stake."

"But he tried to manipulate *my* destiny from the afterworld. That's screwed up, Ed. The whole thing is. Unless you people fix things internally and muster the courage to fight the *brujos,* you're all lost. If I'm going to reach Esperanza, I'll do it under my own steam, on my own terms. I don't intend to be a pawn in anyone else's drama."

She went over to the bar, settled the bill for dinner and drinks, and asked the bartender how to get to the bus station. When she turned to leave, Granger was slumped over at the table, head resting in his arms.

It had grown considerably colder. The stars looked crisp, bright, close enough to touch, the Milky Way stretched from one end of the sky to the other, Led Zeppelin's *Stairway to Heaven.* Maddie and Lauren waited by the SUV. "Good work, ladies. You creamed him."

"Idiots are easy targets," Maddie said.

Tess told them about the blog, the gathering in Dorado, the buses. "It sounds like just the sort of grassroots uprising you were talking about in there, Maddie."

"Awesome, this is awesome," Maddie breathed. "We can take turns driving."

"I like the idea of safety in numbers," Lauren said. "Let's check it out."

The route to the bus station took them through the center of Tulcán. The streets bustled with pedestrians, restaurants and bars were crowded with tourists: Americans, Europeans, South Americans, Asians, blacks, whites, everything in between. Ecuador, someone had once said to her, was the heart of the universe. It certainly had become the heart and soul of *her* universe.

As they approached Tulcán's topiary cemetery, famous for its above-ground tombs and garden sculpted from cypress bushes, Maddie asked if they could stop briefly to take photos. "The guy responsible for starting it in 1936 is buried there and called the cemetery so beautiful that it 'invites one to die.' We should at least have a picture."

"In the dark?" Lauren asked.

"Photoshop performs miracles."

Tess felt uneasy here. The pedestrians, restaurants, and cafés were behind them, she had no desire to see a cemetery so beautiful that it invited you to die, and she wanted to get over to the bus station. "I'll park in front of the entrance, leave the headlights on, and you can snap pictures from inside the car. How's that?"

It wasn't what Maddie had in mind, but she didn't argue. Tess turned into the cemetery, dimly lit by street lamps that cast an eerie pall over the dizzying array of giant green geometric shapes and arches, the perfectly sculpted angels and animals, and the bleached white tombs that resembled the ruins of an ancient civilization.

She stopped in front of a huge hedge shaped and clipped into an archway so perfect that it seemed to invite you within, just as the creator of the gardens had said. Maddie opened the rear door and stepped out to take her pictures. Tess's arm began to itch, then burn. *Shit.* "Get in, Maddie."

"I'm not done yet. There—"

"*Get in,*" Tess yelled.

As she did, ribbons of fog swirled through the giant green arch, hugging the ground, wisps of the stuff drifting upward into bushes, strands wrapping around the green like a string of pale Christmas lights. Tess threw the SUV into reverse and peeled away from the arch with her heart pounding in her throat. Her eyes flicked from the rearview mirror to the side mirror.

"It's still coming, Tesso!" Maddie shouted.

It also was expanding like some mammoth carnival balloon, perhaps bolstered somehow by the dead in the cemetery's tombs. Tess looped back toward town, hoping she could lose the fog in the maze of narrow streets.

As the ball of fog rolled after the Expedition, it kept growing larger, thicker, denser. Tess knew that if it followed them into neighborhoods, residents might be seized. But if she didn't turn somewhere, Lauren and Maddie would be at risk. She estimated that the fog was half a mile behind them, giving them a slight edge. She turned into a neighborhood of small family-owned businesses, most of them closed for the night, and stopped at the curb.

"What're you doing?" her mother asked, alarmed.

"I'm not running anymore. They can't seize me, so I'm going to confront these bastards. We seem to have cell service here in town, so keep your cells on. Go back downtown, stay in crowds. I'll call you when it's gone."

"But . . ." Lauren stammered.

"Tesso, this is nuts," said Maddie. "You can't . . ."

She got out, bag over her shoulder, cell zipped into the pocket of her jacket. She loped toward the end of the block and heard the Expedition's engine coughing, revving, then it peeled off in the opposite direction. When she reached the intersection, she could see it, the fog now a densely compact globe five feet high, wider at the circumference, still in motion. It looked luminous, as if all the *brujos* within it radiated a kind of energy that kept the fog lit, moving with purpose. Tess stepped off the curb, walked out into the middle of the road, mouth dry with fear, the mark on her wrist burning. Curiosity drove her forward. *What are you?*

The globe stopped, ribbons of fog stirring in the night air, light from the old street lamps spilling over it. Two cars sped toward it on the other side, approaching from the border with Colombia, and both screeched to a halt about a hundred yards from the fog. Doors flew open, the drivers and passengers piled out, young travelers, maybe college students, with their digital cameras, camcorders. They probably thought the huge globe in the middle of the road was a UFO. In an hour, the spectacle would be on YouTube.

Tess was afraid they would attract the *brujos'* attention, so she trotted toward the globe, shouting, *"Here I am, you bastards . . . Estoy aquí, pendejos . . ."*

The fog moved rapidly now, streamers shooting outward, information-gathering surrogates that eddied toward her, across the pavement. She barely suppressed an overpowering desire to run. She kept shouting, taunting the *brujos.* "That's right, c'mon, you bastards, I'm not running anymore."

The first streamers curled around her ankles, sending a chill into the soles of her feet, through her socks, into her calves. More streamers twisted around her legs, thighs, down her arms, between her fingers, an insidious touch, creepy in the extreme. A dry, rustling sound filled her head, the whispered voices of the dead. Then the entire globe of fog rolled over her, swallowing her.

The dry whispers grew to a loud, irritating chatter. It was as if she were in the middle of a cocktail party with hundreds of guests, everyone talking over everyone else so that no single voice could be heard. A bone-deep cold cut through her, turning her eyes as dry as paper. Her wrist felt scorched. An almost unbearable pressure pushed against the base of her skull, as if they were exploring her in some way, as if she were an alien country to them.

A chant exploded in her head. *Find the body, fuel the body, fill the body, be the body,* louder and louder, until the chant hammered at every part of her. Terror and pain buckled her knees, she went down, hands gripping the sides of her head, then doubled over, arms covering her head. Suddenly she reared up, yelling, "Who speaks for you?"

Find the body, fuel the body.

"No one?" Her voice rang with false bravado. "Where's your leader? Where's Dominica?"

The chants abruptly stopped. In the subsequent silence, she heard the frantic thundering of her own heart.

"Who speaks for you?" she shouted again.

"We are one voice."

She sensed the *brujo* spokesperson was female. "Then hear this. Your battle is not with me. I only want to return to Esperanza and find Ian. We just want to be left alone."

"Your presence will destroy us."

"Wrong. Your battle isn't with me and this battle isn't mine."

The chanting started again, then the cold bit into the back of her neck and the pressure against her skull grew so intense that it drove her, shrieking, onto her side. The base of her skull felt as if it were being pried open with a dull blade and Tess gasped and curled into a fetal position. Blackness spread like India ink across her peripheral vision. Seconds, she was only seconds away from losing consciousness. They couldn't seize her, but they could cause her such agony that madness or death looked appealing.

She rolled, struggling to escape the globe, but it simply drifted outward, always remaining just beyond her, trapping her inside of it. The prying sensation reached the top of her skull and she reared up, hands clawing at the sides of her head, lungs screaming for air, her stomach in revolt from the pain. She suddenly heard her father.

Laugh, Slim, laugh until your sides ache, laugh until tears roll down your face.

Laugh? She rolled onto her knees and flung herself back, then forward again, and air flowed into her lungs. She sucked it in and exploded with laughter. She laughed until her sides ached and tears streamed down her face. The pain ebbed, drew back, and she forced herself to keep laughing as she got shakily to her feet. The globe didn't withdraw, but the chanting stopped, she was completely without pain now.

Her dad stood at the edge of the fog, fist pounding the air. He said something, but she couldn't understand him. Charlie, ever innovative, held up a blackboard. *Station liberation follow.*

Then Charlie faded away, and she said, "Tell Dominica that she can't stop me from entering Esperanza. Tell her I know the way in."

The luminous globe rapidly withdrew and a young man, camcorder hanging from his neck, stumbled forward, moving as if his own body were foreign to him. "Tell me yourself." His companions tore away from him, back to their car. They understood something terrible and terrifying was happening to him. The kid's cheeks were ruddy from the cold, his handsome, youthful face skewed with pain. In his eyes, Tess recognized Dominica.

"You can't stop me."

The kid's head jerked back and he laughed, but it sounded unnatural, like loud hiccups. Dominica was having trouble with the kid's body. "If you continue your journey, I will do to Dan what I'm going to do to this young man."

"Why?"

"Because I can."

"But what's the point?"

"Esperanza belongs to my kind. It was stolen from us. We intend to take it back."

"Fine, take it. But you don't have to kill to do it."

"You're an outsider. If you really understood what Esperanza is, you would not be so cavalier about our taking it."

"Like I said, this isn't my battle. Or Ian's. But if you make it our battle, then we'll defeat you precisely because we *are* outsiders."

A siren sounded—not cops, but like an air-raid siren—and metal grates in the road suddenly clattered open and cyclones of air exploded upward, dispersing the globe of fog that hovered to the kid's left.

Tess slapped him across the face, yelled, *"Fight her, fight, fight!"*

The kid wrenched back, tripped, slammed to the ground. Tess kept hollering and dancing around him like a referee at a wrestling match. The powerful bursts of air continued to explode through the grates, carrying her voice across the darkness.

Then he went still, sprawled on his stomach. A dark mist drifted from the top of his head and the wind took it away. *Please don't be dead.* Tess knelt beside him, turned him over. No bleeding. "Hey." She touched his neck. Heartbeat strong, steady. "Hey, wake up."

He opened his eyes, groaning as he pushed up, looking wildly around, rattling off something in German. *"No hablo alemán,"* she said.

He switched with ease to English. "Is it gone?"

"Yes. I'm not sure where your friends went. Do you have a cell phone? A way to get in touch with them?"

He patted the pockets of his jeans, brought out his cell. The face was smashed.

"Use mine," she said. "Call them and get out. You fought well."

He took her cell, and as they quickly crossed to the other side of the street, the explosions of air from the open metal grates chilled her. "My friends are close by," the kid said. "I heard you . . . shouting at me to fight. It . . . what *was* that thing? I remember seeing something in the road . . . and you . . . you were inside it and then . . . I felt violated, it pushed me down . . . inside a metal room without windows, doors, or light . . . and took over my body . . ." His eyes brimmed with tears, he looked away, embarrassed.

Tess squeezed his shoulder. "If you see fog again, run fast in the opposite direction." She punched out her mother's cell number.

"Slim?"

She hated hearing the frightened tightness in her mother's voice. "I'm okay, Mom."

"Thank God. We're on our way."

Tess rubbed her eyes. She and the German kid huddled together on the deserted road, where the city's blowers kept the fog away. Her father's message kept playing through her head, *station liberation follow.*

Twenty-six

Dominica fled the center of Tulcán and returned to the mountain pass where she'd left Dan Hernandez in a deep sleep in the car. But he was gone. So were the backpack, bottles of water, food. Maps and papers were tossed in the passenger seat, crumpled cellophane wrappers littered the floor. He'd awakened and escaped, and because he couldn't remember tossing the keys to the side of the road, he had fled on foot. She drifted through the area, searching for him. The terrain here was wild, rough, unpredictable, with numerous dips and rises in the land. The altitude rose from six thousand feet to just above eight thousand, challenging for any human in good shape, probably a breeze for Dan, whose physical body was one of the healthiest she'd experienced. He wore well-made hiking shoes with thick, sturdy soles, a huge point in his favor.

She focused, again, on Dan's body and started following the hum, the frequency unique to him. It eventually led to Punta, one of the few prospering villages in this region. It had paved roads, new schools, well-stocked stores, inns, restaurants, cafés, and thermal springs that had put it on the tourist map in the last thirty-five years. Its church boasted a new rectory, a new language school. But the distance Dan had traveled since she'd left him in the car was too great for him to have made it on foot. She was sure he'd hitched a ride.

Why were the streets so empty? The bars and clubs should be open, she thought. This town rarely slept. But Punta looked like a ghost town.

Dominica drifted down toward the church, peered through the stained-glass windows. She couldn't see anything. She slipped inside, senses attuned for Dan, and felt that he was beneath the church, in the underground rooms, the sanctuaries from her kind. She couldn't bring herself to descend into the tomblike maze. Many *brujos* refused to enter churches at all, placing themselves squarely in the realm of vampires, werewolves, all those silly legends about full moons, crosses, wooden stakes, clusters of garlic.

She moved to the far side of the church, looking for the rectory door. Here, she sensed another frequency, one so familiar and strong it shocked her.

Wayra. From when? She couldn't tell. But since he couldn't possibly move through time with the American or anyone else, he must have been here in the present before he and Ian had gone over that cliff in 1968. He had to be dead, his truck had plunged off a cliff, her people had combed through the rubble of the crash, and found nothing. Besides, if he were here now, he would sense her and show himself—to gloat, whisper sweet nothings, to try to manipulate her somehow.

Dominica thought herself to the back of the church, seeking someone she could seize so she could get inside without feeling the full brunt of the bunker, that sense of being buried. The rectory was back here, where the priests and some of their staff lived, and so was the small greenhouse that supplied fresh vegetables and fruits year-round. Since the greenhouse didn't have fancy electronic shutters like those in Esperanza, she slipped inside easily enough.

She found an acolyte stealing a smoke at the far end, beneath papaya trees growing with wild abandon.

She seized control of him swiftly and within moments convinced him she was God. He immediately began to weep and begged forgiveness for every lustful thought he'd ever had. While he pleaded, she dug around inside his mind and learned why the streets were deserted. Thanks to the wireless Internet the church had brought to Punta, everyone here knew about the assault in Tulcán. The alarm had sounded shortly after a video had been posted on YouTube several hours ago, probably by one of those college students who traveled with the young man she'd seized. So now the bunker beneath the church was crowded with terrified villagers who believed the *brujos* were on their way.

As if her kind could monitor every single stupid village in this ridiculous country when they had so many issues and concerns of their own. She told the priest to please put out his cigarette and return to the rectory to say three rosaries and a Hail Mary.

The priest hurried back through the hallway that connected the greenhouse and rectory to the church, fingers moving swiftly over the beads of his rosary, mouth trembling with prayers. He trotted down the steep stairs, one hand gripping the railing, and emerged in a warren of underground rooms. As soon as the priest entered the cafeteria, she scanned the faces, didn't see Wayra or Ian, but spotted Dan, one gringo among frightened villagers, serving breakfast. If she took him now, she risked annihilation. Even churches kept an arsenal of flamethrowers to be used against *brujos,* and she was certain there were sentries keeping watch on the crowd for signs of possession.

She slipped out of the acolyte and into one of the pretty young village women, a schoolteacher seated at a long wooden table with other adults and children. The priest whose body she'd vacated seemed briefly confused, then hastened out. The teacher twitched a little but not enough to call attention to herself. Dominica urged her to get up for a refill on her coffee, to flirt with Dan. Because he was lonely and confused, he succumbed to her charms. They exchanged names—Katrina and Dan—and it didn't take long for him to hang up his apron and turn his serving spoon over to someone else.

"We probably shouldn't go outside yet," the teacher said. "But we can walk through the greenhouse. It's really quite impressive."

"Is it safe from *brujos?*"

"Quite safe. I honestly believe everyone overreacted to that video. Just because *brujos* attack in one part of Ecuador doesn't mean they'll launch a full-scale attack elsewhere."

"They'd like to," Dan said.

"You think so?"

"I'm sure of it."

He knew more than he should, Dominica thought. "Well, there hasn't been an attack on Punta in the last few years," the teacher said. "The town's not big enough to bother with."

"But there're a lot of tourists. *Brujos* enjoy seizing tourists."

"It sounds as if you know a lot about *brujos,* Dan."

"More than I'd like to. You speak English well. Where did you learn it?"

How smoothly he turned the conversation back to her, Dominica thought, and was delighted when they slipped away from the others.

The teacher was a wonderfully compliant host, unaware that she was compromised. And Dan, a sucker for a pretty face who was still troubled by what had happened to him, enjoyed the moment. Dominica wasn't sure yet how she would escape Punta once she seized him again, but surely one of the vehicles out back had keys tucked above a visor. One way or another, she would take him, they would get to Esperanza, and she would use him to kill Tess, thus ending whatever plan the chasers had.

They made their way through the corridor to the greenhouse, talking quietly, discovering they had quite a bit in common. Katrina had graduated from Dan's alma mater, the University of Miami, on an international scholarship, and they knew some of the same people, frequented many of the same clubs and restaurants in Miami, shared a common passion for certain movies and books. They walked around the greenhouse, through the lush, tropical odors, and finally settled on the ground to share a plump, ripe mango. As Dan leaned forward to kiss her, howls filled the greenhouse and Nomad shot toward them at the speed of light.

The howls, so primal and electrifying, echoed in the greenhouse, an alarm to anyone within hearing distance. Katrina, certain the dog was rabid, shrieked and scrambled to her feet, her terror so extreme that Dominica couldn't control her, was forced to leap out of her toward Dan. But Wayra suddenly stood between them, tall, enraged, and threw open his arms, catching her.

Never in all these centuries had she dared to seize him, had she thought such a thing was even possible. As her essence sank into him, her shock and horror were as great as his, but she was stunned into senselessness, unable to grab control of any part of him. Wayra shouted, *"Warn the others,"* and Katrina and Dan tore out of the greenhouse.

Then Dominica felt a terrible compression in the center of her being, heard the snapping of bones, tasted an alien blood. She realized Wayra was shifting, that she wouldn't survive the transformation—and he knew it. He intended to annihilate her. She leaped out of him, soaring through the roof of the greenhouse, and thought her way back to Esperanza, to the cave. She immediately assumed a human form and fell to her knees, her sobs echoing in the dark womb.

One moment Ian was asleep in the rectory and the next, Wayra was shaking him awake. "We're leaving. I'll meet you out back."

Ian leaped out of the hard, narrow bed in the rectory where he had slept for—what? Seven uninterrupted hours? By the time they'd gotten settled here in the rectory last night, Ian was so exhausted that he'd collapsed around nine. Wayra had warned him that the jump forty years forward might have physical repercussions and had advised him to sleep as much as he needed, to stay hydrated, and had given him a bottle of vitamins and herbs to take for the next five days.

They'd planned to leave this morning, but the urgency in Wayra's voice, his obvious haste, worried Ian. The likeliest scenario was that *brujos* had tracked them here. But how had they done it so quickly? Even after he'd regained consciousness in his old life, it had taken the *brujos* a while to locate him. And he'd been in Ecuador for nearly three weeks before they had found him in Otavalo—and that was only after Wayra had shown up.

Was it easier for *brujos* to find Wayra because he had once run with them?

Within minutes, Ian was outside, in the church's back lot. Wayra was with Father Pedro Jacinto, the priest in charge of the church, and another man—blond, blue-eyed, bearded, who looked to be in his late thirties. They appeared to be arguing. The blond man glanced around uneasily, twitching, shifting his shoulders as if his jacket were too small for him.

"What happened?" Ian asked as he reached them.

His question was directed to Wayra, but Father Jacinto answered. "I believe you haven't met Dan Hernandez, Ian." The priest touched the blond man's shoulder. "He arrived last night, not long after you had gone to bed. You two have more in common than you realize."

Dan's shoulders kept twitching as he thrust out his hand. "Pleasure, Ian." Then he quickly added, "I think."

Staggered by the man's name, Ian was speechless.

"I, uh, won't even ask how it's possible that you're here," Dan said. "In 2008."

"Some things," the priest said, "are better left unknown."

"You're Tess's Bureau partner," Ian blurted.

"Was."

"Tell him what you know, Dan," said the priest.

Dan raked his fingers back through his hair. "I . . . was possessed by a *bruja* in Miami, so she could kill Tess. I think . . . she made me blow up Tess's mother's house."

He looked on the verge of tears and was so obviously traumatized that Ian barely resisted the urge to pat him on the shoulder. The priest expressed their collective compassion. "It's okay, my friend. We understand what *brujos* can do."

Dan stared down at his shoes, struggling with his demons. "Tess . . . told me . . . all of it . . . about Esperanza . . . I laughed at her. I thought she'd lost her mind. When she, Lauren, and . . . Maddie fled, this . . . thing inside me . . . forced me to pursue her. I have huge holes in my memories of these past weeks. I'm not sure when I realized I was in Ecuador. One day in Quito . . . I heard voices . . . it must've been her, the *bruja,* telling me what to do . . . I thought I'd gone totally over the edge. Then, last night, I woke up in a car . . . in the middle of nowhere and . . . knew that whatever had been inside me was gone. So I . . . started running. I . . . hitched a ride and ended up here in Punta. She . . . found me a little while ago, she was inside . . . a local teacher and—"

"Dominica nearly took him again," the priest finished. "But Wayra chased her off."

Ian wondered if that was why Wayra looked like shit—forehead beaded with sweat, a sickly pallor, eyes bleary.

"While she . . . used me," Dan went on, "I learned . . . about her plans, the plans of her tribe. I don't know what it all means, but maybe you will. She thinks you and Tess, Ian, are a chaser experiment that will be expanded if it's successful." He made air quotes around that last word. "And that's . . . why you and Tess were allowed into Esperanza. She believes that *brujos* outnumber chasers right now and they . . . need physical helpers who can do what they do. She's facing an insurrection in her tribe. The majority of them just want to . . . to sweep into Esperanza, seize everyone, make it a city of *brujos*. If they can do that, then they'll . . . move through Ecuador and take over the entire fucking country." He blinked, looked guiltily at the priest. "Sorry about the F word, Father."

"No problem. Go on, please."

"There were some memories . . . of a fog rolling through the . . . streets of Frisco . . . thousands of *brujos,* chanting. She couldn't seize you there, Ian. Something about restrictions she encountered when she . . . traveled back in time. But . . . when thousands of *brujos* descended, they were . . . able to take people, use them up, feed off the collective terror." He rubbed his hands over his eyes. "Jesus, her memories were so . . . so dark. So alien."

"You're fortunate you survived the possession," Wayra said. "Not many make it."

"She ordered her tribe to isolate Esperanza by shutting off power, establishing a perimeter of defense around the town. They plan to . . . to seize as many people as possible and the rest will assume forms, whatever that means, and prevent anyone from entering the city."

"It explains why I haven't been able to get through to anyone in Esperanza," Wayra said.

"She knows . . . the *brujos* know . . . that an attack on them is imminent, that it'll happen during a festival celebrating Inti. I don't have any idea what that means."

Wayra looked alarmed. "Is that possible, *Pedro*? That they could know?"

"Priests all over Ecuador have been taken," Father Jacinto said. "It has made us more vigilant. Our plans are in flux."

Ian didn't have a clue what they were talking about.

Four men loped out of the rectory, carrying a large plastic bin, a cooler, and four ten-gallon containers of gasoline. They set everything on the ground in front of the priest. "Our contribution to the cause, gentlemen. Food, water, forty gallons of gasoline, eight flamethrowers. Fire will obliterate a *brujo*. You won't get far without them."

"You're . . . a priest advocating *murder*?" Dan burst out.

Father Jacinto turned his woeful dark eyes on Dan. "My friend, the *brujos* are already dead. When they're obliterated, they're freed to move on in the afterlife."

Dan gave a sharp, nervous laugh. "Dead. Right." He blanched and looked like he was on the verge of puking. "She . . . messed with my brain, my blood chemistry . . . my memories."

"It's something at which they excel," Wayra told him.

"There are also two high-powered rifles and two handguns in the bin," the priest added, then gestured for the men to take the supplies to a small, decorative bus parked nearby.

"Why a bus?" Ian asked.

"It's not an ordinary bus," Father Jacinto said. "The windows can be tinted and sealed with just the flick of a switch. Mounted in the middle of the luggage rack is a rotating camera that provides a three-hundred-sixty-degree view. It has a satellite mounted on the roof, too, and an onboard computer. A panel in the roof can be opened for surveillance in case the camera fails or to shoot at the enemy. It was built by a Swiss company to transport valuables across the Alps and we simply modified it to fit our needs. We have six of these buses that we use for church-sponsored events. I'll show you both how to operate everything."

"Are you joining us, Dan?" Wayra asked.

"Me? No fu—I mean, no way, man." He looked horrified at the thought. "I'm going back to Miami, try to pick up the pieces of my life." He looked at Ian. "But would you do me a favor if you find Tess? Give her this." He passed Ian an envelope. "It's just an apology. For everything. I scribbled cell numbers on the back for Tess, her mother, and niece. I've called their cells several times, but never got through. Their service may not work here."

"I'll be sure she gets it, Dan," Ian said. "And thank you for the cell numbers."

"And Wayra, everything Dominica does, every . . . decision she makes, is ultimately about getting even with you," Dan went on. "In her mind, you broke her heart, used her, betrayed her time and again. I mean, this is all in her own head, but it's how she sees it."

"No doubt," Wayra replied.

In Spain, in the fourteen hundreds, I was killed because the father of the woman I loved hated me. Was *that* woman the *bruja* known as Dominica? Ian wondered. It made a terrible kind of sense.

"Dan, go get yourself some breakfast," Father Jacinto said. "Then we can make preparations for getting you home."

"Thanks, I appreciate it." He nodded at Ian and Wayra and offered a small, wan smile. "Good luck, you two."

He seemed to limp away, shoulders hunched as if he were carrying an impossible burden. Ian felt as if he were watching a broken man struggling to appear whole. "You need to protect him from being seized again," Wayra remarked.

"He'll have an escort to Quito." The priest gestured at the bus. "Let me show you a few things inside."

The interior of the bus was impressive—five rows of leather seats that would seat three across on either side of the aisle, for a total of thirty passengers, storage bins overhead, a built-in cooler and restroom at the back, a console covered with buttons, switches, screens. Father Jacinto sat in the driver's seat and proceeded to demonstrate what each switch and button controlled, how the satellite and GPS worked, what the computer could track. "Internet reception is not so good. Like the cell phones." He explained that the sides of the bus were reinforced steel, the windows were made of bulletproof glass, that the bus was basically a tank that could get through almost anything.

After Ian climbed back down, Father Jacinto said, "You will not be alone when you cross the Río Palo. By our estimates, there could be as many as twenty thousand from all over South America, men and women whose loved ones have been seized by *brujos*—and killed."

"The liberation group," Wayra said, glancing at Ian, and gave him a quick rundown on what it was. "They often refer to themselves as the people's army. Or as avengers."

"The churches all over Ecuador have been working with this group," the priest said. "It's why the churches have set up sanctuaries, supplied villagers with weapons, why we created alarm systems. So now the *brujos* are about to learn what happens when the people rise up. Because they have learned of our plan, you'll stop at the Santa Clara church first, just outside of Dorado, and will be given instructions on how to proceed. We're trying to keep everything self-contained, with only a few people knowing the full plan."

"Where's Dorado?" Ian asked.

"Just four hours from here. It's where this liberation group is gathering."

"How far is Dorado from Río Palo?"

"Less than a quarter of a mile."

A stone's throw, he thought, his excitement surging. "Why did they wait until now? Why didn't they attack years ago?"

"They were waiting for you and Tess to return to Ecuador," the priest replied. "They looked at it as some sort of sign."

"How could they possibly know about us?"

"Your entry into Esperanza as transitionals was heralded as the beginning of a new era, Ian. And the liberation Web site has contacts throughout Ecuador. I suspect they knew the moment Tess entered the country. But you, my friend, since you came via other means"—he looked at Wayra—"there's probably no record of you at all. The other reason they chose today is that it's the summer solstice. Hundreds of thousands in Ecuador and Peru will be celebrating Inti Raymi, the Festival of the Sun. In the five years the liberation Web site has tracked bleed-outs, there has never been one at a Festival of the Sun celebration."

Twenty-seven

By early morning, they were high in the mountains again, one of the Dorado 13s chugging along in front of them, a chain of vehicles behind them. The paved road was two lanes and, in some spots, barely that. Most of the time, there was no guardrail and the sheer drop-off on the right distracted Tess. She kept expecting to see fog creep up over the edge. Now and then, she heard a troubling clunk in the Ford's engine or beneath the car. She wasn't sure. *Please don't break down out here.*

They'd taken turns driving in two-hour shifts, and Tess was now on her second stretch, the final hour to Dorado. Lauren and Maddie were sacked out, Tess's eyes ached, she only wanted to get somewhere. Anywhere. They had made two stops, a dozen vehicles pulling into the same roadside restaurant, then a lonely gas station, neither of which could easily accommodate fifty-two hungry people who also had to pee. It meant lost time, increased anxiety, but bonds were forged while waiting to use the restroom, to pay for a snack or a bottle of water.

Tess came to understand that everyone in this little wagon train was here to take a stand against the *brujos*, against the evil that had killed their loved ones with such indifference and broken so many lives. There would never be an official record of this battle, nothing that would go down in the history of Ecuador as a decisive turning point against oppressors. Everyone was here to stop the killing—and to rid the country once and for all of this scourge of the dead.

The businessman driving the lead Dorado 13 had watched his wife bleed out while they were having dinner on the island of Chiloé, off the coast of Chile. He had run across Vivian Ortiz's Web site in late 2005 and, since then, had culled several thousand cases from both Chile and Argentina. The Brazilian woman driving the rusted old VW bus lost her brother, a physician, to the *brujos* while he was conducting a conference on alternative healing in Rio. A Peruvian yoga teacher had been windsurfing on the island of Margarita when his son had suddenly begun bleeding from the eyes and keeled over while still on his board. An American congressman had seen a colleague bleed out in a hotel bathroom in La Paz. A California screen-writer had seen her daughter and a colleague bleed out during a film festival in Cannes, the only European incident in the group.

Fifty-two stories in just their group. The experiences had landed some of these people in therapy, caused others to lose their jobs and pensions, branded others as unemployable. But they knew they'd left the rational world when they began to post on the liberation Web site.

As the road leveled out, the morning light carved the landscape into stark relief—trees blown into odd shapes by wind that swept up over the edge of the mountains, memorials for roadside fatalities decorated with clusters of wildflowers, then buildings made of stone, wood, and tin, where old people sat on porches, watching the procession of vehicles. At the summit, stood a sign: BIENVENIDOS A DORADO. Honking erupted up and down the line of vehicles, and on Dorado 13, passengers stuck their heads out the windows, shouting and waving.

The Río Palo was less than a quarter mile from the center of town, Tess thought, and the Bodega del Cielo, the place where her journey had begun, was a short distance beyond it. Excitement and dread rolled through her in equal measures.

The trees gave way to a town so beautiful and pastoral that it possessed a fairy-tale quality. Stone buildings looked gold in the morning light, bells rang, the sonorous notes echoing across the summit, an open-air market burned with colors. A church dominated the skyline, a throwback to ancient times with a fountain out front, doves cooing in the eaves. The town's tremendous plaza was filled with people and dozens of stalls where locals sold jewelry, food, coffee. Near the fountain, five men played flutes and guitars, the haunting notes rising toward the cloudless sky.

"Ladies, we've arrived," Tess announced.

"Somewhere, like, maybe a Hilton with a hot shower?" Maddie raised herself up from the back seat, face visible in the rearview mirror. "Never mind. The answer's no."

"I'll settle for a Jiffy John," Lauren remarked.

Tess parked in a pasture the size of a football field. Row after row of small buses, all Dorado 13s, lined up with several thousand cars, trucks, vans, jeeps. Colorful banners welcomed all to the Festival of the Sun. From a stall in the pasture, they bought coffee and vegetable empanadas that steamed in the chilly air. Tess couldn't distinguish festival goers from those who were here to avenge the death of loved ones, those here to take back Esperanza. Safety not only in numbers, she thought, but in camouflage.

The driver of the Dorado 13 in front of them was directed to a side street, to a church and its adjoining school to regroup and pick up their directions. But it was a mob scene inside, the place jammed with *vengadores*—the avengers against the *brujo* incursion. Everyone talked at once, the PA system crackling with static as a woman explained what was supposed to happen next. It was too crowded and noisy, and Tess couldn't deal with it. She told Lauren and Maddie she would meet them outside.

Tess wandered into a field behind the church, face turned into the sun, and watched a herd of llamas. Beyond the field, Río Palo's glistening waters meandered beneath the shade of giant ceiba trees, beckoning, tempting her.

She returned to the sidewalk and joined a group of tourists headed toward the river. Her heart beat wildly, she just wanted to see it—and see across it. The road dipped steeply and flowed seamlessly into a two-lane concrete bridge that crossed the half-mile-wide river into *brujo* land.

She paused at the top of the steep banks, shocked at how fast the water moved, rushing over volcanic rocks, into and out of the sunlight, sweeping away everything in its path. A road cut through the vast rolling landscape on the other side. Everything was a deep emerald green, vibrant wildflowers blooming in clusters, the pines and ceiba trees partially hiding homes, squares of pasture, grazing llamas, horses, goats, a *community*.

Kids tossed a Frisbee in a front yard, people were getting into cars, small groups walked toward the bridge, presumably to join the celebration to the ancient sun god. It surprised her that people lived on that side of the river. Her memories were of a lonely building, isolated in thick fog. She sat on the grassy bank to get a better view and there, in the distance, stood the bodega, cars parked out in front, buses idling, their exhaust creating gray plumes in the air, passengers waiting around outside. Was the edge of the mesa right behind the bodega, as she remembered? Were the outhouses still there?

Are you out there somewhere, Ian?

An intense, powerful wave of emotion swept through her. She had made it, the river and bodega existed, and she was terrified it would be torn from her again. As she stood, her father strode up the banks, Charlie with his inimitable smile of optimism, his usual buoyancy. "Not much farther now, Slim."

"You *played* me, Dad."

"I did not." He looked indignant, then angry. "At every juncture, every—"

"You played me just like you played the court system all those years."

"Slim, c'mon . . ."

"Go plead your case with Mom."

"She's, uh, not exactly receptive."

"Gee. I wonder why."

"Look, I've always just wanted what's best for all of you, Slim. No one's forcing you three to go up the mountain."

"Going up the mountain is the only way I'm going to find Ian. I do thank you for that, Dad."

"Just remember, Slim, these *brujos* are tricky, they've seized nearly every-one in town, and in their host bodies, they can do whatever you can do. But you and yours have purity of purpose. That will go a long way." He paused, listening to something. "Gotta run. Some more people are headed this way." He winked. "Love you, Slim."

Then he became a glowing white hummingbird, his little wings beating so rapidly she could barely see them. He soared across the Río Palo, swooped down once, as if to say, *Later,* and vanished against the blue of the sky.

Purity of purpose? She didn't know about that.

Tess ran back up the hill to find Lauren and Maddie, tears blurring her vision.

The sun stood high in the sky when Dominica left the cave in her humble peasant form. Her demons were history and Wayra was, at last, truly dead to her.

Out on the street, she turned in place, senses attuned for the faintest hum of electricity. Only an eerie silence prevailed. Her smile grew with her certainty that the *brujos* had won this round—a complete shutdown of the city's electrical grid. That meant that Rafael and his minions had done their jobs—windmills blown up, hydroelectric plants sabotaged. Some build-ings, those with underground sanctuaries, would have backup generators, but eventually generators would run out of gas, sanctuaries would run out of food, and these desperate human idiots would have to emerge. People in rural communities, where greenhouses were abundant, might fare better for a while. But eventually, even they would have to surface.

As she walked through the streets of Esperanza, she saw that many in her tribe had seized residents—not for sensual pleasures, but for the defining battle ahead. Blockades were going up on the main arteries into the city, weapons were being dispersed, snipers positioned. As she crossed through the park into El Corazón, four *brujos* seized three men and a woman trying to escape the city by car.

She located Rafael, whose host body was that of a muscular black man, a young Ali who taught boxing at one of the local gyms. He was directing a group to surround a government building, one of the official underground sanctuaries.

"Nica," he exclaimed when he saw her. "Why haven't you chosen a host?"

"I will. How many are hidden in the sanctuary beneath this building?"

"We believe there are between sixty and a hundred."

"How many have been seized so far?"

"More than three thousand. By dusk, we expect double that. You were smart to order your followers to join us, Nica."

"Let's get something straight, Rafael. I didn't order my followers to join *you*. I ordered them to join all *brujos* and isolate Esperanza."

He offered a small, sly smile. "In other words, you recognized the wisdom in my plan."

"I recognized that it was time to make the city ours." Before he could gloat or contradict her again, she went on. "We know that Ed Granger rescued Tess in Otavalo and was last seen in Tulcán. But where are the others? Sara? Juanito? Illika and her Quechuan advisors? And what about Manuel Ortega?"

"We haven't found them yet. But we will, Nica. We will." His eyes glistened with hunger and excitement for the battle ahead. "Can you taste it? Smell it?" He lifted his head and sniffed at the air. "Our victory."

"The city is not ours yet, Rafael. But we're close. In an hour, I will address the tribe from here, in the park." Close to where Atahualpa and his army had marched against the Spanish, she thought, and across the street from the buildings that covered an Incan religious site where Inti, the sun god, had been honored daily with sacrifices. *May Inti shower us with his blessings.*

"Well, I hope you have a host by then."

"And I hope you won't have to kill anyone, Rafael. You already had one breakdown and it certainly wouldn't do anything for your supposed reputation as a leader to have another."

With that, she swept past him, vowing to banish him as soon as Esperanza was theirs.

After so many failures these past weeks and months, the host she chose had to do what Pearl had suggested, it had to make a statement, to say, *Do you see how truly powerful we are as a tribe?* Only a member of the Esperanza hierarchy would accomplish that.

Dominica shed her form and thought herself to Saint Francis Church, where Ian and Tess had spent their final hour in Esperanza before returning to their physical bodies. Across from it was the orchard where Wayra had made love to her only to keep her from the transitionals. But that day, fog had filled the orchard, the field, and obscured the road. Now, there wasn't any fog, just brilliant light showering the orchard.

The church looked deserted, not a car in sight, the fenced fields to either side of it empty of llamas and horses, even the chicken coop was deserted. She thought herself to the barn on the church's left, alert for traps. But she sensed nothing like the low-frequency field that had surrounded Otavalo's ExPat Inn. Apparently Illika hadn't bothered learning anything from her neighbors to the south. Quechuans were a proud people and she suspected that Illika considered the Otavaleños too materialistic and their technologies too expensive.

She drifted through the roof of the barn, and found an old truck, VW Bug, and Harley parked inside. She sensed eight people beneath the barn, in the private little sanctuary for Esperanza's elite. She really had no desire to descend into that underground place, but if she wanted to make a statement when she addressed her tribe, she would have to.

Dominica reminded herself that she was already dead, that the mounds of earth could do nothing worse to her than what had been done already. Just as she readied herself to descend, Persephone into the underworld, a door opened at the far end of the barn. Pretty Sara Wells stepped out, an Amazonian parrot riding on her shoulder.

The parrot squawked constantly. "Hungry, where is Nomad? *Cómo estás?*"

"*Cálmate, Kali,*" she said quietly, and hurried over to the truck and opened the door.

As she leaned inside, Dominica seized her, and quickly took control of her. The parrot fluttered off toward the ceiling, shrieking and squawking loudly, *"Peligro, brujos, peligro."*

Dominica forced her to get into the truck, to insert the key in the ignition, to press the remote-control button that opened the barn door. The parrot flew off, its shrieks and squawks echoing through the still, cold air, *Brujos, peligro.* She commanded Sara to back out of the barn and met no resistance.

Very good, Sara. Keep doing what I tell you and you'll enjoy breakfast tomorrow. Defy me and you'll wish you'd fled with the younger residents when you had the chance.

Sara's essence spoke softly—not from fear, but with disarming certainty. *You won't win this battle, Dominica. But there's a certain karmic justice in all this. Your kind brought me to Esperanza. So lead the way,* jefe.

Jefe. As if she were some macho jerk searching for a piece of ass. She resented it. But in all fairness to Sara, she resented nearly everything these days. While Sara drove fast over deserted roads, Dominica plundered the treasure chest of information she carried. She learned that in the hours just before the power had gone down, Sara had heard from Ed Granger, who said that Tess was no longer in his "possession," as if she were a bag of gold or jewels that he'd lost. She discovered that Father Jacinto at the church in Punta was doing stations of the cross for the success of the revolt against the *brujos.*

You will lose, Sara said.

You've lost already.

You'll be annihilated or forced to move on.

Shut up.

She learned that Wayra and Ian had left Punta early this morning. The shock of it—that it wasn't enough that he had tried to annihilate her, but that he was now pursuing her, that he intended to be a part of the final battle—caused her to pull to the shoulder of the road.

Sara laughed and laughed. *You thought he was going to sit around on the sidelines? You really are delusional, Dominica.*

The information was phony, Sara was trying to trick her.

Why would I bother with tricks? You seem to do that well enough on your own. While you've been busy all these centuries perfecting ways to kill, Wayra has been fine-tuning all his shifter abilities. Dominica ignored her and tried to reason her way through all these new revelations. He had survived that crash by moving through time and taking Ian with him, which meant she never had known him. That he was now pursuing her, that he would be a part of this battle, meant she had never known his heart, his soul, that their one hundred and thirty-seven years together had been lies. A great wave of sorrow abruptly filled her—and then Sara started laughing again.

You never knew Wayra and never will, Dominica, because your heart went cold centuries ago.

You know nothing of my relationship with Wayra.

Actually, I know quite a bit. And with that, Sara's memories of Wayra rose up and crashed over Dominica. Through Sara's memories, she heard Wayra talking about *her,* discussing what their relationship was like in the very early years, how Dominica changed, how she became corrupted when she joined the *brujos.* Then there were more of Sara's memories, a tsunami of memories so intimate and profane that Dominica couldn't think, couldn't bring the body to move.

He brought me to Esperanza, actually drove me here from the Bodega del Cielo when I was a young anthropologist and full of myself. We were lovers for years, and to this day are still lovers when the spirit moves us. He will love others, as will I, but that's not something you understand, Dominica. It's the spirit you lack, the human soul that you will never understand. It's why you and yours will lose.

Dominica snapped out of her torpor, slammed the truck into gear, pressed her foot against the accelerator, and tore onto the road, Sara's laughter pursuing her.

You will die hideously, I promise.

I will die gladly to join the chasers in their battle against you and your kind.

Shortly afterward, the truck hit the first of the roadblocks into the city. Dominica stopped and two men approached, physical men, and within them she sensed *brujos.* "Esperanza is in lockdown, ma'am. What is your business here?" asked the taller of the two, a goth type with spiked hair, tattoos, nails painted black.

Dominica addressed him by his tribal name. "Good job, Cooper. Now how about letting me through so I can address the tribe?"

He stooped over and looked in the window. "Dominica?"

"Who else could take the great Sara Wells?"

"Holy shit."

"Who's your companion? I don't recognize him."

"From another tribe, down south. *Buena suerte.*" He slapped his hand against the roof of the truck and waved her on through the roadblock.

A tribe down south? Where? How far south? Southern Ecuador? The tip of South America?

Sara laughed hysterically. *You don't know? You're really that clueless? You should get out more, Dominica, meet the other tribes. Some of them are quite innovative, and it won't be long before they're larger and more powerful than your tribe and they won't want you as a leader. You represent the old ways.*

Dominica shoved her down inside the metal room she had constructed long ago. Moments later, the car squealed to the curb and Dominica got out to great fanfare, a rock star's welcome. Her followers cleared a path for her to the most elevated spot in the park, the base of a large statue of Atahualpa.

As she stood before them in the beautiful body of her rival, she did what she had been born to do six hundred years ago—inflamed the crowd, stoked their tremendous passions, their rage, their profound hunger for physical life. As she beat her fist against the air, cheers and applause went up from the burgeoning crowd. *"The city is ours,"* she shouted. "And just as the Incas made sacrifices to the sun god, Inti, right over there, beneath those buildings, I now sacrifice this body so that Inti's blessings are with us in this battle."

Then she slammed her virtual fist into Sara's brain. As the body began to bleed out, Dominica leaped from it, assumed her peasant form, and watched Sara Wells twitching and writhing with agony as she died, her blood spilling everywhere. The crowd went wild.

She wondered why it didn't feel all that good.

At Santa Clara Church they picked up twenty-three passengers, five hundred flamethrowers, and hundreds of other weapons that ranged from grenades to handguns to high-powered rifles with scopes. Ian was astonished that a church had amassed such an arsenal, but was grateful for anything that might give them an edge against the *brujos.*

Wayra and one of the priests spent an hour on a basketball court behind the church, demonstrating how to use the flamethrowers and grenades and how to load the rifles and guns. He also spelled out some basics, first in Spanish, then in English.

"It's likely that anyone we encounter in Esperanza is a *brujo*, that they now inhabit everyone in the city who is not in hiding. These are our fellow countrymen, so don't shoot to kill. Aim for a leg, foot, shoulder. An injury is often enough to cause a *brujo* to vacate a host body.

"Anywhere north of the Río Palo, a *brujo* can assume a virtual form. Sometimes you'll recognize that there's something not quite right about it, something *off*. But these forms are convincing, so when in doubt, use the flamethrower. Just the threat of fire will cause the *brujo* to shed the form or leave a host body. Fire obliterates them. And remember that these forms can interact with most things in the physical world—they can open doors, drive cars, fire guns."

"How many of us will there be?" asked one man in the crowd.

The priest answered. "Around twenty thousand. There are five hundred buses parked in the pasture on Dorado's north side, where people will board. The rest will go by cars. We aren't sure what kind of defenses they've erected, what the conditions are. But we hope to simply move in and overcome them. Most of you who are here understand the ways of *brujos*, know how dangerous they are. What we're about to do is perilous, I cannot emphasize that enough. No one will think badly of you if you decide to back out now."

A woman raised her fist and shouted, *"Libertad de los brujos! No más tiranía! Sí, se puede!"*

A roar went up, a call to the end of *brujo* tyranny, and Ian felt a tectonic plate shifting, something so profound that he lacked the language to describe it.

"Bueno, vámonos!" the priest yelled, and motioned the group forward, toward the bus.

As the crowd dispersed, Wayra suddenly doubled over, clutching his arms against him. Ian grabbed his arm. "Jesus, what is it?"

Air hissed through Wayra's clenched teeth. He tried to straighten up, couldn't, and Ian helped him over to a bench. Even once he was sitting down, he remained doubled over, unable to speak, barely able to breathe. His body began to change, fur appearing on his cheeks, the backs of his hands.

"Wayra, you can't shift now." Ian looked around anxiously, worried that someone would see. "There're a bunch of people here."

The fur vanished into the pores of his skin. He finally raised his head, his face eggshell white, his eyes dark pools of sorrow. "Sara . . . Dominica seized her . . . killed her . . . a sacrifice to Inti, the sun god."

Sweet Christ.

"I'm done walking circles . . . around Dominica. We must . . . hurry, Ian."

"Can you get up?"

He inhaled deeply, sat up straight, but the effort cost him. Sweat poured down the sides of his face, he grimaced. "The pain . . . is passing. Just help me stand."

Ian helped him up, he swayed, then seemed to gain control of himself and strode forward. Color returned to his face, his pace became more certain. By the time they reached the bus, he acted almost normal. But he wasn't, that deep sorrow was still evident in his face. "I'll drive," Ian said.

"Good idea."

Several men from the church had put the weapons into large plastic bins, and as passengers boarded, Wayra handed out flamethrowers, rifles, handguns, additional ammo. They loaded the bins into the rear of the bus and covered the remaining weapons with quilts just in case the Dorado cops were checking vehicles. As Ian slipped behind the wheel, the ghost of Sara Wells suddenly appeared on the hood, sitting there in a lotus position, staring in at him.

"The others are in the church where you and Tess spent your last minutes as transitionals. The *brujos* are now trying to smoke out the bunkers and underground shelters. Pablo, Charlie, and I and the rest of us will do what we can to help once you get into the city, but it's going to be bad, Ian."

He had dozens of questions, but she evaporated before he even opened his mouth. He started the bus, pulled out onto the road. Wayra was on his cell, chattering away in Spanish, then snapped it shut, frustration rolling off him like an odor. "It seems that the only cell service that's working is right around Dorado. They've got their own tower and it doesn't work for Esperanza. We're just a few miles from town, so we're going to head straight to the bridge. Buses are moving across already."

"Do you know how to get to that church where Tess and I were just before we left here?"

"Of course. Why?"

Ian repeated Sara's message.

"That's all she said?"

"That's it."

"Shit. Drive faster, Ian."

The Ford trundled over the bridge, the rushing Río Palo sweeping past below them, the beauty of this small valley utterly breathtaking. Tess felt as if she were returning home after a long journey abroad and could barely contain her excitement as the bodega came into full view. It was larger than she remembered, made of stone, with half a dozen small windows bordered by dark blue wooden shutters.

Passengers waiting outside with their bags waved and shouted, drivers honked in return. Employees stood in the open doorway, applauding, and held up signs in Spanish and English that read, NO MORE BRUJO TYRANNY! DEATH TO TYRANNY! Men and women waved posters that bore photos of loved ones who had been killed by *brujos,* other groups simply stood there, watching the procession, weeping, their fists raised in solidarity.

But suppose this was a trap? Suppose the *brujos* knew about it? They had to know, Tess thought. There was nothing subtle about their approach. And the clunk and clatter in the Ford's engine continued and worsened every time they hit a pothole.

Maddie, busy in the back seat with her digital camera, recording everything, suddenly said, "Maybe it's just me, because I'm tired, but I really don't like the sound the car's making."

"I'm getting kind of creeped out by all this," Lauren said. "You think these people cheering us on are *brujos*? That maybe they're cheering because we're the lemmings who're about to jump over the edge of the cliff?"

"My wrist doesn't burn," Tess said. "I think we're fine. We're all just worn out."

"Yeah, even the car," Maddie remarked.

The road twisted upward like a strand of DNA and was perilously steep, one hairpin curve after another. The mountain blocked most of the afternoon light, so headlights came on, glancing off trees, creating a strobelike effect. She tried not to focus on how narrow the road was, the lack of a guardrail. One of the buses was so close to the lip of the cliff that as its right rear tire struck the skinny shoulder, a chunk of mountain fell away.

Tess smelled something burning now, an odor like scorched fabric, not smoke. She hoped to hell it wasn't the engine overheating. The car behind her suddenly pulled out into the other lane—the lane that went down the mountain—the driver honked twice and flashed a thumbs-up as he drove past. Other vehicles immediately followed. It made sense. Esperanza and the villages that surrounded it like planets revolving around the sun were the only hubs of civilization up here. She doubted cars would be coming down the mountain. Anyone who could leave probably had left already. Two lanes of traffic would get them there twice as fast.

The burning odor grew. She came out of a turn and the road briefly leveled off, then dipped steeply downward. Tess tapped the brakes—and her foot went clear to the floor. The brakes weren't just mushy or soft, they were *gone.* "Aw, shit, shit," she breathed, and quickly pulled out into the other lane to avoid rear-ending Dorado 13.

"Don't tell me that's what the smell is," Lauren said, her voice sharp with alarm.

"Start looking for a place where I can pull off. Preferably a level place, with a guardrail."

"You've got a hill coming up," Maddie said. "Get back in the right lane when you can. We'll be okay."

Until the next descent, Tess thought, and hit the horn, then the blinker, and darted into the right lane, cutting dangerously close to the Dorado 13 that she had just passed. The driver slammed on his horn, letting her know he didn't appreciate it, and swerved into the left lane, gaining on her. Tess lowered her window, shouted, "My brakes are gone!"

But the bus had only a door on the right side, no window that could be lowered, and the driver couldn't hear her. She made frantic hand gestures. Dorado 13 sped on.

"We're going to have to bail," Lauren said anxiously.

"*Bail?*" Maddie exclaimed. "Into what? We bail, we'll go over the side of a mountain."

Or the Ford would roll backward, down the mountain, crashing into every vehicle behind it, a domino effect that could kill hundreds. Tess gripped the wheel, bleeding off as much speed as she safely could while in a climb. Fifty to forty to thirty-five, then down to twenty miles an hour. She let the speedometer needle slip to fifteen. As the cars behind her started pulling into the other lane, she hit the hazard light. The top of the hill was visible, a clump of wilted flowers marking a roadside fatality, no guardrail, no place to pull off. She frantically pumped the brake, hoping it would kick in. Nothing happened.

"Mom, get into the back seat with Maddie, both of you bail out on the right side. *Hurry!*"

Lauren scrambled over the seat, Maddie hurled open the door, and they threw themselves out. Then the car reached the top of the incline, which looked to be about two heartbeats long. Tess turned off the engine, grabbed her pack, and swerved the wheel to the right, aiming the SUV for the edge of the cliff. She jerked up on the door handle, but it wouldn't budge, it was stuck, and the trees at the edge of the cliff were rushing toward her. *Jesus.* Tess climbed over the seat, kicked open the back door, dived for the ground. She slammed into it, rolling, air rushing from her lungs, dust biting at her eyes.

The Ford crashed into several large boulders, the rear end flipped upward, over, and the SUV vanished over the edge of the mountain. An explosion sundered the air, a fireball soared through the trees, incinerating everything in its path. Embers rained down, other trees caught fire, the dry branches crackled and burned like money. Clouds of smoke rolled across the road.

Coughing, rubbing her eyes, Tess pushed to her feet, aware that something had gone awry in her right leg, the one that had cost her thousands, the one with all the metal inside. Or maybe it was her knee, her ankle, she couldn't tell.

She limped forward, shouting for Maddie, Lauren, only vaguely aware of the shriek of tires against asphalt, the squeal of metal hitting metal around her. At some point, she realized her hair—her long white hair—was burning and she scooped up handfuls of sand and slapped it against her head, smothering the fire. She tripped over something, it was Maddie, groaning as she lifted up, face smudged with soot and dirt. "Tesso, Jesus, where's Lauren?"

"Running like hell," Lauren shouted. "Can't see shit through this smoke. Keep talking to me, keep talking."

She emerged from the smoke, face and hair gray with ash, eyes leaking with tears, blood rolling down the right side of her face from a gash in her temple. She fell into Maddie and Tess, and they held her up. Tess tore off her jacket and pressed it against her mother's temple. "Hold it there, Mom. Keep moving your feet. Left foot, right, good, good."

A bus covered in ash squealed to the side of the road, its windows black with soot, and people poured out to help them. They coughed, stumbled, and limped into the bus. The doors whispered shut behind them. When Tess could finally see again, when the aching, pulsing burn in her eyes began to ebb, she and Lauren were in seats at the back of the bus, where a man and a woman with first-aid kits tended to their injuries.

Someone else handed Tess a large bottle of cold water and a damp cloth so she could wipe the ash off her face. The woman examining Tess's ankle—not her leg, not her thigh—announced that she had sprained it. "And your knees look like my son's the first time he fell off his bike," the woman said in Spanish. "I'll wrap the ankle and clean the scrapes and you'll be good as new."

"Thank you so much," Tess croaked, her voice as dry as paper.

She took a long swig of deliciously cold water and then wiped the damp cloth over her face and neck. It came away black. She poured water over it and wiped again. When she raised her eyes from the cloth, a tall man stood in the middle of the aisle, staring at her. Soot was smeared across his face, ash had turned his hair and beard a dirty white. Ash even coated his lashes, so that when he blinked, bits of it fluttered away like tiny insects. But it was his eyes that spoke to her, his eyes that drew her up from the seat, his eyes that she remembered.

"Ian?"

His eyes flooded with incredulity, hope, then gratitude and love. "Slim?"

As they moved toward each other, figures in a dream, Tess was vaguely aware of the hush that settled through the air, that the other passengers watched them. Then none of it mattered, his arms tightened around her, he was real, achingly real. He buried his face in the curve of her neck, said her name again. He ran his fingers through her singed white hair, kissed the ash from her mouth, explored her face with his eyes and fingers as if to divine her journey to this moment.

Behind them, applause and cheers erupted from the other passengers.

Twenty-eight

Dominica and her tribe knew the so-called liberators were on their way and that they numbered in the thousands. Even so, the sheer number of buses, trucks, cars, and SUVs that poured into the city shocked her.

Snipers, positioned on rooftops, in trees, in windows high above the streets, opened up as the first wave of vehicles entered El Corazón. Windshields shattered, tires blew, vehicles ran amok as their drivers were killed, other vehicles were overturned and set on fire. The human idiots stumbled out into the streets, across the parks, only to be mowed down. Great, billowing clouds of black, greasy smoke rolled through the streets.

She stood on a rooftop in her host body, a nobody female bureaucrat in the Esperanza scheme of things. From here, she had a panoramic view of the city and could see the weaknesses in their defenses. So she threw up her arms and summoned the fog, just as she had in San Francisco. It tumbled in from every direction, filling the streets, rising against the buildings, reducing visibility to zero. The hungry ghosts inside shrieked and chanted, *Find the body, fuel the body, fill the body, be the body . . .* The sounds sliced through the screams of the invaders. And then the fog swallowed entire blocks, sped up the trunks of trees, covered the tops of buildings like an intricate white lace, and moved with incredible swiftness toward the next ring of vehicles.

Her tribe had prevailed for ten years through intimidation and terror but now terror wasn't enough. Fearless men and women armed with flamethrowers, guns, rifles, grenades, and homemade explosives swept up and down the streets of El Corazón, forcing her tribe to fight in a way that was foreign to them. Hand to hand, face to face. *Brujos* in their host bodies fell like ducks in a carnival shooting gallery. Blockades were breached and the armada of vehicles tore on through the city, horns blaring, flames shooting from windows and open doors.

Enraged, Dominica commanded a thousand host bodies to close off the city to the south and west and summoned a second, darker fog to block the eastern and northern boundaries of the city. Everywhere she looked, in every corner of the city, fires blazed, smoke and fog mixed with the cacophony of battle, the screams and moans of the dying. But the humans kept on coming—Ecuadorians, Argentineans, Chileans, Venezuelans, Brazilians, Colombians, pouring into Esperanza like some sort of plague. In every country where her tribe had seized someone since they had constructed the twin peaks twenty years ago, they had fostered the enmity of countless humans, and here they were, eager for blood, victory, freedom, revenge.

Karma. Dominica sent out a call to Rafael, requesting that he dispatch a thousand of his special followers to the northern edge of the city so that the avengers couldn't fan out through the countryside. These followers had seized the strongest men and women in Esperanza, street fighters who had battled *brujos* for years. It was only fitting that now they would kill their fellow humans.

Suddenly, she felt it, that hum, that auditory beacon that was the mark on Tess's arm, and she leaped out of her silly human body, left the bureaucrat stumbling around on a rooftop, confused and terrified, and swept toward the sound. It led her to one bus among many that barreled through Esperanza, flames shooting from its windows, its rooftop. She came up behind it and entered through the rear door, the only unguarded spot, safe from the flames.

The diversity of humans shocked her—white, black, brown, indigenous, all of them armed, doing their part to annihilate her tribe. She moved among them to the front of the bus where Ian drove madly, Wayra shouted directions, and several dozen people, including Tess, her mother and niece, fired from windows, the open door.

Dominica seized an Argentinean woman next to Maddie. The moment Dominica was inside of her, she knew this woman's cousin had been seized by a *brujo* four years ago in Buenos Aires, and the young man had bled out. *Oops, sorry. Time to join him.* And suddenly the woman shrieked and her eyes started to bleed as she stumbled blindly through the bus.

Maddie scrambled away, yelling, *They're here, in the bus,* and Dominica leaped into a middle-aged man, an Otavaleño with a graying *shimba* that fell to his waist. A pair of *brujos* had taken his parents, proprietors of a leather shop in Otavalo, and had bled them out two days after seizing them. Now he lusted for vengeance. Dominica had underestimated the passion for revenge among humans. Didn't matter. She squeezed his brain, he started to bleed, squealing like a dying pig, and she jumped out of him.

The chaos and terror inside the bus reached epidemic proportions. Passengers shouted, the bus swerved through the streets, and Wayra leaped up from his seat—and shifted. Did it right there in front of everyone, nothing hidden, no camouflage, no grace, just the transformation, man to dog or wolf or whatever the hell he was. Then he hurled himself at her, but without snarls, howls, or drama.

His powerful legs slammed into her and the next thing she knew, they were on the beach of the Lago del Sueño.

Ian saw Wayra shoot to his feet, then he transformed at the speed of light, and Nomad leaped toward something that only he could see—and vanished. After that, Ian drove like a man possessed, shouts rising throughout the bus for towels, blankets, something with which to cover the dead.

Another roadblock loomed just ahead, large refrigerated trucks parked across the road, several dozen snipers on top of them firing at everything that approached. Ian couldn't tell if the snipers were host bodies or virtual forms, but the distinction no longer mattered. "Slim, grab a couple of grenades," he shouted. "Get up to the rooftop and blast those fucks to the Stone Age. I'm going to their right, over the sidewalk, where the smoke is thickest."

"Done."

He watched her briefly in the rearview mirror, tearing down the aisle, her burned white hair flopping around. At the back of the bus, Ian saw Maddie already gathering up grenades from the bin of weapons. Then both women clambered up the ladder to the rooftop and vanished from his sight. It scared him, that he couldn't see her anymore.

Fog now moved around the blockade of refrigerated trucks in front of him. Firelight turned the stuff an eerie pumpkin orange. He sensed the brujos waiting within, could hear their whisperings again, that sound like sandpaper drawn across satin, grating yet slippery and soft.

Ian slammed his foot against the accelerator, shifted gears, and the bus tore over the curb and barreled up the sidewalk, crashing through tables and chairs and anything else in the way. The fog rushed toward them, that terrifying chant reached out to them. Ian hollered, *"Flamethrowers, fast!"*

Flames blasted from the windows, the rooftop. The fog recoiled swiftly, but the snipers on top of the refrigerated trucks kept shooting. The smoke, so thick and dark and oppressive, offered excellent cover, and before they sped out on the other side of it, two refrigerated trucks went up. Grenades, he thought. Tess and Maddie had hit their marks.

The explosion hurled flaming debris fifty feet into the air and spewed it in every direction. Stuff rained down around them, chunks of metal and pieces of bodies slammed into the top of the bus. Maddie and Tess reappeared and hurried back up the aisle armed with flamethrowers again.

Ian pressed a button on the dashboard and a shield covered the front windshield, with a four-inch horizontal opening that allowed him to see the road. Another button raised shields along the side windows, but left enough open space for weapons to be extended. Then he gunned the accelerator, shifted gears, and the bus tore free of the smoke. The air echoed with gunfire, explosions, the shriek of sirens. It sounded like Armageddon.

He slammed on the brakes, the engine racing, staring at the road ahead. He recognized it. It was the one he'd followed out of the city when Juanito was so badly injured. The church where he and Tess had spent their last hour as transitionals lay some distance beyond it. The same church where Illika, Juanito, and others were trapped. One way or another, he would get there.

But first, he had to take the bus through the army of host bodies that occupied the road as far as he could see. Men and women, even teenagers, stood shoulder to shoulder, armed with guns, machetes, pitchforks, rifles, assault weapons.

He had no idea how the *brujos* had gathered so many weapons. But he understood *this* strategy: put a human face on the enemy. March out the strongest host bodies, all of them locals, most of them Ecuadorians, and dare the avengers to kill their Latino brothers and sisters.

Vehicles lined both sides of the road—more refrigerated trucks, vans, cars, all with headlights blazing. Ian suspected that if he and the cars and buses behind him dared to slam through the army of host bodies, these vehicles would pursue them to the gates of hell.

"How many buses and cars are behind us?" Ian asked Tess.

"Dozens."

He radioed the drivers of several other buses, and within moments, vehicles lined up on either side of him, engines revving. *"Assume positions,"* he shouted. "We're going first and we'll shoot straight through them. They're heavily armed. Anyone who wants to get down on the floor, do so now."

No one moved to the floor.

"End the *brujo* tyranny!" shouted someone at the back of the bus, and the chant went up.

Ian looked at Tess and mouthed, *I love you.*

Tess's beautiful eyes latched on to his. *Back at you, bigger than Google,* she mouthed. Then she, Lauren, and Maddie moved back to their seats, flamethrowers ready.

He revved the engine once more, a signal to the other vehicles, then released the emergency brake, and the bus sprang forward.

Tess didn't know how long it took to slam through all the host bodies that filled the road. Seconds, hours, days. But she felt every horrifying thump, every shriek of agony, every *brujo* annihilation. When flames shot from her weapon, she smelled the burning of clothes, hair, skin, and saw the survivors scattering, fire leaping from their backs and legs and heads.

Trucks and cars exploded, but other vehicles careened away and vanished into the dark countryside. Pieces of smoldering metal fell from the sky. *Thump, thump, thump,* went the bodies that hit the bus, each thump interspersed with a hail of gunshots, knives, machetes.

Just as her flamethrower ran out of fuel, they broke free of the host army, and the bus shot up the road. But vehicles pursued them, and fog tumbled toward them from both sides of the road and quickly grew into a wall.

"Grenades!" Tess shouted.

Moments later, four quick and furious detonations on both sides of the bus set trees ablaze, forcing the fog back, and the road opened up in front of them.

But for how long?

The fog chased them for miles, closing in, backing off, closing in again. Then it rolled over the bus, swallowing it completely, and the insidious whispers filled the air, *Find the body, fuel the body . . .*

"Make sure the fog isn't getting in through the windows and doors," Ian shouted.

Tess shot to her feet, but suddenly, through the horizontal slit in the windshield, she spotted lights moving against the distant horizon, dozens of them in formation. *Choppers.* Their brilliant searchlights swept across the landscape, then great furious bursts of fire exploded beneath them. The fog rolled away so fast it was as if it never had been there.

"Look," she hollered, pointing. "Remove the shields from the windows, Ian."

As he did, everyone on the bus saw the lights, the choppers, their firebombs plunging from the sky. Excited cheers and shouts reverberated through the bus.

Ed Granger had finally come through. Tess didn't have any idea how he'd done it, what strings he'd pulled, what favors he'd called in, or how he had convinced the pilots to fly into the city at night. But he apparently realized that the liberation of Esperanza was going to happen with or without him, and had done the right thing.

Lauren and Maddie made their way forward and threw their arms around Tess, Ian, around each other. Then Ian swerved down the church's driveway, blasting the horn, and glanced over at Tess. "Do you remember this?"

"Yeah. Last time I was driving," she said, and he laughed and the garage door began to rise.

Once Dominica and Nomad were inside the mysterious cave at the edge of the lake, he became a man once more, Wayra so tall that he couldn't stand upright. They regarded each other with open wariness, their long and convoluted history a presence between them. She took solace from the tea-colored eyes of the man she'd loved so long ago and hoped that man still existed somewhere inside of him. Then those eyes darkened with rage.

"It ends here, Nica. Now."

"Oh, please, you and I have reached this juncture too many times. So much of this was unnecessary, Wayra."

"Everything you have done in the last five hundred years has been unnecessary and cruel. The woman I loved had a good heart, but yours has turned to stone. The woman I loved was compassionate, warm, loyal to the people who loved her. But you lost all of those qualities when you joined the *brujos*. Now you seize the living because it's the only thing you know how to do."

"Such sanctimony, Wayra. It isn't like you."

"Your seizure of Sara Wells was for display, to boost your standing, to make yourself look good to the rest of your tribe. That's unforgiveable, Nica."

She rolled her eyes. "Spare me. The only reason you see it as unforgivable is because you two were lovers."

There. She'd said it. Let him try to deny it.

His mouth twitched into a slow, sad smile. "We were more than lovers. My relationship with Sara predated yours and mine. Our history was longer and richer than anything you and I ever knew together."

She just stood there, shocked beyond words or feeling, unable to comprehend that Wayra, born in the last light of the twelfth century, had loved anyone before he had loved her. She started laughing and laughed until phony tears rolled from her virtual eyes. "What? She was a shifter? Is that what you're saying?"

"Spiritually, she was my other half." He spoke softly. "I met her when I was twelve years old. In that life, she was the daughter of a shepherd. I was with her the day I was bitten and . . . and when we were confronted by the shifter, I screamed at her to run. And she did. And that's why, in her life as Sara, she was so drawn to myth, and then to Ecuador."

Dominica felt many human emotions just then—sorrow, despair, hatred, jealousy, and rage. "Lies," she hissed, and her arms flew up and she pushed him. He stumbled back, the top of his head scraping against the roof of the cave. "Everything you've just said is a lie—to hurt me, weaken me, to . . . to . . ."

"Perhaps. But you'll never know for sure, will you, Nica? And not knowing will drive you mad." He laughed at her, the sound of it echoing through the cave.

"You said you loved me. That you loved me as a soul mate, that you—"

"We never loved like that. It was all in your mind, Nica. You fooled Ben with that kind of talk, but you never fooled me."

His words twisted the dagger in her heart even deeper and her rage propelled her to violence. But as she slammed into him, his arms closed around her, tightening like a hangman's noose, and he began to shift.

The agony caused her to scream and writhe, to fight for her very existence. She threw up her last best hope, an image of the two of them in the moments after she had died as Dominica de la Reina six hundred years ago, and he had galloped toward her on his black stallion like a hero from a romance novel, and swept her up into the saddle. But the memory didn't affect him. It was as if, for him, it had never happened. He kept shifting, his grip so tight, so powerful, it threatened to suffocate her even in her virtual form. She suddenly realized he intended to absorb her into his shifter form. Was such a thing possible? *Does it matter?*

Dominica shed her virtual form, but it didn't make any difference. Her essence was being sucked into the shifter, like dust into a vacuum cleaner. As he absorbed her, his sensory abilities became available to her. She could *see* herself being absorbed, could *feel* her own disintegration, could *taste* the strangeness of Wayra's world, *hear* the whispers of his ancient past gathering around her. But these sensory experiences were intended to distract her so that she didn't struggle. They were a lure, a seduction, the ultimate trick and betrayal.

Dominica shrieked, *No, never, never,* and as she struggled to break his hold on her, she heard her tribe's keening, screams of agony, pleas for help and redemption and salvation, all of it echoing her own near-annihilation. This was her tribe, the world she and Ben had built over the last twenty years. It was being destroyed by humans—and, ultimately, by a shifter who had never loved her. Who had never considered her the other half of his soul.

The calls of her dying tribe infused her with strength and she tore away from Wayra, screaming, "You are now dead to me, shifter. Always. Forever."

Below her, Wayra's form fluctuated wildly from animal to human to animal again, as if he were trapped in some crazy evolutionary loop. He lunged for her, reared up on his human legs, with his snout and front legs still those of an animal. But Dominica leaped away from him, hoping he died here, and soared free.

Twenty-nine

Dominica wandered aimlessly for a long time, days, weeks, months, she didn't know. Time held no meaning for her now. She thought she might be insane, slipping in and out of scenes from her long, strange life as human, as *bruja,* sometimes with Ben, sometimes with Wayra, always loving the one she was with. But in the end, none of the men she'd loved were there for her—not her father, not Ben, not Wayra. So when she was drawn back to the city, she looked for him, for Wayra, trying to understand what had happened, who she really was, what had gone wrong.

Parts of the city looked devastated, trees and parks charred, buildings just scorched shells, windows gone, roads torn up. Bulldozers moved through the city, gnashing their teeth, engines roaring, scooping up wrecked cars, burned trucks, pieces of buses and ravaged lives. In one neighborhood, clothing flapped from trees, children's toys littered sidewalks. Torn books, ravaged tools, and computer parts were stacked on long tables, as if in preparation for a bargain-basement sale. Throughout the city, church bells tolled, long mournful notes—but not for the *brujos* who had perished.

She didn't encounter a single one of her kind. Those who had survived had fled.

Dominica finally found Wayra in a neighborhood that looked to be in the throes of recovery. Everything was green, lovely flowers bloomed in ceramic pots. Trees were being planted in the parks, buildings were being constructed, renovated. She believed that months had passed.

Wayra sat outside a café with the horrible woman who had killed Ben, one arm resting on the back of Lauren's chair, the other slung out along the back of Maddie's chair, as she tapped away on the keyboard of her stupid laptop. Ian, goddamn his wretched soul, whispered sweet nothings in Tess's ear and sipped hot coffee from a tiny cup. Manuel Ortega, Juanito, Illika, Granger, all of them were there, talking and laughing, obviously enjoying themselves. Even the ridiculous parrot, Kali, perched on the back of Tess's chair, seemed content. How she hated them.

Tess sat up straighter and started scratching at that faded mark on her arm. But it was an absentminded scratching, she hadn't connected it to the mark, and Dominica didn't intend to give her that chance. She slipped into the niece, into Maddie with her strong, youthful body, her optimistic heart, and Dominica dispersed herself through the woman's cells.

No reaction. Maddie had no idea she had been seized. Like the silly woman in Otavalo, she was clueless. Here, Dominica would listen, watch, and wait for the moment when the *brujos* would rise again. Already, she thought she heard them calling from somewhere to the north.

After a few minutes, she prompted Maddie to pack up her laptop, stand, and walk away from the others, toward the north.

"Hey, Maddie, where're you going?" Tess called after her.

Maddie raised her arm and waved. "Later," she called back, and crossed the street to the shadowed park.

North, we're going north, Dominica whispered, and Maddie walked on.